The chanting had fluttered up through the trees, filling the Glades like water, like air, and McCleary had followed it. Now he was flattened out on his stomach on the edge of a mound, peering down into the source of it. Into an eerie blue light and a scene so bizarre, it took him a few moments to assimilate what he was seeing.

When he understood, when he had somehow managed to shuffle the pieces around in his mind like pawns in a mental game of chess, death cackled in his ear. Death laughed at him. Death galloped on his great black horse across that blazing white desert, his laughter rising and falling inside McCleary's head.

WE MAY NOT GET OUT OF THIS ONE, QUIN. BUT WE'RE GOING TO GIVE IT A BLOODY FIGHT.

Also by T.J. MacGregor
Published by Ballantine Books:

DARK FIELDS

KILL FLASH

DEATH SWEET

ON ICE

KIN
DREAD

T.J. MacGregor

BALLANTINE BOOKS • NEW YORK

Library of Congress Catalog Card Number: 90-93128

ISBN 0-345-35766-3

Manufactured in the United States of America

First Edition: October 1990

for Megan Maya
and Rob

Prologue

From the Confession

I COULD TELL them outsiders was going to be easy.

The guy was a fatso who wheezed while he was carting gear from the canoe to the site. His bimbo pranced along behind him in real tight shorts, whining that the campsite was so dirty, there was bugs everywhere, and how could Charlie expect her to spend the night in this place? He set her straight, as straight as you can set a woman like that, and said they was either sleeping here or in the canoe. Then he told her to get the food.

She gave him one of them looks I knew all about, the look a woman gives a man when she'd like to put her hands around his throat and squeeze till he turned purple. "Whatever happened to that other campsite you told me about that was supposed to be so *comfortable?*" she said.

"We won't make it by dark, Vi."

She looked around once more, wrinkling her nose, her painted nails tapping those plumpo hips. For a second, I thought maybe she'd seen me because she was staring at the bushes where me and Opal was hiding. But then she turned and marched off toward the canoe, and the guy dumped the gear on the ground and stared at it like he didn't know what to do next.

Even from where me and Opal was hiding, I could see that gear. Nice stuff. Expensive. Sleeping bags, a tent, one of them stoves that folds up like a chair, lanterns—things the band could use. Things we needed. And when you was in need, my old man used to say, it was okay to do what you had to do. It was okay to borrow, especially if you was borrowing from someone who had a lot more than you. And I could smell money on that fat man. I figured he lived in one of them swanky homes on the

3

beach, a place with fifty rooms where the air was like perfume. Fat Man had; the band didn't. It seemed right simple.

"I want her rings," Opal whispered. She was crouched beside me, lean as a cat, her bow and arrow hooked over her shoulder. "Jus' look at all them rings she's got on, honey. And we could use that canoe."

"Gotta wait till they's settled in for the night. Till they's sleeping."

"That could be hours."

"Don't matter."

Me and Opal had stopped at Lard Can on our way back home to look for stuff campers left behind and had come upon Fat Man and Bimbo. I knew we shoulda left; Opal was trouble when it came to outsiders. She got these ideas in her head and forgot I was boss. But it seemed like Charlie and Vi were put there just for us, you know? And that gear was mighty nice. It sure was. It'd been a while since the band had gotten anything new. This had been a slow season for campers on account of the heat and all.

We watched Fat Man trying to set up his tent. The breeze flapped at it, he dropped the stakes, he swore to himself. He wasn't getting no help from the bimbo, either. She was too busy spraying the ground with shit to kill insects and complaining about how dirty her shorts was getting. God, I hated her voice. It zipped along my nerves like the pain of a toothache, making my fingers twitch against the shotgun in my lap.

I sure liked the way that shotgun felt.

I borrowed it from a poacher six, seven months back, when I was on another expedition. The stupid bastard figured I was no smarter than the 'gators he was tracking, but I showed him a thing or two. I got his shotgun and airboat and supplies and left him baking in the sun on a spit of land in the middle of nowhere. I guess one of his buddies picked him up eventually. And since he was poaching, he couldn't report the thieving to the rangers, now, could he?

"What're we waitin for?" Opal whispered.

"We don't do outsiders 'less they're sleeping," I told her. "You know the rules."

4

"Aw, c'mon, honey. So what if they report it to the rangers? What they goin do about it?" She grinned; her teeth were the color of an old floor. "Come lookin for us?"

Opal just wanted to shove ahead, get their gear, head home. But I didn't want to be seen. I knew how outsiders were; I'd lived with them for a spell. But I figured she was probably right about the waiting and I didn't feel like waiting.

"C'mon, honey," she said again.

"You gotta do what I say."

"I will."

I thought about it, but not for long. We slipped out of the bushes and came up behind Fat Man and Bimbo. "Evenin', folks," I said.

Their heads snapped around. Fat Man's eyes was as wide and round as dinner plates. Bimbo looked like she didn't know whether to scream or to puke. "Wh-what's going on?" Fat Man stammered.

"What's it look like, asshole?" Opal laughed, her bow in position, an arrow fixed and ready to fly.

I waved the shotgun toward the gear on the ground. "What you're goin do for me, Charlie, is load all that there stuff into our canoe." I swung the shotgun toward the bimbo. "And you just kneel right there, sweetheart, with your hands flat against them thighs, where I can see 'em."

"You can have everything." Fat Man was real cooperative; he knew the score. "Go ahead. Take it. It's yours. And I . . . I have money, too, a lot of money." He pulled out his wallet, flipped it open, and held it up like a prize fish. "See?"

I didn't want his money; I had no use for it. But just in case I ever had to go out into the world again, I told him to toss his wallet over to me, then get his fat ass moving.

He did.

"Good, Charlie. Long as you follow directions, no one's goin to get hurt, okay? We understand each other?"

"S-sure thing." He started picking up the gear.

"And you, honey," Opal said to the bimbo. "Start

5

takin off them rings. Put 'em in that tin cup there and bring the cup over here."

"They're j-just junk." Bimbo's eyes got real shiny with tears. "Worthless junk."

"Uh-huh," Opal told her. "You got three seconds, lady. Otherwise this here arrow's goin to find you mighty quick."

"Jesus." Fat Man stood there with his arms piled high with gear, looking like he might puke. "Just do what she says, Vi. Hurry up."

"But . . ."

"Do it!"

Opal grinned. "Better listen to him, lady. I'm real good with this here bow. Want to see how good I am?"

Bimbo shook her head and worked them rings off her fingers, twisting them, grunting, tears tracking down her cheeks. She was scared, all right, good and scared. And that was okay. When folks was scared, they wasn't likely to make trouble. The rings clinked against the sides of the tin cup as she dropped them in.

"Get movin, Charlie," I told the fat man. "I want that stuff in the canoe fast. And don't try nothin. I'm right behind you."

He waddled back and forth from the campsite to the canoe, and I could tell the noise of insects and frogs and things rustling in the brush bothered him. He was a typical outsider that didn't really much enjoy being here but felt like he needed to experience it.

When the canoe was loaded, I told him to kneel beside the bimbo, who was blubbering. "Stop your noise, lady. It's gettin on my nerves."

"Y-you're not taking our canoe, are you?" Bimbo's eyes was bright red; her chest heaved. "We n-need our canoe. It's n-not safe here without a canoe. I mean, how're w-we going to g-get—"

I grabbed her by the hair and flung her head back and pressed the end of the shotgun against her throat. "Shut up! Or I'll blow your vocal cords outta your throat. Got it?"

"Oooh, G-God. Y-yes." Her eyes bulged in her cheeks. She swallowed, and I could hear the saliva going down.

6

"Yes, sir," I told her.

"Yes, sir." She hiccuped.

"The rope, Weston, get the rope and tie his hands," Opal said. "It's near dark."

When I let go of the bimbo's hair, she spat at me. "You're a dirty, filthy man," she sobbed. "Dirty dirty dirty."

"You stupid bitch," Opal hissed, and let her arrow fly. It whispered past the bimbo's head and slammed into a tree trunk behind her. "You hear the sound it makes? Ain't that somethin? Next time you pull shit like that, it'll be your tit."

The woman pushed her hand against her mouth. She looked from Opal to me. I wiped the glob of spit off my cheek, then hit her across the face. "Spittin's nasty, lady," I told her, and I hit her again, knocking her backward. She sprawled in the dirt, crying, rubbing at her cheek.

Suddenly the fat man wailed, "You bastard!" and charged me from behind.

I spun, but Fat Man was already stumbling, his eyes wild with pain, confusion, surprise, his hands clawing at his back, where Opal's arrow had sunk between his shoulder blades. He toppled forward and landed in front of the bimbo. She scrambled up, screaming like a stuck hog, and raced toward the water, still screaming. Jesus, but it was a horrible noise. I didn't have no choice but to shoot the bitch.

The explosion from the shotgun echoed across the water and through the trees, scaring the blue heron into the sky. Opal and me just looked at each other. I felt like shoving my fist into her mouth but didn't because of the bow. I was scared of what she could do with that bow.

"That was a gawddamn stupid thing to do, woman."

"I told you he was an asshole." She marched over to the fat man's body and started to work the arrow out of his back.

"Leave it. Let's get the rest of their gear and cut the canoe loose. 'Gators will finish 'em off."

"We need the canoe."

"We got plenty of canoes. We just take the gear. Hurry."

But she didn't budge. "We gotta move 'em." The last of the light was bleeding from the air, and her voice sounded weird and hollow. "In case there's campers here tomorrow."

'There's hardly no campers now. Weather's too hot. And them who come never come during the week."

"Them two did," she replied.

She had a point.

"And if campers show up tomorrow, Wes, they ain't goin to camp in the trees. We can cover 'em up with leaves. It'll be weeks before anyone finds what's left of 'em."

I was thinking right then that it might be better to take the bodies with us and dump them in the saw grass. But I was starting to feel real uneasy about things, so I said okay, we'd cover them up with leaves.

I saw her smile and then heard the soft sucking of the guy's flesh and muscles as she jerked the arrow free.

PART ONE

Everglades
May 9

"There are no other Everglades in the world."

Marjorie Stoneman Douglas

Shoving Off

1.

SHRIVELED PERIWINKLES WEPT against the curb.

One of them had been stepped on and its squashed petals had bled lavender into the concrete. The stain, Quin knew, would withstand just about everything except the brutal assault of sunlight, which would eventually bleach it away. There seemed to be a lesson in this about scars and the passage of time, but it wasn't something she wanted to think about just now. It was easier to list her complaints about the lawn service that had been here yesterday and hadn't cleaned up before it left.

All right, so the yard was now a suburban dream, clipped and manicured like a poodle. But the driveway where she stood was a mess. Weeds curled against the asphalt, as simple as commas, stickers clung to the cuffs of her jeans, blades of grass were everywhere. The lawn-service people apparently thought that just because McCleary was no longer paying the bills, they could get away with shoddy work. If she'd been home yesterday when they were here, she would've fired them on the spot.

She peered down the road, looking for McCleary's car. But there was only the stop sign at the end of the block, its red faded and anemic from the sun, the letters almost gone. Thunderheads were building to the west, moving toward the Everglades. By the time they got the canoes into the water, it would probably be raining. Leave it to McCleary to be late when three people were waiting for him.

"He probably got held up in traffic," said Lydia Nichols, coming up behind Quin.

"Yeah, maybe." More than likely, he'd been having a

11

late breakfast in his favorite Cuban café in Little Havana and had lost track of the time.

"Hey, we're officially on vacation, right? No timetables. No schedules. It's no big deal, Quin. Really."

Lydia: ex-schoolteacher, ex–social worker, ex-hippie, a college friend of McCleary's. Time meant as little to her as it did to him. Laid-back Lydia, with her shiny black hair that never frizzed, neon-blue eyes, high cheekbones—in short, a face worthy of romantic poetry—still subscribed to the old hippie motto, *Don't sweat the small shit.*

Quin had seen her uptight only once, when her husband, Beau, had misplaced her stash of grass. That fell into the category of major shit. It had happened during a trip to Key West, shortly after McCleary had introduced her to the Nicholses six years ago, before any of them were married. The incident had gotten blown out of proportion and Lydia and Beau had argued for four days. It was the first time—and the last—that they'd traveled anywhere with the Nicholses. Until now.

And this trip was against her better judgment.

It had been planned since early last summer, when Quin had backed out because she couldn't stand the thought of spending four days with Lydia. She'd gone to Canada with her sister instead. The very weekend they would have been in the Everglades, McCleary was found unconscious in a motel room in Fort Lauderdale, with a dead woman in the other bed and twenty years of memories on ice. He was charged with murder one, and although he was later cleared, that experience coupled with his amnesia had eventually resulted in their separation after five years of marriage. He still occasionally handled cases for their private-investigation firm, but mostly he practiced by himself in Little Havana.

All because she'd gone to Canada instead of camping. So for her this trip was a kind of penance. Besides, she was too superstitious to back out of it a second time, and it was only for four days. Then the Nicholses would fly back to their lives in Atlanta, where they owned a sporting-goods store, Quin's conscience would be appeased, and she wouldn't have to deal with Lydia again.

"Hey, could I get some help with this?" called Nichols.

Quin and Lydia hurried up the driveway, where Nichols was struggling to lift one of the canoes on top of his van. The canoe was aluminum, silver, as shiny as a wet fish; the van was maroon and tan; Nichols was blond and fair-skinned. At first glance, it was the sort of odd arrangement and contrast that would have made an interesting photograph, if she'd had a camera handy.

But with closer scrutiny she realized the picture would seem unbalanced or disproportionate because everything in the arrangement was so large. The van, the canoe, even Nichols, the friendly giant. And the picture would invariably remind her of the trip she hadn't taken last summer and what had happened instead. It always came back to that.

When McCleary had first mentioned this camping trip to her, her first impulse was to say no, she had too much work to do, she couldn't afford to take the time off. But instead she'd said she'd think about it. A couple of days later, Nichols had called and asked her to please come along, it'd be fun, and he'd be outnumbered without her. *"I'll have to hear those stories about the good ol' days all by myself."*

Maybe it was Nichols's way of trying to get her and McCleary back together. Maybe he thought that with just the three of them, he'd be the odd man out because of Lydia's longstanding friendship with McCleary. She could only guess at his real reasons for calling. But she liked Nichols more than she liked his wife, and since she was already feeling guilty, she'd said yes, fine, she'd go.

"You two get the other end, will you?" Nichols asked. Although he was a big man, an ex–college football player who looked as if he could lift a house single-handedly, this was a question of balance, and he was losing. His face was bright with sweat. His biceps rippled with exertion as he hoisted one end of the canoe while Quin and Lydia maneuvered the other end.

"Mike call?" He grunted as he let his end of the canoe down carefully on the rack.

"Not yet." Quin scooped up the rope and bungy straps from the ground and handed them to him.

"Do I hear a hint of irritation?"

"A hint."

"He'll be along." He glanced at his wife. "You sure you packed the sleeping bags?"

"Of course I'm sure." Lydia pulled a joint out of her shirt pocket, ran her fingers over it, licked the end shut. Then she lit it with the dramatic flourish that punctuated everything she did, as though she were always onstage. "They're in the van."

"What about the food?"

She gave Quin a look that said *He gets like this sometimes* and let out a loud, exaggerated sigh that escaped with a puff of sweet-smelling smoke. "Yes, Beau. I packed the food."

Nichols fixed his wide eyes on Quin and spoke as though Lydia weren't present. "She forgets things when she smokes that loco weed."

"Well, I didn't forget the food or the sleeping bags. Just the booze." Lydia laughed. "But you remembered that, so everything's fine, Beau." Then she flicked her hair off her shoulders and sauntered off toward the end of the driveway, her narrow hips swaying.

Nichols gazed after her, frowning with disapproval. "I told her not to wear shorts on a camping trip to the Everglades. She's going to get eaten alive by bugs."

"She'll find out soon enough."

"And once she does, she won't do anything about it because if she did, that'd prove I was right." He shrugged. "Go figure." He secured the front of the canoe to the rack, then walked around to where Quin was standing and did the same to the other end. "I hope Mike's got maps and everything for this."

"Don't worry about it. He's probably had this trip mapped out to the second for weeks."

"Yeah." Nichols smiled and brushed his hands together. Large hands, like paws. The backs were covered with fine, light hair. He looked down at the second canoe, rubbed the heel of his hand against his chest, and shook his head. "This is how guys my age end up with coronaries. Mike can help me with that one."

"*Your* age?" Quin laughed. "My God, Beau. You're only forty."

"Some days I feel fifty."

Married to Lydia, Quin thought, a man who was twenty would feel like fifty.

"And sometimes at night I wake up with chest pains. Lydia says it's my imagination."

"So go to a doctor."

"I did."

"And?"

"He said my heart's fine. But, hell, he's not inside my body. I am."

Nichols, the hypochondriac.

He limped over to the van, favoring the knee he'd injured more than twenty years ago, an injury that had squashed any chances he'd had of playing pro ball. "I need a cold beer. You want one?"

"No, thanks." Not at ten in the morning.

But for the Nicholses a joint and a beer took precedence over morning coffee. Not always, not every day, just when they traveled.

McCleary turned into the drive, announcing his arrival with two quick blasts on the horn. He pulled alongside the van and hopped out in his usual garb: jeans, a T-shirt, running shoes. Today he also wore a green baseball cap she didn't recognize with CAFÉ DE ORO on it. Symbol of his new life, his life separate from her, the life that was still in its infancy and in which her role was minimal. And of course he bought clothes and accumulated things in this life she wouldn't recognize. What'd she expect, anyway?

At six feet tall, he possessed a runner's leanness and a certain economy of movement. He had recently shaved off his beard, and although it wasn't the first time he'd done it, it always took her a while to get used to it. Beardless, his jaw seemed more square, more stubborn; his eyes looked bluer and clearer; and the symmetry of his face was somehow more balanced, as though the beard had weighted the flesh and bones.

"Sorry I'm late, guys. Traffic in Little Havana rivaled Tokyo's."

You've never been to Tokyo, she thought, irked that he

15

hadn't compensated for the traffic by leaving his place a little earlier.

Nichols raised his cold beer in greeting. "How about helping me with the second canoe?"

"Sure thing."

"See?" said Lydia, stopping alongside Quin. She was puffing on the last of the joint. "No big deal."

"Hmm," Quin murmured, watching as the two men lifted the canoe.

The canoes belonged to McCleary. He'd been storing both of them at the house since they'd separated, because the house he rented in Little Havana was too small. They had certain memories attached to them that offered up quick glimpses of simpler times: a jaunt through the Adirondacks one summer, camping trips in the Everglades before they were married, a trek in Minnesota's north woods. She had no idea which memories he'd retained. Maybe none of them.

Even though he'd regained many of the memories that amnesia had stolen from him last summer, the more recent years remained sketchy. She imagined that his recollections of their private-eye business, of their marriage, were unconnected dots of bright lights, half-hour sitcoms devoid of plots. At one time she'd believed that when— *if*—he recovered the missing portions of the last five or six years, things between them would snap back to the way they had been, as though the rescued memories would fill in the emotional blanks. Now she knew better. Now she understood it was more complicated than that.

If his memories of the marriage had returned within weeks of the blow on the head that had caused the amnesia, things might have turned out differently. But emotions were like talents. Unless they were nurtured, fed, exercised, they atrophied or transmuted. Nothing was static.

She wasn't even sure that a reconciliation was what she wanted anymore. In seven months, she'd carved out a new life for herself, just as he had done, and rather enjoyed her singular existence. She liked staying up late to read if the urge hit her. She liked eating breakfast alone. She liked coming and going as she pleased, answering to no one, not balancing the checkbook, eating crackers in bed, leaving her den in complete disarray without having to listen to McCleary's mumbling about how disorganized she was. And she liked seeing other men.

There was no one special, no one with whom she felt any kind of psychic closeness, no one whose absence from her life would make a difference. But that was how she preferred it. The common interests she and McCleary had once shared were now divided among several men: one whose delight in food matched hers, another with whom she ran a couple of evenings a week, a third with whom she often did things on weekends. Though her life now sometimes lacked a certain excitement, it was infinitely simpler than it had been when she was married to McCleary.

And that counted for something.

2.

After Quin helped Lydia load things in the back of her van, she went inside the house to get the cooler and her backpack. She paused at the hallway mirror, scrutinizing her reflection, wondering why she always felt like the ugly stepsister when she was around Lydia.

At five ten she was taller than Lydia and thinner, but one look at Lydia made her feel like the fat girl on the block. Her umber hair was just as thick as Lydia's, just as long, but it was curly to her straight and invariably frizzed. In the face department, she definitely fell short when compared to Lydia. Freckles dusted her cheeks; Lydia's skin was flawless. Her mouth was okay, although the upper lip was a bit too thin; Lydia's mouth was a perfect bow. Her cheekbones were high, but Lydia's were higher. Her pale blue eyes—spooky eyes, McCleary used to call them—were her best feature. And yet they didn't hold a candle to the blue jewels of Lydia's eyes.

Lydia was gorgeous and Quin wasn't. Bottom line, she thought, and turned away from the mirror to find Merlin, one of the cats, peering up at her. The other two felines were positioned between her and the kitchen. "Feeling insecure, guys?" she asked, brushing past them.

Already disturbed by all the activity outside, the cats now acted like neurotic children, fussing to be fed, picked up, reassured that her impending absence wouldn't be permanent.

"Yeah, yeah, I know," she said as they padded after her into the kitchen. "But you'll get over it when Benson arrives twice a day with tuna fish."

Tim Benson was McCleary's old partner from his days in homicide at Metro-Dade; he was like family. And knowing Benson, she thought, the cats would probably feast not only on tuna but on a cuisine of steak and chicken as well. She would come home to cats that were candidates for the Pritikin diet.

She finished packing the cooler and added some last-minute items to one of the paper bags: trail mix, more fruit, a couple of pop-top cans of tuna fish and salmon, four cans of soda. This bag, she decided, would be stashed in the canoe with her. Her metabolism would probably be jammed in overdrive and she didn't intend to go hungry en route to the campsite. She also made up an emergency munchie bag and a survival kit for her purse. You couldn't be overprepared for the Everglades.

She set out extra dry food for the cats and scribbled Benson a note, which she tacked to the fridge. Then she walked through the house, checking doors and windows to make sure they were locked. Merlin, the oldest cat, tagged along behind her. Now and then he nipped at the back of her leg just to let her know what he thought of the arrangement.

Merlin was pre-McCleary, a twelve-year-old stray who had appeared on her doorstep one day, thin as a pencil, his black fur matted, his eyes haunted by life on the streets. Now he was plump and sassy, his muzzle was graying, and his eyesight wasn't what it used to be.

During the five years she and McCleary were married, Merlin had become more his cat than hers and had gone through the feline equivalent of separation anxiety when McCleary had moved out. He'd peed on the carpet, torn apart curtains, stolen food from dinner plates. As the vet had put it, separation or divorce affected animals just like it did kids and perhaps joint custody was in order. So Merlin had lived with McCleary for a while and, sure enough, most of the weird behavior had stopped. But the cat was still a tad neurotic.

18

She picked him up as she went back downstairs. McCleary was in the kitchen, emptying another bag of ice into the cooler, and Merlin jumped to the floor when he saw him. He rubbed against McCleary's legs, asking to be picked up, and McCleary, naturally, obliged him.

"How goes it, guy?"

Merlin gazed up at him, those bright copper eyes blinking slowly, in a kind of code only McCleary seemed to understand.

"No kidding. Hepburn did that?"

Blink, blink.

"So what'd you do?"

Blink.

"That's easy," Quin said. "Two days ago, he peed on the dining-room table because I didn't let him out."

"You should've let him out."

"There was a dog in the yard."

"He would've climbed a tree."

"He would've *tried* to climb a tree and not made it because he isn't that fast anymore."

"You can't keep him locked up in the house for the rest of his life, Quin, just because you want to protect him."

As if they were talking about an elderly, incontinent relative whom she'd sealed shut in the attic. "Oh, forget it."

She slammed the lid shut on the cooler and yanked open the door of the fridge to see if there was anything else to take with her. She felt McCleary's eyes on her back.

"Beau's worried the van won't be safe unless it's parked in a lot near the ranger's station," he said.

Changing the subject. An old McCleary trick. But she let it pass. "If he parks it far enough into the trees, no one will even see it."

"That's what I told him. But you know Beau. If there's something to worry about, he'll worry."

Like me. That's what he's really saying. That I'm a fretter like Beau. Fair enough. "Just do me a favor, Mac. If he wants to drink and drive, tell him we'll take our own car."

"I already told him."

19

"And?"

"He says he never drinks before five."

"Yeah, right. He's got a ton of beer and a quart of Scotch with him."

"Hey, relax, okay? I read him the riot act."

He ruffled her hair, a signal that their conversation about Merlin was already forgotten. It was also a gesture of affection from the old days that used to make her heart seize up in her chest; now it only irritated her. She stepped away from him to pick up the bag of food.

"Something else bothering you or what, Quin?"

As though he couldn't figure it out. As though being late had never been a bone of contention in their marriage. "Having to wait an hour always bothers me." She headed for the door, hoping she didn't live to regret this trip.

3.

The Everglades covered five thousand square miles spread throughout five Florida counties. It began at Lake Okeechobee to the north and was bordered by Big Cypress Swamp to the west, Florida Bay to the south, and the Atlantic coast to the east. Less than a seventh of the area was a national park, the third largest in the country.

The Everglades was actually a river that was two hundred miles long, seventy miles wide and six inches deep, flowing through saw grass to the sea. Its flat expanses of marshes and wet prairies of saw grass were broken up by bay heads or tree islands and hammocks—larger elevated stands of tropical forests.

The saw grass was aptly named. The tiny, numerous ridges on its leaves were sharp enough to flay the skin on a man's hand. But at a distance the stuff looked as innocuous as a field of wheat, filling in the vast spaces between the verdant clusters of mangroves.

To Quin, the saw grass was a metaphor for the savage beauty of this place, a subtle thing, an acquired taste, not for everyone. Some people visited once and once was enough. Others returned but never went beyond the walking trails. Then there were people like herself who came back again and again, and each time ventured a little farther into the wilderness.

It was not a passion for camping that attracted her and kept drawing her back. There were, after all, more comfortable spots in which to camp. More civilized spots. Parks in the Keys, Ocala National Forest, places with showers and electricity and a 7-Eleven just down the highway. She returned because all things seemed possible here. It was as if the Everglades were a magical vortex of some kind where the real and the imagined coincided, overlapped, merged.

They put the canoes into the water at the entrance to Hell's Bay Trail. The mangroves on either side of the channel were so overgrown, the branches had braided together. McCleary, naturally, was the only one of them who'd thought to bring a machete and hacked at the growth until there was an opening wide enough for their canoes to get through. Then they loaded their gear.

Just as they were ready to shove off, Nichols decided he wanted to move the van across the road, into a clutch of trees where he thought it would be safer. Never mind that they'd miss their projected departure time by three hours, Quin thought, and would be lucky to reach a campsite by nightfall. All he cared about was the van.

While they stood alongside the road waiting for him, it started to sprinkle. "Shit," Lydia muttered, scanning the sky as if the forecast for the rest of the day was written in the sagging leaden clouds. She'd evidently forgotten that South Florida's weather was rarely predictable. Rain at three was often followed by bright, sunny skies at a quarter after. "Maybe we should hold off for another day. Then we could get a real early start tomorrow."

"No thanks. For me, it's today or never."

McCleary shrugged. "It's just a shower."

Lydia rolled her lower lip against her teeth. "I didn't even bring a raincoat."

"I've got an extra poncho in my bag," he said.

Lydia smiled at him as though he were her precocious younger brother. "What *didn't* you bring, Mac?"

"Toothpaste."

They laughed. "That's the *one* thing I didn't forget," she said. "You can use mine."

As they walked over to the canoes to get the ponchos, it struck Quin that they looked good together, like a TV couple with unblemished lives. She saw the way Lydia hooked her arm through McCleary's, how he leaned toward her as she said something, and wondered what would have happened if their college friendship had become something deeper. Would they have married? Gotten divorced? Would Lydia still have met and married Nichols? Would she and McCleary have met and married and separated? Were they all born with the broad strokes of their scripts cast in stone?

She glanced back down the highway. There wasn't a car in sight. The black pavement shot off toward the horizon, straight as a ruler until the trees on either side of it met in a perfect point.

A sudden desolation, an elemental fear and urgency, filled her. It was as if they'd survived a terrible cataclysm that had left the cities in chaos and were escaping into a wilderness that was safer.

Quin rubbed her hands over her arms and turned her face upward to the warm drizzle, the strange, forbidding sky. A damp breeze lifted strands of her hair, blowing them across her eyes, her cheeks. She brushed them away, wondering if the abrupt darkness in her mood was hormones, McCleary, or a premonition.

Bound for Hell's Bay

1.

THIS PARTICULAR TASTE, thought McCleary, was connected to memories.

It was the taste of rainy air in the wilderness, which was unlike the sullied taste of rain in the city or that chilled sweetness of rain that swept in over mountains. It was a clean, simple taste, undomesticated, raw, visceral. It satisfied that deep craving he'd been feeling for weeks for something he hadn't been able to name or identify and seemed to awaken a long-dormant part of himself. He could feel that self shaking loose of its deep sleep like a hibernating creature greeting spring, and he reveled in it.

But his enthusiasm, he knew, wasn't shared by the Nicholses. Their collective misery moved in waves between their canoe and this one, placing the blame on him, as though he were personally responsible for the weather. Okay, so he was wrong about this being just an afternoon shower—*wrong, but not sorry*—and yes, they probably should have postponed the trip a day.

And yet, thanks to the awning of green they were gliding under, the rain hardly touched them. It dripped through the mangroves, dimpling the dark waters, keeping a soft, steady rhythm like a heartbeat. As long as it didn't pick up once they reached the open waters of Hell's Bay, they would probably make the chickee by late afternoon. Their tents would be up before dark and dinner would be ready by eight. No problem. Even the Nicholses, who were as fussy as kids when it came to creature comforts, would find the chickee an adequate shelter.

The first chickees were built by the Calusa Indians,

who settled the gulf coast of Florida. They were open platforms that were roofed and thatched with palmetto leaves. Erected at the mouths of rivers, in sheltered inlets, they often were constructed on pilings that lifted them out of the water. The Seminoles later lived in similar habitats.

The chickee's contemporary counterparts, which now served as campsites scattered throughout the park, had tin roofs and were equipped with charcoal grills and Jiffy Johns. The chickee in Hell's Bay was large enough to accommodate the four of them, even with their two frame tents and all their gear. It would also protect them from the rain, unless the wind blew hard and fast. But even so, the chickee would still be a far sight more comfortable than a campsite on land.

He heard a disgruntled rumble from Nichols and glanced back. "Everything okay?"

"A weird bug just took a chunk out of my hand," Nichols griped.

"He likes the booze in your blood," Lydia remarked drolly. Seated at the front of their canoe, Lydia was alternately puffing on a joint and paddling. Inside the hood of the poncho McCleary had lent her, her face was a damp, white moon. She waggled her fingers and grinned, trying to be a good sport about things. "We almost there, Daddy?"

McCleary laughed. "Once we pass marker one forty-eight, it's probably another thirty minutes to Hell's Bay."

"And then what?" asked Nichols, popping open a beer. "How far to the chickee from there?" He was totally entrenched in his fretting mode now.

"Depends on the wind. An hour if it's with us, more if it's not."

"Jesus," Nichols moaned. "I've been using muscles I didn't know I had. I may not be able to move in an hour."

Lydia rolled her eyes and winked at McCleary. "He *never* exaggerates, does he." She shifted slightly and offered Nichols the joint. "A couple hits from this and you won't even know you've *got* muscles." He took the joint. "How about if we stop for a while and eat up some of these sandwiches? I can't be the only one who's hungry."

24

"Stop where?" Nichols glanced around, making a face. "There's no land."

"Right here. We can tie the canoes to the trees," McCleary replied.

"Sounds good to me," Quin said. "I'm starving."

Nichols snorted. "That's nothing new. Will we still be able to make the chickee by dark, Mike?"

"If we don't hang around here too long."

"What's too long?"

Lydia sighed. "Relax, Beau, will you? Have another beer or something. Better yet, open that bottle of Scotch."

"Oh, yeah, I like that idea." Nichols grabbed on to a nearby branch, tied up the canoe, chugged the rest of the beer, and pulled out his bottle of Scotch.

"Take it easy," McCleary said. "Hell's Bay can be tough to paddle even when the weather's perfect."

Nichols patted the air with a hand. *"No problema, amigo."*

McCleary and Quin exchanged a glance; he knew she was thinking the same thing he was. The last time Nichols had said those very words, he was drinking and driving and they'd nearly ended up in a canal. He wondered why unpleasant memories seemed to have come back so much more quickly.

"You remember that?" Quin whispered.

"Yeah." He turned away to tie up the canoe.

2.

". . . so we're driving around D.C. trying to find a parking spot, right? And the car's filled with the smell of grass and we've got handkerchiefs in the glove compartment coated with Vaseline just in case the cops use tear gas at the march," Lydia was saying. "Remember that, Mac?"

Sure, he remembered. He had no trouble with the older memories these days, and this was definitely an older memory. 1970. A trip to D.C. with Lydia and three other people to protest the killings at Kent State. They'd made the eight-hour trip in his black VW, all five of them jammed into the bug, barreling down the New York State Thruway, the radio blaring. They'd smoked enough dope, he remembered, to catapult themselves into the ozone for a week.

"... we found a parking spot in front of a park. We figured we'd catch some sleep until the march started, but instead we missed the march." Lydia laughed and lit another joint. "So we hung around Georgetown for a couple of days and crashed with some friends of mine."

Not quite true, McCleary thought. Lydia had barely known the people they'd stayed with. It turned out that the guy who rented the apartment peddled grass and acid to put himself through college. She'd talked him out of five tabs of Owlsley acid, which they'd dropped one night at a party.

At some point during that long, involuted acid trip, Lydia had lost it. Lost it bad. Crying jags, vapid staring, fetal positions, hallucinations. All of the terrible things you ever heard about LSD had happened to her that night. She had later blamed the bum trip on McCleary, saying that he had started it all by rejecting her when she'd come on to him. But that wasn't quite true, either. He hadn't *rejected* her. He'd simply been honest: they were friends and he wanted to keep it that way.

Yeah, he remembered the trip to D.C. Remembered it clearly.

"We've heard this story a million times," Nichols interrupted, glancing at Quin.

"I haven't," she said, looking interested and somewhat bemused.

"We did some Owlsley at this party," Lydia went on, dropping her head back and blowing smoke into the air. "Then we walked around Georgetown looking at churches, wondering why they were all locked." She lifted her head again and glanced at Quin. "That's when I stopped believing in God."

"Because the churches were locked?" Quin asked.

Lydia laughed. "Naw, just because."

"I thought that was the trip where you decided to go to India or something," Nichols remarked.

"Nepal."

"Wherever."

"And then you and Mike decided to go to the library so you could look up stuff on Nepal," Nichols continued.

She gave him an exasperated look. "Mike wanted to go to the library, Beau. He was on his reincarnation binge then and thought the university library might have some books on it."

"So what happened?" Quin picked up another peanut-butter-and-banana sandwich.

"The library was closed," McCleary said.

Lydia's bright blue eyes glinted mischievously. "You said you could pick the lock on a window."

"What I said, Lydia, was that it'd be easy to pick a lock on one of the windows."

And what you said was, Let's do it here in the bushes, Mike, under the windows of the halls of knowledge, and then you started giggling and lowered yourself to the ground and reached out for my hand and then you weren't giggling anymore, it wasn't a joke anymore, was it, Lydia?

Nichols capped the bottle of Scotch. "Hey, it was twenty years ago. Who cares who said what." He held his hands at his sides, palms up. "It's starting to rain harder. Let's go."

"Doesn't anyone want to hear the end of the story?" Lydia asked.

"I do," Quin piped up. She looked at McCleary as if to ask why he hadn't shared this particular episode of his life.

"Fine, it'll be one of the campfire tales tonight at supper," Nichols said, and untied the canoe.

Lydia poked him. "You a teeny bit jealous, Beau? Is that your problem?"

"Jealous of what? An acid trip you took twenty years ago?"

She rolled her eyes at McCleary. "He's jealous because I've known you longer than I've known him, can you believe it?"

"He's jealous," said McCleary, "because he was too busy playing ball to drop acid."

"You got it." Nichols's laugh was a little too hearty, and McCleary wondered just how far Lydia had stretched the truth when she'd told him the story.

3.

When they reached marker 148, McCleary steered left, into a new channel. It was clogged with branches, and for the first hundred yards, he had to cut a path through it with the machete.

After that, the channel widened a little, although they were still close enough to the mangroves to see the curved, tannin-stained roots that grew from the fertile soil beneath the water. According to the rings on the roots, clearly marking the water level in years past, the channel was at least a foot shallower than it should have been. Not surprising. This was the first hard rain since January; no wonder the canoes scraped bottom.

They had to backtrack and return to marker 145 before they found an alternate route to Hell's Bay. By then, they'd lost an hour, the rain was coming down harder, and the light within the tunnel of green was dim and murky, like contaminated water.

Near the end of the channel, where it emptied into the bay, the skies opened up. Rain poured through the tunnel of green, sweeping dry leaves and bugs with it. Then they were out from under the canopy, headed across the open waters of the bay, and the wind slammed into them. It whistled around McCleary's head, burned his eyes, whipped up whitecaps and waves. The rain fell in thick, silver sheets; he couldn't see the other side of the bay even when lightning cut a jagged blue path through the downpour.

"Which direction?" shouted Nichols.

"North," McCleary called, and tried to steer the canoe to the right. But the wind was invisible concrete, poured wet and thick from somewhere inside the light, in the swirling heart of the rain, and it knocked them left, to the west.

He and Quin paddled frantically on the left side, the right, the left again, but they went nowhere. A wave crashed over the side; water poured off his poncho and ran down inside it, soaking his clothes. Puddles sloshed over his running shoes and seeped through his socks to his feet. He dropped to his knees and shouted, *'Left!'*

Then he leaned with the wind and paddled hard and furiously on the left side until the canoe slowly angled north. The wind whistled, seized a flap on the tarp, and hurled it back, offering the supplies to the rain. Quin twisted around, slapping the plastic with her hands, trying to secure it, but to no avail. McCleary jerked the small cooler from the supplies and slammed it down over the corner of the tarp, but knew it was too late. Water was rising from the floor and oozing through the gear and supplies. At this rate, there wouldn't be so much as a dry paper towel when they reached the campsite.

The canoe pitched violently to the left and the cooler slid with it. McCleary grabbed it before it tumbled into the water, then yanked the corner of the tarp over the supplies and fixed it under one of the soggy sleeping bags. Water washed over his shoes again and again; a Styrofoam cup floated out from under the tarp. He shouted at Quin, but the wind swallowed his words, so he leaned toward her and gestured wildly at the mangroves behind them. She paddled like a woman possessed, her body a hunched yellow shape in front of him.

They turned. McCleary saw the Nicholses' canoe off to his right and slightly ahead. It bounced like a beach ball in the waves and tracked a haphazard path toward the mangroves. McCleary paddled faster to catch up. As he and Quin struck the right rhythm, the canoe crabbed into the wind, gaining speed. The rain hit them at an angle now, drumming against the hood of his poncho, deafening him.

As they drew alongside the other canoe, Nichols shouted something, but McCleary couldn't hear him and motioned for him to travel parallel to the trees. He signaled that he'd understood, and a moment later, his canoe swung left. McCleary and Quin quickly followed.

The mangroves provided some protection against the wind, but they were still traveling into it, losing a foot for every two they progressed. Unless something changed, which seemed unlikely, they would never make the chickee by dark.

He pulled in his paddle and told Quin to grab on to one of the trees and hold them steady while he took a look at the park map. He slipped it out of his poncho, then leaned over it to protect it from the rain, his nose almost touching the tarp that covered the gear.

It took him a minute or two to locate Lard Can campsite, about half a mile beyond this clutch of trees. It was nestled in a curve of mangroves that would probably provide some defense against the storm. He scanned the map for an alternate spot, but the thing was soaked, the ink had started to run, and finally, the wind tore it out of his hands, lifting it.

The map flapped wildly in the rain, a bird with a broken wing trying to gain altitude, then pinwheeled across the water and vanished. He shouted for Quin to let go of the tree and they were suddenly moving again.

They reached an indentation in the mangroves where the Nicholses were waiting. The wind wasn't as loud here and he could explain where they were headed without having to shout. Lydia, her eyes glazed with fatigue, grimaced as a roar of thunder swept across the water.

"I'd really like to go back. Not tomorrow, not when it stops raining, but now."

Like what everyone else wants doesn't count.

"Now?" Nichols exploded with laughter and slapped his hands against his wet thighs. Water rolled off his hood, down onto his forehead, and he blinked rapidly to keep it out of his eyes. He reminded McCleary of a seal that was struggling to juggle several things at once and not succeeding. "No way we're going back now. That'd be worse. How long do you think it'll take us to get to the campsite, Mac?"

"An hour tops."

Lydia ran a hand over her face. "I'll be psychotic by then."

"You've been psychotic for the last hour," Nichols said. "C'mon, let's get going."

Lydia glanced helplessly at Quin, seeking support. "Don't Quin and I have any say in this?"

Both men turned to Quin. She was still kneeling on the floor of the canoe, rocking as it rocked, a hand clutching either side. "Just get me wherever is closest."

"An hour to the campsite," McCleary repeated, dropping his paddle in the water.

"Fine." Quin nodded rapidly. "That sounds fine. Now

let's just get going, huh?'' With that, her face seized up, her skin turned absolutely white, and she leaned over the side of the canoe and threw up.

Lydia didn't say another word.

4.

Fifty minutes later, they approached the tongue of land on the eastern side of the mangroves. True to the map, it was set back in a half-moon bay that sheltered them from the wind. But the last of the light was oozing from the sky, the rain still swept across the bay, and tempers were short. They were like a family afflicted with cabin fever, McCleary thought, and it wouldn't take much to set one of them off. A wrong word, a misplaced look, one more snafu.

It was tricky finding an opening to the shore. The thick trees huddled over the water like thugs. Several spots that looked promising were blocked closer to shore by branches the storm had blown down. They had to twist back and try another entrance.

They finally made their way through a tunnel of leaves that smelled old and stale, of stagnant water, of dead things. The wind shook the branches, knocking loose twigs and leaves and more bugs. Big bugs, tiny bugs, fat bugs, bugs that crawled and flew and wiggled.

They were poked and scratched. The light died. The canoes struck ground and they scrambled onto land, digging for flashlights and lanterns. Light was suddenly more important than comfort, food, shelter. It was the magic that banished that primal fear of the dark, and once they had it, McCleary sensed an attempt among them to hold on to humor, the way people were supposed to do in situations like this. As they unloaded the canoes, Nichols cracked one-liners. They weren't very funny, and even though everyone laughed, the laughter was weak and brittle, a nervous release that might topple any second into something less civilized, perhaps even a little ugly.

Nothing was dry. The sleeping bags would probably take several weeks to dry completely, the stove was shot. They might be able to salvage some of the food in the paper bags, but McCleary guessed most of it was inedible. There also didn't seem to be any spot in the small clearing to pitch the tents. The ground was either as soft as angel-food cake or had turned to mud.

Quin suggested they look for a place in the trees to camp, where it might be drier.

"Drier?" Nichols's laugh was a fraction this side of ugly. "What difference does *dry* make when everything we've got is so wet it's already rotting?"

"I don't want to sleep in the woods." Lydia jammed her hands inside the poncho and huddled close to Nichols. "There might be snakes."

"Snakes don't come out in weather like this," said McCleary. His eyes followed Quin as she trudged away from them, the beam of her flashlight preceding her into the trees. "They're too smart."

"Which says a hell of a lot for us," mumbled Nichols, slipping an arm around Lydia's shoulders.

Her head bobbed in agreement.

Great, thought McCleary. Now it had turned into a *them-against-us* routine. "Do what you want. We're setting up our tent in the trees."

He picked up an armful of gear and hurried after Quin. She marched on, the ubiquitous beam darting here, there. She didn't slow down when he caught up to her. "Good idea. About the trees."

"Right about now, I'd sleep in the water if it meant getting away from them."

"They're probably saying the same thing about us."

"Yeah." Quin's laugh was sharp. "No doubt."

"I'm really sorry about this."

"Don't be. It's not your fault. You didn't know the weather was going to be shit. We should've gotten a forecast."

"I don't mean the weather. I mean Lydia and Beau."

She shrugged. "Forget it." The light stopped under a tree. "How about right here?"

"Looks good enough to me."

He dropped the gear and fixed the hurricane light so it faced up, dispersing its light against the underside of the nearest trees. They worked silently, quickly, and erected the tent in record time. Its floor was relatively dry, but without the sleeping bags, it was going to be about as comfortable as a sidewalk on the streets of New York.

Quin, however, had packed a couple of blankets in a plastic dry-cleaning bag. They were damp around the edges, but dry where it counted, which was more than he could say for the rest of their things.

They redeemed what they could of their food and supplies and stored the stuff in the corner of the tent with their backpacks. Then they wrapped everything else inside the tarp, put it under one of the trees, and zipped themselves up inside the tent.

Rain drummed against it, but it seemed distant, no longer connected to them, no more real than noises in a movie. Off came their wet ponchos. Quin's hair tumbled in damp umber curls to her shoulders. She combed her fingers through it, ran her hands over her wet shirt and jeans, and made a face. "Somewhere in here I've got dry clothes." She gestured toward her backpack. "And dry matches for that lamp you're fiddling with."

"How about extra batteries for the hurricane light? I don't know if matches are going to salvage this thing."

"No batteries. That was your department." She dug through her backpack and shoulder bag and brought out a pair of nectarines, a plastic bag filled with trail mix, a canteen of water, and two sodas. "Dinner." She lined up everything in front of her like a child taking inventory of her most prized possessions. "And dessert." She held up the fattest joint this side of the sixties and grinned.

"From Lydia?"

"Who else. She gave me five more the size of this one."

"Let me guess. You went to the store for some last-minute items and she didn't have enough cash to pay her share. When you got back to the house and she asked Beau to pay you, he said he needed to cash a traveler's check. So she paid you with the joints."

Quin laughed and rocked back on her heels, her palms flat against her thighs. "Close."

Yeah, he thought. Real close. Lydia had never left the sixties. "Can you find those matches?"

"Matches, matches." Her hand vanished inside a flap on her backpack; out came another plastic bag with several boxes of matches inside. "Still dry. If only I can be so lucky with a change of clothes."

She tossed him the bag of matches, then embarked on a meticulous exploration for dry clothes. She came up with a cotton workshirt and a pair of khaki shorts. She sat on the floor of the tent, removed her running shoes and socks, then turned away from him as she took off her wet shirt and bra. Her bare back gleamed damply in the light; he could count the steps in her spine.

He suddenly wanted to touch her, to love her, to apologize for everything that hadn't existed between them since their separation and before, when he couldn't remember her. He wondered if this was what he'd actually had in mind when he'd asked her to come on this trip. He hadn't really given it much thought at the time. It had just seemed right that Quin should come along, as though the trip were a natural extension of their occasional dinners together. Now he realized he had been insensitive, considering her dislike for Lydia, and felt he should apologize for that as well.

But the time for apologies about anything was long past. The best course seemed to be the one they'd followed for months now, in which they rarely discussed the separation or the marriage or why neither of them had filed for divorce. These details comprised a third presence they had both chosen to ignore, like sounds in a haunted house.

The evasion, he supposed, was a form of denial similar to what happened when someone was diagnosed with a fatal disease. *If I ignore it, it'll go away.* Like that. As for the fact that neither of them had taken any steps toward divorce . . . Well, maybe at some level she felt as he did, that as long as they were only separated, a reconciliation was possible. But, on the other hand, it was likely that she hadn't filed because it was just simpler not to.

She slipped on the dry shirt, stood, and peeled off her wet jeans. Even though the shirt ended at midthigh, she seemed to be all legs, five-ten and still growing. Considering the amount of food she packed away, she should have weighed two hundred pounds. But she was blessed with a metabolism that burned calories the way an air conditioner did electricity and was happiest when she ate every two hours, like an infant. Which meant that right about now, she was probably ravenous.

She pulled on the shorts and sat down Indian-style, eyeing the spread of food. "So what'll it be first, Mc-Cleary?"

"Dessert."

She smiled and lit the joint.

Just as he took a hit, a high, shrill scream cut through the din of the storm. Lydia's scream. It broke into quick, staccato bursts, as though she had hiccups and couldn't catch her breath, then settled into a long, mindless noise.

5.

McCleary and Quin were on their feet and out of the tent in seconds flat, their flashlights dancing through the darkness, but barely penetrating it. Suddenly Lydia flew directly into the light, her hair wild around her head, her arms flailing at the air. She was no longer screaming. But her breath erupted from her in loud, terrible rasps that sounded as if she had a tube stuck in her throat that she was trying to spit out. Her panic was so extreme, she probably wouldn't have seen them if McCleary hadn't grabbed her.

"What is it? What's wrong?"

She gasped and stuttered and tripped over her words like someone who didn't speak the language. She stabbed at the darkness behind her. "In th-there. I . . . I needed to go to the bathroom and I . . . two bodies . . ."

Nichols tore into the woods just then, waving his flashlight, and Lydia ran to him, ran as though McCleary and Quin were the enemies. "Bodies?" Quin asked, staring after her. "Is that what she said?"

"Stay here with them. I'll be right back."

He sprinted into the trees, his soggy shoes sinking into ground so soft that it would be a river of mud in another six hours. It didn't take him long to find what had frightened Lydia. The bodies were face down in the wet leaves and had been there long enough for the bugs to get to them. The woman had been shot at a fairly close range. At first McCleary thought the man had been stabbed in the back with a knife, but when he examined the wound more closely, he realized a knife wouldn't have torn the flesh like this when it was removed.

He went through the man's pockets and came up with a handful of change and a wallet empty of bills but crammed with credit cards and ID. According to his license, he was Charles Crawford III and lived in Coconut Grove. The address was in an expensive neighborhood, if McCleary remembered correctly. There was nothing on the woman to identify her.

"Christ." Nichols stopped beside him. The steady patter of the rain made his voice sound like that of a three-year-old lost in a department store. "What the hell are we going to do?"

McCleary shook his head and pushed himself to his feet. "Nothing tonight. But tomorrow we've got to head back and report this to the ranger's station."

Nichols continued to stare at the bodies; the glare of his flashlight washed across them from head to toe. "Maybe we should move the tents closer together."

"Good idea."

"Sorry about before."

"Don't worry about it."

Nichols rubbed his hand across his mouth. "You got a gun with you?"

"No."

"Any kind of weapon?"

"Swiss Army knife."

"Shit."

"What about you?"

"Nope. Nothing. You think whoever did it will be back?"

And because Nichols was a fretter, McCleary shook his head. "I doubt it." He said it with far more conviction than he felt. "Why would they bother?"

"Yeah."

The two men looked at each other, back down at the bodies, then turned and walked toward the clearing where the women were.

Visitors

1.

THE RAIN CAME in fits and starts, like a tired engine that couldn't decide whether to die or keep on fighting, Quin thought.

Rolls of thunder were followed by brilliant bursts of lightning that turned the inside of the tent the color of faded denim. She counted by thousands during the lapses between one and the other, then couldn't remember what it was supposed to measure. The distance of the lightning from where she was? The storm's distance from her? *Does it matter?*

Her eyes ached with fatigue, but every time she closed them, she was racing into the trees after McCleary, then watching as he and Nichols turned the bodies over. The man and woman were supine in the wet leaves, ants scurrying over their cheeks. In her mind, she saw the worm inching across the bridge of the woman's nose and the torn flesh of the wound in the man's back. Lucid images, as bright as aluminum.

She had seen a wound like the man's before but couldn't remember where or when. At a seminar? In the Dade County coroner's office? In a movie? Well, it would come to her. Maybe then she would be able to sleep. Or, better yet, it would be light when she remembered and they would be on their way out of here and the wound and the bodies would be someone else's problem.

So much for the subtle beauty of the Everglades.

She flipped over onto her stomach, trying to find a comfortable position on the blankets. But she could feel every pebble, every root, every depression in the ground. Something poked at her hipbone. She rolled onto her side and stared at McCleary's back. She wished she had something to cover herself with. She wished she hadn't come. She wished she had her own tent. She wished she were anywhere but here.

She sat up, peeled off her shorts, dug in the backpack until she found the jeans, and pulled them on. She felt safer with her legs covered. She lay back on her side, brought the backpack against her, and hugged it like a pillow. Her eyes closed. Opened again.

What time was it? Nine? Ten? What time did the sun rise? How long before they could leave? Ten hours? Eleven? A lot could happen in eleven hours.

The rain might stop.

She might consume all of the food in the backpack.

The rain might get worse.

Lightning might strike the tent.

Whoever killed the man and woman might come back. But the killer had gotten what he wanted—a canoe, supplies, camping gear, the money in the man's wallet—so there wasn't any reason to return, was there?

No. Definitely not.

So close your eyes.

She did, and saw the man, the woman.

The man has a name, Quin.

Charles. Charles Crawford III, of Coconut Grove.

With a name like that, he probably came from a family with money. Or a family that wished it had money.

He had driven—what? A Mercedes? A BMW? Or something flashier, like a Porsche?

A Porsche, she decided. And he lived in one of those *very* expensive town houses in Coconut Grove and probably owned a yacht and . . .

It could have been us. Mac and me. The Nicholses.

Timing, she thought. Everything in life was timing.

If she hadn't come on this trip, if Lydia hadn't gone into the woods to go to the bathroom, if Charles Crawford III had chosen a different campsite, if the Nicholses hadn't visited Miami, if she hadn't taken that trip to Canada last summer . . .

Timing.

Ififif.

She pressed the heels of her hands against her eyes. *This is not my real life.* This was a mistake, an illusion, some sly trick the Glades had played on her—on all of them. When they awakened tomorrow morning, the bodies would be gone because they'd never been there to begin with. McCleary would whistle a couple of bars from the *Twilight Zone*. Nichols would make some crack about Lydia's loco weed and break out the Scotch again. And for the rest of the camping trip they would puzzle over this inexplicable event in the privacy of their own heads, and twenty years from now, each of them would have a different memory of what had actually happened.

None would be true.

Or all would be true.

2.

"Quin? You awake?"

"Yeah."

McCleary rolled onto his back; so did Quin. "Do you still carry that bottle of mace on you?"

The mace had never been intended to ward off anything but canine attacks when she ran. She hadn't carried the stuff for several years. "You remember that?"

"Sure."

Sure. As though all his memories were in place. As though none of them had ever been missing.

"But I can't remember whether you replenished it when it ran dry," he added.

"I didn't. Why?"

"Just wondering."

"It could hardly count as a weapon."

"I know."

"Do you think we should take the bodies ourselves tomorrow or just notify the ranger's station and let someone else pick them up?"

"We should take them. If we can get them in the canoes with the gear and everything."

She didn't really want to talk about the bodies and apparently he didn't, either. Rain filled their silence. Quin stared at the ceiling of the tent. There was a piece of clear plastic in the center of it, a skylight, a window to the world, a transparent eye. But it was too dark to see it or anything outside unless the lightning flashed.

During other camping trips, the skylight had opened

to moonlight, stars, sunrise, a hawk circling through a patch of blue sky. She wondered if McCleary recalled any of that.

"You mind if I ask you something?"

He laughed. "Since when do you have to ask permission?"

Since you moved out of the house. But she didn't say it. "Just what *do* you remember? About us?"

"Small things mostly."

"Like what?"

"Like the first time I saw you. After Grant had been killed. You were sitting on the front porch when I drove up. I remember thinking you looked like a schoolteacher."

"Thanks a lot."

He chuckled. "I was only ten years off base."

She was suddenly grateful for the dark, which made it easier for them to talk, and for the distraction of conversation. "I didn't like you much that night."

"Can't blame you. I thought you might've killed him."

The marriage went sour, she thought, because things between her and McCleary started with a death. Sure. It made a terrible kind of sense. Grant Bell's death. She'd lived with him for more than a year before McCleary's partner and the woman he'd been in love with had killed him.

Another death. Infidelities. Mac and I never had a chance.

But the Grant part of her life no longer seemed real. It had happened to another Quin. Any vividness that still lingered in the details were like those from a book she'd read or a movie she'd seen. "What other things do you remember?"

He recounted incidents that had happened during cases they'd worked on together. A surveillance that had gone haywire, a break-in at the home of a small-time crook that they'd nearly blown, the pound of fresh shrimp she'd eaten the night they'd sat in a bar waiting for a contact who'd never shown. The details and events were oddly selective and sometimes didn't match her own recollections.

It was the sort of thing she sometimes encountered

while investigating a case. A pair of witnesses to the same event could describe it so differently, it was like two separate incidents. This disparity was an adult version, of the old children's game of Pass It On, where you gave a person a phrase or a sentence that he was to pass on to the person next to him. By the time the phrase had gotten back to the first person, it wasn't even remotely similar to the original phrase. No two people perceived the same event in exactly the same way.

So listening to McCleary's reminiscences made her feel that the terrain of their marriage was still new, undiscovered, that its geography had undergone a subtle transformation during the months they'd been apart. The change, if that's what it was, had come about without their active participation, as though the marriage possessed a life, a momentum, of its own.

But then he spoiled it. He asked why she hadn't filed for divorce, and she had the impression that it was what he'd intended to ask all along. When she spoke, she tried not to sound defensive but didn't entirely succeed.

"Why haven't *you* filed? You're the one who moved out."

He hesitated. "Divorce seems so . . . I don't know. So final, I guess."

Why couldn't he, for once, just be direct? She lifted up on an elbow, wishing she could see his eyes, his face. "Meaning what, Mac?"

"That I don't want things to be final."

"Then what *do* you want?"

"What do *you* want?"

"For you to answer my question."

"I'd like to try again."

So the trip had been a setup for this, for McCleary's pitch for reconciliation, she thought. As if the last year could be wiped out because he'd said the magic words. Yes, there were extenuating circumstances. Yes, the separation had been the wisest decision at the time. But what about the months when *her* desires hadn't mattered? What about the days and weeks when his absence in her life loomed as large as the county landfill? Now that he'd apparently made a decision, he seemed to think she would simply accept it, that she'd been waiting around for this.

"I don't know if that's what I want."

Silence. Then: "Is there someone else?"

Typical. Just because she didn't feel the same as he did, the reason had to be another man. "It's just how I feel, okay? For all I know, you decided a reconciliation is the way to go because there's no one else in your life and good ol' Quin is available and you've already invested nearly six years in the relationship."

"That's unfair."

Unfair? You want to talk about unfair? Her anger was sudden and probably unreasonable, but she didn't care. She sat up, grabbed her backpack, pulled it over to her, then patted the floor for the flashlight. "This whole thing was a big mistake." She found the flashlight, switched it on, shone it around until she spotted her shoes. "I knew that, but I came. That was stupid. They're *your* friends, and hell, Lydia doesn't like me any more than I do her." She yanked on her wet socks, jammed her feet into her running shoes. "Really stupid."

He sat forward. "What're you doing?"

"Sleeping outside. Under the tarp or something." She shrugged on her poncho and grabbed her backpack. "I should've done it earlier."

She expected him to reason with her, argue with her, or make some snide remark, but he didn't. He scooped up his poncho, his flashlight, and pushed himself to his feet. "Forget it. I'll go."

She rubbed a hand over her face, started to say something, but McCleary suddenly whispered, "Turn off the flashlight."

Her thumb hit the switch; the tent went dark. "What is it?" she whispered.

"I heard something."

She listened but heard only the rain. "What? What did you hear?"

"I'm not sure." He brushed past her as he moved toward the front of the tent and unzipped it partway.

"See anything?"

"Nothing. I'm going to have a look around."

"Wait for me."

He drew the zipper down the rest of the way and stepped outside, Quin right behind him. They stood for a moment with their backs to the tent, clutching their flashlights but not turning them on. She pulled air into her lungs, air that smelled of incredible richness, of water and black soil, of moss and fish and unimagined things. But it felt wrong.

Years ago, she'd felt this same wrongness at an amusement park seconds before a car on the Mad Mouse had veered off its track and crashed into a popcorn stand, killing the two people on board and five more on the ground.

That kind of wrongness.

McCleary touched her arm; she leaned closer to him. "You feel it?" he whispered.

She nodded.

"Let's check on Beau and Lydia."

She glanced uneasily at the woods. So much darkness. And now it would be at their backs.

3.

The Nicholses' tent was at the edge of the trees, where they'd moved it after Lydia had found the bodies. They crept toward it. Wind skipped through branches. Leaves fluttered around her, caught in her hair, kissed her cheeks, stuck to her poncho like leeches. She looked back, saw nothing, and was beginning to feel ridiculously paranoid when a twig snapped somewhere to her right.

She froze. So did McCleary.

Suddenly there was light everywhere, bright, white, blinding. She threw up her arm to cover her eyes. "You move and you're dead," promised a man she couldn't see. The loud, distinctive sound of a pump shotgun punctuated his words. "Now just toss them flashlights on the ground . . . uh-huh, real good. You keep followin directions and no one'll get hurt. Hands locked on top of your heads . . . that's right."

The beam of light danced to the side. Black dots popped inside Quin's eyes. She blinked rapidly to clear her vision and immediately wished she had not. The first thing she saw, illumined in a circle of light, was Nichols, slumped on the ground, motionless.

The beam darted from him to a sinewy woman who

might have been thirty or fifty and looked like every child's image of the wicked witch. A snake tattoo started just under her right eye and twisted down her cheek. Her gray-streaked hair hung loosely to her shoulders. She was dressed in a dark raincoat, jeans, and alligator boots. She stood with one leg slightly in front of the other and her body angled with almost careless precision in a classic archer's stance. Her bow and arrow were trained on Lydia, who was sitting on the ground, her arms wrapped around her knees.

Terror had skewed her features, upsetting the delicate balance on which her beauty depended. One eye seemed lower than the other, as if an invisible finger were pulling it down at the corner. Her mouth was slack, her nostrils flared like a horse's, strands of her black hair were plastered to her cheeks. She kept rolling her lower lip against her teeth, and her eyes darted like nervous insects from the archer to her companion.

"The lady with the bow is Opal," said the man. "You ain't wantin to fuck with her."

Now the light slipped to a very thin man who must have been six-four or -five. His shoulders were stooped, as though he were self-conscious about his height, and his dark hair was pulled back in a ponytail, accentuating the gauntness of his face. A face, she thought, that whispered of generations of incest. He was popping chewing gum and clutching what looked like a homemade spear. "This boy here is Judd. My son. He does things with that there spear that'll make your head spin. And I'm Weston."

He aimed the flashlight at himself. It struck the underside of his jaw and threw his face into a chaos of light and shadows. *Weston, the ugliest of them all.* He could have been a character actor playing an Indian. His features bore that same incestuous taint as Judd's but with traces of other blood, Seminole or Miccosukee, Spanish, Caucasian, Negroid, as though his genes contained the vast history of the peoples who had inhabited the Glades. His low, sloping forehead, topped by bushy brows, gave him a faintly simian appearance. His eyes were so deeply set they existed as nothing but pockets of shadow in his face. All sorts of things hung from his belt: an extra flashlight, tools, ammunition, lengths of rope.

"You've made your point," McCleary said. "Now what do you want?"

The woman exploded with laughter. "Hear that, Weston? The man's askin what we want. Show him, hon. Just go on and show him."

The light skipped across the wet ground and stopped ten yards to Opal's left, illuminating the two bodies Lydia had stumbled across in the woods. "We come back to get rid of Charlie and Vi," said Weston. "They was stupid. Stupid people end up dead. We just wanted their supplies, but Charlie got it in his head to show off for Vi." The light found McCleary. "You goin to show off for the ladies, asshole?"

"Not as long as you've got a weapon."

Judd let out a weird sound that was supposed to be a laugh, a *yuck yuck* followed by a wheeze. He stabbed at the air with his spear. "He ain't stupid, Pa."

"Coulda fooled me. Get them flashlights they tossed."

Judd looked like a pogo stick when he moved, lifting up on the balls of his feet, settling down, lifting again. He scooped up the flashlights, stuck them in a battered flight bag slung over his shoulder, glanced at Quin. Their eyes momentarily connected; his were as vacant as the moon.

"Just take our supplies and leave us alone." Lydia's voice cracked with fear. "We haven't done anything to you."

"I'd like that, little lady," said Weston. "I'd like that a lot. But you folks'll be comin with us, for a spell, anyway. Can't have you goin back to the ranger's station and spillin your guts. That won't do none of us no good."

"Once those people are reported missing, the rangers will come looking for them," Lydia rushed on. "And for us, too."

Shut up, Lydia, just shut the hell up, Quin thought.

"I got no problem with that," said Weston. "Them rangers don't know the Glades like us."

"Like us. That's right." Judd yucked again.

"So here's what we're gonna do," Weston continued,

and swung his shotgun toward McCleary. "You help Judd. Get your buddy there on the ground. And don't try nothin. Otherwise these ladies and your buddy ain't gonna see the sun. Got it?"

"Yes," said McCleary.

Judd waved McCleary over with his spear. "Get the guy."

As McCleary crossed the clearing to where Judd stood, Weston pointed his weapon at Quin. "You. Get over here and sit down next to her. Toss that pack over here."

All things are possible in the Glades, she thought as she walked over to them. But this wasn't what she'd had in mind.

Quin threw her pack toward Weston and lowered herself to the ground, her thoughts spinning, racing, seeking a way out, as McCleary crouched next to Nichols. "He's got a gash on his forehead." He paused. "And an arrow stuck in his thigh."

This elicited another yuck from Judd. "Yeah, Ma never misses 'less she wants to." He jabbed the spear within inches of McCleary's face. "C'mon, hurry up."

"Jesus," Lydia whispered.

"Shut your mouth," snapped Opal.

If they had a chance to make a break for it—and that prospect seemed damn bleak at the moment, Quin thought—Lydia was going to be as useless as her unconscious husband. Somehow that realization drove Quin's alarm back into a corner of her mind, where it circled, dark and fleet, waiting.

McCleary lifted Nichols by the arms and draped him over his shoulder. As he turned, Quin saw the arrow protruding from Nichols's thigh and understood what had made the wound in Crawford's back: an arrowhead yanked from skin and muscle.

"Which way?" McCleary asked.

Judd fumbled in the flight bag, pulled out one of the flashlights she and McCleary had been carrying, switched it on. "Down there." He pointed left.

"The canoes are to the right."

"Not now they ain't. *Move.*"

"I'll cover them two here, Opal," said Weston. "Check through the tents for shit we can use."

She relaxed the bow and hooked it over her shoulder. The arrow went back into the quiver. "All their gear's soaked from the rain."

"It'll dry, Opal. Jesus. Just get what we need, huh?"

She turned on her heel and strutted off toward the Nicholses' tent, her narrow hips swaying. A flash of lightning overhead marked her departure.

"Sometimes," Weston muttered, "she ain't too bright." He pointed his shotgun at Lydia and asked what her name was. When she told him, he rolled it over his tongue, pronouncing it Lee-dee-uh, and nodded with approval. "Pretty name. And your friend?"

"Quin," said Quin.

"Quin?" He laughed. "What the hell kinda name is that?"

Ask my mother. "Foreign."

"You got that right." He laughed again, and Quin looked away from him, fixing her gaze on the darkness where McCleary and Judd had vanished. It was like a curtain, that blackness, and she kept waiting for it to part, for McCleary to appear, to sneak up behind Weston the Ugly and slam something over his head. But nothing happened.

Beside her, Lydia's arms were still locked around her knees; her forehead rested against them. She was sucking air in through her teeth; it made soft, hissing sounds, like steam escaping from a teapot. Quin couldn't tell if she was crying or trying to calm herself. She hoped it was the latter.

Opal returned to the clearing with things from the Nicholses' tent rolled inside one of the sleeping bags, which she dragged across the ground. She left everything in front of Weston, fixed her hands on her hips, said, "But it'll dry, won't it, hon," then strutted off again.

Weston swung his flashlight up so that the beam struck her back. "Bang," he said softly. "You're dead." Then he laughed and looked around. "Hey, Judd, everything okay?"

Silence.

"Judd?"

Quin worked her fingers into the wet ground as she and Lydia exchanged a glance. No words were needed.

She knew Lydia was thinking the same thing she was. *Get ready to hurl mud and run.*

But run where? Just where the hell were they going to run?

Away. Just away.

Minutes passed.

"Hey, Opal," shouted Weston. "Go check on Judd."

"Judd can take care of hisself," she called back.

His flashlight found her midway to the clearing, pulling another sleeping bag through the rain and the mud. On top of it was Quin and McCleary's cooler.

"We ain't got ice for that cooler," Weston said.

"I want it for some of my things."

"We got four extra people and too much stuff for the canoes."

She deposited the gear with the other things, brushed her palms together, brought a hand up under her stringy hair, and flicked it off her shoulders. "How come when it's stuff *you* want, we got plenty of room, and when it's stuff I want, there ain't no room?"

"Because he's the boss," said Lydia.

Quin winced as Weston's head snapped toward Lydia. "Keep your mouth shut."

"He ain't," said Opal. "We're equal. Tell her, Wes. We're equal. That's how it is in the family."

Not *our* family, Quin noted, but *the* family. Like the Manson gang.

"Go check on Judd," he told her again.

"I'm taking this stuff," she replied.

"Not the cooler."

"I *want* the cooler. I need it. I can tie it behind the canoe and float it."

"Fine, Christ, fine. Now go check on the boy."

Her smile said she knew she'd won and she didn't care who knew about it and just what was the big fucking deal about Judd, anyway? As the darkness swallowed her, she was preparing her bow.

4.

Quin counted the seconds.

The seconds melted into minutes.

Weston got antsy. He stepped back and, without taking

his eyes from Quin and Lydia, shouted for Opal. When there was no reply, Quin moved her left fist closer to her thigh. Her fingers clutched mud, bits of stone.

Her heart sped up. She blinked raindrops from her eyelashes.

Please, McCleary, hurry and do whatever you're going to do.

Weston yelled for Opal again, Judd, Opal. He swore to himself. His thin legs danced back another step, forward, back again. His head jerked around once, but it happened too quickly and he was too far away for Quin to get a good shot at him. A shot that would count.

Suddenly Weston pumped the shotgun and yelled, "Your lady gets it first, pal. You got five seconds." He grinned at Quin and started counting, the shotgun aimed at her head.

"One thousand . . ."

Her stomach rolled through acid.

"Two thousand . . ."

"Sweet Christ," Lydia whispered.

"Shut up, bitch!" he shouted. "Three thousand . . . You hear me, man? The skinny broad goes first." He marched over to Quin, grabbed her by the hair, jerked her head back. "Call him. Call the bastard."

She gasped, shouted, "Mac, he means it!"

Then her arm flew up and the fistful of mud and pebbled struck Weston in the eyes. He bellowed and dropped the shotgun and the flashlight as he clawed at his face. He stumbled backward and Quin lunged forward and grabbed the shotgun just as McCleary burst from the trees, shouting "Head for the canoes!"

He slammed into Weston and both men went down, rolling, grunting, fists punching. Quin scooped her pack from the ground and danced around them, jabbing at Weston with the end of the gun, waiting for the moment when she could club him without also hitting McCleary. When the moment came, she swung the gun high and hard and brought it down against the backs of Weston's legs. The small of his back. The side of his head. He shrieked, he groaned, he writhed. McCleary stumbled to his feet and they tore into the trees.

5.

Light: They headed toward it.

Quin's breath balled in her chest. Her legs were rubbery. Her pack felt like some hideous tumor that weighted her right shoulder.

Behind them, Weston's shouts cut through the dark, pushing her faster, faster. Her eyes fastened on the light. It came from Lydia, who was in one of the canoes with Nichols. He was conscious and trying to start the tiny outboard engine; he yelled for them to hurry.

Just before they reached the water, they passed Opal, sprawled in the mud and dead leaves, as still as a fallen stick figure in a cartoon. Three yards beyond Opal was Judd and he wasn't moving, either. But there was no question that he was dead: his own spear protruded from his back.

The outboard kicked over, the light went out, and the Nicholses' canoe chugged away. Weston charged through the trees behind them, raging like a madman. McCleary grabbed the shotgun and shoved the flashlight into Quin's hand. *"Go!"* he hissed. "Start the motor in the other canoe!"

As she ran, he spun and fired twice into the darkness. The shots rang out, pure and clear, like musical notes the wetness held together.

She reached the water. Switched on the flashlight. Three canoes. Only one with an outboard. It was tied to a nearby tree and she lost precious moments fumbling with the rope because her fingers wouldn't work right; they felt thick and awkward, twice their normal size.

By the time she got it loose and scrambled into the canoe, McCleary was cutting loose their own canoes. He shoved them out into the water. They wouldn't go far; the foliage would stop them. But it would compensate for the time she'd lost with the rope, for the time she was losing with the outboard, trying to crank it up. Time, Jesus, time was everything.

He pumped two more shots into the trees. The engine sputtered, popped, gasped, and for an instant, she thought it was going to die altogether. Then it caught and the canoe pitched as McCleary leaped in. They putted out into the black, the rain. *Away, away.*

Aftermath

I DIDN'T HEAR nothing for a long time except the sound of the outboards going north. When I couldn't hear them no more, my head and back started screeching from where the bitch had hit me with the shotgun. Blood oozed from a gash at the side of my head. I could feel Opal behind me, knew what she was doing, knew I oughta go over to her, but my legs wasn't listening. There was this huge aching hole in my chest and I needed to fill it with something. With anything.

Finally, I unhooked the flashlight from my belt and walked over to where she was. She didn't look up. Didn't speak. I hated that silence. I shone the flashlight on her son.

My son.

Our son.

He was on his side. The spear done gone straight through his chest and come out on the other side. I just looked at it. At the beads of water that sparkled in his hair. At the emptiness in his eyes. The hole in my chest got bigger.

I dropped to my knees, blinked, squeezed my eyes shut, opened them again. Judd still hadn't moved.

"Jesus God."

I touched my fingers to his neck. No heartbeat. The skin was cold and wet. "Judd." I patted his cheek. "Wake up. Wake the hell up."

"The big man done it." Opal's voice was hard and dead. "The one with the arrow in his leg. He did it. I seen him do it."

"He was out."

"Uh-uh. He come to. I seen him, Wes. He come to."

It didn't matter to me who done it, the big man or the

51

other. They was all going to pay. No one did this to the band and got away with it. No man, no beast, no one.

I closed my boy's eyes, then I stood, handed Opal the flashlight, grabbed hold of the spear. I worked it slowly out of his back.

"They took our canoes. One of them broke my bow."

"Yeah." I didn't want to listen to her. *"Take the woman back into the trees and dump her. I'll take the guy. We ain't got room for them in the canoe."*

"We have to paddle home."

"We gotta catch a canoe first. The fuckers cut 'em loose." I pulled the spear free.

"And then what, Weston?"

"You know."

"Tell me. Tell me, anyway."

"Go get the woman, Opal." I lifted Judd, cradled him. He didn't weigh nothing at all. *"I'll take care of Judd."*

She grabbed my arm. "Tell me." Tears stood in her eyes. I'd never seen Opal cry. Never. Not in all the years I knowed her. "Tell me what we're gonna do to them, Wes. I need to hear it." She wiped the back of her hand across her cheek, across the snake tattoo.

"We'll hunt 'em down."

"Can we find 'em?"

"You know we can. There's more of us than them. We know the Glades. They don't know shit."

"They's armed. They got your shotgun."

"I got other guns."

"When we catch 'em, Wes, what're we gonna do to 'em?"

I thought of the old ways. I thought of my people, men who'd worked on the Panama Canal and survived the mosquito sickness, the fever, the heat, the jungle. I thought of how when the canal was finished, they came here to Florida because the climate was what they was used to. Some pushed into the Glades, where they bred with the Seminoles and Miccosukees and each other.

My grandpa was half Seminole, a renegade medicine man who married a white lady, another man's woman. My pa was the youngest of their boys and my ma was a full-blooded Seminole. I was the youngest of their four boys—with other half brothers and sisters—and I married Opal, my cousin, who was three-quarters Seminole. We got three boys and a girl and Judd was the oldest. The firstborn.

Now he was dead and the old ways was whispering to me, telling me what we had to do. And them ways could kill a man just from fear, I knowed it, I seen it happen. I seen the look in an outsider's eyes when the medicine man brought the gold box out and took off the lid.

"Wes?" Opal squeezed my arm. "Tell me. Tell me what we'll do to them. For killin Judd."

"We make 'em pay," I said, and told her how.

PART TWO

Flight
May 10

"If geographic areas could be put in human form, the Everglades National Park would be a schizophrenic."

The Miami Herald

Refuge

1.

FLIGHT: THE WORD assumed new meaning for McCleary.

Until now, it was something birds and outlaws did. Or it had numbers after it, as in Flight 407. But it had never meant hauling ass in a canoe with this breed of crazies on his tail.

And they are *coming,* whispered a voice inside him. *Weston and his lethal lady. They're coming because they believe one of you killed their son.*

McCleary wasn't sure how long it had been since they'd fled from the campsite. One hour, two, maybe much longer. He'd lost his watch in their scramble to escape and now his senses of time and direction were skewed.

Wrong word, old buddy. Your sense of everything is missing, got it? Missing. Gone. Absent. Dead.

The head wind was eating up gas in the outboard, hurling rain in their faces, flinging water into the canoe. The odds, in fact, seemed quite good that the storm would never stop, the sun would never rise, the puny outboard would ferret them deeper and deeper into the Glades until it ran out of gas, and he would never know exactly where they were in relation to Hell's Bay or anywhere else. He suddenly felt like a character in a scene that had been abandoned when the author got writer's block. Now he and Quin—who'd sneaked into this scene—were destined to repeat these events over and over again, without variation, forever.

If I had a map . . .

Who was he kidding? A map wouldn't make any difference at this point. It was too dark to see landmarks or channel markers. It was too dark to see if landmarks or markers even existed. It was too dark to see a god-damn thing at all. Even Quin.

Sometimes, just to reassure himself that she was still there, he shouted, "You okay? Can you keep paddling?" And she would shout back or switch on the flashlight and shine it around to make sure they weren't too close to the trees. Or about to run aground. Or putting through floating branches and weeds that would tangle in the motor.

At the beginning, as they'd sped out of the bay, he'd been able to see the flashlight in the Nicholses' canoe. It had bobbed in the blackness, small and trite and hopeful, and he'd followed it, willing Nichols to slow down, to give him and Quin an opportunity to catch up. But the light had long since vanished. McCleary guessed they'd turned off somewhere or the batteries in the flashlight had burned out. He worried about the arrow in Nichols's thigh. About the pain. The risk of infection. His weakness from the blow on the head he'd sustained before he'd fallen.

The blow that had knocked him out. The blow that had turned the outing from a bad experience into a nightmare. He worried because he liked Nichols, because he felt responsible for him and Lydia. But most of all he worried because what affected the Nicholses would ultimately affect him and Quin as well.

Her flashlight found the water puddled on the floor of the canoe, an alarming amount of water that seeped up around the supplies the crazies had left behind. Even though the stuff was wrapped like an eggroll in a tarp it wouldn't be long before the water got to it—and to the shotgun, which he'd wedged under the tarp.

"We need to stop and bail!" Quin shouted.

He wished she wouldn't shout. He wished she would stop saying the obvious. He wished his eyes would quit following the light every time it appeared, holding on to it like a lifeline, like a magical thread that would lead them out of here. Now the light was aimed to their left, and he tracked it, and yes, he saw the mangrove looming like a hunchback whale, and yes, it was probably a safer place than here, wherever here was. But he didn't want to stop—not to bail, not to rest, not to eat. He didn't want to stop until dozens of miles separated them from the crazies.

But if these supplies were ruined, they would be left with nothing except what was in Quin's pack. Which probably didn't amount to much more than a couple of joints and some fruit.

He veered toward the mangrove, cut back on the power. Quin aimed the light at the water; it was difficult to tell just how deep it was. The storm had stirred the silt and moss on the bottom, turning the water as murky as ink. Just to be safe, he killed the engine and pulled the motor up and out of the water.

The wind immediately caught them, pushing them dangerously close to the mangrove. He grabbed the paddle and fought the currents, struggling to keep them clear of the trees until they spotted a channel. But the wind was stronger, it was a howling bitch with a will of her own, tossing the canoe around like a fallen branch, spitting out his paddle, driving them closer and closer to the trees.

Quin's light skipped across the wet, dripping green. "Just ahead. I think I see a channel."

But the paddle was useless for steering. The only way he could control the canoe was by grabbing onto a branch and pulling them closer to the mangrove. Quin dropped the flashlight and did the same. Then, slowly, laboriously, they moved hand over hand through the branches fighting the wind every inch of the way into the channel.

The muscles in his shoulders ached, the branches, rubbed his palms raw, his eyes burned from the wind and lack of sleep. He forgot about the crazies, the Nicholses, and eventually he even forgot his discomfort. The focus of his existence had been reduced to this singular, obsessive purpose. *Get into the channel.*

As the nose of the canoe poked into the pass, the wind's shrieks grew fainter. Quin dropped back. He heard her patting around frantically, her hands splashing through the water on the floor, slapping the wet tarp. "I can't find it. The flashlight. I can't find it."

Panic fluttered through her voice, and he thought, again, about light and the absence of light, about the way his own throat went tight and hot at the possibility that their only source of light had gone overboard. It was like being told that what you believed was temporary blindness was actually going to be permanent.

He wanted to say, *Don't worry about it, we'll find it later, the flashlight's still in the canoe.* But the only thing that came out was, "Just paddle."

He had no comfort to give.

Branches snapped at his head, bit at his cheeks, stabbed at his neck as they passed. He could hardly hear the wind now, could barely feel the rain. But the dark didn't diminish, didn't go away, didn't change one iota. It closed in on him like a clammy fist and squeezed at his deepest fears, all of which seemed imminent, huge, overpowering. He could think only of light. Light and its numerous sources. The sun. A bulb. A flashlight. A match. Flint. A blowtorch.

He dropped his paddle inside the canoe and thrust his hands into the water on the floor. Flashlight. Here. Somewhere. It had to be. He dug wildly into the crevices between the tarp and the canoe, and his mind kept shouting, *Light, light, light* in a voice that was not his own, couldn't be his own.

Then there was light—dim, weak, watered-down—and Quin was shaking the flashlight, repeating, "The batteries are low."

The batteries are low. How mundane, how simple, how absolutely ordinary. He threw his head back and laughed, and then Quin started to laugh and quickly turned off the flashlight to conserve the batteries.

The canoe drifted through the rustling darkness.

2.

He dozed and awakened in a cycle that wasn't predictable, that had no rhythm, no rhyme. Sometimes he dreamed, although he couldn't have said of what, and sometimes his wakefulness possessed the quality and texture of a dream, even though he knew it was not.

Once he woke up to a splash and realized Quin was bailing water with her hands. He started to help and lost himself in the endless repetition, dip and heave, dip and heave, until the water was lower. It occurred to him that they should find land, a hammock, someplace where they could turn the canoe upside down and empty it. But the mere thought exhausted him and he dozed again.

During another period of alertness, he understood that his fatigue was cumulative. Despite catnaps, it had acquired the weight and substance of a possession, and when it grew too heavy, it simply claimed him, like narcolepsy. He could not wish it away. He could not shake loose of it. He could not control it any more than he could control the weather. Like his sudden panic attack earlier, like his amnesia last summer, the fatigue happened despite his best efforts to prevent it. He knew there was a warning in this about the Glades, about man in the Glades, but didn't know what it meant.

Perhaps he wasn't meant to know.

Not yet.

3.

"Mac." Quin nudged his leg. "Mac, wake up."

"I'm awake." A lie. He was still drugged with sleep. "What's wrong?"

"I think I just heard an airboat."

He listened. He heard the wind, whistling through treetops, slapping wet branches together. He heard water sloshing against the sides of the canoe and something stirring through the leaves to his right. Then he heard the high-pitched whine of an airboat as it sped toward them, an anomalous sound that somehow didn't fit in this wilderness of rain and wind. There was no way of telling whether the airboat belonged to rangers, poachers, or crazies, but why take chances?

"Let's paddle farther in." He slipped the shotgun out from under the tarp, balanced it across his lap, and covered it with the corner of his poncho.

They paddled for several minutes. The whine of the airboat drew progressively closer, their heads scraped against the low ceiling of branches, something obstructed the channel—weeds, grass, muck—and it entangled their paddles, slowing them down.

"What the hell *is* this shit?" Quin flashed the light over the side of the canoe long enough to illuminate the growth they were struggling through. Water hyacinth. And it was everywhere. It covered the channel, snaked up trees, hung from the lowest branches at precipitous angles like a troupe of trapeze artists. It looked almost thick enough to walk on and there was no point in even trying to get any farther down the passage.

They stopped. Neither of them spoke. He heard Quin going through her pack.

"Matches," she whispered.

"Wait until the airboat passes."

"Here." She pressed the canteen into his hands.

Until now, thirst and hunger had simply been part of his general discomfort. But as he lifted the canteen to his mouth and drank, his thirst consumed him. He gulped at the water, coughed, felt his stomach seize up.

"Take it easy," Quin said. "All we've got is that canteen and two sodas."

He paused, then forced himself to take small sips that he swirled around in his mouth before he swallowed. Better. Now if he could just put on dry clothes, eat, and sleep for a while, he might feel human again.

As he handed the canteen back to her, the airboat roared past the mouth of the channel. It was close; the canoe rocked in its wake. "You think it was them?"

"Maybe." He didn't want to talk about the crazies. "Light a couple of matches, will you? Let's see where we are."

The flame flickered dimly in all the darkness, a solitary firefly seeking refuge in the storm. Quin touched it to the wick of a candle she dug from her pack; it burned bright and lovely and made one thing immediately obvious. The channel was so clogged with hyacinth and branches, they wouldn't be able to move ahead without a machete. There was no dry land to either side of them, but McCleary spotted what looked like another channel behind them. He paddled toward it while Quin held the candle above her head. Liberty with her torch.

The new pass was just as narrow, but the hyacinth wasn't as thick and the branches didn't lean as low; they could sit without hunching over. When they'd gone about half a mile, McCleary tied the canoe to one of the trees and he and Quin took inventory of their supplies.

Between what was in her pack and what the crazies had wrapped in the tarp, their total food supply was hardly impressive: a bag of trail mix, two bananas, a can of tuna, a can of pork and beans, and two ginger ales. But Quin had packed hooks and lines for fishing, which would help compensate for what they didn't have. And thanks to the crazies, they now had a sleeping bag that was actually dry because it had been wrapped in plastic; a Sterno stove with a lightweight frying pan; another flashlight; four Cyalume lightsticks, each one good for twelve hours; a hunting knife; a box of long kitchen matches; a can opener; and a pair of socks.

"It could be worse," she said. The lambent light created dark, slippery hollows in her face, and where it illumined her features, the skin was the color of butter. "I mean, it's not like we're going to be stuck in here for weeks or anything. Once it's light, we can find the Nicholses and get out of here, right?"

"Right." He wished he really believed it.

4.

They divided the supplies between the bow and the stern of the canoe, then covered the floor with the tarp and unrolled the sleeping bag on top of it. Even with both of them stretched on their sides, feet to feet, it was a tight fit, Quin thought, and damned uncomfortable.

The chill of the aluminum seeped through the sleeping bag. Water dripped from the branches and struck her cheek in a steady, maddening rhythm. Mosquitoes feasted on her. Every time she or McCleary moved, the canoe didn't just rock, it churned, it danced, it shook. When she closed her eyes, when she tried to focus on deep breaths, relaxation, she heard rustling in the trees. Not wind or rain, but critters. Alligators. Snakes. Bugs the size of the canoe. Panthers. Then her breath quickened, her muscles tensed, and finally her eyes snapped open and darted about, seeking shapes within the blackness.

She never saw anything, but it didn't make any difference. She sensed something out there, in the landscape the darkness kept submerged, beneath the river of grass, in that part of the Glades man would never touch. Perhaps the spirit of the Everglades was most evident in the unseen, the hidden, the implied. Even Weston and his group, materializing as they had at the campsite, seemed to be spawned from this very spirit. They were this wilderness made manifest in flesh and bone.

There wasn't much they could do about the crazies except avoid them. But she could at least tackle her gnawing hunger. She sat up slowly, trying not to rock the canoe, and patted through the supplies.

Lightning seared through the dark, followed seconds later by a crack of thunder that brought an involuntary jerk to her shoulders as they pulled in closer to her body. Wind moaned through the trees, a long, haunted sound that belonged in abandoned houses, along deserted highways, but not here. The rain came down a little harder.

"You can't sleep either?"

His voice startled her. She'd grown so accustomed to the noise of her own thoughts that his voice had no more place here than the haunted sound of the wind. "I'm too hungry to sleep. You want half a banana?"

"Sure." He sat up; the canoe pitched.

Quin peeled the banana, divided it, passed McCleary his portion. Her first bite set off a furor in her stomach. "What happened at the campsite earlier?" The calmness in her voice seemed wrong; it was as if they were sitting over dinner and she'd just asked how his day had gone. "With Judd?"

"It was an accident." He made a strange sound, part sigh, part yawn, part something else that said he wished he could undo everything that had happened up till now. "Beau must've come to when I picked him up and realized what was going on. I didn't know it until we were headed toward the canoe and he poked me in the back."

McCleary had then told Judd that he needed to switch Nichols to his other shoulder, that he was awfully heavy, and Judd had said, Yeah, okay, but make it quick. As McCleary had let him down, Nichols had sprung up and kicked Judd in the gut.

In her mind, Quin saw this happening, saw it with the clarity of a memory, as though she'd been there. But she could not see the detail that mattered the most. "Who killed him?"

"It was an accident. The kid tripped on something and fell on the spear. We left him where he fell and waited for whomever was going to come next. About the time

Opal showed up, I heard you scream. I came up behind her and knocked her out."

Quin heard him uncap the canteen. Sip from it. He passed it to her. "They didn't look like campers to me."

"I think they're poachers or backwoods weirdos who live out here somewhere."

Funny, that possibility hadn't occurred to her. In fact, she hadn't given much thought at all to who they were or where they came from. "There's no place for anyone to live out here. There's hardly any dry land."

"About five hundred Miccosukees do it."

The hardcores. She wondered how McCleary could remember such minutiae about the Everglades but not about her.

"What worries me," he said, "is that if they think Beau or I killed Judd—which is probably what they do think—then they're still out there looking for us."

"Mac, even if they were able to follow us in the storm, which I doubt, we were using outboards. They were paddling. You also set their canoes adrift. That bought us some time."

"Maybe." He didn't sound convinced. "But *if* they're looking for us, it's not going to make much difference to them who they get."

The words hung there, dark and powerful.

Then the rain fell in earnest again, pouring through the branches, and they scrambled to cover the supplies, the human threat forgotten.

River to Other

THERE WAS SOME things in the Glades a man never got used to. 'Gators, heat, bugs, snakes: it depended. For me, it was the saw grass.

I hated it. I hated the way it looked, the way it glistened like dust when the light hit it, the way it bit into your hands when you forgot how sharp the blades was and grabbed for it. I hated the way it ruled the channels, the bays, the river. But most of all I hated how it sounded.

When the wind whipped through it and those jagged blades rubbed together, it made this terrible sound, like hundreds of fingernails scraping across wood. Or it was the high cries of dredging equipment bringing the outside in closer and closer. Then there was times that it sounded like something from another world, a critter that lived in the dark world under water, the place of mud and bad dreams.

That's how it was when Opal and me was bringing Judd's body home. The voice of the saw grass raised the hairs on my arms, clawed at the inside of my head, raced along my spine until I was clenching my teeth against it. I didn't want to be where we was. I hated crossing them wet prairies, and we did it only because they was short-cuts to places deeper in the swamp, places like where the band lived.

The stretch we passed through that night was called River to Other. It covered nearly two square miles, with blades that sometimes reached as high as ten feet. It was a secret passage through the grass. If you didn't know it was there, you wouldn't see it, and even I had to look hard for it. When you was in the middle of it during the daylight, it was all you could see. But when you was in the heart at night, in a storm, it was the world.

It took us a long time to cross it. We was fighting a headwind till we turned south, and by then, I was so tired I couldn't hardly see. Sometimes I touched Judd's shoulder with my foot like I used to do when he was just a boy curled up between me and Opal in a boat like this one. I could still hear Judd's sleepy boy-voice saying, We there yet, Pa? How much farther, Pa? I'm hungry, Pa. I reckon I'm going to hear that voice for the rest of my natural life.

The firstborn is always special.

The sound of the wind got worse as we neared the end of the saw grass. The blades was shrieking and crying. The inside of my head felt thick and prickly, like there was something in there that wanted out. I decided that before the hunt started, I'd ask Grandpa to make me a potion. He was once a medicine man of the highest rank and his bundle, his yaholi, was powerful. Even though his tribe hadn't recognized him or the bundle since he'd up and married that white woman, I knowed the truth of his power. I believed in it, most of the time. We all did, most of the time. And I wanted the potion the color of piss that made me feel as strong and fast as a panther.

We glided free of the grass and cut into a strait as narrow as a Band-Aid. The wind died and so did the voice of the grass. My jaw was throbbing something fierce from clenching my teeth. My body hurt. All I wanted to do was lay down and close my eyes. Then I saw the lanterns and my body went soft and quiet.

But the hole in my chest was big enough to fit a truck into.

And for that them outsiders was going to pay.

2.

Lights. Dozens of them.

They was like stars in the wet dark of the lagoon and I loved the sight of them. They was home.

The band lived on ten chickees that shot up from the water in twos and threes at the shores of the lagoon. They had walls, windows, roofs made of thatch and tin. We had twelve places like this we done built over the years. Whenever one was found by people who ventured where they didn't belong, the band abandoned it and moved to another. And another. That was the way.

The band was the smallest it'd been since I was a boy—thirty-two adults and five children under twelve. There wasn't no mystery about the children. The women usually lost their babies when they was three, four months along. Them that was born was usually deformed, so we drowned them. We'd had a lot of drownings in the last five years.

With the adults, disease had claimed some and others left because they got pissed about doings in the band. But the rest . . . Well, I guess I blamed it mostly on the stories that was brought in from the outside by people like me who'd been there and come back. TVs, cars, movies, magazines, them fancy video machines, microwaves: Things and the magic of things lured our people from the band and out of the Glades.

I knowed about them things. I knowed how they could trap a man. I knowed because it's what happened to me when I went into the world. But the real problem wasn't that people like me had left and come back; the world was just too close. Every year it got nearer to the Glades, to our secure places, and pretty soon there wasn't going to be no other place to go.

Sometimes at night I laid awake thinking about the outside. I could feel it closing in on us, stalking us, waiting for us. I shoulda knowed that what happened at Lard Can was a sign, that we wasn't meant to go that close to the outside. I shoulda knowed when I looked down at my boy with that spear sticking out of him. But all I could think about was making them outsiders pay for what they done, and I still believed that the band was always going to exist, just as it had for nearly ninety years. I thought survival was in our blood. That it was basic, like food, water, children, that in the end only the basics mattered. The band. Survival. Revenge. The old ways.

But I was wrong.

3.

I steered the canoe toward the lone chickee to the right of the last pair. The shutters opened into darkness, but I could feel the old man waiting.

He always knowed when something done happened. When I was a boy, I used to think Grandpa's power could reach almost anywhere, even into the darkest, most forbidden parts of the Glades. Maybe I still thought that.

The wind gusted, grabbed a shutter somewhere, slammed it open, shut. The sound made the dead crawl on my skin. In my head, I could see the old man clapping his hands and shouting at the wind, ordering it to grab the shutter just then to show he was still powerful enough to control nature.

The canoe bumped up against the ladder that climbed the side of the chickee. Opal held on to it and looked back at me. "Go on. I know what I gotta do. The old man ain't got nothin' to say to me and I ain't got nothin to say to him."

We had argued about the old man enough, so I just kept quiet and touched my hand to Judd's forehead. The skin was damp and cold now, like plastic. Or wet leaves. My throat closed up and I quickly climbed the ladder. Then I stood in front of the chickee, the wind at my back, and watched Opal paddle out into the wet, gray light.

I hated her for her freedom from the old man.

4.

The door behind me squeaked. Grandpa greeted me in Spanish, the tongue of his dead wife, then switched to English. His voice was low, hoarse, a rasp like the wind. When I turned, we stared at each other. His hair was long and white and blowed around his wrinkled face. His shoulders was rounded, but he held himself tall, rigid, the way a man's s'posed to. His dark eyes was shining like polished stone, eyes that had awed and terrified me as a boy, eyes that locked on mine now.

"You know what must be done," he said.

"It's the way."

"And you'll do it?"

"Course I will."

Grandpa smiled. It creased the corners of his mouth, his eyes. "With help."

"The band knows?"

"The word has spread. Preparations are being made." He waved an arm toward the dripping sky. "The weather helps. It will not be clearing today or tomorrow or the day after." His smile cut his face in half. "The enemy, Wes, rarely does well unless there is sunlight. Blue skies. How many are there?"

"Four. Two men and two women in two canoes. Our good canoes."

"We are already twenty." He motioned toward the chickee. "Come. We have much work to do."

Inside his chickee it was quieter, calmer. I felt like the storm swirled around outside without touching the old man's little house. A single lantern flickered in one of the back windows. The air smelled of kerosene, of herbs, of band history. The walls was covered in skin and hides and heads—panthers, 'gators, bobcats, deer, snakes. Some was gifts, others was creatures Grandpa done killed himself. The shell of a two-hundred-pound turtle hung on the longest wall. Capturing it was part of his initiation when he inherited his medicine bundle from his pa.

We went into the tiny kitchen. On the wall over the sink was a green banner that said MIAMI TOMMY. It was the name Grandpa used when he owned a trading post at the edge of the Glades years ago and the name we called him. Herbs covered the tops of the wooden boxes next to the sink. Herbs for his potions, his teas. Sweet bay, willow, cedar leaf, snakeroot, others I didn't know. They was used for magic and to heal things like the mosquito sickness, the rat sickness, the sickness dreams and wandering caused. They could bring on pain, ease pain, confuse a man, make him see clearly. They could create the dreams of knowledge. They could weaken and kill. If one magic didn't work, Grandpa created another.

On the table under the window was a CB I borrowed from a truck when I was in the world. It was Grandpa's link with the poachers, trappers, smugglers, fishermen, and Indians the band sometimes traded with. "One of our canoes was seen an hour ago in Whitewater Bay, near the Wilderness Waterway. Two people were in it. It

70

is being watched.'' Tommy's fingers stepped through the bunches of herbs, pulling out this one, that one. He poured water from a jug and filled the rusted kettle, which he put on the two-burner stove. *It was one I borrowed a few years back from some campers. But I did it while they slept, so they never knowed. I never shoulda listened to Opal.*

"I'll prepare a tea to take with you. For strength, clarity of vision, for triumph. Before you leave, we'll get a precise location for the canoe.'' He pulled out a wooden stool. "Sit, Wes.''

I shrugged off my raincoat and hung it on a hook behind the door, then kicked off my shoes. My toes was cold and wet; I curled and uncurled them against the hard floor and watched Tommy move around the kitchen.

From a drawer, he pulled out a box of kitchen matches and an aluminum can filled with long, thin splinters of wood. I knowed what they was for and I swallowed hard, swallowed hard and noisy, just like Vi had. "Why them?''

"Physical pain consumes the pain of the soul.''

It was a crock of shit. "But—''

"You question a medicine man?''

His voice stayed calm, but them dark, frightful eyes went through me and suddenly I was a boy again, twelve years old, about to be initiated into the band through the test of splinters.

"Do you?'' Tommy repeated.

I shook my head and looked away. *He was lying, the old man was lying, this didn't have nothing to do with pain in the soul or anywhere else. It was just another test, one of many, a lifetime of tests. Ever since my ma and my half brother up and left the band too many years ago to remember, the old man had tested me for weaknesses, for some sign of the bad seed.*

And, like always, if I passed the test, then the old man would back me up in whatever I was doing. And with this it meant he would see that the band was behind me. He would lend his magic and we would catch the outsiders and Tommy would bring out his gold box with its sweet, dark secrets and we would win. So I rolled up my sleeve and held out my arm.

I thought of Judd.

Of them outsiders.

Of the band.

I thought of how when me and my brother was boys, we would hunt together, canoe together, fish together, do everything together. That's how it was with Judd and me, too.

Tommy picked up the first splinter and I looked at it, remembering.

"Think of what your son felt. And don't forget. Ever."

Tommy let the tip of the splinter slide nice and easy over the skin on the underside of my wrist, where the flesh was soft. The muscles knowed what was coming and started to twitch. It was still raining, I knowed it was, and the wind was still blowing, but the storm seemed far away. The only thing I heard clearly was my breathing and the hiss of the lantern.

I licked my lips. Watched the splinter sliding slowly up the skin and down, light and easy. The muscles stopped twitching. He'd tricked them. A part of me knowed that. But the part of me that was tired, that grieved, didn't listen. It felt good, that splinter tickling my arm. It calmed me. It made me sleepy. Then the old man suddenly drove the splinter deep into the skin and twisted it and I bit back a scream.

Blood bubbled up around the splinter as Tommy pushed it in deeper, through tissue, muscles, tendons. I held on to the edge of the table with my left hand; my knuckles turned white. Bubbles popped inside my eyes. Tommy watched me, waiting for me to scream, expecting me to, like the man I was could stand less than the twelve-year-old boy who done got through the test of splinters without flinching.

The splinter poked out the other side of my wrist. I nearly puked from the pain. But I didn't scream. I would never give the bastard the satisfaction.

Now he took a piece of cotton from the aluminum can and squirted lighter fluid on it. He ran the cotton down both sides of the wood, soaking it. He lit a match. His eyes went into mine, looking for weakness. I pressed my lips together. The flame touched one end of the splinter and then the other, and the tongues of hot light raced toward each other, toward my wrist, the hairs, my skin.

I thought of my boy.

Of the hunt.

Of revenge.

And when the flames reached where they was supposed to reach, I didn't make a sound.

I passed out.

Lydia and Beau

1.

"DON'T MOVE, QUIN."

McCleary's voice was barely a whisper. It slid over the surface of her sleep like a breath of air, but possessed such urgency, such intensity, that only the muscles in her face functioned. Her eyes snapped open instantly.

The first thing she saw was the dripping green twilight overhead, with patches of milky light seeping through it like pus. Rain struck her forehead, her cheeks, and trickled down over her chin into her poncho. She felt the muscles in her hands twitching to wipe it away. But McCleary had said *Don't move* in a tone she recognized, a tone that meant exactly that. So she remained as she was, flat on her back, legs drawn up, head at an uncomfortable angle.

Her gaze dropped from the trees to the stern of the canoe, where he was kneeling, the paddle rising over his head, his eyes fixed on something to her right. She knew she didn't want to see what he was seeing, that she wasn't going to like it if she did, but she looked anyway.

A small snake, perhaps sixteen inches long, was sliding along the edge of the canoe. It was striped on top, with a belly the color of a nicotine stain that was divided neatly down the middle by black spots like a perforated line. Its tongue flicked mindlessly at the wet air and its tiny, dark eyes slipped around in its hideous head like shiny marbles. Its skin glistened with water, making it look as if it were wrapped in cellophane. As it steadily inched closer to her, these details assumed an unnatural clarity, as though she were peering at the thing through a zoom lens.

Centuries glinted in its primal eyes, a light that would

74

never be extinguished. Its body made a soft, slithering sound against the aluminum. A hot, metallic taste filled her mouth.

"Jesus, Mac." She could barely get the words out. "Do something."

"When I tell you to, roll to the left."

Time screeched to a crawl. She saw the paddle coming down, the snake slithering closer, the leaves stirring overhead. "Roll," McCleary hissed, and she did.

Her cheek sank into the wet sleeping bag, into the stink of rotting leaves, moss, soil. She scrambled up on her hands and threw herself back. The paddle clanged against the side of the canoe and flung the snake up, up into the branches, the leaves, the ashen light. A second later, it fell, struck the water, and whipped away, vanishing into the hyacinth. Quin stared at the spot where it had disappeared, certain that it would leap suddenly from the green and shoot straight toward them.

"You okay?"

McCleary touched her shoulder and she turned. Shadows slipped across his face but didn't hide his stubbled jaw, his bloodshot eyes, his fatigue. He looked like she felt. "Other than heart failure, yeah. Thanks."

She hoisted herself onto the wooden bench and eyed the floor of the canoe, making sure there were no more surprises. Other than a few bugs floating in the puddles of water, the canoe seemed to be free of wildlife hazards. She tilted her head back, scanning the branches. Rain struck her face; she didn't see anything that wiggled or slithered, and drew her hood over her head.

"What kind of snake was it?"

"I don't know." He gestured toward the hyacinth. "But he's probably got a bunch of friends in there."

"How comforting." She looked around, hoping to see a bit of dry land, a large rock, anyplace where she could stretch her legs, relieve the pressure in her bladder, set up the tiny stove and cook something edible. But dry land was as rare as rain in the Sahara. "Any idea where we are in relation to Hell's Bay?"

"Given the wind last night, I'm pretty sure we got pushed past the bay and to the northeast."

Pretty sure. She didn't like the sound of that. Mc-

Cleary's sense of direction was usually infallible. "Which would put us where?"

"Somewhere near the Wilderness Waterway, I think."

"Christ."

It might as well have been the middle of the Amazon. The waterway was nearly a hundred miles long and extended south from Everglades City to Flamingo on the Florida Bay. Quin had never canoed it, but she knew people who had, and they considered it the most challenging trail in South Florida. Under optimum conditions, it was a seven-day trip that twisted through rivers, creeks, open bays, and some of the most desolate wilderness in the Glades. Compass and navigational charts were essential even for experienced canoeists, which they weren't.

"If we can figure out which way is south, we can take our chances in reaching Flamingo by nightfall and then get help and come back tomorrow morning to look for the Nicholses. Or we could look for them now and hope we find them by dark."

"Look for them where? We don't even know for sure where *we* are."

"They were headed in the same direction we were. They've got to be somewhere nearby."

He made it sound like a trip to the grocery store. "Let's get out from under all this stuff. . . ." Her gesture encompassed the hyacinth, the mangroves, the claustrophobic tightness of this little alcove. "And then decide."

"Aye, Skipper."

He saluted and Quin laughed. It elicited a smile from him that was quick and brilliant, like the old McCleary, like the man she'd married. And for a moment there in the moist, humid shadows, something warm and companionable flowed between them. "It's never as bad as it looks," he said.

She didn't know whether he was referring to their present circumstances, their marriage, their separation, things in general, or all of the above. It irritated her that the remark was veiled in ambiguity. "Yeah. And sometimes it's worse than it looks."

His smile faded, and the connection between them snapped. He picked up his paddle and thrust it in the water, steering the canoe clear of the hyacinth. Then he started the outboard.

Quin immediately regretted speaking so brusquely, started to apologize, then changed her mind. What was the point? Why should she be so concerned about offending or hurting McCleary? He certainly hadn't taken *her* feelings into consideration when they'd separated. And what about his brief fling several years ago with Sylvia Callahan? Had he been thinking about her then? And what about that time—

"You think you'll ever get to a point where you stop blaming me for everything?" McCleary asked.

The question was so direct, so *un*ambiguous, it caught her by surprise. She didn't bother turning around. "I didn't have anything to do with your screwing Callahan, Mac."

Silence. Waves of resentment slapped her across the back. *Like it's my fault,* she thought. *Like I drove him into Callahan's bed.* "You *do* remember Callahan, don't you?"

Tersely: "Yes." Then: "Your version of what happened and my own version."

She refused to ask how *his* version differed from *hers* but knew it would be another example of the Pass It On game.

Their silence followed them as the canoe putted free of the trees, where the wind and rain struck with a vengeance, whipping across a savannah of saw grass that stretched between them and the mangroves on the other side. McCleary killed the outboard and pulled it from the water. She didn't think they would be able to paddle their way through the growth, but it was either that or go back and find a way around it. When they reached the grass, the fierce-cutting sedge clawed at the canoe and gnawed at their hands as they paddled through it. The grass whipped in gusts of wind; the sharp, glasslike edges rubbed together, whispering, singing.

Its song was strange and lovely, a timeless ballad of life and death and rebirth, a history of how the saw grass sprang up from the black soil of its own decay, year after year, century upon century, for millenia. In some spots, the grass grew to ten and twelve feet. There were other places, Quin knew, where the depth of the silt and muck were equal to the height of the grass. This was the secret heart of the Glades, where the river ran deepest, where the currents moved and flowed forever while the saw grass stood as rigidly as a battalion of soldiers at attention. They could not get through it. The growth was impenetrable unless you sheared your way through it with a machete or on an airboat and they had neither. They had to retreat and look for a way around it.

As they turned, the wind struck Quin from behind. Rain pelted her hood and poured over the tarp they'd secured across the center of the canoe, where the supplies were. It ran off the rubber in streams that struck the long, folded leaves as they sang and sang. Even a hurricane couldn't decimate the grass, but just flattened it here and there, as though a giant had trundled through. Its only enemy was fire. Fire set by lightning, by man, fire ignited by the sun when the rains hadn't come. The muck at the bottom contained layers of ash from old fires and was as much a part of the saw grass's history as its savage, passionate song.

The irony, she thought, was that they were being driven back to the mangroves by a place that was a fitting metaphor for their marriage.

2.

As they neared the border where the grass ended and the sweet blue waters began, the whine of an airboat pierced the noise of the wind and rain. Quin jerked in her paddle, threw back the edge of the tarp, and dropped to her knees. She glanced back and saw that McCleary had done the same. Underneath the tarp, his hands were moving; she knew he was clutching the shotgun.

Immobilized by the threat of crazies, her stomach suddenly shrieked for food. It cramped, tightening like a fist; she fought back a wave of nausea. Water coursed over the hood and down her face when she clutched her arms to her waist and leaned forward. She tasted it on her lips, warm and oddly sweet, an ambrosia, and realized the only fresh water they had was in the canteen and it was only half full.

The whine of the airboat drew close. Closer. And then

it appeared, a silver blur against the gloomy sky, skimming the prairie of grass like some tremendous insect. It turned sharply, passing within yards of where they were hidden.

Quin glimpsed two men riding high on the pilot's seat, beneath a canopy that flapped in the wind. Their raincoats were dark smudges against the sky, the grass. When the airboat suddenly slowed and swung into another turn, it was almost as though the men had sensed her and McCleary's presence. She could see their faces now. Although neither of them was Weston the Ugly, both were armed.

They might have been park rangers, but she doubted it. Poachers seemed likely. Or smugglers. Or more crazies. The bad possibilities definitely outweighed the good, and she crouched lower in the canoe, waiting.

The airboat slowed to a putter. One of the men stood up, then gestured to his left with the rifle. The pilot nodded and the airboat putted across the grass, close enough so that Quin could smell gasoline and hear the scratch of the saw grass as the airboat passed over it.

"There!" shouted the man with the rifle.

A canoe shot out from the edge of the saw grass and headed for the mangroves. Quin recognized McCleary's poncho and Lydia's black hair, flying wildly behind her in the wind. She didn't see Nichols.

The airboat turned sharply in pursuit but didn't speed up. It didn't need to. It would reach Lydia's canoe long before she got to the mangroves and the pilot knew it. He toyed with her, swerving when she swerved, lunging ahead to cut her off, then swerving again.

They struggled through the last few feet of grass, then McCleary shouted for Quin to change places with him and crank up the engine. She opened it up all the way, which wasn't saying much, and it wouldn't have made any difference if the airboat had been going any faster. But the gap between them gradually narrowed as she steered wide and to the left of the airboat.

McCleary steadied himself at the bow, raised the shotgun, aimed, and fired. The explosion startled a flock of snowy egrets from the nearby mangroves. They lifted into the air, white as angels, and fluttered off over the saw grass as the airboat veered in a smooth, neat arc. It kicked up water, picked up speed, and bore down on them.

Quin slammed the steering mechanism all the way to the right just as one of the men fired, missing them by ten yards. McCleary returned the shot. It must have hit something on the airboat, something strategic, because the boat suddenly flew wild, churning a ragged path toward the saw grass. The pilot leaped off and, a moment later, so did the second man. They vanished in the sharp swords of grass. A beat or two passed, then the airboat slammed into the mangroves on the other side and exploded.

A ball of fire and smoke surged into the air, spitting debris. Tongues of flames sped through the gas spill, briefly igniting trees, brush, and the edge of the saw grass before the rain stamped it out. Plumes of black, greasy smoke hovered in the wetness, until the wind whisked them away. Then there was only the rain again and the sound of the outboard, straining, as Quin steered it toward the mangroves where Lydia had disappeared.

3.

The channel Lydia had taken twisted like a pretzel through a canyon of red mangroves and buttonwood trees where everything echoed: the rain, the wind, the splash of their paddles, McCleary's voice as he shouted her name.

Now and then they passed a tongue of dry land where branches sagged with Spanish moss, where ferns that were eight and ten feet tall grew with lush exuberance. Within all that green flashed the brilliant red of wild poinsettia and the bright yellow and pale lavender buds of orchids that had rooted in the trees. Fallen petals floated on the surface of the water like tiny, colorful ships that drifted aimlessly through light and shadows. This was a softer, less savage world, McCleary thought, a refuge of color and exquisite excess, a secret folded up inside the thick, brutal fist of the Glades. And he suspected that Lydia had headed into this channel intentionally because she and Nichols had been hiding here, perhaps since last night.

The channel was an artery with numerous veins shooting from it, some closed off by hyacinth and fallen
branches, others as clear of obstruction as the interstate
at four in the morning. Lydia might have turned down
any of them. So he kept shouting her name, hoping the
water would carry his voice, trying not to think about
the men who'd leaped from the airboat, trying not to
think at all.

They had putted along for perhaps ten or fifteen minutes when, off to the left, Lydia appeared on a finger of
land. She stood in milky light under a buttonwood tree,
a dark, wet figure with wild hair, shorts smeared with
mud, waving her arms furiously. She looked like a character in a Gothic tale, someone of dubious ancestry with
black, terrible secrets that had driven her utterly mad.

Quin cut back the power and they chugged closer to
shore. Within the frame of the poncho's hood, Lydia's
face was absolutely white, as though she hadn't seen the
sun for years. She motioned them around the buttonwood
tree, under the sagging shawls of moss, to a waterway
that wasn't visible from the main channel. Then she followed them, running along the shore like a small child.

The waterway led to a hammock filled with cabbage
palms, red mangroves, buttonwood trees, and shrubs.
Lydia's canoe was tied there, bobbing in the brackish
waters, rain sloshing around inside it. McCleary stopped
alongside it, turned off the motor, tipped it back and out
of the water. Then he and Quin pulled the canoe onto
land.

When Lydia reached them, she was breathless and
stumbled over her words, mixing up her prepositions,
misusing verbs, dropping the articles from in front of her
nouns. It was as if whatever had happened to her since
last night had short-circuited the speech centers in her
brain. She was no more coherent than a patient recover-
ing from a stroke.

McCleary and Quin hurried after her as she led them
toward wherever she'd left Nichols. The deeper they went
into the trees, the more surreal the place seemed to
McCleary. He felt as if he were inside a Disney cartoon,
a child's rendition of a lost world. The light was almost
painfully soft, gentle. The extensive prop root systems

on the mangroves, curving with a strange and graceful symmetry toward water, always toward water, created yawning nooks and crannies, magical places where talking rabbits lived, where dragons breathed fire, where a princess from a faraway land was being held captive by a wicked king. The kind of world where good was good and bad was bad and there was nothing in between.

The trees had trunks that were sometimes seven feet in circumference and seventy and eighty feet high. They blocked out much of the already exiguous light and most of the rain. In parts, where the trees weren't as tall or growing as closely together, the ground was so soggy it had turned to mud. The three of them trekked through it, sinking in up to their ankles, their shins. It seeped down inside McCleary's running shoes, into his socks, between his toes. Its smell was overwhelmingly rich, fecund, a sweetness so intense it was almost unpleasant.

Lydia alternated between silence and quick bursts of words where her small, white hands jerked about in the murky air like a puppet's. She jumped around in time, a traveler who touched down here, there, with no regard to sequential events. But at least when she spoke now she was relatively coherent, and McCleary was able to piece together some of what had happened to her and Nichols since last night.

They had fled in and out of channels for several hours, seeking a refuge from the storm, from Weston and his people, until Nichols couldn't paddle anymore because of the pain in his leg. Lydia had taken over and had somehow gotten them here. She'd set up a makeshift camp with the supplies and gear in the canoe. At first light, they'd moved farther inland, and by then, Nichols was so feverish, he had told her to leave him in the camp and get help. Not long after she'd left the channel, as she was approaching the prairie of saw grass, she'd spotted an airboat and had ducked back into the channel for cover. Whoever was on board had seen her as well and had searched up and down the perimeter of the trees for twenty or thirty minutes looking for her.

Were they the men they'd just encountered on the airboat? McCleary asked. She didn't know. Was it Weston? No, she didn't think so. What happened once the men had left? She'd gone back to camp to check on Nichols. It was pouring, so she'd slept a while and tried to feed him something, but all he wanted to do was drink. Booze killed the pain in his thigh.

Was the arrow still in his leg? McCleary prodded.

Yes, yes, of course, *she* wasn't about to pull it out. She didn't know anything about first aid, and even if she did, there was no first-aid kit in the supplies, and suppose he started bleeding badly or something?

But he had a fever, right? Quin asked. Hadn't she just said he had a fever? Well, yes, he did, but she couldn't do anything for his fever, now, could she? She didn't have any aspirin, she didn't have anything for first aid, she'd just finished telling them that.

"Okay, calm down," Quin snapped. "It was just a goddamn question, Lydia."

But Lydia turned on Quin with astonishing fury; McCleary didn't know how she mustered the energy. "Miss Fucking Efficiency. Jesus. I've done the best I can." Her eyes turned the bright blue at the bottom edge of a flame. "I'd like to see you do any better. I mean, this stupid camping trip wasn't *my* idea." She poked herself in the chest. "I don't even *like* the outdoors, and quite frankly, Quin, I would've been a *lot* happier if you hadn't come along. I don't know why Beau made such a big fucking deal about you coming."

"Then you don't know Beau very well," Quin replied.

"And just what the hell is *that* supposed to mean?"

"Beau's insecure when it comes to your friendship with McCleary. He figured that with me along, he wouldn't have to worry about you coming on to Mac. Simple, Lydia."

"Did he tell you that?"

"He didn't have to."

Lydia's eyes darted to McCleary, seeking confirmation, denial, support, anything that would reassure her he thought Quin was lying, that he sided with her. She acted as if this were some sort of high-school war between members of an opposing clique; she'd already forgotten what had just happened out in the saw grass. It was exactly the same thing she'd pulled last night at the campsite, but then it had been with Nichols. Them against us. Us against them. Her world reduced to a game of fucking Ping-Pong. He refused to play.

"C'mon, let's get going." He touched Quin's shoulder.

Lydia was evidently accustomed to winning these little games, and that she had lost this one seemed to surprise her. She stood there staring at him, at Quin, then she flung off her hood, raked her fingers through her sopping black hair, and marched past them without a word.

Quin rolled her eyes toward the cathedral of green overhead, gave McCleary's hand a quick squeeze, and fell into step behind Lydia. His hand warmed where she'd touched it and he felt absurdly grateful for small things. Land, for instance. Shoes. A poncho. Their escape from the crazies.

They crossed a mound where the ground had been built up with silt and shells, a sure sign that this place had once been inhabited by Seminoles or Miccosukees. A few of the trees had been cut down, leaving stumps that air plants and vines had claimed. He saw charred firewood, aluminum cans, plastic wrappings. Campers had also been here, so they couldn't be *that* lost.

But then again, in the Glades, the concept of *lost* was relative. You could be lost in a channel that had no marker but that wasn't more than a couple of miles from a ranger's station. You could get lost in one of the open bays, in a river, in a hammock at the edge of civilization.

Hardly reassuring.

As the hammock became dense and squalid with foliage, the air grew more still, more humid. Mosquitoes dived for his head, his cheeks, and bit wherever his skin was exposed. Lydia slapped at her neck and swore. She pulled an aerosol can of repellent out of a pocket in her poncho and sprayed it on her hair, face, and hands. When she didn't bother offering to share it, Quin looked over at McCleary, her annoyance as palpable as the gloom.

Deep in the hammock, they reached a wooden platform raised about three feet from the ground. The steps were missing, part of the thatched roof had long since caved in, many of the boards were rotted. But the area where Lydia had strewn her meager supplies was the driest place McCleary had seen in twenty-four hours. In the center of it was Nichols.

He was curled up on a sleeping bag covered with a soiled rubber tarp. A thin blanket was drawn over him. A nearly empty bottle of Scotch stood upright beside him. He smelled of sweat and booze, of a sickness that seemed to radiate not only from his thigh but from the very depths of him.

As McCleary crouched beside him, the odors stirred an old memory, a lost memory. First it rushed at him in strobelike flashes, then it gradually evened out so that he could place it in time, in fact.

A singles place in Coconut Grove. Eight years ago, before either of them was married, before McCleary had even met Quin. Loud, grating music came from a band onstage that wasn't very good: the details were suddenly clear. They were standing at the bar, where Nichols was hitting on an attractive blonde who was nearly as loaded as he was and trying not to show it. McCleary hadn't driven his car and signaled to Nichols that it was almost closing time and why didn't they shove off? But Nichols was intent on taking the lady home and kept mouthing *Five more minutes, buddy, just five more minutes.*

After fifteen minutes of it, McCleary finally leaned between Nichols and the woman to tell him he was splitting and the smell of sweat and booze and sickness had struck him. This odor.

As though his malaise now and his lust for the sweet young thing at the bar then were part of a deeper misery, perhaps something that had pursued him since his knee injury had killed his dream of a career in pro ball.

"Hey, man," McCleary said quietly, gently shaking Nichols's shoulder.

He didn't stir, didn't open his eyes, didn't do anything except lie there, his eyes shut, his breathing a shallow wheeze.

"He's bombed, Mac," said Lydia.

McCleary pulled back the blanket to take a look at Nichols's thigh. Lydia had cut open his jeans and one of them had broken the arrow off to within a couple of inches of the skin. The arrow's barb was buried under the skin; the flesh around it was inflamed, with red streaks already shooting down from it. "We've got to get the arrowhead out and let his leg drain."

Lydia pressed her knuckles against her mouth and made a face. "Get it out with what?"

"Quin's got a first-aid kit."

"And just who's going to cut it out, Mac? You? Me?" She pulled her fingers back through her hair again. "Jesus, none of us knows anything about first aid. And we need an antibiotic to put on it afterward."

"There's an antibiotic salve in the kit," Quin told her.

"A salve's not going to be enough. He'll need penicillin or something."

"We'll use what we have," McCleary replied.

Quin offered to fetch the kit, which was in the canoe. Before he could say he would get it, she was gone, evidently preferring the solitude of the woods to being left alone with Lydia.

He looked back down at Nichols, at the broken arrow, and knew the task of removing the damn thing was going to fall on him.

4.

As far as Quin knew, McCleary had never taken a first-aid course, CPR, or anything else even remotely related to medicine. And yet, when he went to work on Nichols's thigh, he did it with the careful precision and steadiness of a surgeon who'd been cutting on people all his life.

After pouring alcohol over his hands and the blade of his Swiss Army knife, he swabbed Nichols's thigh with Betadine. He asked Quin and Lydia to hold Nichols down at the legs and the shoulders, just in case he came to, and made a small incision to the left of the arrowhead. Nichols didn't stir. Pus and blood poured out of the cut.

"Christ," Lydia murmured, and turned her head as McCleary made an identical incision on the other side of the arrowhead.

The blade scratched metal. Pus streamed around it. He handed the knife to Quin and hesitated, his face skewed with that same concentration she saw on it when he painted. His vision had narrowed to nothing more than the arrow.

Lydia looked back. "Aren't you going to take it out?"

He didn't answer. He pulled gently on the arrow, then stopped. "Damn."

"What?" asked Lydia.

"The thing's in there real deep."

"Meaning you can't get it out?"

"Yeah, I can get it out, but I don't want to rip his leg to shreds."

"Then cut around it some more."

McCleary's mouth twitched with annoyance, but he had the admirable good sense not to pursue the conversation. Quin dabbed a square of sterile gauze at the pus and blood oozing from the incisions. She wished Lydia would vanish, fade into the trees, become the laid-back, stoned, and unhassled woman she usually was. Instead, she paced back and forth on the platform, the boards creaking under her feet.

"I just want this whole goddamn nightmare over with, that's all. I can't believe this has happened. I told Beau I didn't want to go camping, I told him, but do you think he ever listens to me? No, of course not. What I want doesn't count. What I think doesn't matter. You know where I wanted to go? Miami Beach. To one of those nice Deco hotels. I wanted to bake on the beach, drink piña coladas, go dancing." She stopped, threw her arms out at her sides, laughed. "And look where we ended up. Christ, I—"

"Shut up, Lydia," McCleary snapped. "Just shut the fuck up."

"Don't you *dare* speak to me like that."

He spun around and held out the knife. "You want to do this?"

She hugged her arms to her waist. "Don't be absurd."

"Then shut up."

She looked at Quin, realized she wasn't about to get any support from her, so she climbed down from the platform and marched off into the trees. "Three cheers for you, McCleary," whispered Quin.

He held out his hand. "Knife, nurse."

Then he was sealed up inside his concentration, and the only sound was the rain and the soft sucking of Nichols's skin as the blade found it again.

Benson

1.

IT WASN'T NOON yet, but Benson knew today had all the markings of a day he was going to wish he'd skipped.

His alarm hadn't gone off this morning and he overslept an hour. Then, thanks to the rain, there was an accident on I-95 that had delayed him forty minutes. He lost another hour at the McClearys' house, where he'd gone to feed the cats. Hepburn had escaped and he had to chase the little bugger into the park before he caught her. It was past ten when he got to the station, and his desk was buried in telephone messages, all of them urgent. While he was returning them, a call had come through from the mayor's office reminding him about the meeting this afternoon.

It was the mayor's monthly bullshit meeting and promised to be boring, a waste of time, and steeped in bureaucracy. If he was going to get out of it, the reason would have to be damn good, and at the moment, he didn't have any good reasons. Unless the woman sitting in front of him provided one.

She was short, rather chunky, with soft, pale skin and strong features. Her hair was very long, very blond, very shiny, and she wore it in a single thick braid that hung over her left shoulder. She wasn't pretty, but there was something oddly appealing about her, an openness you didn't see much in South Florida these days. Her name was Stevie Ibson and she was here, she said, to report a missing person.

"... Charlie was due back last night and he never got home, and I'd like someone to look into it," she was saying.

"I'm Homicide, not Missing Persons, Ms. Ibson. You

should see Lieutenant Gerald on the first floor.'' So much for a reason to skip the meeting, he thought.

"Look, Captain, I've got a lot of friends at the courthouse and I called a few of them before coming here. They all said the same thing. See Benson if you need to get something done. So I took their advice. I'd really appreciate anything you could do.''

Put like that, he supposed the least he could do was listen. "What makes you think your friend is missing?''

"He should've been back late yesterday afternoon.''

"Then he hasn't even been missing twenty-four hours.''

"Well, no, but—''

"We don't even take a missing-persons case, Ms. Ibson, unless the individual has been missing at least forty-eight hours.''

"I realize that. But you don't know how Charlie is, Captain. He's very prompt. If he says four, he means four, not a quarter after.''

"Where'd he go?''

"Camping in the Glades.''

"Well, the weather's been pretty lousy. That might've held him up.'' He thought of Quin and McCleary.

She shook her head and flicked her braid back over her shoulder as she sat forward. Her expression was tight and intense and her voice, soft. "No. Something's not right.''

The way she said this was vaguely disturbing, and it impelled Benson to pull a legal pad out of his desk drawer. "What's your friend's name again?''

"Charles. Charles Crawford.''

"Address?''

She gave him an exclusive address in Coconut Grove.

"He left yesterday?''

"No, the day before. Tuesday. He was supposed to be back yesterday afternoon.''

"Do you know where in the Glades he was going?''

"Hell's Bay. It's a campsite in the park.''

The same place the McClearys were headed, he thought. "So he was canoeing. Did he have his own canoe?''

"No. He said he was going to rent from someplace in the park.''

Lead one. "Was he alone?"

She shook her head. "No, his wife was with him."

Benson suddenly understood the situation. But before he could think of a tactful way to ask, she said, "Yes. That's right."

"Excuse me?"

"About me and Charlie." She smoothed a hand over her flowered skirt. "On this camping trip, he was supposedly going to tell his wife he wanted a divorce."

"Weird place to break the news."

She smiled. "Not really. Not for Charlie. He even took the settlement papers with him. I guess he figured that since Vi hates the outdoors so much, she'd be more willing to listen to him out there." She paused. "You don't know who he is, do you?"

"Should I?"

She shrugged. "Well, maybe not. Crawford Chevrolet. Crawford Jeep. Crawford VW. Crawford Mazda. Sound familiar now?"

Very. Crawford car dealerships were as indigenous to Florida as sunlight and beaches. If Benson remembered correctly, Crawford himself was a well-known philanthropist with a penchant for privacy who was probably worth upwards of five or six million. That made abduction a possibility.

"Have you contacted the FBI?"

"No. There hasn't been any ransom note or anything."

"How do you know there hasn't?"

"His only living relative is a sister. She'd be the likely one to receive a call or a note. But she hasn't heard anything. I talked to her before coming over here."

"So she hasn't contacted the FBI either?"

"No."

"Does his sister know about your relationship with him?"

"Yes."

"Does anyone else know?"

"A few of his close friends and mine, but no one else."

"His wife doesn't know?"

"She might suspect, but I doubt if it'd concern her too

much. Fidelity isn't real high on her list of values. She's stayed married to Charlie because she likes his money. And until I came along, he didn't really have any reason to divorce her. It would've been too damn expensive. It's still going to be expensive. But at least now he's got proof that she's seeing other people and he's going to use that as leverage to get her to accept his terms for a settlement."

"How long have you been involved with him?"

"About two years. I'm a physician's assistant for his doctor. That's how we met."

Usually when you asked people questions like this, there was a lot of hemming and hawing. But not with this woman; he liked her for it.

"Would it be possible for me to talk to his sister?"

"No problem." She ticked off the phone number and address. "Are you going to drive out to the park to check with the canoe rental place?"

"I'll call them and the ranger's station and see what I can find out."

She looked disappointed. "You're not going down there?"

"I really don't think that's necessary at this point." Not to mention that it was at least an hour's drive. "I'll call you when I find out something."

2.

But finding out anything over the phone was tougher than he'd thought. Although Crawford's sister verified everything Stevie Ibson had said, she didn't provide any new information. When he called the canoe shop, no one answered. Then he had to go through three people before he was finally connected with a ranger named Joe Farrel. Benson introduced himself, and Farrel, who was evidently hard of hearing, said, "Petrol made? What's that?"

"Metro-Dade," Benson said.

"Ah. A Miami cop. Okay. So what can I do for you, Sergeant?"

Benson didn't bother correcting the "sergeant." "I need to locate someone who went out to the Glades on Tuesday to go camping and was due back yesterday."

"I can't give out information to just anyone who calls up and claims to work for Metro-Dade. How do I know you are who you say you are?"

Shit. "Look, why don't you call back here and go through the switchboard? Then you'll know I am who I say I am. Okay?"

Farrel didn't seem particularly enthused about the idea but consented to it rather grudgingly.

His call came through twenty minutes later. "Well, I reckon you are who you say you are, Sergeant. Now who is it you need to locate?"

Benson told him what he knew, which wasn't much.

"Did this guy have his own canoe?"

"No. He rented one. But no one answered at the shop when I called."

"At the hop? What's that?"

"At the *shop*. The canoe shop."

"Ah. Well. Sammy probably closed up early. With the bad weather and all, business has been real slow. But to be quite honest with you, Sergeant, the chances of your friend making Hell's Bay in yesterday's weather are pretty slim. The winds were gusting to forty-five here. That's hell when you're canoeing. He probably took refuge in the mangroves and that's why he isn't back yet."

"So there's no way you can get in touch with campers?"

Farrel chuckled. "Nope. No phones at the campsites out here, Sergeant."

"Anyone at the canoe shop after hours?"

"Nope."

Drop it.

He started to thank Farrel for his time when the ranger said, "Don't know if this has got any bearing on your business, Sergeant, but maybe I ought to mention that there was an explosion near the Wilderness Waterway this morning. Airboat, from the sound of it. Airboats aren't allowed in the park. It was probably poachers, but no one around here is crazy enough to check it out in this weather."

"How far is this waterway from Hell's Bay?"

"A good piece. But with the wind and the rain, it's

easy for a man to get disoriented in there. That's the only reason I mention it.''

The Crawfords and Hell's Bay, the McClearys and Hell's Bay, an airboat explosion, a possible missing-persons case. And not just *any* person. It bothered him, bothered him down deep. But no crime had been committed, and missing persons wasn't his department, and short of driving out to the park, there was nothing he could do about any of it.

But a VIP like Crawford was certainly reason enough to skip the mayor's meeting, wasn't he?

Benson smiled to himself and picked up the phone to call the mayor's office.

3.

Route 27 was a straight shot south and then west to the Glades. It cut through acres of farmland that glistened in the rain—fields of beans, strawberries, tomatoes; groves of mangoes and papayas. For mile upon mile, there was only the lush, relentless green unbroken by concrete, condominiums, or shopping centers. It reminded Benson of how South Florida had looked when he was a boy, before developers had razed the land in the name of progress, before snowbirds had created an industry of tourism.

With every mile south that he traveled, the sky grew darker, the rain fell harder, the clouds dipped lower. It was as if all the gloom and strength of the storm system had stalled over the Glades, which needed the rain the worst. Lightning sutured the sky, blazed across treetops, flashed like a strobe gone berserk. The road was virtually empty; anyone with any sense, he thought, had already gone home.

When he turned west at Florida City, the rain had reduced visibility to a couple of yards. He slowed to forty, thirty, twenty-five, and for miles crawled along in second or third gear. It was the equivalent of seeing the world from a horse and buggy. Interesting if you were on vacation, frustrating as hell if you weren't.

He reached the park entrance at five-thirty, just as it was closing. The man in the guardhouse, an old coot with a hooked nose who smelled of smoke, directed him to the park headquarters. "You'll find Ranger Joe in there."

He sounded like a character on *Sesame Street*. "Right. Thanks."

The old coot touched his fingers to his forehead in a salute and grinned. "Don't mention it, Captain."

The park headquarters consisted of a single wooden building. It boasted long front windows that winked like eyes in the gloomy light, a wide front porch with a railing, and a line of faded rattan rockers. Two of them were occupied by Seminoles. They watched him with a kind of predatory interest as he dashed through the rain from his car and up the front steps.

Both men were examples of the uneasy alliance between the white man's world and their own. They wore their black hair long and loose, but dressed in jeans. One had on a long-sleeved blue workshirt; the other wore a T-shirt with MIAMI DOLPHINS on the front and had a baseball cap pulled low over his eyes. A scar on the left side of his face carved a jagged line from the corner of his eye to his jaw.

"Afternoon," Benson said.

They both nodded.

"Ranger Joe around?"

The man with the cap jerked a thumb toward the door. His companion fixed his dark eyes on Benson as he raised a can of Coors to his mouth and sipped noisily. Benson walked past them.

The inside of the place looked like someone's cozy living room. Sofa and chairs, floor lamp, TV tuned to the local news. The rain against the roof was a steady, comforting sound. "Mr. Farrel?" called Benson.

"He doesn't hear so well," said a voice behind him.

Benson turned to see the Seminole with the scar. Who hadn't made a sound.

They were both reflected in the window, Benson a couple of inches taller than the Indian, his wire-rimmed glasses glinting with light, his chestnut hair damp from the rain, his spine too erect, too rigid, too telling. The Seminole was still holding his can of beer, and as he spoke, he brushed his long black hair away from his face.

"If you want to get his attention, you do this." He

flicked a switch on the wall; the lights blinked off and on.

Sure enough, a man materialized in the doorway on the other side of the living room. He looked like a retiree from Miami Beach who loved the sun and shuffleboard, not like a ranger. Benson guessed he was in his mid to late sixties.

"Mr. Farrel?"

"Ayup."

"Tim Benson. I spoke to you earlier today."

He frowned as if he couldn't remember.

"From Metro-Dade?"

"Ah. Right." He nodded as he strolled over and shook Benson's hand. "I thought I answered all your questions, Sergeant."

"And raised some new ones. I was wondering if you could direct me to the entrance of the Hell's Bay Trail."

"You going canoeing in *this* weather?" the Seminole exclaimed.

"Not tonight." Benson glanced at the Indian, then back at Farrel. "But tomorrow I might want to borrow an airboat and go in myself."

"Then you'd best go to Lard Can campsite. It's on this side of the bay and it could be that your friend didn't get any farther than that."

"Someone missing?" asked the Seminole.

Farrel explained. The Indian, whose name was Billy Tiger, jammed his fingers into the back pockets of his jeans and shook his head. "That's three hours from the entrance of Hell's Bay if the weather's good and a lifetime if it isn't."

"Look," said Farrel, rubbing his jaw. "Before you go chasing off on a airboat tomorrow, how about if we do this. Billy and me will drive you over to the canoe shop to see if your friend's car is there. If it is, we'll know he hasn't gotten back yet and I'll leave Sammy a note to get in touch with me first thing tomorrow morning. Go bring the Jeep around, Billy."

When the Seminole had left, Farrel said he wanted to show Benson something on the map. It was a huge thing, pinned to the far wall, and Farrel drew his fingertip down a twisted blue line that ran the length of the Glades.

"Here's the waterway I was telling you about. Toughest trail you'll find in these parts." He circled an area. "The explosion I mentioned happened right here. I didn't want to say anything with Billy around."

"Have you found out anything more about it?"

"Nope. But you can see all the mangroves and how easy it'd be for a man to get confused in there, especially at night. In a storm."

Benson wondered if even someone with McCleary's sense of direction could get lost in such a maze.

The Jeep's horn sounded twice. Farrel grabbed a raincoat from the hook on the back of the door, and they went outside. The porch was empty. Billy Tiger's companion was inside the Jeep in the passenger seat. "They work for you?" Benson tilted his head toward the Jeep and zipped up his raincoat.

"What was that?"

"The Seminoles. Do they work for you?"

Farrel slipped his raincoat's hood over his head. "More or less. They get on my nerves sometimes, but they come through in a pinch, if you know what I mean. You'd be surprised at the things these boys know about the Glades. About what's going on in there."

"Then wouldn't they know about the airboat explosion?"

Farrel flashed a smile that had a history of dental problems. "Yeah, probably. But the point is that they didn't tell me about it. So I don't talk about it around them." With that, he hurried out into the rain to the waiting Jeep.

4.

The rental shop was tucked back in a clutch of pines, and on the door it had a sign with big yellow letters that said CLOSED. The parking lot to the right of it contained maybe a dozen cars. "What kind of car does your friend drive?" asked Billy Tiger.

"A red 1989 Camaro."

The Seminole pointed. "There it is."

He stopped behind the Camaro and Benson checked the license plate number against what Crawford's sister had given him. They matched. He got out, tried the Camaro's doors and trunk, which were locked, and peered in the windows. Nothing inside.

"Where to, boss?" asked Billy Tiger when Benson was back in the Jeep.

"I'd like to see the entrance to Hell's Bay," Benson said.

"Not much to see," the Seminole remarked.

"If that's where the man wants to go, Billy, let's go." Farrel's tone was sharper.

"Okay, boss."

They followed Route 27 south through the park, past walking trails and hammocks, freshwater sloughs, and stands of cypress trees. The rain tapered to a drizzle. Light seeped from the air. Billy Tiger's mute companion, whom Farrel had introduced as Buffalo George, shifted around in his seat and looked at Benson.

"Your friend missing or what?"

"He's a friend of a friend who says he was due back yesterday."

"No way he could've crossed Hell's Bay yesterday or the day before or even today. The bay's as big as a lake, and when the wind's blowing out there, you get waves. Whitecaps. Just like the ocean. If he's smart, he's probably waiting out the storm somewhere in the groves."

"Or the clan got him." Billy Tiger snickered.

"The who?" Benson asked.

"Foolishness," muttered Farrel.

"What's the clan?" Benson asked again.

Billy jerked a thumb toward Buffalo George. "Ask him. He knows more about them than I do. Hell, they're his anthropology project."

"Sociology," George corrected.

Farrel emitted a soft, practiced sigh, as though the clan were a topic he and the Seminoles had long since exhausted. "The clan's just one of the local myths, Sergeant."

"No one knows that for sure," said George.

Billy Tiger laughed. "Shit, man, they aren't real."

"Think what you want," George replied.

Benson felt like he'd stumbled into the middle of a family argument. "So who are they?"

"The story is that there's a small band of white Indians

living deep in the Glades," said Farrel. "They've been blamed for everything from droughts to slaughtered panthers to the theft of camping gear and canoes in the park. But as far as I know, no one's ever seen them."

Buffalo George snorted. "Hell, you don't have to see something to know it's there."

"What's a white Indian?" Benson asked.

"White people who live like Indians," replied Buffalo George. "The story is that in the early 1900s, people who were working on the Panama Canal came back here. Some of them settled in Davie." It was a small town south of Fort Lauderdale. "That's why Davie was first called Zona. Anyway, some of the others supposedly went into the Glades and intermarried with Indians and each other. Their descendants are the clan. They allegedly have adopted some of the Indian ways for their own. That's why they're called white Indians."

"Poppycock," muttered Farrel.

"Hey," said Billy Tiger. "You're either an Indian or you're not. And I don't care what they tell you in those classes, George. That's how it is."

Benson asked how large the group was supposed to be and George shook his head. "You hear different things. Personally, I think it's small and that they move around a lot. I've seen abandoned chickees out there that are similar to what you see among my people, but these have walls and tin roofs and wooden shutters and are built in clusters. Nearby, there is usually a hammock or a bit of dry land and a midden. These chickees are in places that are inaccessible to the ordinary canoeist."

"Doesn't prove anything," said Billy Tiger.

George shrugged. "I know what I know."

"Tales," scoffed Farrel. "Nothing but fanciful tales."

The Jeep pulled off to the right side of the road and stopped. The headlights illuminated a sign that said HELL'S BAY TRAIL. "That's it," said Farrel. "Not much to see until you're on the trail."

"And Lard Can campsite's on the way?"

"On the bay?"

"En route," Benson said, raising his voice.

"Yeah."

"Any other way to get there?"

"Airboat, but you have to approach from Whitewater Bay."

"Where can I rent an airboat?"

Farrel shook his head. "You can't. Not within the park. But one of us could take you in tomorrow morning, weather permitting. What's the forecast, Billy?"

"More of the same."

"Well, we could see how it looks in the early morning," said Farrel.

Billy Tiger pulled back onto the road and crossed it, entering a dirt turnaround the storm had reduced to puddles and mud. The headlights struck the rear of a van with out-of-state plates.

Benson frowned and asked Billy to stop.

"Here?"

"Yeah. I want to take a look at something."

The van had Georgia plates; the McClearys' friends were from Georgia and were driving a van. There was a canoe rack on top of the van; the McClearys and the Nicholses were going canoeing. *So?* So nothing. Hell's Bay was a popular trail. McCleary wasn't a beginning canoeist. They weren't due back until Saturday. Then why was he memorizing the license plate number? Why was he going to run a make on it and confirm that it belonged to the Nicholses? Why the hell was he thinking like a cop when there was no reason to, where the McClearys were concerned?

Because if he were a superstitious man, he would think he'd been led here. Because nearly twenty years as a cop had taught him to pay attention to this kind of coincidence. Because he did not believe in coincidences. Because he had a hunch, and a hunch was what had brought him here. Because, that was all.

Just because.

Roberts River

1.

WHEN QUIN WOKE up, it wasn't just dark, it was pitch
black. An unforgiving, fathomless black.

She blinked her eyes, touched them to make sure they
were open, that she hadn't awakened inside a dream. She
listened for human sounds but heard only the noise of
the rain and the night: branches whispering in the wind,
frogs, crickets, a cacophony of the wilderness. She
pushed herself up on her elbows; the wet sleeping bag
squished like mud beneath her.

"Mac?" She whispered it; the dark swallowed it
whole. She cleared her dry throat and said his name
again, louder this time. When there was no answer,
prickles of fear tightened the skin around her mouth and
across her cheekbones like a bad sunburn. "Lydia?" Silence. "Beau?" More silence.

Something has happened.

Wrong. If something had happened to *them*, it would
have happened to her, too.

*Like what, Quin? What kind of something are we talk-
ing about here?*

Slaughter by the crazies.

Very good. Start with the worst possible scenario.

She clenched her fingers and rubbed the back of her
hand across her mouth. She drew a strange kind of comfort from the odor of sweat and mud on her skin, from
the feel of her knuckles, from the reality of her own body,
damp and smelly as it was.

It helped her remember.

They'd all collapsed from fatigue sometime after
McCleary had finished cutting on Nichols's leg, before
it had gotten dark. But she couldn't recall exactly when

that had been. Morning? Early afternoon? Midafternoon? Hard to tell. She wasn't even sure when they'd gotten here. The hours blurred together, punctuated only by hunger, fatigue, discomfort.

But she remembered clearly that the three of them had devoured a can of beans and a can of tuna fish and had shared water from the canteen. Lydia had tried to wake Nichols so she could give him something to eat, and when McCleary had suggested she let him sleep off the Scotch, she'd told him to mind his own goddamn business, that she and Beau were going to leave while it was still light. She'd tried to lift him, to drag him and the sleeping bag off the platform. But he was too heavy and she'd finally given up and settled down beside him.

Quin remembered the look McCleary had given her when that had happened: a certain twist of his mouth, a roll of his smoky eyes, a parable in code that even Lydia could have broken if she'd seen it, a story about college friendships. And a rather nasty one at that, she thought.

Sometime later she and McCleary had fallen asleep.

She turned her head right, left, then shifted around on the sleeping bag and peered behind her. *Light.* She needed light.

She sat up and patted around for the flashlight. She was sure she'd left it somewhere nearby when she'd lain down. But she couldn't find it. Matches then. She dug down inside the soggy sleeping bag, nauseated by the fetid, musty odor that now emanated from it—and from her clothes. She smelled like the swamp. The inside of her mouth tasted of the swamp. And the swamp was growing on her teeth. Her head ached, her eyes burned, her stomach growled; she had to go to the bathroom, bathe, brush her teeth, change her clothes, eat. Yes, that most of all.

Her needs suddenly overwhelmed her and she jerked her canvas bag out of the sleeping bag, unzipped it, jammed her hand inside. Her breath was coming in sharp, ragged bursts. Things poured out of her pack. Brush: no. Comb: no. First-aid kit: no no no no.

Stop it. Not so fast. First things first.

Quin pressed her hands hard against her thighs and

forced herself to take long, deep breaths. *Slow and easy. Light first of all.*

She needed light before food, light before she budged from the sleeping bag, light before everything. Light.

She sat with the soles of her feet touching and then emptied her pack in the space between her legs and sifted carefully and slowly through the contents. Her fingers defined each item, touching it all over like a blind person. Once she'd identified something, she set it on the left. A piece of Dentyne floating free at the bottom of her pack alleviated the sourness in her mouth. A pre-packaged wipe cleared the grit from her face. A rubber band got her damp hair off her neck. The deeper she dug in the pile, the fewer complaints she had.

When she finally found the box of wooden matches, she hesitated before striking one. If the crazies were nearby, a flicker of light would be all they needed to pinpoint a location. And just what the hell good would a single tiny flame do in all this darkness? She still wouldn't be able to see more than six inches or a foot from where she sat.

But at least she might be able to recover the flashlight.

Quin struck the match. It flared with a singular beauty that made her breath catch in her throat and stirred an intense longing for every ordinary convenience she'd taken for granted all her life. She held it up; it winked out. She lit three at once.

The platform was empty. Nichols and the sleeping bag he'd been lying in were gone and so were all the supplies that had been strewn around. Her only thought was that McCleary and Lydia had departed without her, departed together; that they'd picked up where they'd left off twenty years ago, during the acid trip, and this was nothing more than a repeat of the past, a repeat of McCleary and Callahan.

Excellent, Quin. What else can we conjure? Laughter bubbled up in her throat. Here she was, stranded in Bumfuck, Egypt, and the first thing that entered her head was that McCleary had run off with another woman? Wonderful. And with Lydia? My God. She'd accused *him* of having problems?

And so what if he did run off with someone? What difference did it make to her?

Disgusted with herself, she lit several more matches and rocked onto her knees. She found the flashlight under the foot of the sleeping bag. Simple, very simple. If only her entire life could be so simple.

She blew out the matches, pointed the flashlight down, switched it on. The glow was so dim, it didn't really count. She shook it, rattling the batteries, and the light brightened.

"Turn it off."

McCleary's voice hissed from the darkness just beyond the platform. She turned off the light. "Where the hell were you?"

"Getting Beau and the supplies in the canoes. I tried to wake you, but you were out of it. Lydia's down by the canoes."

Simple, again. "Where're we going?"

"Anywhere." He climbed onto the platform and crouched beside her. "I don't think it's safe to stick around any one place too long."

"How can you see so well in the dark?"

He chuckled. "This helps." The thin beam from a penlight struck her hand and washed across the stuff she'd dumped out of her pack. Its spill of light created crevices and hollows in McCleary's face where none had existed before, aging him. "I found it tucked inside a pouch in my poncho."

She gathered up the things from her pack and shoved them back inside. "I woke up and no one was here and everything was gone. You wouldn't believe what went through my head."

"Yeah, I'd believe it."

From the tone of his voice, she knew he knew exactly what she'd thought. And even though he turned off the penlight just then, the darkness didn't make her feel any less transparent. "Yeah. Well." She shrugged. "How's Beau?"

"Worse. He needs something a lot stronger than an antibiotic salve." He started to roll up her sleeping bag.

"What about Lydia?"

"Less weird now that she's slept."

"And the weather?"

"The rain seems to have let up some and the wind isn't as strong. If we can get someplace else and wait until dawn, then we can figure out which direction is south. If the sky is clear enough."

A big *if*, she thought.

"The one thing I forgot besides my toothbrush turns out to be the most important omission of all. A compass."

"It'll work out okay," she said, but she was no longer sure.

He stood, her sleeping bag tucked under his arm, and she slung her pack over her shoulder as she got to her feet. As they climbed down from the platform, he turned on the penlight again and kept the beam aimed at the ground so they could see where they were going.

"The engine on the Nicholses' canoe is out of gas," he said.

"Then how're we going to work this with Beau and the canoes? We won't all fit in one, and I doubt if our engine is strong enough to pull theirs."

"He's too out of it to sit up, so he's stretched out in their canoe. I figured you, Lydia, and I could ride in ours and tow theirs or one of us could paddle his canoe."

Quin doubted that Lydia could paddle the canoe alone in weather like this, at night, with Nichols a dead weight inside. "What's Lydia want to do?"

"She hasn't said."

"Then either you or I should paddle the canoe with Beau in it. In the long run, it'd be less trouble."

"In the long run," he said, "it'd be less trouble if we just left them here, went for help, and came back for them."

There was no hostility in his voice. He was simply stating a fact, even if it was a fact neither of them would seriously consider. "It'd be better if I rode with Beau," she told him. "Lydia would just resent it if I were in her canoe."

"Tomorrow we'll switch off."

"Fair enough."

"Nothing happened, you know."

"With what?"

"Between Lydia and me."

"I didn't say it did."

"You didn't have to say it. You've been thinking it ever since she told the acid story."

"So?"

"I'm just setting the record straight."

As if "the record" were a physical thing, a little black book where their transgressions were listed and tallied like columns of numbers. "Okay." A few moments later, she added: "I get the feeling Lydia's never forgiven you for it."

"Probably not."

She thought of how, throughout their marriage, it seemed she had been the caretaker of the relationship, the one who'd watched its barometer. She'd pushed to restore its balance when it tilted out of kilter, to confront, to talk things out, while McCleary had remained more reticent, stepping back, preferring to allow things to take their own course. She was too much one way and he was too much the other. But since the separation, she'd ceased to question, to confront, and he'd become increasingly self-contained. Until last night, when their roles had suddenly reversed.

"Hey, Quin."

"Yeah?"

"Truce?"

She looked over at him. "Are we battling?"

"Before."

When before? Before this trip? Before tonight? Before five minutes ago? It didn't matter. "Yeah, sure. Truce." The dirt on her face cracked when she smiled.

2.

"I'd like to check on Beau, Mike. And change the dressing on his leg. Would you mind if we stopped for a few minutes?"

Lydia's voice strained with the politeness of her family background—servants, boarding schools, summers in Europe—a family where manners were valued above all else and could compensate for even the most despicable behavior of the night before. It brought back flashes of the family estate in Scarsdale, where McCleary had visited once. Single rooms as large as the outdoors, stables, tennis courts, an Olympic-size pool. And none of it had united a family as divided from one another as politicians on opposite sides of an issue.

All of it seemed out of place here, where for a long time now there had been nothing but the splash of their paddles and the distant moan of the wind. But it was the first time all day that she'd sounded in control of herself.

"There's no place to stop," he said.

"If we turned on the flashlight for a couple of seconds, we might spot some dry land. Maybe a hammock."

"I doubt it."

An uneasy silence ensued. He knew she was either concocting an argument or figuring a way of winning Quin's support. He wondered if she'd always been this way, so singularly obsessed, so . . . hell, so *spoiled*. He decided she probably had. But it wasn't as noticeable twenty years ago because everyone was obsessed with something. The war. The women's movement. Drugs. Music. Politics.

And in the years since, he hadn't been around the Nicholses enough to see this side of Lydia very often. Other than the disastrous trip to Key West, there had been the usual dinners and parties and barbecues, then a couple of weekends in Atlanta after the Nicholses had moved. And yeah, from time to time, Lydia had done things that were a little tacky—"But not without style, Mac," she always said afterward—and that he'd overlooked because they had known each other for so long. But there had been nothing like this. Nothing so prolonged. Nothing quite this obnoxious.

"How about shining the penlight around? You've been using it to navigate," she said finally.

It wasn't the argument he'd expected, although it happened to be true. But he'd been keeping the thin beam pointed down at the water, to make sure the channel wasn't blocked, and for only brief moments at a time. "How about if Quin changes the dressing?"

"She can't do that plus hold the light." She sounded stubborn and spoiled again. "Besides, what the hell's the difference between using the penlight to look for land and using it to change Beau's dressing?"

McCleary's annoyance overpowered his better judgment; all he wanted was for her to shut up. "Fine, fine. Start looking." His thumb hit the switch on the penlight. The tiny beam brushed the shore, skipping over mangrove roots, fallen branches, leaves, weeds. Everything glistened. The bark of the trees looked reddish black. Shadows loomed like buildings just ahead, where the channel twisted to the left. But there was no land.

As they turned, the canopy sagged like an old mattress. McCleary snapped some of the branches with his hands and pushed others out of the way with the end of the paddle. He let the light linger so that Quin would see them. She ducked and batted at them with her paddle.

"What's with the light?" Her voice echoed in the tunnel of foliage.

"We're looking for dry land," Lydia replied.

He noted the *we* and qualified it with, "Lydia wants to change Beau's dressing."

"His dressing is fine. I just checked it."

Lydia brought her hand up under her hair and flicked it off her shoulder as she turned. "You don't know what to look for."

"Since when are you a medical expert?"

"It's my goddamn leg." Nichols's voice was hoarse and low, but clearly audible. He sounded hung over, which wasn't surprising, considering he'd packed away three quarters of a bottle of Scotch. "And the dressing's fine, but the leg hurts like hell. Where are we?"

"Beau? Honey?" Lydia turned all the way around. "Can you sit up?"

"No. Where are we?"

"Stop paddling, Mike." A command. "C'mon, Quin, get up here closer. I want to see Beau."

McCleary grabbed Lydia's paddle before it slipped into the water. "Sit still. You're rocking the canoe."

"Would someone tell me where the fuck we are?" Nichols said.

"About two miles from where you and Lydia were last night," Quin replied. "At first light tomorrow, we'll get out of here and into the open so we can figure where south is."

"What's south?"

"Flamingo, where there's a ranger's station. Stop squirming, Beau. It's hard enough to paddle this thing as it is."

The canoes bumped into each other as Quin drew alongside. Lydia leaned over and touched Nichols's cheek. "You're still hot." She looked at McCleary. "He's still hot."

"Quin turned on the flashlight and shone it at Nichols, who winced when the light struck his face. He looked like a man coming off a week-long binge. "What day is it?" he asked.

"Thursday."

"How did we find you guys again?"

"Lydia can fill you in later. Let's keep moving," McCleary said.

"I want to be in the same canoe as Beau." Lydia glared at Quin, just daring her to say no.

Quin sighed, rubbed a hand over her jeans. "It's going to be a little awkward to change places now."

"I don't care."

"Fine, fuck it. Whatever."

Quin, hunched over like a cripple, her backpack slung over her shoulder and the flashlight tight in her hand, climbed out of one canoe and into the other just as Lydia stood. The canoes pitched and Lydia lost her balance and toppled back. Her arms pinwheeled, hands grappling for a hold on something, anything. McCleary's senses were so skewed by fatigue that it seemed to happen in slow motion: Lydia falling back into the dark as if into a cushion, her mouth wide open, her wet hair floating up around her face like oil-coated weeds. Then she struck the water and the world snapped forward again.

She was screaming, "Oh God, oh God, get me outta here, oh God, something's biting my legs!" Her yellow poncho filled with water and billowed around her like a huge lily pad as her arms slapped the water. She grabbed for the canoe, struggled to hoist herself over the edge, fell back again, shouting Nichols's name. He was already leaning over the side, all two hundred pounds of him, and the canoe tilted steeply to the left, spilling supplies into the water. A sleeping bag, the canteen, a couple of cans, the frying pan, Christ knew what else.

McCleary scrambled into the canoe and shoved Nichols against the floor. The canoe rocked back. The beam of light impaled Lydia as McCleary leaned over the side and seized her by the hair. She screeched and kept screeching even as he took hold of her arms and hauled her over the side. He clamped a hand over her mouth.

"Shut up, Christ, shut up. You're all right."

She wrenched free, sobbing, rubbing at her face. Bits of moss and weeds clung to her cheeks, her eyelids, her forehead. "She did that on purpose. Quin did that on purpose," she gasped. "She wanted me to fall over."

"Right." Quin shone the light directly on her. "I wanted you to fall over so we could be treated to another terrific example of your goddamn hysteria. Uh-huh. You got it, Lydia."

"You saw what happened, didn't you, Beau?" Her head snapped toward Nichols, who was sitting with his back against the rear bench. His right hand covered his wounded thigh; his left gripped the edge of the canoe.

"I'm gonna puke," he said, and turned his head and did exactly that.

"He's sick," Lydia said to no one in particular, looking at Nichols as though she'd never seen him before. "He's sick. We need to do something."

"He's hung over," McCleary said. "And we need to get moving."

The expression on her face brought new meaning to the adage, If looks could kill. But she gave a curt nod, pulled off her soaking poncho, and said, "I can paddle just fine, thank you very much."

A few minutes later, they started down the channel again. McCleary had the uncomfortable feeling that the greatest threat to their survival, to their getting out of here, wasn't the crazies or the Glades or the weather.

It was Lydia and Beau.

Weston and Opal

"THERE." OPAL STABBED the paddle toward Wedge Point. "I seen it there."

"You sure?"

"Yeah."

Opal's eyes was like a cat's in the dark. If she said she seen a light, then that was what she seen, all right. I steered the canoe toward Wedge Point, less than five miles from where the airboat had exploded that morning. The wind wasn't too bad; the islands in the bay broke it up. Even the rain had backed off. Good signs: Tommy's magic was with us.

Around ten that morning, one group of eight and another of twelve left the chickees in airboats and dugouts to explore the saw grass where the poachers' airboat had gone up. Me and Opal took our airboat across Oyster Bay and headed south to Joe River, where we searched some of the small creeks for the outsiders. I didn't think they was that far west, but I wanted to be sure.

Once we finished searching the creeks, we went east toward the Wilderness Waterway. I was afraid the whine of the airboat might alert the outsiders, so we ditched it in some groves in Midway Pass and put our dugout in the water.

Even before Opal seen the light, I sensed the outsiders somewhere nearby. It was almost like they left a spoor in the air that the wind carried, a scent I could smell, a scent that wasn't nothing like the other smells in the Glades.

Sometimes, when I was thinking about Judd, about what I was going to do to them outsiders when me and Opal found them, the odor got away from me. But when I relaxed, I found it again, a trail cut into the wet night as clear to me as the way home, as the memory of Judd's face.

A few times, when I was really connected to the scent, when it pulled me in, it was like I could feel the outsiders as separate people. The woman with the pretty name, Lee-dee-uh, the skinny broad, the dude who said he'd never argued with a gun, and the big man.

And I knew they was in deep shit, and yeah, that made me feel mighty good.

As we got near to Wedge Point, the wind fought the dugout. I started the outboard so we wouldn't get carried upstream and hoped the wind took the sound of it. But even if it didn't, them outsiders would have a tough time figuring where the sound was coming from. You gotta know the Glades pretty good to be able to do that. It's something band children learn early on. My half brother, in fact, was the best when it came to that. When we used to go out on fishing trips, just the two of us, he would show me how you could track a sound as easy as you could track a deer or a 'gator. He showed me lots of things that last year before he and Ma up and left. Things I ain't never forgot. Sometimes, still, I miss him real bad. If he was with us, we woulda catched the outsiders by now.

Once we was past the point and moving east along the shoreline of groves, I killed the power. Opal aimed her flashlight at the trees, looking for a shimmer of metal, a blur of movement, anything that would tell us where them outsiders was. A couple of times she flashed the band's signal, waited ten seconds for a response, but we didn't see nothing. I figured the others had gone farther north, around the Watson River, and was coming south from there.

The outsiders was doing what I'd do if I was them. They was traveling at night on the rivers, inside the channels, staying hid. It'd make it tougher to find them, but not impossible. I could track an amateur through the groves any day. Also, one of them was wounded, which was slowing them down. But even if they was all in perfect health and knew what they was doing, it wouldn't matter. I growed up in Glades. It was my world, not

111

theirs, and they didn't have a chance in hell of getting out alive.

I kept thinking how they didn't have no idea what the band really was; no one did. How could they? To most people, we was just stories. To them that traded with us, seen us, we was a bunch of weird backwoods folk, mean and tough, with our own way of doing things. Them that found the truth didn't live to tell it.

When I was in the world, I used to think a lot about that truth, about how it set me apart from other people. I would see a pretty woman—on the beach, in a store, on the street—and I would try to put her inside the band, inside the old ways, and she never fit. I would see her screaming.

As the canoe glided out from behind the protection of some mangroves to the left, the wind and rain slammed into us again. I paddled hard toward the mouth of the Roberts River. The wind whistled and moaned, fighting us, then we slipped into the mouth of the river and the wind was just a little whimper again.

Opal's light flickered from right to left through the rain. The beam paused on a pair of red eyes glowing from the stand of trees.

"Wes, you see it?" she whispered.

Yeah, I seen it. A 'gator looking for a place to ride out the storm. "Keep paddlin. It ain't doin nothin."

"Just make sure you got that shotgun ready."

"Don't worry about it none, Opal."

She hated 'gators the way I hated the sound of wind in the saw grass. A long time ago, when the band was friendlier with some of the Seminoles and Miccosukees that lived in the Glades, we used to bet on alligator-wrestling matches. Opal was the only one in the band that never went to the matches. Miami Tommy kept after her to deal with her fear, to drink a potion that would give her courage, to go through a test to train her mind. Then, like now, she refused. No one except Opal defied him. The old man respected her for it, even though he never done admit it.

I rubbed my sore wrist and wondered if he respected me.

The glowing pricks of the 'gator's eyes vanished. A

112

moment later, there was a splash to the left. Opal's beam tracked the 'gator for a few yards as it swam off toward the mouth of the river. Then she turned it on the nearest branches, looking for them that had been snapped by a hand or the passage of a canoe.

"I smell gasoline," she whispered.

I sniffed the air. "Me, too."

"They's in here, Wes. Somewhere."

She turned off the light. The dark closed around us again, tight and wet. I felt her head moving right, left, as her eyes swept through the blackness, seeking the presence of the outsiders.

The Cutoff

1.

FOR A HALF mile or so, the left twist in the channel was as thin as a coat hanger.

Quin had to paddle on her knees and pull in her shoulders to keep her head and body clear of the profuse growth. She kept turning on the flashlight to check for fallen branches and areas where the foliage had tangled across the channel, blocking it. But the passage remained unobstructed, and it gradually began to straighten and widen and was relatively easy to follow in the dark.

The worst problem they encountered in this two- or three-mile stretch was mosquitoes. They swarmed around the canoes, so hungry for blood they bit through ponchos and denim and seemed impervious to the repellent Lydia had finally shared. She didn't realize just how thick the swarm was until she turned on the flashlight and its beam struck a wall of insects, hundreds of them hovering in the dense foliage, diving toward their heads, swooping through the light with the mindlessness of moths. Lydia sprayed the repellent into the cloud, then passed the can along so that the others could do the same. It helped until the mist dissipated, then the mosquitoes swarmed in again.

"We've got to get out of here." Lydia's voice skimmed the surface of the darkness, small and tired, one more noise in the symphony of night sounds. "We're getting eaten alive back here."

McCleary swore softly. "Just where the hell do you suggest we go, Lydia?"

"Out in the open. In that bay where I got chased this morning."

"It wasn't safe," he said.

She'd conveniently forgotten the airboat, Quin thought. In fact, her memory didn't seem to span more than the last fifteen minutes.

"I don't know why we had to leave that other place, where the platform was. There was nothing wrong with it."

"Then you should've stayed if you thought it was so safe," Quin said.

Testily: "I didn't really have a choice."

"You've always got a choice."

She didn't have anything to say to that. They kept paddling. Quin flicked on the flashlight again. Just ahead on the right the trees seemed to recede, revealing a finger of land. She signaled McCleary to steer toward it. As the canoe brushed up against a tuft of weeds sprouting like whiskers from the shore, Quin pulled in her paddle. Mosquitoes whined through the light as she shone the flashlight on the weeds and branches, checking for snakes, spiders, critters of any shape or size. When she was satisfied that the nearest branch was okay to touch, she grabbed on to it and pulled them in closer.

"Beau, honey," said Lydia. "It's land. We've found some land."

Nichols grunted; he didn't sound too interested in land.

"We'll get you fixed up real nice, honey," she promised.

Quin rather doubted that *nice* was the adjective to describe this place. The land barely looked solid and, about a foot in, was thick with tremendous ferns and weeds. Branches were connected by webs of Spanish moss that hung so low, they almost brushed the ground. Rain beat against the treetops and dripped through the branches. The idea of traipsing through this, especially in the dark, was not particularly appealing. But neither was the other option: sleeping in the canoe.

McCleary tested the solidity of the ground with the end of his paddle, then hopped out, took hold of the rope, and pulled the canoe forward so there would be room for the other one. He tied the rope to a branch and hurried back to secure the Nicholses' canoe as well.

"God, there're so many *weeds*," Lydia griped.

"Don't worry about the goddamn weeds," McCleary told her. "Just pass me what's left of the supplies."

"You don't have to say it like *that*," Lydia snapped. "What do *you* have to be upset about? *You* didn't get pushed into the water."

"Neither did you," he replied. "Can you walk, Beau?"

"Limp, maybe," came the weak reply.

"He's going to need help." Lydia again, talking as though she were speaking to a servant. "He can't possibly walk through that shit by himself."

Fine. You help him. The words pushed up against the inside of Quin's mouth, begging to be spoken. She swallowed them and concentrated on unloading the canoe. When everything was on the ground, she divided it into two piles. Distressingly small piles.

Even if she added the Nicholses' supplies to these, the piles wouldn't be much larger; too much had gone overboard with Lydia. One more day in here, she thought, and she was going to be eating roots and dirt. But food was the least of their problems; they could always fish. The most pressing concern was water. They couldn't replenish the fresh water that had been in the canteen.

Survival question number one: *How long can you live without water?*

She didn't know the answer.

The water in the Glades was three percent salt, the result of freshwater rivers and creeks, named and unnamed, flowing down from Lake Okeechobee and mixing with the warm, tropical waters of the gulf and the Atlantic. But rain was the source of it all. *Rain.*

She tilted her head back, grinning. *Rain rain rain.* Of course. It had been there right along, buckets of rain, rivers of it. They could catch rain in something. In cups. Did they have cups? Were there any left?

The skillet, then. No. It had gone overboard.

The tarp. They could rig up something with the tarp to collect the rain and then pour it into something.

Into what?

Anything. The important thing was the rain, rain that had been falling since . . . When? How long had they

116

been here? What day was it? Hadn't Nichols just asked a while ago? Hadn't McCleary told him? Or was it yesterday when he'd said it? When had time ceased to touch her as minutes and hours and become this strange, surreal thing whose passage was marked only by periods of light and dark?

What's wrong with my memory?

She suddenly couldn't recall the color of the walls in the kitchen at home. Were they white? Peach? Were they papered? And why couldn't she visualize her bedroom? Did its windows overlook the driveway or the pool in the backyard? And, yes, the pool. Had she ever planted that Mexican heather along one side of it as she'd planned? Had she put in those dwarf oleander bushes along the back of the house? These were simple facts, as basic as her name and her age, and yet they eluded her. It was as if the Glades were absorbing bits and pieces of her, of all of them, feeding off their energy, their personalities, their memories, a psychic vampire. And as it fed, as it soaked up their civilized veneers, they were becoming something else, new versions of their old selves, which were not necessarily better versions.

She wondered if this was similar to what it had been like for McCleary last summer, when he'd awakened in that motel room with a dead woman in the next bed and twenty years of memories wiped clean. *To be lost*, then, could be more than just a geographical confusion; it could also be a misplacement in personal space and time.

And as long as the rain kept coming down like this, compensating for last year's dry summer, they were going to remain lost, geographically and perhaps otherwise as well. They were going to awaken tomorrow morning to gray skies and more rain, with no more sense of where they were than they had now.

Lost with the Nicholses.

". . . that's good, Beau, honey. Lean against me and Mac. Yeah, fine, you're doing fine."

Quin glanced over.

McCleary had twisted the end of the flashlight into the wet ground, so the light was dispersed across the Spanish moss and the undersides of leaves the size of small dogs. In its pale illumination, Nichols looked like an injured bear, his bulk wedged between McCleary and Lydia, a huge arm around each of their shoulders as he limped to the nearest tree. He leaned into it, breathing hard. Water glistened against his blond hair, sweat gleamed against his cheeks. She didn't think he was even going to make it a half mile.

"I can carry the supplies on my back," he said to his wife. "Just wrap them up in the sleeping bag and help me get it on my back."

"Okay, you just rest there a second. Could I borrow the flashlight, Mike?"

McCleary gave it to her, turned on the penlight, and walked over to where Quin was. His expression was a faithful reflection of everything she was feeling just then. "That's it?" He gestured toward their meager supplies.

"That's it."

He crouched next to her and unrolled the soggy sleeping bag and the tarp. Then he began placing the supplies on them, fashioning them into backpacks. "Hope you've still got that hook and line handy."

"Sure." She patted her pack.

"You ever fished?"

"You don't remember?"

"No." He looked at her. "Is that something I *should* remember?"

She smiled. "Not really. We only went fishing once, before we were married, at one of the lakes outside Orlando."

"And?"

"I got seasick. The trip was a disaster. It's a good thing to forget."

Softly: "I have a feeling this is a trip I'm going to wish I could forget." Then he touched her arm and held up the sleeping bag. "I'll help you get this on."

It fit as snugly as a papoose against her back and was surprisingly light. "Okay?" he asked, slinging the tarp over one shoulder and her pack over the other.

"Yeah, it's fine."

"If it gets too heavy, just holler."

"Okay."

This new version of McCleary that was emerging was gentler. The new versions of the Nicholses, however, were wretched. *And what about me?* Well, hey, that was easy. The emerging Quin possessed a certain meanness of spirit that had probably always been there, settled inside her like silt at the bottom of the jar.

They started into the trees, the mosquitoes hounding them. McCleary took the lead with one flashlight, Quin brought up the rear with the other, and the Nicholses were in between. They were on a mahogany hammock that was dense with tremendous ferns, dwarf cabbage palmettos, vines, and air plants that clung to the branches like marsupials. Spanish moss draped the branches in flamboyant swirls that seemed luminescent in the dark. The air vibrated with the sounds of wildlife. Leaves rippled with movement that had nothing to do with the wind or the rain. There was something distinctly primeval about the place, as though it had stood like this for millennia, untouched, undisturbed.

But after the first hundred yards or so, they stumbled across a footpath, so they weren't the first canoeists to discover the place. Even though the ground wasn't packed hard from frequent use, the foliage on either side of it had been cut back. Quin hoped a chickee or a campsite lay at the end. It would mean they weren't lost, that a marked channel would be somewhere nearby. And once they were on one of the designated channels, their chances of encountering other campers or reaching a ranger's station were good.

They trudged along very slowly for perhaps a quarter of a mile, stopping frequently so that Nichols could rest. No one said much of anything, not even Lydia. Talking required too much effort. What little energy they had was consumed by the simple act of placing one foot in front of the other. Quin was so tired, her bones literally ached. Every time she blinked, her eyelids felt weighted and sluggish. A couple of times she actually nodded off for a few seconds, then came to when she stumbled.

After that, to stay awake, she counted the number of times she was bitten by mosquitoes. She counted the bones in her body that hurt. She counted imaginary grains of rice on an imaginary plate of *arroz con pollo*. Not just any old rice, but that succulent, almost sweet yellow rice that Cubans made so well.

Her mouth watered. Her stomach cramped and fussed for food, *real* food, not trail mix and bananas and tuna fish. Her hunger was suddenly cyclopean, a beast that ranted and raged and flung itself from side to side. She dug in the pack on Mac's back for gum. Yellow Chiclets. She popped a square into her mouth, sucked off the white coating. Her teeth sank into it, saliva rushed into her mouth, the sweetness ran down the back of her throat. Nothing had ever tasted this good. Nothing. It made the inside of her mouth feel cool and clean again, opened her sinuses, burned all the way up to her eyes. She dug the box out of the pack, drawing a look from McCleary as she did so, emptied it into her hand, and counted how many pieces were left.

Five.

One before bed, one after breakfast, one for a midmorning snack, one after lunch, and another after dinner. But it wouldn't come to that. By tomorrow, they'd be home and gum wouldn't be farther than a two-minute walk to the nearest 7-Eleven.

Home.

Home was a hot bath, clean hair, clean clothes, clean teeth, a full belly, air-conditioning, electricity, a bed, feather pillows, coffee, a fridge jammed with food, Dan Rather and the evening news, *The Today Show*, a three-mile run in the park, cats, phones, traffic, crime, Miami, her office. Home was creature comforts and civilization with all its accouterments, good and bad, and everything she'd taken for granted for forty years. It had never looked as good as it did right now.

Just to prove that she really believed she would be home by tomorrow, she allowed herself another piece of gum. A moment later, as though her leap of faith with the gum was a kind of portent, the path widened into a small glade. It was bordered by huge ferns, young pine saplings, and, beyond it, live oaks. Needles, leaves, and fallen Spanish moss cushioned the ground. The scent of pine and the deep humus odor of the soil sweetened the humid air.

But there were no chickees, no platforms, no refuse left by other campers.

While McCleary and Nichols rigged the pair of tarps

120

between trees, creating two separate shelters from the rain, Quin set out one of the empty cans to catch some water. Then she opened the wet sleeping bag under the shelter she and McCleary were going to use and collected fallen palmetto leaves to place over it. They were like giant fans and three of them covered the sleeping bag completely. Although they were damp, as was the blanket she smoothed over them, the end result was a bed far more comfortable than just a sleeping bag on the ground.

"Where'd you get the blanket?" Lydia asked, coming up behind her, her light pointed at the blanket.

"It was in the canoe."

"Which canoe?"

"McCleary's."

"I was in that canoe, too, and there was a blanket that belonged to me and Beau."

Not now, Lydia. Don't start with this shit. "A blanket you brought on the trip or that belonged to the crazies?"

"To the crazies. It was in the canoe we took off in."

Quin glanced up at her. "Well, it wasn't this one."

Lydia's mouth twitched. She folded her arms at her waist. She looked deranged. "I think it was, and I'd like it back, Quin."

"Look, Lydia. If you had a blanket and it isn't in with your things, then it probably slipped overboard with you earlier."

"It wasn't with all that junk. Now let me have the goddamn blanket." She extended one hand and fixed the other to her hip. "I'm not lying on top of a wet, smelly sleeping bag."

"Neither am I."

With that, Lydia swooped down like a vulture and snatched up the blanket. It was like getting your purse ripped off your shoulder in a crowd. It happened so fast and was so unexpected that Quin was shocked into passivity.

"I'm sick of you and Mac bossing us around." Vitriol cracked her voice. "I don't know who the fuck you guys think you are, but we're not taking it anymore, you understand me, Quin?" Then she fluttered away, clutching the blanket against her.

When McCleary came over, Quin was still crouched

beside the sleeping bag. She was imagining things she would like to do to Lydia, concocting paybacks the way a spurned child would. How about a spider in her sleeping bag? Or a dead roach in her coffee? Or, better yet, how about burning the rest of Lydia's dope?

"What was that about?" McCleary asked.

"We just lost our blanket."

He flashed his light on the bed of palmetto leaves, then glanced at Lydia. She was kneeling under the other tarp now, fixing the blanket over *her* bed and whispering to Nichols. Conspiring with him, Quin thought, planning an overthrow, a mutiny.

"Forget it. The inside of my poncho will do the trick." McCleary set the flashlight down, shrugged off the poncho, shook it. Then he turned it inside out and spread it across the leaves. He patted it, looked up at her, grinned. "See? How could you ask for anything better out here?"

Quin smiled. "Brilliant. It's perfect." She pulled off her own poncho and tied both ends to the rope that held the tarp to the trees. It fell far enough down so that the Nicholses wouldn't be the first thing she saw in the morning. "Voilà. Privacy."

McCleary laughed, stripped down to his underwear, pulled on the last of his dry clothes, and flopped back on the bed. "Not bad. Not bad at all."

"Don't hog the space, you."

He rolled onto his side, arms under his head like a pillow, and was asleep in seconds. She retrieved the flashlight and the shotgun from his side and placed both things between them just in case Lydia had designs on them as well. Then she went through her pack, taking stock of her dry clothes. Shorts, a long, loose cotton shirt, black cotton jeans, a pair of socks, cotton panties. Just the shirt, she thought, and peeled off her wet clothes, noticing that her polish had chipped, that dirt had pushed up under her nails, that her fingertips were wrinkled from all the water. Rain, rivers, bays. Water.

But none for a hot bath.

Even though the mosquitoes weren't too bad here, she wished she had insect repellent to coat on her arms and legs. Quin wadded up the dry jeans to use as a pillow. She put the pack next to her, then stretched out on her side, drawing her legs up against her. She turned off the flashlight and lay there in the utter blackness, surrounded by noises.

There was no point where she felt sleep washing over her, where she felt her body surrendering, melting away, becoming something else. She simply sank.

2.

"Quin, wake up, c'mon, wake up."

The sound of McCleary's voice jerked her instantly from a dream of water: oceans, rivers, creeks; water that was black, that was blue, that was white with sunlight; water that she drank, that she bathed in; water through which she swam like a fish. Even the air was filled with the song of water—rain beating steadily against the tarp and drumming through the trees.

She pushed up on her elbows, instantly aware of her body's small complaints. Bones that whined, eyes that felt like sand had been ground into them, skin that stank of sweat, fingers and feet that throbbed.

"What?" she whispered. "What is it?"

"Put on your shoes. I want to show you something."

She unrolled the dry jeans she'd been using as a pillow and pulled them on. She slipped on her shoes—without socks—untied her poncho, shrugged it on. She picked up the pack, the flashlight. McCleary already had the rifle. "Mac?"

"Right here." He touched her arm; his fingers slipped down it to her hand and he helped her up.

Once they were safely away from the Nicholses, he switched on the light. "You didn't need to bring everything."

"I'm not taking any chances. Where're we going?"

"You'll see."

A little mystery. A tourist's jaunt to parts unknown. Swell. Just what she didn't need.

They cut through a low wall of ferns, moved through a stand of pines, and emerged at the shore of a lagoon. Rain swept in great silver sheets across it, spraying their faces as they huddled under a live oak. It caught the glare of the flashlight and reflected it like metal, tossing it back at them, spilling light onto a crescent of limestone sand that sloped gently into the water.

"I followed the shore for probably half a mile," McCleary said, making a semicircle in the air with his finger. "It looks like it curves around into another river."

Once a detective, always a detective. "Is that what we were on earlier? A river?"

"Yeah, I think so. And I think this is some sort of cutoff between the two."

"But a river to where? We need to get to some marked channels."

"Maybe this will lead us to one. I just want to stay clear of that bay tomorrow. We were too exposed."

"You really think those weirdos are still looking for us?"

"I don't know and I don't want to find out."

Quin set down the pack and the flashlight, held her hands out beyond the borders of the tree, and cupped them, letting the rain fill them. The water was warm and tasted faintly sweet. It reminded her of her dream, the dream of water, and suddenly all she wanted was to feel it against her bare skin, to wash away the grime and the sweat and the dirt of the Glades.

She shucked the poncho, her blouse and jeans, and kicked off her shoes. She ran down to the beach, dropping to her knees in the sand. The rain poured over her, silky, light, tepid as bathwater. She rubbed handfuls of sand against her skin, scrubbing herself down. She combed her fingers through her hair, washing out the stink of the Glades, and turned her face up toward the black, wet sky. She opened her mouth to the rain, gulped it, coughed, gulped again. It streamed down her gullet, beaded on her lips, her lashes, rolled down the length of her nose. There was only this, the water and the blackness and the rough sand against her knees.

Then she felt hands against her shoulders, McCleary's hands, McCleary behind her, drawing her hair away from her cheek and nuzzling the skin there with his stubbled jaw. She turned; he put his arms around her. Her hands sought their old spots on his shoulders, his neck, the back of his skull. His mouth tasted of rain. When he pulled her up and against him, his skin felt smooth and slippery and new, like an infant's, not at all like she remembered. It shocked her.

They sprinted to the shelter of trees and stumbled onto the discarded ponchos. They rolled; they laughed; they pressed up against each other with the kind of urgency born of relief, not of passion.

"This doesn't mean I've changed my mind," she said.

"I know."

He kissed her, and the taste of rain and the past was still there, but it mixed with something new. Her hands recognized him; her hands had never forgotten. She wondered if his had. She wondered if her body felt different to him, if his hands discovered changes in her body that had escaped her own scrutiny: a pleat in her skin that hadn't been there last summer; wrinkles in her forehead, at the corners of her eyes that she no longer saw because she was used to them; maybe a slackness in her thighs that running hadn't touched.

He pulled a poncho up around them, sealing them inside it, little pigs in a blanket. At first, they made love shyly, awkwardly, as though they'd never been together before. But gradually his hands and mouth became more practiced. They knew where to touch and how and when. His fingers, his tongue, drew her skin into sharp, almost painful peaks of pleasure. When he slipped a finger inside her, he drew back a little, watching her face, and she whispered, "You're embarrassing me." He smiled and said he was remembering, that was all, just remembering. And his finger kept moving in that slow, maddening way, into her and out, then in tight, moist circles around her until her breath grew short and she couldn't stand it anymore, she wanted him inside her, please, she said, please.

But it was as if he hadn't heard her. And now her hips pressed up against his hand, moved as if of their own volition, and she started to come, her mouth opening against his shoulder, muffling her cry. He slid into her, and their movements became those of small fish swimming upstream against impossible currents. And in the end they struggled against each other, enacting some ancient ritual of birth and death and renewal, the life cycle of the Glades. The rain swelled around them, carrying the scent of the lagoon, the trees. It became the black, rich soil, the moss, the river of grass, the embryonic waters of their marriage.

3.

Afterward, she wanted to say, *I don't think this will work, Mac.* Whether it was true didn't really matter right now. What mattered was that the words would protect her, like an amulet. But the most she could muster was a repetition. "This doesn't mean I've changed my mind."

"You already said that. Besides, it worked for a long time with us."

"That was before."

"Before what?"

Before Callahan, before his amnesia, before last summer, before their marriage had begun accruing unpaid interest. "Before everything."

"Nothing comes with guarantees, Quin."

"I don't want guarantees. I just want better odds." And stability. She wanted to know that when she got home from work in the evening, her life there would be waiting for her, like the cats. She wanted to know that she wasn't taken for granted, that the marriage mattered enough to him to be nurtured. Was that asking for guarantees?

They were on their sides. The faint glow of the flashlight some distance away, on the ground where McCleary had left it, spilled onto his cheek, his eyelid. He was touching her again, a slow, intimate touch that had nothing at all to do with the conversation. Their bodies carried on without them.

"I'm just asking you to give us another chance, that's all. You want to start over, we'll start over. We'll go on dates. We'll be proper. I'll send flowers. I'll call two weeks ahead for a date. Whatever." A pause, then: "Did I ever send you flowers?"

"A few times."

His hand slid up the inside of her thigh; the muscles there rippled in response. "You have an unfair advantage, you know." She touched a finger to his mouth and felt its shape change as he smiled. "Real unfair."

"I know."

126

"And considering where we are, this is an absurd conversation."

"I agree."

"Maybe we could just have an affair."

"Champagne and candlelight?"

"And dinners in the Grove and rainy afternoons in a bungalow on a beach somewhere."

"In the Caribbean." His fingers drew hieroglyphics against her belly, then slipped lower, touching her lightly, absently. "On an island."

"Barbados?"

"Or Curaçao."

"Or both."

"You never liked candlelight dinners," he said. "Before."

She felt an absurd delight that he'd remembered such a small detail. "Yeah, I guess I didn't. But maybe I would now."

He laughed and kissed her again, and just then, the strange, diluted glow from the flashlight suddenly moved, expanded, and burst with a blinding brilliance.

"Well, well, looky here. Folks grabbin nooky on *our* beach. What do you think we oughta do about that, hmm?"

"Nothin," replied another voice. "They's Wes's. You know the rules."

Quin and McCleary scrambled to their feet. She scooped up the poncho to cover herself and winced against the light, against the voice that had come from inside it. A man's voice with the same uneducated twang to it as Weston's. But it wasn't Weston's voice.

Now shapes stepped out of the light, from behind the trees, surrounding them, trapping them in a circle.

"If I was you, buddy, I'd cover my dick and then I'd stand real still, jus' like your lady friend here," said the voice. "Otherwise you'll be makin me do somethin we'll both regret. Do I make myself clear?"

"Perfectly," said McCleary.

"Good." His wadded-up clothes sailed out of the light from one direction and Quin's from the other. "Now put on them clothes. We got to get movin."

White Indians

1.

THEY NUMBERED A dozen—six men, six women.

Two men carried rifles—the lean, sinewy character who'd first spoken and another man who was brawnier, taller, but looked to be about the same age, in his late forties or early fifties. Everyone else had bows similar to what Opal had carried, store bought, top of the line, with strings tightened with such precision that they probably sang with perfect pitch when an arrow flew, McCleary thought.

The men all wore jeans and cotton shirts, with boots and belts made of alligator skin. Their clothes were covered by cheap, transparent raincoats, the kind of thing you found at K mart for $1.59, which folded into a neat square. The women also wore jeans and alligator boots, but their blouses looked handwoven, with colorful designs similar to what Seminole women wore. Their raincoats were the same variety as what the men had on, but all were a dark tan, the color of taffy or of wet saw grass.

The uniformity of their clothes reminded McCleary of the dress code at military and parochial schools, where its purpose was to make everyone equal. But perhaps this was simply a paucity of supplies and materials or a lack of imagination or maybe both. He found it as unsettling as the disturbing sameness of their faces—flat noses, full lips, small eyes set deeply in gaunt cheeks—that weird mixed heritage he had seen in Weston, Opal, and Judd. Some of them had snake tattoos, just as Opal had, and all were in visible places—on a cheek, a forehead, the back of a hand, the palm. Regardless of who they were or where they'd come from, it was clear that these were people you didn't fuck with.

They maintained a wide circle around him and Quin as they moved toward the glade. Their powerful hurricane lanterns stripped back the darkness with the efficiency of stadium lights, revealing details he'd failed to see earlier. Like the hard-packed ground of the path they were on, the thatched lean-to near the glade, the way the lowest shrubs had been cut back. Details, he thought, that might have made him think twice about staying here.

But retrospection was pointless. He needed a plan, a strategy, answers. If escape was even a remote possibility, where would they escape *to*? Was the hammock connected to land? Was it large enough to hide in? Could they remain hidden in a place these people probably knew as well as he did the streets of Miami? What chance did they have of escape once they were on the water? And if they *did* escape, either on land or on water, just how much of a hindrance were the Nicholses going to be?

The only question he had an answer for was the last.

As they came into the glade, he saw Lydia and Nichols. They'd been gagged and tied to either side of a pine tree. Their gear and the McClearys' had been packed up in a tarp that had been lashed together with rope. The fact that all of this had happened without so much as a sound from the Nicholses, with no warning of the group's approach, meant these weirdos were as acclimated to darkness as they were to this goddamn swamp. And that was more unsettling than the monotony of their clothes, of their appearance.

The man who'd first spoken gestured toward the Nicholses with his rifle and spoke to a young man with cheeks so pitted, they looked like volcanic rock. "Ticker, get them loose from that there tree, then tie their hands behind them. Take out them gags. If they scream, they's dead. Same goes for these two."

Ticker smiled. He had a severe tic under his left eye that made his cheek twitch constantly. "I gets to shoot 'em, Pa?"

"That depends," Pa replied, then swung his rifle up and pointed it at a woman with a missing front tooth. "Josie, you's in charge of the tall woman." He looked at Quin. "What's your name?"

She told him.

Josie snickered. "Quin. It rhymes with sin."

"Never you mind what it rhymes with, woman. Jus' make sure she's never outta your sight."

"Yessuh, Pa." She poked one end of her bow at Quin's chest. "Turn 'round and put your wrists together."

Quin did exactly what she was told.

"Ain't you the skinny one." Josie pulled a length of something that looked like rope out from under her poncho. She wrapped it around Quin's wrists, jerked on it, knotted it, jerked on it again. Then she slid the bow up under Quin's hair and flicked it off her neck. She rocked toward her on the balls of her feet, her mouth only a few inches from Quin's ear. "You kill Judd, Miss Bones?"

"No one killed Judd," McCleary said. "He tripped and fell on his own spear."

Pa fixed his small, dark eyes on McCleary and sank his fist into his sternum. A white-hot pain exploded in the center of his chest. He gasped, his knees buckled, and he sank to the ground. His vision blurred. The glade tilted like a sailboat in a storm, trees rushed together, bile poured into his throat. McCleary swallowed it back, coughed, then slowly pushed himself to his feet.

"No one asked for your oh-pi-nion, asshole. We knows 'xactly what happened to Wes's boy."

"You want that I should teach him manners?"

The man who spoke had a nose that looked like a squashed grapefruit. A boxer's nose. It made him wheeze when he breathed, so that his voice was hopelessly nasal. He was grinning at McCleary and gripping the center of his bow the way a thug clutched a bat he intended to beat you with.

"Jus' tie his hands, Rusty." Pa turned the powerful beam of the hurricane lantern on McCleary's face; his eyes narrowed against the brightness. "Rusty gets . . . hmm, what's that word, Josie?"

"Overzealous," she said.

"Right. That's how Rusty gets sometimes, Mr. Lover Boy. So if I was you, I'd be *real* careful what I do and say 'round him. You understandin what I'm sayin?"

McCleary's chest burned fiercely and the fire seemed to be radiating up into his throat, closing it off. He managed to nod.

"What was that?" Pa asked. "Cain't hear you, Lover Boy."

"Yes," he rasped.

"Yes what? Yes you enjoyed fuckin the skinny lady? Yes your chest is hurtin somethin bad? Yes what, Lover Boy?"

The others laughed.

"Yes, I understood what you said."

"Good, Lover Boy. That's good. Tie his goddamn hands, Rusty."

"Should I put somethin in his mouth?"

"Your fist if he don't do what you tell him."

Rusty grinned, told McCleary to put his hands behind him, then tied them with what felt like a strip of rawhide or maybe a root or a vine of some kind. Whatever it was didn't burn his skin like rope would have when he worked his wrists, trying to loosen it. But the dampness constricted it.

Ticker brought Lydia and Nichols over. Blood oozed from her left nostril; tears glistened in her eyes. "She told me to fuck myself," Ticker said. "I had t'hit her."

"Maybe you shoulda fucked her instead," piped Josie. "*If* you could even git it up," she added, and exploded with laughter.

Ticker looked helplessly at Pa, who shrugged as if to say, *Deal with it yourself.* "What d'you know," Ticker muttered finally.

Josie silently mimicked him, then plucked once at the string on her bow, and yeah, it had perfect pitch, just like McCleary had suspected.

"So," said Pa. "What've we got here?" He walked over to Lydia and touched a grimy hand to her chin, turning it left, right, scrutinizing her. "Bet you're the lady with the pretty name. Lee-dee-uh. Right?"

Lydia rolled her lower lip against her teeth; her head bobbed.

Now Pa's attention focused on Nichols. "Big man." His eyes dropped to the soiled dressing on Nichols's leg. "But even big men get theirselves hurt, now, don't they, boy."

Nichols didn't make any wisecracks and didn't just nod his head the way McCleary had done. He said yes, big boys sure did get hurt sometimes, and he said it like they were just standing around at a cocktail party having a friendly chat. Either he was a damned good actor, McCleary thought, or he was too out of it to know he should have been scared shitless.

"You got nothin smart to say, Big Man? Like your buddy here?" asked Pa, still trying to get a rise out of Nichols.

"Nothing," Nichols replied. "But I'd like to ask a question."

Josie snickered again. "My, my, ain't we police, huh, Pa?"

"Ask away, Big Man."

"Could I have a drink of water?"

"Me, too," said Lydia, her voice feeble. "Please."

"Please," Pa repeated softly, nodding, chuckling to himself. "Please. Ain't that somethin. Pretty lady like yourself sayin please to the likes of me." He touched Lydia's chin again. "Maybe I'll keep you for myself, Lee-de-uh."

"Ma would have your hide," Josie told him.

Pa laughed. "Your ma don't even know what a hide is, girl." Then he snapped his fingers at Ticker. "Give 'em some water."

Ticker slid the canteen off his shoulder.

"But you keep hold of the canteen. Don't want 'em touchin it."

"Is it bad luck or somethin?" Ticker asked.

"Jeez-uz, boy, ain't you got no sense? Bad luck's got nothin to do with it. Jus' try to think it through, huh?"

Ticker looked confused; McCleary could almost smell the circuits in his brain overloading. But he nodded and said, "Yessuh," and walked over to Lydia.

"You be wantin water?" Pa asked, glancing at McCleary, then at Quin.

"Yeah, thanks," McCleary said.

Quin echoed the response, her voice quiet, controlled, her eyes cast toward the ground in a pretense of submission, of surrender. But in the set of her mouth, a mouth that he remembered, a mouth that he had painted, kissed, watched, a mouth that he loved, he read a flurry of con-

132

flicting emotions. He willed her to look at him and she did, but only when Pa had turned his attention elsewhere.

Be ready, his eyes signaled.

Just say the word, her eyes whispered back. Then, for an instant, a smile brushed the corner of her mouth, a smile meant just for him, for what had happened on the beach.

It's going to be okay, he thought at her.

But she was already watching Ticker as he ambled over with the canteen.

2.

From what McCleary could determine, the group had come ashore on the leeward side of the hammock. The entrance was through a cypress swamp that, in the wash of light from the hurricane lamps, looked spooky, self-contained, a scene transposed out of Sleepy Hollow. Great shawls of Spanish moss hid their canoes.

And there were a lot of canoes to hide.

The group had four cypress dugout canoes that were short, shallow, and large enough for one person and gear. They were equipped with 15-horsepower outboards, half as powerful as the engines on the other canoes. But their lighter weight and smaller size made them ideal for scout vessels. Fleet and perfect for the Glades. There were also four aluminum canoes identical to the ones the McClearys and the Nicholses had been using, which accommodated the other eight members of the group. As soon as McCleary saw them, he knew he probably wouldn't be in the same canoe as Quin, that the four of them, in fact, were going to be separated.

As they stood on the grassy bank, waiting while supplies and people were rearranged, only Ticker was left to keep an eye on the four of them. McCleary was able to get close enough to Quin to whisper to her. "I think we should try to make a break for it."

Her pale blue eyes seemed to recede in her cheeks. "We'll get ourselves killed." She hunched her shoulder up and rubbed her cheek against it, streaking dirt on her jaw. "Even if we managed to get away, we're not going to have a canoe. And if we *do* have a canoe, how're we going to paddle with our hands tied?"

"I'm pretty sure I can work my hands loose. What about you?"

"I've been trying. But that witch tied them really tight and this rope or whatever they've used is awfully wet. You have a plan?"

"Not really. We'll have to play it by ear. When you hear a ruckus, you know to jump."

Her eyes flickered over his shoulder to Ticker, then darted back to him. "If only one of us makes it, the other should head south to Tarpon Creek and the Coot Bay area. I heard Josie talking about how the rangers patrol that area pretty regularly."

"Hey, you two, no talkin," barked Ticker as he hurried over. "Talkin ain't allowed. Move apart."

McCleary stepped to the side a few paces; Ticker stopped between him and Quin and glared at McCleary. "You best follow orders, Lover Boy." He tried to emulate Pa but didn't quite make it. McCleary felt like laughing until Ticker pulled an arrow out of his quiver and fixed it in his bowstring. "Otherwise, you gonna make me hurt you. And jus' in case you're thinkin I dunno how to use this, lemme show you."

He reached under his raincoat and pulled out an apple that fit into the palm of his hand. He tossed it up. It rose through the luster of the hurricane lamps, then into the dark where the light didn't reach. He pulled back the bow and shot the apple on its descent. The impact carried it about thirty yards, where the arrow slammed into a cypress tree and the apple fell apart in pieces.

Ticker's lips drew away from his teeth in a grin that revealed sharp, pointed eyeteeth. "See?"

"Impressive," McCleary agreed, the back of his throat dry with fear.

Ticker cocked his head and frowned, as if he were listening to a voice McCleary couldn't hear. As the frown smoothed out, Rusty lumbered over and said, "Okay, we're ready."

Ticker tapped McCleary's chest with the end of his bow. "You's comin with me. The skinny lady's goin with Josie." He looked at Nichols, who was standing with most of his weight on his stronger leg. "You's ridin with Pa's brother. He's the other guy with a rifle. You don't wanna fuck with him, Big Man." He glanced at Lydia and grinned again. "You and Pa goes in the lead canoe. He likes you. That makes you lucky." Ticker laughed. "Till Ma hears about it. Now move. Toward the canoes."

Ticker fell into step behind McCleary, and Quin and the Nicholses were behind them, with Rusty at their backs. McCleary felt like a condemned man about to walk the plank.

3.

The caravan of canoes putted through the eerie silence in the cypress swamp. The soft luster from the hurricane lamps eddied across the ceiling of branches and leaves and washed through the webs of Spanish moss. Insects shrieked and cried from the nearby shores. Schools of tiny fish, pursued by something Quin couldn't see, rose from the black waters in shimmering silver blurs, only to splash down again. A pair of alligators, half submerged in a shallow nook, watched them pass, the glow of their eyes luminous and strange in the dark.

I can't do this. I can't jump off the canoe.

The perils of the water and of what lay beyond it seemed infinitely worse than whatever their captors might do to them. Until she thought about it. Until she remembered the voice that had said, *They's Wes's. You know the rules.*

Weston the Ugly, who thought they were responsible for his son's death.

Weston with his thirty-ought-six, Opal with her bow. Weston and Opal, the nightmare couple of the year.

Quin worked her hands a little harder. Even though Josie was behind her, steering the canoe, she didn't have her lamp on. Quin hoped it was too dark for her to see what she was doing.

But the rope or rawhide or whatever it was that bound her wrists held hard and fast. And as they moved out from under the protection of the trees and into the rain, the thing got wetter than it already was and tightened.

They entered what appeared to be a wide river or maybe a bay. The rain struck with a vengeance, transforming the glow of the hurricane lanterns to nothing more than faint ghost lights, a memory of light, a distant dream of redemption. If she jumped overboard here, with her hands still tied, she would drown. And that was only if she didn't become some alligator's gourmet delight.

Please don't try anything, McCleary. Please please. I don't want to be left here alone with these people.

And for a long time, he didn't.

For a long time, there was just rain and more rain and the incessant chug of the outboards, ferrying them deeper into the darkness. She had moved closer to the side of the canoe and now sat with her back to it, where she worked the rope against what felt like a loose screw.

If she'd been able to move her hands as quickly as she wanted and at the proper angle, she knew she could cut through the rope in no time at all. But with Josie behind her, with the canoe rising and falling against the currents, it was a slow, tedious task. And yet the rope did seem a bit looser, and when she allowed herself to think about it, her hopes soared. Until she looked down at the water.

Until she imagined what it would be like to be in it.

In the dark.

Alone.

Her clothes weighting her.

The canoes circling her like hawks.

She'd have to swim underwater.

If she could swim at all.

The caravan started to slow down. The lights bounced across a channel with land on both sides. Islands, she thought, or a hammock with a passage through it. As the lead canoe entered it, Quin glanced around, trying to make out the canoe McCleary and Ticker were in. Two back. But there wasn't enough light to see and the rain was still falling too hard.

Josie cut the power to a bare minimum; the canoe's nose poked into the pass. Quin kept working her hands, moving the rope against the screw, blinking rain from her eyes. She sensed that McCleary would do whatever he was going to do here, while the group was distracted by the logistics of getting through this narrow pass. This perfect pass with land on either side of it.

Land.

It meant she wouldn't have to leap into the water. It

meant it didn't matter that her hands weren't free yet. On land she wouldn't need her hands to run. On land they would have a chance to hide without being confronted immediately by other dangers.

Suddenly, shouts went up behind her, slapping the wet air, rising above the noise of the rain. A voice inside her screamed, *Now, do it now.* She leaped up just as Josie turned to see what was going on. The canoe lurched and Quin, robbed of her arms for balance, fell forward. Her knee struck the edge of the bench she'd been sitting on. Pain flashed through it, hot and fierce, biting through cartilage, muscles, down to the bone. She struggled up, the rope around her wrists popped loose, freeing her hands, and she lunged from the side of the canoe. For land. For freedom. But something slammed across her midsection, stealing the air from her lungs, knocking her back, and pain exploded across her stomach, her ribs.

The dark shape of the island slid left, the canoe seemed to slip out from under her, and she knew she wasn't going to make it. Then her head hit the other side and she slumped to the floor, the blackness closing around her like the petals of some huge and poisonous flower.

4.

One moment McCleary was airborne, the wind and rain whipping his face raw, and the next moment his shoes smashed against land. He started to slip, found purchase, and charged ahead blindly, crashing through brush, thorns, water, mud. Light from the hurricane lamps found him. Shots rang out. He dived for the ground and crawled on his belly for the nearest cluster of trees.

The lights passed over him and he froze, his cheek squashed against a bed of wet ferns. Insects swarmed over his hands, stinging, clinging to the skin even when he slammed the backs of his hands against the ground trying to get them off. When the lights had passed, he leaped up again and ran.

Branches snapped at his ankles, bit at his cheeks, slapped at his arms. The air was blacker than ink and he never knew when a root, a vine, or a palmetto brush was going to jump out at him, tripping him. He fell half a dozen times, crashed into low-hanging branches, got tangled up in Spanish moss. Now and then he heard shouts somewhere nearby, much too close for comfort, and saw lights flickering through the rain, the dark, seeking him.

He kept moving deeper and deeper into the trees, moved until his body refused to go another step, until his legs finally gave way and he sank to his knees, hunched over, trying to catch his breath. His lungs were on fire. His hands burned and itched from the bites. He tasted dirt in his mouth. Felt mud squishing between his toes, his fingers. Blood pounded in his ears.

Get up, asshole.

He wanted to sleep.

Move.

His eyes closed.

You looking to die, turkey?

He lifted his head, wiped his hand across his mouth, then peered around him into the blackness, the endless, fathomless blackness. He let out a short laugh; his forehead dropped to the ground again. Warm. Soft. *Sleep, just a few minutes of sleep.* But something in one of the poncho's zippered pockets poked into his chest. He sat up, his hand sliding inside, his fingers thick and awkward as they dug around and closed over the penlight and one of the Cyalume lightsticks. The weirdos had neglected to check his pockets. He bent the lightstick, snapped and shook it. The green glow flared in the dark, an infant's finger seeking the black hole of its mouth.

With light, he had a chance.

The shouts were more distant now; the bastards were moving in the wrong direction. He checked the poncho's numerous pockets, taking inventory. He wasn't as bad off as he'd thought. Besides the penlight and the lightstick, he had two slices of beef jerky, his Swiss Army knife, two sticks of Juicy Fruit gum, a pair of dry socks, a pack of matches, one of Quin's tangled fish lines and hooks, and one of the joints she'd laid out in the tent that first night.

He remained as he was for a few minutes, forcing himself to empty his head of *ifs. If* Quin didn't get away, *if* the crazies caught up with him, *if* he couldn't stay awake until it was light, *if* the rain didn't slack off.

If.

138

His life seemed to be predicated on a string of probabilities, and none of them looked encouraging.

But I've got light, food.

He started to move again, the phantom glow of the lightstick washing through the dark in front of him, and reminded himself that people beat the odds every day. Against cancer. Against plane crashes. Against five-car pileups on I-95. Against assault, rape, murder.

But had anyone ever beat the odds against survival in the Everglades with crazies on his tail and no fresh water?

Bad question, he decided, and moved on.

PART THREE

The Band

May 11

"I had done battle with a great fear and the victory was mine."
>—Marjorie Kinnan Rawlings,
>from *Cross Creek*

Morning

I

1.

THE LAST TIME Benson had been up and moving at five in the morning was when he was a rookie cop, working the seven A.M. streets of Miami. The hour hadn't bothered him then, but it did now. At some point during the last two decades, he had ceased to function well before ten. Even coffee didn't help; it pooled in the pit of his stomach like acid. The only good thing he could say about the hour was that there wasn't any traffic.

He made it to the ranger's station in just over an hour. Buffalo George was sitting on the porch just as he'd been yesterday afternoon when Benson had driven up. He was still wearing his baseball cap, which was pulled down low over his eyes, and jeans. He was motionless in the old wicker rocker until Benson darted up the walk to the steps. Then his index finger popped up against the visor, nudging the cap back on his head.

"Morning," Benson said.

George nodded. "Joe's having his coffee. He said he'd be out in a minute. He doesn't like to be disturbed when he's having his coffee." He shrugged as if to say the vagaries of the old man's quirks were beyond his comprehension. "Have a seat." He gestured toward the other chairs, all of which looked as old and faded and rickety as the one George was sitting on. "Don't know that Joe's going to want to go out in the Glades in weather like this."

"It's better than it was yesterday."

"Not for long." He pointed at the black sky, a huge abscessed boil that hung over the heart of the Everglades.

Lightning flashed around its edges. "That sucker's going to pop before long."

Benson saw the scars on the lower part of his arm as he pointed at the sky. They looked like a connect-the-dots picture. "All I need is the airboat. He doesn't have to come," Benson said as he sat down.

"You won't get far out there alone when that cloud breaks. It's real easy to lose your sense of direction in the Glades even on a good day."

"With maps, I think I can manage."

The screen door creaked open and Joe Farrel stepped out. "Morning." His eyes swept across the sky. "It's not looking good, Sergeant."

"All I need is the airboat."

"Yeah, a man could float in that, all right." He laughed and scratched at the back of his neck with an unlit cigar.

"Look, if you could just lend me an airboat, I can get to Lard Can on my own."

"Yeah, you'd get there. Eventually." His gaze slid lazily toward George. "But you'd be better off with George. He knows these parts. What d'you say, George?"

"I say fine."

"Course, George isn't on the park payroll. And he's got those college bills to pay."

Pay or stay. Like it hadn't been set up beforehand, Benson thought, irritated. He poked his wire-rims back on his nose and sighed. "All right, what do you charge an hour?"

The Indian shrugged and looked down at his hands, pretending to think about it. He named an exorbitant fee. Benson came back with a lower figure. George shook his head and bargained for something a little higher. *What the fuck,* Benson thought. "Okay, fine. I'd like to stop by the canoe rental place first."

"George'll take you," Farrel said.

Don't do me any favors.

2.

Spider.
Small. Brown. Ugly.

On my hand.

The words popped into McCleary's head the moment he opened his eyes and saw the creature scampering across the red welts on the back of his right hand. But they failed to make an immediate impression. It was as if he were watching a nature documentary on PBS, something with fantastic zoom-lens closeups of a spider on another man's hand. Any second now he would get up and walk into the kitchen to get a beer. Or he would switch the channel. Or the doorbell would ring and it would be Quin and . . .

Quin.

Quin and the Glades and Ticker and the weirdos in the canoes. Run, Jesus, run.

He flipped his hand over, smashing the spider against the ground, then rolled into a crouch, head snapping right, left. His breath was a hot wheeze in his chest. Gray light filtered through the branches, pooling like spilled milk on leaves, ferns, and brush. The rain had dwindled to a drizzle. He didn't hear shouts or gunshots. He didn't hear much of anything at all except the things you'd expect to hear in the early morning in the Everglades. Birds. The buzz of insects. The chatter of squirrels. Creatures scurrying through the brush. He hoped they were the benign variety—marsh rabbits, opossums, deer. He didn't allow himself to consider the other choices.

He rocked back on his heels and examined his hands. Tiny red welts dotted the backs and palms, and they itched terribly. But other than the welts and some scratches, he seemed to be relatively unscathed.

He dug out one piece of beef jerky, broke it in half, and savored it bit by precious bit. The salt increased his thirst, which he managed to slake somewhat by licking rainwater from the surface of leaves. He was tempted to devour the rest of this piece and the other one as well, but restrained himself.

Off came his running shoes. His filthy socks. He curled and uncurled his toes in the damp, humid air, then massaged his feet, working out the stiffness, the soreness. He pounded the shoes against the ground, getting rid of the dirt and caked mud. It didn't help much; they still felt like concrete.

Next: dry socks. They were cool and soft against his aching feet and improved his disposition almost as much as the jerky and bit of water had. A dry change of clothes would have gone a long way toward mitigating his discomfort, but he was lucky just to be alive. And free.

He pulled out the Swiss Army knife and checked the blades: three different sizes, none of them longer than three inches. Good enough to kill a grasshopper, but it sure wouldn't do much on a full-grown man.

Miserable again, he stood on legs that felt as if they'd been frozen, thawed, and frozen again. His joints were stiff, his neck didn't work right, his knees cracked as he moved. But once he'd gone several hundred yards, the aches and complaints diminished. His body had apparently remembered what it was supposed to do.

And where're you moving to, pal?

Toward water and away from the pass where they'd been last night: that was his first goal. From there, he would try to get his bearings and find a way off this island. If it *was* an island. If he could believe what Ticker had said during his last few moments on the canoe, before McCleary had jacked his legs up and slammed his shoes into the weirdo's chin.

Ticker, for all his expertise with the bow and arrow, for all his macho tough talk, had been easy to bring down because he hadn't been expecting anything. And because McCleary had freed his hands. Easier, certainly, than Pa would have been. Or Rusty with the squashed nose. Easier than Josie.

Quin never had a chance.

He didn't want to think about what had happened to her, about where she was, about what they might do to her. But the possibilities marched through him with impunity, tossing up dire visions, each worse than the last.

He kept moving through the green twilight.

3.

If George drove an airboat the way he did the Jeep, Benson thought, they were in big trouble. He whipped the vehicle around potholes in the road as if they were knots of cars, shifted gears with no attention at all to what speed he was doing, and used the horn liberally.

He honked as they sped around a curve, honked again when a Key deer paused in the middle of the road, honked a third time as they screeched to a stop in front of the canoe shop. "Door's open and Joe's note is gone. Sammy'll be expecting you," George said.

Sammy Petrellis was young and exuberant and looked like an avid outdoorsman: Coppertone tan, the musculature of a man who took bodybuilding seriously and wasn't shy about showing off the results. He wore shorts and a sleeveless T-shirt and had a habit of flexing his biceps and watching them as they bulged. He said he'd gotten Farrel's note and had pulled Crawford's paperwork. He flipped open a file and turned it around for Benson to look at.

Benson glanced through it, but it didn't tell him much. "You remember him?"

"Sure. It hasn't exactly been weeks. He and his wife strolled in here early Tuesday afternoon. She looked like she was dressed for the mall, not the Glades. You know the type—real tight shorts, halter top, high heels. I told her she'd be better off in jeans and a long-sleeved shirt and tennis shoes. She really took offense, like I'd told her her feet smelled or something. But Crawford laughed; he was kind of cool. Anyway, she changed into a shirt and sneakers but kept on the shorts. Weird woman."

"Did they say where they were going?"

"Wedge Point if they could make it before dark, otherwise Hell's Bay." Petrellis flexed his bicep and touched it, admiring it. "Personally, I didn't think they'd make the point. It's a long trip and I could tell he was no canoeist."

"When were they supposed to be back?"

"Crawford said maybe Wednesday, but probably as late as Friday."

"Today's Friday."

Petrellis smiled. "All day."

Which meant that Crawford probably wasn't missing at all, that he'd simply lied to Stevie.

"Look, Captain." Petrellis leaned forward, arms resting on the desk. "Crawford wasn't a canoeist, but I could tell he was really looking forward to this trip, you know? *If* he and the missus made Wedge Point that first day, it's possible they moseyed on up the Wilderness Waterway for a mile or so the next day, even with the storm and all. Course, the rain would've driven them to a shelter eventually. And that's probably where they still are." He paused. "If they've got any sense at all."

"Would you venture out in this?" Benson stabbed a thumb over his shoulder.

"Not unless I had provisions coming out the kazoo."

"Did they have a lot of provisions?"

"Nope."

"Did they have maps?"

"Yeah, maps they had. If I were you, I'd check as far north as the North River Chickee. It's possible they could've gotten that far."

"How did Crawford and his wife seem together?"

Petrellis frowned. "What do you mean?"

"Did they argue?" *Did they look like a couple on the verge of divorce?* "Did they look like they were happy? What?"

"I wouldn't say they were exactly in honeymoon heaven, if that's what you're asking. All she did was bitch about everything and he pretty much ignored her. I was sort of curious about how they'd be when they got back, you know? Camping in the Glades isn't like a little trip to your local park, Captain. And if you're going with someone, you'd better be damn sure the two of you get along, because the Glades have a way of bringing out the worst in people if the conditions aren't good. And the conditions this whole week have sucked."

"Where'd Crawford leave from?"

"The entrance to the Hell's Bay channel, about six miles down the road."

"How'd he get there? His car's in the lot."

"Usually I take the customers to wherever they're going if they leave their cars here. But that day we were pretty busy. One of Ranger Farrel's boys took them."

"Yeah? Who was that?" Benson asked.

"Billy Tiger. He hires out as a guide from time to time."

Considering that Billy had driven them over to the entrance to the channel last night and hadn't mentioned

148

taking the Crawfords, it was an interesting omission. Benson wondered what it meant.

"You know anything about Buffalo George?"

"What's there to know?" Petrellis shrugged. "He's one of those Seminoles who's got a foot in both worlds. A crossover. He, Billy, and some others hang around here doing odd jobs. George is really the only one in the bunch who's got any ambition. He's taking courses at the community college and hires out here as a guide on weekends and during the week when he doesn't have classes."

"How well does he know Billy?" Benson asked.

"They're friends."

"Good friends?"

"Hey, just friends, Captain."

Did that mean George knew his buddy had driven the Crawfords over to the Hell's Bay Trail?

"Joe said something in his note about you going out there in this mess to look for Crawford and his wife," Petrellis said.

"He's lending me an airboat."

"He going with you?"

"No, George is."

"Good thing. Joe's a nice old guy, but compared to George he doesn't know squat about the Glades."

On impulse, Benson asked Petrellis what he knew about the white Indians; he laughed and shook his head. "Nothing except what the tourist brochures say. They're part of the local color, you know? Like the skunk ape. Like the UFO sightings out here. They contribute to the mystery. They're good for business."

"So you don't believe they exist?"

"Nope. Not till I see one."

The door opened and Buffalo George shuffled in, rain beaded on his baseball cap. "We'd better get a move on. The rain's starting up again." His dark eyes skipped to Petrellis. "How's it going, Sammy?"

"Not bad, George, not bad. Where's your sidekick this morning?"

"Sleeping off a hangover."

"Take care of the captain here."

George grinned. "That's what they pay me for."

"Stop here on your way back, Captain," Petrellis called after them as they turned to leave. "Maybe your friend will be back by then."

"And maybe not," George replied.

Petrellis gave a soft, nervous chuckle, and Benson had the sudden, uneasy feeling that everyone knew more about all this than he did.

4.

McCleary stood at the edge of a stand of denuded cypress trees, gazing across a vast stretch of water. A gulf of water. An ocean. Beyond it lay what might have been another island or the other side of the bay. It might as well have been the other side of the world. It looked like a floating green stain, a discolored oil spill, a stoned artist's abstract rendition of Everglades beauty.

Rain moved through this corridor of water in concentrated spurts, as it often did in the tropics when it poured on one side of the street while the sun shone on the other. Beams of sunlight, the first he'd seen since leaving Miami two days ago, penetrated the space between two cloudbursts and shot the rain through with silver and pale gold. Rainbows shimmered inside it. It dazzled, it blinded, it blazed with a singular grace and beauty and fit the name that Spanish mapmakers had given this region. *La Laguna del Espíritu Santo.* The Lagoon of the Holy Spirit.

At any other time in his life, he would have stood there mesmerized, absorbing everything so that he could try to reproduce it later on canvas. But the sight only increased his gloom, nearly overwhelming him with the sheer logistics of how, short of walking on water, he was going to get off this island.

He moved through the drizzle to the edge of the water and followed the grassy shore to where the land curved like a paw and grew dense with buttonwood and tetrazygia trees, pines and live oaks. A channel angled through it; he guessed it was a shortcut to the pass between the islands. If he followed it, he would have to backtrack. But what was the point? He doubted that it would lead him to a bridge of land that would carry him off the island, and at the moment, that was the only thing that interested him.

He sat in the grass, the drizzle warm against his face. He stood. Paced. No matter how you cut it, he thought, the only way off the island was to swim.

He tried to estimate the distance. One mile? Two? Maybe as much as three? He wouldn't know for sure until he was out in the middle of it. That would mean soggy beef jerky, wet matches, not to mention the possibility of alligators and whatever the hell else lived in these waters.

McCleary peeled the wrapper on a stick of gum. It was so old it broke into pieces in his palm. He plucked up the largest bit, popped it in his mouth, sucked off the sugar, chewed. Saliva filled his mouth, easing the rawness at the back of his parched throat.

How long would it take him to become dehydrated? What were the symptoms? Did the saliva dry up first? Could he drink his own piss if he had to?

He chewed harder on the stick of gum.

He crouched, untangled the fishing line, removed the hook, bent it, put it inside the gum wrapper. Then he wound the line around a stick so it wouldn't get knotted again, and slipped everything in one of his pockets. He kept studying the water and the land beyond it.

The sorry truth was that he wasn't ready to attempt a swim.

He might never be ready.

He wanted to think about it, to explore a little more. Maybe there were other options.

McCleary went down to the place where the land curved, where the channel twisted through trees and weeds. It wouldn't necessarily lead him back the way he'd come, he thought. Nothing so far had been the way he expected it to be, so why should this be any different? He decided to follow it.

Now that he had something definite to occupy him, something concrete, something that demanded concentration, the Everglades intruded. The brush grew denser. The brilliant fans of the cabbage palms, glimmering like wet metal in the silky light, distracted him. Ferns leaped out at him, vines swung toward him in a sudden gust, moths swooped in front of his face. The assault, benign as it was, slowed him down and seemed almost intentional, as if to keep him away from something.

Sure thing. And what other paranoid delusions can we come up with, Mac ol' buddy?

He trudged through brush and mud for a quarter of a mile. The air was oppressively humid, and pretty soon he shed his poncho and tied it at his waist. But the mosquitoes were so bad, he had to drape the poncho over his shoulders to keep the little fuckers off his neck and back.

He remembered reading that the Indians had smeared themselves with mud to ward off mosquitoes and slapped some on his cheeks, arms, and hands. It worked surprisingly well and even took the sting out of the welts on the backs of his hands.

The channel forked about half a mile in. The right arm dead-ended three hundred yards later, blocked by tangled swirls of dead branches and a cloud of dragonflies. So much for his little exploration, he thought. Time for a swim. He started to run away when a glint of something caught his attention.

He grabbed on to the nearest dead branch and yanked it toward him. The entire tangle fell away, revealing an airboat that was just sitting there like a huge bird with clipped wings. To get to it, he would have to step into the water and swim about thirty yards through weeds. But thirty yards was an improvement over two or three miles.

Never mind that he would need a key or jumper cables to start the damn thing. Never mind that he knew next to nothing about airboats or whether, in fact, they could even be jumped. Never mind. He would think of something.

He dropped the poncho on the ground, started to strip off his jeans because they would weight him down, then looked at the tall grass he had to get through first and changed his mind. He moved toward the shore.

The stuff wasn't saw grass, but it was dense, a forest of grass as tough as rope that reached to his chest. When he walked into it, he couldn't see his shoes; that bothered him. He wanted to know where he was stepping—and on what. He pushed through it; his right shoe vanished underwater and sank into the muck. Miles of muck down there. A continent of muck. *And China's on the other side.*

He brought his left foot even with the right. *The jeans are going to weight you bad.* He peeled them off, then wadded them up and tossed them over his shoulder. He looked down at the water; insects swam the backstroke on the surface. They bumped into his ankles, caught in the hairs on his legs.

Get one of those suckers up a nostril and no telling what's going to hatch in your sinuses.

Move it, snapped the drill sergeant in his head.

Right foot again. Left. The mud sucked at his shoes. The drizzle tickled the back of his neck.

"The hell with it," he muttered, and eased himself into the water.

He swam a fast and furious breaststroke toward the airboat, the longest thirty yards he'd ever traveled. He managed to keep his head above water, but just barely. Things crawled on his neck, wiggled inside his shirt and down inside his shorts. His arms fought strings of weeds, long, dead blades of grass, dark buttons of hard mud that looked like turds.

He scrambled up over the side of the airboat and tore off his shirt and shorts, slapping at the tiny bugs that scampered this way and that across his skin. He didn't know what the hell they were, but the names of things had ceased to matter. They were bugs and that was enough.

When he was sure he'd gotten them all, he kicked up the water right next to the airboat, churning it enough to scare off anything large or small, then rinsed his shirt and shorts. He spread them on the boards and turned his attention to the airboat.

It wasn't as large as some he'd seen, but it was big enough for two small men on the elevated seat. The rack on the floor was for a canoe. Behind the seat were an engine and propeller encased in wire mesh that was smeared with the remains of squashed insects.

He checked the ignition for a key, but that kind of luck only happened in the movies. He looked under the seat and in the metal storage box on the floor. It contained tools. Rusted tools. Wrenches, screwdrivers, a hammer, bolts, nuts, screws. He picked up a screwdriver and a wrench and moved over to the engine.

It looked like an ordinary automobile engine that had been rigged to accommodate the propeller. He didn't know if that was typical for airboats or not, but he started fiddling around with it to see if it could be hot-wired.

And that was when he heard it.

The chug of an outboard and voices.

Campers, poachers, or crazies?

The odds were stacked in favor of one of the last two, and chances were good that they were coming back for the airboat.

There was no place to hide on board and he wasn't armed. So he did the only thing he could do. He pulled on his shirt, his shorts. He held the wrench in his mouth—it would make a good weapon—sat on the edge of the airboat, and dropped into the water.

Then he swam like hell for shore.

II

ME AND OPAL lost the outsiders' trail and spent what
was left of the night on the North River Chickee.

I slept real good, deep, the way I always did when I
was moving. I dreamed about my half brother. It was a
dream I'd had plenty of times since he and Ma left.

We was at the Mound—the bad place, he called it—
and was picking through the shells and shit around there,
hoping to find bones or whatever. In the dream, his face
wasn't real clear, but, Jesus, I could see them eyes of
his, darker than mine by a mile, eyes that could dig down
inside you like Tommy's could, but not because they was
looking for weakness or a goddamn bad seed. In the
dream, he was looking to connect. And he was good at
it.

Like this, he said, and took my smaller hand in his
and held it gently. His thumb moved over the knuckles,
the back, the palm, reading the lay of the bones, the skin.
When you connect, he said, you look for something that
belongs to that person, something familiar, something you
can see in your head. And then you try to find it.

In the dream, like in real life, he made it sound easy.
So we played a weird game of hide-and-seek where he
would hide somewhere around the Mound and I would
try to find him by seeing his eyes in my head and locking
in on them. It was like memory, this dream, and when
the picture of his eyes in my head kept fading and I
couldn't find him, I got afraid. I shouted for him. He
didn't answer. I thought he done left me alone on the
Mound and started crying. I just sat there in all them
shells and dirt, the trees big and mean around me, and
waited for him.

After a while, I heared a noise behind me and looked

around and there was this man watching me. He had my brother's eyes, but he was grown and he was saying my name, Wes, Wes, and it spooked me bad, and I woke up with Opal whispering, "Wes, wake up."

I looked at her and I knowed.

I knowed sure as anything that something had happened to someone in the band. That's how it is sometimes—what happens to one, happens to all. And Opal knowed it, too. The first thing she said to me was, "Who?"

I shook my head. "Don't know. Hurt or dead?"

She thought about it. Her hair was a wild black web around her face and she stabbed her fingers through it, head cocked to one side like she was listening to something. "Hurt. I think he's just hurt."

"Who?"

"One of Pa's boys, maybe. Yeah, one of Pa's boys. But I don't know which one or where it happened."

"We'd better get back."

So we packed up our gear and headed toward the pass to get the airboat. It was raining hard, but it was a good rain, warm and steady, the kind of rain we'd needed this winter and never got. It'd bring more fish into the lagoon, and more fish meant more food for us. And it'd bring the 'gators, and with 'gators we'd have hides, and with hides we'd have traders, and with traders more of the outside would come to us. But the outside was killing us.

Two men the year before last, one man last year, Judd this year, and now another injury. But we needed the supplies the traders brought, and in the end, traders was safer than tourists.

I kept thinking how the gold box hadn't held the outside world away from us, how maybe it didn't have the power it used to, how maybe the old man's magic just wasn't strong enough for us no more. I said this to Opal, the only person in the band besides Josie who I could say such truths to, and Opal laughed.

"I tol' you that, Wes, but you never believed me. You somehow got it into your head that Tommy's so strong he can do anythin and that just ain't so. The gold box is only as good as the medicine man who commands it."

"You ain't afraid of him. How come?"

156

She turned and looked at me. "You want truth or lies?"

"Truth."

"You see us doin good, Wes? You see a lotta food on our tables? You see children born that ain't got somethin wrong with 'em? You see the band prosperin like before? You see Judd alive?"

I shook my head.

"Well, then. How can Tommy be so strong if we ain't seein those things that matter?" Her eyes went away from me; her truth became sadness. "But it don't matter what I think if the rest of the band don't see it."

"We dyin, Opal? Is the band dyin? Is that what you're sayin?"

She shrugged and wouldn't answer.

When we got near the pass, I could feel that the band had gone through. Opal felt it, too. It bothered me some, bothered me down deep, even though there wasn't no reason it should. The band used the pass whenever they came into Whitewater Bay. It was like the saw grass fields, a shortcut.

The feeling got stronger when we slipped into the channel, under the mangrove branches. "Don't like this none," Opal whispered.

"Me neither."

"Someone's been here, Wes."

"One of ours?"

"Uh-uh, don't think so."

"An outsider?"

"Uh-huh."

"One we met?"

"Can't tell."

"Shit, Opal. Try."

"You try."

But she always connected better than me. The women usually did. "I am tryin and I ain't gettin nothin."

"You ain't tryin hard enough."

"I am."

"Hell, that's what you always say."

She went silent, the way she did when she knowed one or both of us was going to get hopping mad. She done that since we was young, since before we was initiated into the band. I didn't like it much then and I didn't like it much now, but you couldn't push Opal to do something she didn't have a mind to do. You couldn't push Opal, period.

So we paddled on in the silence. The hair rose on the back of my neck and them death bumps popped out on my arms, and pretty soon Opal set her paddle down real quiet-like in the canoe and fixed an arrow in her bow, ready for whatever was out there.

III

1.

McCLEARY HAD WATCHED the canoe from behind the wall of grass. Now it emerged from the swell of green like a phantom vessel, dark and silent, a throwback to earlier times, to when the Calusa Indians inhabited the Glades, long before the Seminoles, the Miccosukees; before the Spaniards arrived. The canoe seemed almost mystical to him just then, a symbol of something larger than himself, of a prodigious unknown, just like the Glades itself.

So it was only fitting that the man and woman inside it were Weston and Opal. Weston in his transparent raincoat and alligator boots, Opal with her wild black hair, the two of them paddling along like a couple of tourists who knew exactly where they were.

McCleary hugged the ground and looked around for something besides the wrench and his Swiss Army knife that he could use as a weapon if he had to. Even a good-sized rock would have been welcome. But there wasn't so much as a pebble in sight.

Water slapped against the sides of the canoe; it sounded close enough to touch. McCleary scooted back on his stomach, and when he was far enough from the water, he pushed up from the ground and sprinted back into the trees, headed for the spot where the channel forked.

The wet ground cushioned his footfalls. His poncho, tied at his waist again, flapped against the backs of his thighs. His shoes squeaked. *Think, turkey. Think of something quick or you're going to be swimming to shore.* He had about ninety seconds before the canoe rounded the curve, before Weston and Opal saw that the dead branches that had hidden the airboat had been pulled away, before they realized someone had messed with their machine, before the shit hit the fan.

He reached the fork and shot beyond it to the spot where he'd gone into the water earlier, then pulled out the stick on which he'd wound the fishing line. Five feet of it.

His fingers fumbled and slipped as he tied one end of the line to the lower trunk of a buttonwood tree and back-pedaled, unwinding the rest. He secured the other end to the stem of a low bush. The line was as taut as the string on Opal's bow. He plucked it with his finger, testing it, smiling as he did so.

He moved back a couple of feet. Thanks to the light, the line was invisible, and thanks to the tall grass, who-ever came ashore wouldn't be seen from the airboat.

And one of them *would* come ashore, just as he would do in the same situation.

McCleary heard the slap of paddles and glanced around for a place to hide, praying this would work, knowing he was dead if it didn't.

2.

"Wind musta blowed like crazy last night." Weston's voice: McCleary heard it clearly. "Knocked all them branches away from the boat."

"Hell, no wind done that," Opal replied. "You know it same as me, Wes."

"You still feel him around?"

"Sure do. Go easy in here."

McCleary could see them through the tall grass. They were approaching the airboat now, Opal's bow sliding through the air as she sighted along the shore, Weston's head moving with it, as though the two were connected. McCleary's hand dropped to the ground; he hunkered down. He heard the canoe bump up against the side of the airboat.

After a few minutes, Weston said, "The fuck went through my toolbox. He took a wrench." Then he snick-ered. "But he didn't get the key. . . . Here, take it."

"I got you covered," Opal said.

Yeah, I bet you do, McCleary thought.

"If somethin happens, head home," Weston told her.

"Go careful, Wes."

The tenderness with which those words were spoken surprised McCleary. It didn't seem possible that people so brutal could feel much of anything.

Now McCleary heard Weston climbing into the canoe. And the paddle whispering through the water.

And the grass to his right rustling as Weston pulled the canoe through it.

McCleary saw the faint shadow he cast against the wet ground in front of him. He could just make out the blue of his jeans, the dark of his hair, his shotgun.

C'mon, sucker. A couple more steps.

Weston's head snapped left.

He saw me.

He lifted the shotgun.

I'm dead meat.

Sighted.

Fucked.

"Bang," Weston whispered, and laughed softly to himself, then lowered the shotgun. "Gotcha, asshole."

Relief poured into McCleary, adrenaline pumped through him, and he silently shouted, *Move, jerk, move. Let's get it over with. C'mon.*

Weston moved and tripped over the fishing line. The expression on his face was that of a man who knew he'd just messed up, messed up bad, and knew there wasn't a hell of a lot he could do about it. His surprise was so acute, he didn't utter a sound. His hands flew out in front of him, and before the shotgun smacked the ground, McCleary was up and running.

He kicked Weston in the side before he could push up or turn over, then grabbed the shotgun and slammed it against the side of his head. A soft grunt escaped from Weston's lips before his eyes rolled back in his head and he blacked out.

3.

McCleary nudged Weston with the end of the shotgun. He was out cold and would be for a while.

He rolled him over and worked off his raincoat, alligator boots, socks. He jammed the socks into the boots and hurled them into the trees. Let the bastard walk out of here barefoot, he thought.

He went through the man's pockets and found a wad of bills and a credit card that belonged to Charles Crawford. McCleary unbuckled Weston's belt, let everything on it slide off, pulled it out of the loops. Then he quickly returned the items to the belt and slipped it through the loops on his own jeans. Extra ammo, a flashlight, a hunting knife, a lightweight plastic bottle half filled with a yellow liquid, and lengths of rope.

He shrugged off his poncho, zipped it, folded it, secured it in the waistband of his jeans, then put on Weston's raincoat. "Just evening the score, fucker," he spat, and hurried down to the water. To the waiting canoe.

He didn't know if he could fool the woman, but he would try. She wasn't just his ticket out of here; she could lead him to Quin.

He shoved the dugout off land and climbed inside.

The raincoat's hood was pulled over his head, as if for protection against the rain; he hoped it would obscure his face long enough to delude Opal. As the canoe slipped out of the grass, as light and smooth as he'd imagined, he dropped the engine back into the water, cranked her up, and hitched around, firing the shotgun toward shore. It had the desired effect on Opal.

Believing that Weston was fleeing from someone on land, she dropped her bow and scrambled onto the high seat to start the airboat. It gave him the few precious seconds he needed to reach the vessel. But he hadn't counted on the wind flinging the raincoat's hood off his head or on Opal being quite so quick, so agile, when she glanced back and saw who he was.

He scrambled onto the airboat and they dived for the bow at the same time. The shotgun skittered across the deck, the airboat trembled and rumbled beneath them, the propeller whined as it spun. Opal was faster. She jerked the bow out of his reach and struck him on the shoulder with it. Pain radiated up into his neck. He rolled. The second blow whistled past his ear and slammed into the deck. He lunged for her legs as she leaped up, missed her, and the bow cracked down over the small of his back. He gasped, then writhed like a fish out of water, working his way toward the shotgun.

His hands closed over it.

He rolled again, onto his back, and made it onto one knee before Opal got an arrow fixed in her bow. "Drop it."

She froze, one leg slightly in front of the other, an arm reaching over her shoulder for an arrow. She looked like a nightmare cast in stone, eyes skewed to small, black dots in her face.

"*Drop it!*"

The bow clattered against the deck. Her arm fell to her side.

"Kneel."

"What d'ya done to Wes?"

"Same thing I'm going to do to you if you don't get down on your fucking knees. *Now!*"

Her knees bent slowly, reluctantly, the joints cracking. He stood but had trouble keeping himself erect. The small of his back felt like it was on fire. He jerked some rope from the belt. Weston's belt.

"Turn around. Lock your fingers at the back of your head."

She glared at him, and for a moment, he thought she was going to refuse, that she was going to call his bluff. But she didn't. Her hands came up behind her head. She clasped her fingers together as she shifted around.

"He dead?" she asked.

"No. But he's going to wish he were."

She emitted a soft, strange laugh. "So are you. You gonna wish you killed him."

McCleary came around behind her, pulled the arrows from the quiver, and flung them away. They scattered in the wet, gray air, and as they fell, they looked no larger than matchsticks. He thought of the arrow in Nichols's thigh. "Drop your hands and keep them behind you, wrists together."

She complied and he bound her wrists tightly. "Nice rings. Get those from Crawford's lady, Opal?"

"They's mine," she spat.

"Sure." A turquoise, a topaz, a diamond the size of a knuckle.

"Wes ain't gonna like this none, you know."

"I don't give a shit what either of you likes. You started this and I'm going to finish it."

"You dreamin, mister."

He pressed the end of the shotgun against her shoulder. "Stretch out on your side, ankles together."

She clicked her tongue against her teeth as she lay down; she laughed. No, it wasn't a laugh, he thought, it was an honest-to-God cackle worthy of any witch in any cartoon, a noise that stirred some old childhood dread that made him clench his teeth.

"You shouldn't mess with the band, mister. Ain't you outsiders got a lick of sense?"

Her eyes slid sideways in her head, trying to see him as he knelt behind her and lashed her ankles.

"You hearin me, mister?"

"And you shouldn't have abducted my wife or killed Crawford and the woman." He came around in front of her. "You hearing *me*?"

Those small dark eyes, those insectile eyes, pinned him. "You killed my son," she spat, the snake tattoo dancing.

"Your son tripped and fell on his own spear."

"You lie." The words rushed out in a spray of spittle. "I seen what happened. The big man killed him."

"Wrong, lady. You saw what you wanted to see."

"The band'll come lookin for you."

Wrong again. He was going to look for them. But first he had to get out of here.

As a precaution, he tied another piece of rope around her left wrist and secured it to the wire mesh behind him. Then he climbed up onto the seat, set the shotgun beside him, pushed the stick out of neutral. A cloud of exhaust spewed from the engine as the airboat roared to life. It sputtered, it shook, it snorted. He steered it through the channel, holding the speed steady. It was like trying to keep a new car within the speed limit when you knew a cop was on your tail.

He wished he'd thought to sink the dugout's outboard, but it was too late now. The boat had drifted off to the right and he wasn't going to waste time trying to catch it. Besides, it was far enough from shore to give Wes a run for his money.

When he reached the fork, he took the passage he hadn't traveled yet, certain it would lead him out into the bay. The propeller churned through the wet air, chopping up weeds and bugs and hurling the remains against the wire mesh. He was sitting high enough off the water to be decapitated by low branches and had to hunker down until the boat suddenly shot free of the trees and raced into the open, rain-swept waters.

The wind bit into his eyes and burned his cheeks. Rain seethed over him. But it didn't last long. In minutes, he was on the other side, racing parallel to the mangroves, easing back on the power. When he killed the engine, the boat bobbed in the turbulence.

McCleary climbed down from the seat and crouched in front of Opal. The wind had tossed her hair over her eyes, and she noisily blew strands of it clear so she could see him when he said, "Here're the choices. You tell *me* where they took my wife or I take you to the rangers, who'll book you for murder."

Her grin was a slivered moon, a parody. "Fuck yourself, mister."

"Want me to tell you what it's like in jail for a woman, Opal? Or in a prison? Want to hear it from an ex-homicide cop?"

"You ain't scarin me." But she looked less certain now. "I been through worse than prison, mister. I been through things that'd make your dick fall off."

"Ever hear about old Sparky, Opal?"

"Who?"

"Sparky. Up at Raiford prison, see, there's this chair that looks fit for a torture chamber. The morning they take you to it, you get a last meal, then they shave your head. They strap you into the chair and hook electrodes to your head, your chest—a bunch of places. You know what electrodes are, Opal?"

She didn't say anything.

"They conduct electricity. You *do* know what electricity is, don't you?"

Her mouth puckered and she spat at him. McCleary wiped the spittle from his jaw with the back of his hand.

He ticked through a mental checklist of possible contagious diseases she might carry and hoped to Christ there were no scratches on his jaw. "When you're all strapped in, Opal, they throw the switch and the juice pours through you. You fry. Your brain sizzles like bacon. The stink of burning skin fills the room. Want to hear more?"

"If you tryin to scare me, mister, you ain't doin such a good job. I heard worse. I seen worse."

"And if for some reason you don't get the chair," he went on, realizing he needed to change his tack, "then chances are good you'll get life without parole. That means they toss you in a cell and throw away the key, Opal. It means you don't set foot in the Glades again. Ever."

Her response this time wasn't as quick, as certain. Something—fear, doubt, comprehension—shadowed her eyes. But when she spoke, she sounded undaunted. "First you gotta git where you're goin, mister." Her lips pulled away from her stained, decaying teeth. "And you don't even know where you are."

It was true.

He left her lying there and climbed back onto the elevated seat, wondering which way was south, wondering how far he was from anywhere.

4.

The North River Chickee was not Benson's idea of comfort, an opinion Buffalo George obviously didn't share. He seemed to think this was a double suite at a Holiday Inn.

He was pouring Gatorade into small plastic cups and arranging cheese sandwiches on a paper plate with a flourish that suggested a gourmet meal. It was a long time until lunch, but considering that he'd eaten breakfast in the middle of the night, Benson was famished. Even George's sandwiches, liberally garnished with bean sprouts and avocados and Christ knew what else, looked good.

From the cove where they'd picked up the airboat, they'd gone north to the Shark River Slough and then west across endless prairies of saw grass to get to the Wilderness Waterway. They'd followed it south into

166

Whitewater Bay, checked the Watson River Chickee and the inlets around it, then headed south along the edge of the mangroves to this spot on the North River.

At points along the way, George had radioed their position to Farrel, a precautionary measure with which Benson wholeheartedly agreed. He no longer had any concept of the distances involved. There was simply too much space, too much green, too many twists, too much water, too much sameness. It was the equivalent of looking for the proverbial needle in the haystack, he thought. The only thing in their favor was that the rain was no longer coming down as hard. "How much farther to Lard Can?" he asked.

"A ways," George replied. "Wedge Point and Hell's Bay Chickee come before. There's a couple other places we can look before, like a site a little farther upriver."

"Can we get in there with the airboat?"

"Nope. Got to go in on foot."

"You're kidding."

George laughed. "Yeah, I am."

Benson wasn't amused. "How far is it?"

"Two miles." George held out a cup of Gatorade. "You've got to be less concerned with distances, Captain. Once you start thinking of the Glades in terms of how far one thing is from another, it becomes incomprehensible."

"I'll keep that in mind. This place you're talking about. Is it a campsite?"

"Of sorts."

"Either it is or it isn't."

"Second lesson about the Glades, Captain." He held up two fingers and sipped noisily from his cup of Gatorade. "Nothing here is either/or. That's the sort of thinking that can get you into trouble."

He passed Benson the plate of sandwiches and a cup of Gatorade, then sat back against the railing watching as Benson studied one of his nautical maps. "According to this, the only campsite on North River is right here. The chickee."

George nodded. A gust of wind blew rain through the chickee and nearly lifted his baseball cap off his head. His hand slapped down over it. "The site upriver is an old Indian mound. There're a lot of them scattered throughout the Glades. You could dig down through them and uncover the history of this place in layers. Some of them are still considered sacred."

"What about the one upriver you just mentioned?"

"No. It's too accessible. The places I'm talking about are much farther inland."

"You go any more inland, and you'd be in the gulf."

George chuckled. "Just a figure of speech, Captain. By 'inland' I mean deeper in the Glades. Some of these spots were burial grounds, others were where certain rituals were performed, others are just considered power places by the medicine men."

"I thought medicine men were primarily figureheads these days. Except for the guy who killed the panther."

Benson was referring to a case that had happened the year before last, when a Miccosukee medicine man had killed a panther for one of his rituals and created quite a stink among animal lovers and environmentalists. "They aren't extinct," George said with a laugh.

"Well, they aren't exactly what they used to be."

"We still have a reservation. And a tribe. And as long as we have those things, there'll be medicine men."

Benson caught the "we." It was the first time George had included himself in any discussion about Seminoles or Miccosukees.

"It's not quite the same thing. Not really."

George gazed off into the rain, rubbing absently at the strange scars on the insides of his forearms. At one time, he said, the power of the medicine men was beyond question. Although they were still respected and even feared, the modern world had diluted their mystique somewhat—and thus their power.

"In the old days, a medicine man began his training when he was still a child and then studied twenty or thirty years before he'd truly mastered the art. But who has the luxury of that sort of time now?" He shrugged. "So with every generation, there are fewer medicine men. And no great ones. There hasn't been a great medicine man, really, for decades. The last one was exiled from his tribe."

"For what?" Benson asked.

"Sorcery."

Right. But to be polite, he asked what kind of sorcery, as though it were a commodity available under different brand names, like soap.

"The husband of a white woman whom he wanted to marry met an untimely demise on Tamiami Trail. Actually, the woman and her husband were Hispanic. Farm laborers. Migrants. Anyway, the tribe believed the medicine man caused the husband's death."

"How?"

"Sorcery. Like I said."

His sardonic smile said it was a stupid question. But Benson, in spite of himself, was intrigued. "How'd he do it?"

"How should I know? I'm not a medicine man."

"Where'd he go when he was exiled?"

"There're a lot of stories. He owned a trading post on Tamiami Trail at the time called Miami Tommy's, and after he was exiled, he just never went back. Some say he joined his wife in the white man's world. Others say he returned to the Glades and eventually went crazy. And still others believe that he and the woman joined the clan. The white Indians."

Them again, Benson thought. "What do *you* believe?"

"That he went mad. And that he lives with the clan."

"So you really believe these white Indians exist?"

Softly: "Absolutely."

There was something in the cadence of his voice, in the way the wind blew rain onto the chickee and whistled along the edge of the tin roof just then that gave Benson the creeps. He was suddenly grateful that it was daylight, that he wasn't sitting here in the pitch black of night listening to this.

"So why would he be living with the clan?" he asked.

"It makes sense. He was banished by his own people, he wouldn't fit into the white man's world, and the clan probably welcomed his magic. He also represented a new gene pool, which would be vitally important to a group as isolated as the clan, where inbreeding has probably diminished their numbers alarmingly."

"It's fascinating, George, but your conclusions are all based on supposition."

George smiled; his eyes seemed darkly secretive. "Not

at all. There've been numerous stories. Poachers who claim they've traded with a medicine man who lives with white people; a few traders among the Indians who've exchanged goods for medicines with him; reports from fishermen who've seen white people in areas of the Glades that are unmapped, areas only the Indians know. The clan exists, all right.''

He nodded slowly, as if confirming something for himself. His long, agile fingers worked at a cigarette paper, rolling tobacco into it. ''And I think they travel quite freely throughout the Glades, stealing from poachers and canoeists and, in some instances, from ranger stations as well. In the last few years, four airboats that I know of have been stolen. Hell, talk to Ranger Joe. He'll tell you about the gasoline, kerosene, lanterns, and other supplies his post has lost to theft. But he thinks Indians have stolen the stuff. I know better.''

''If they've been living in here for decades like you say, why haven't people seen them? Why haven't their camps been sighted from the air? We would've heard something about them,'' Benson said.

''Not necessarily. Most of us suffer from a kind of myopia, Captain. We see only the things that fit in with our beliefs about the world. I'm sure it happens in your work, where you don't see the obvious because it doesn't fit with your concept of what something should be.''

Yeah, Benson thought. It was called a dark field. ''Okay, assuming everything you're saying is correct, what's it got to do with why we're out here?''

''Maybe nothing.'' He ran the tip of his tongue along the edge of the cigarette paper, sealing in the tobacco, then looked up. ''And maybe everything.''

5.
Her body felt loose and slippery, as though the skin had been pulled away from the bones in sheets and was filling up with water. Quin let the water carry her toward the surface and then floated there, a lily, a leaf, a shadow without substance, without history.

6.

Memories flickered through her. The storm. The pass. Her attempted escape. Josie knocking her out. And later, someone forcing her to drink something. Then nothing, until now.

When she opened her eyes, her vision was fuzzy. She saw only shades of light and dark that kept shifting, melting together. Her body suddenly woke up. Pain oozed across her stomach and ribs. It hurt to move. The back of her throat was a desert. A sour taste clung to the surface of her tongue and the roof of her mouth. The throb in her head rolled into a temple and clawed down into her sinuses. She squeezed back a moan. The muscles in her limbs strained as she tried to sit up, to rub her eyes. She couldn't move.

I'm paralyzed and something's happened to my eyes.

Panic broke loose inside her. Sharp, startled sounds lurched through her throat but never made it into the air. She flung her head from side to side, which made the light and shadows slip and eddy. Whatever she was in began to sway, to rock. Her elbow slipped through a hole. Her stomach threatened to heave. Then, gradually, her vision started to clear. The light brightened; shapes swam into focus.

Hammock. She was on her side in a hammock, hands tied behind her, ankles bound, cheek pressed against the netting. A hammock in a cabin of some sort. No, a hut.

Wrong again. It's a chickee with walls.

Yes, okay. She was in a chickee.

Directly in front of her was a doorway, and through it, in another room, a kitchen, she could see an old man. He was sitting on a stool in front of an open window, whittling a piece of wood. Wind blew through his long white hair.

She squeezed her eyes shut. *No good. Run that reel again.* But of course the man was still there when she looked again, and of course she didn't know who he was or where she was or how long she'd been here or what had happened to McCleary.

Never mind. Don't make a sound. Get those hands free. Fast. But the ropes held.

She rolled onto her back, eyes flitting around, touching

down here, there, taking in everything. The crude pieces of pine furniture, the pale squares of light in the open windows, the sway of trees beyond them, the slap of water, the noise of rain, the closed door to her right, the wooden spears upright in a corner, the bow hooked on a nail with a quiver of arrows, and the trophies. The head of a panther, its teeth bared, the skin of a ten- or twelve-foot alligator, the skin of a diamondback rattler, a skull.

A human skull.

The bone was so white, it looked as if it had been bleached, then polished until it reflected light like marble, like new snow. The black, empty sockets stared at her. The dark rictus of the skull's mouth seemed to smile.

"Do you like it?"

Quin's head snapped left, toward the man's voice. He stood in the shadows, but she could see that he wasn't very tall, maybe five-six at the most. His checkered shirt was too big for him and was tucked into faded jeans with bell bottoms that had gone out of style at the end of the sixties.

As he stepped toward her, the light from the window filled the creases in his face. Hundreds of them. Perhaps thousands. They shot across his skin like a huge, fine web, each with a story, a secret, a passion, an obsession. His sparse brows, as white as his hair, stuck out like whiskers on a dog's muzzle and were long enough to cast thin shadows on his cheeks. But his eyes were what held her, intrigued her, terrified her. They seemed to be all pupil and shone from a nest of wrinkles. Rasputin's eyes, huge and black and utterly mad.

"Do you like it?" he repeated.

"Not particularly." Her voice was surprisingly calm, controlled. "What's there to like about it?"

He slapped his palm against his thigh and laughed. The sound fluttered through the room like a flock of birds. "A wise answer." He strolled over to the wall where the skull hung, unhooked it, pushed his fist up the opening at the bottom, and carried it over to the hammock. "I suppose it's a matter of taste and perspective, like with anything." He turned it slowly, admiring it. "It belonged to my dead wife's first husband."

172

As though it were a personal possession, like a wallet or a set of keys.

"I had to get it after he'd been buried." He wrinkled his nose with distaste. "It was a rather unpleasant job. But necessary." He looked at her. "One does what one must. What circumstances at the time demand." He rubbed his old, wrinkled cheek against the skull and laughed again. "See this crack?"

He held the skull uncomfortably close to her. She could smell the Glades embedded in the polished bone, and beneath it was the stink of something else, something dark and bad and incomprehensibly evil.

The odor radiated from the old man, not from the skull.

"See it?" he asked again, holding it closer to her face, close enough so that she was peering into the black, empty sockets.

Quin pressed back into the hammock. "Yes." It was barely a whisper. She wanted to wrench her eyes from the sockets, from the ugly crack that raced in a jagged line from the top of the skull down toward the right side. But if she did, she knew he would understand the full depth of her terror. If he didn't already.

"It killed him." He ran his palm over the skull, a languid, intimate gesture. "Poor José. One day he was a robust, healthy man of twenty-eight, a field hand who worked twelve-hour days under the blazing sun. And the next day he was dead. Killed on Tamiami Trail by a horse that was spooked by something."

A horse? How long has it been since there were horses on Tamiami Trail?

He leaned over her, those old puckered lips pulling away from teeth that were nearly rotted in the gums. "And I got the lady." Then he threw his head back and exploded with laughter.

Jesus God. Get me out of here.

A crack of thunder silenced the old man. His head turned toward the window, his eyes narrowed to slits, spicules of sweat rolled down the sides of his face. He'd momentarily forgotten her. She watched him, afraid to move, to speak, to breathe too loudly.

The skull seemed to absorb whatever light there was in the room, sucking it into itself like a black hole and giving nothing back. All sound drained away. The air thickened, bristling until it seemed electrified. Quin sank back into the netting, held there by a sudden, horrible pressure in her head. Blood pounded in her ears. It was as if she'd been diving at two hundred feet and something with the decompression chamber had gone terribly wrong. The oxygen had turned to hot syrup, the pressure of gravity had doubled, her blood was starting to boil.

I'm about to die. That's what this means. I'm going to die here, now, and I don't even know where I am.

Then it broke.

Just like that, sound rushed back into the room, the light evened out, the old man turned. Smiled. Replaced the skull on the hook. Right then, he could have been any old coot, crazy as a loon but harmless.

"Ask your questions." He walked over to the hammock again, hands clasped behind his back. "This is the only chance you'll get."

"Where're my friends?"

When had Lydia become a friend? Jesus, why split hairs?

He nodded toward the closed door she'd noticed before. It wasn't the answer she was looking for; she wanted to know if the Nicholses were alive. But she hadn't asked the right question. She still didn't. Not about them. "Who're you?"

"Miami Tommy."

"A Seminole?"

"No longer."

"Where am I?"

He held out his arms, as if welcoming her. "My home."

"What was poured down my throat earlier?"

"An herbal tea. To make you sleep."

"Who gave it to me?"

"Does it matter?"

No. Yes. Yes, damnit, it matters. "Yes."

"Josie."

"What do you want with me?"

"It is not what I want, but what the old ways demand."

She definitely didn't like the sound of that. "Look,

Judd fell on his own spear. He and his parents had come back to get a couple of tourists they'd killed, and I think they had the same thing in mind for us. They were taking us with them."

He was looking at her, but she had the impression he'd tuned her out. Never try to reason with a crazy.

"A man is dead. And someone must pay. The rules are quite specific."

"Which rules?"

"Those of the band."

"What band?"

"My band, of course."

Of course of course. Sorry. How stupid of her. "What do the rules say?"

He rubbed his palms together and touched his chin with his fingertips in an attitude of prayer. He regarded her with those fathomless eyes. "The rules say that the rules cannot be explained until it is time. And it isn't time yet."

With that, he walked out of the room.

7.

Was that a CB over there near the window?

Quin craned her neck, trying to get a better look at the oblong box near the window. It *did* look like a radio, but it was hard to tell for sure because a couple of shirts were draped over it.

"Yes," said the old man.

She turned her head toward his voice. He stood right next to the hammock, his hands folded in front of him, that strange, knowing smile touching his mouth but not his eyes. He'd approached soundlessly, on feet of cotton, and that was more unnerving than his simple "Yes."

"Yes what?" she asked.

"Yes, that's a radio. A CB. But don't even think what you're thinking, my dear." He held up his hand, showing her the battery, then threw back his head and laughed.

Afternoon

I

1.

THE AIRBOAT SHOT from the veil of rain like a bullet and raced toward McCleary from the field of saw grass to his left. He hadn't heard it, hadn't seen it coming, but he wasn't about to stick around to see who was driving it.

He opened the throttle all the way. The boat took off, skimming the blue waters with the fleetness of a creature born and bred for the Glades. The wind lanced his eyes like sharp glass, making them water so badly that everything blurred. Mangroves turned to lumps of green, the leaden sky dropped, the briny spray felt like needles against his cheeks.

"You ain't gonna outrun him, mister!" Opal shouted over the din.

McCleary wiped his eyes and glanced back. The boat cut a neat, slick path through the blue, narrowing the path between them. He veered right and the other airboat swung right almost instantaneously, as though the pilot had anticipated his move. McCleary steered into a sharp left. The airboat tilted; a wall of spray shot up. Opal bellowed and worked her legs frantically to keep from sliding off. McCleary wasn't sure if the rope that secured her to the wire mesh would hold. Since she was his only lead to Quin, he straightened the boat again and headed for the open stretch of water in front of him.

When he looked back again, his pursuer had turned in a wide arc and was coming up on his right. He could see two men on board now. One of them was standing up, shouting something he couldn't hear, and raising a rifle.

He cut into a series of jagged turns to make himself a tougher target. A moment later, the rifle's explosion pierced the noise of the engines, frightened birds from trees, rocked across the water in waves.

They shot into the air. Not at me.

He slammed his hand back against the throttle, killing the power. The airboat bobbed in its own wake. Rain poured over him. "You is one dead fucker," Opal cackled.

"I don't think so." He moved the rifle out from under the protection of his poncho, so it was in clear view, and kept his hand on it just in case he was wrong.

As the airboat drew alongside, Opal realized who was on board and yelled, "Help! Help me! He's got a shotgun!"

"Won't work," he muttered, and stood, raising his arms well above his head.

The airboat stopped, its engine idling. The ranger leveled his rifle at McCleary, his eyes flickering once toward Opal and then back again. "Sure hope you've got a good explanation for this, mister."

"She and her husband killed two people," McCleary said. "We found their bodies on—"

"He's a lyin son of a bitch!" Opal shrieked, struggling to get loose. "Untie me, someone untie me. Don't believe nothin he says. He's lyin!"

"Quiet down, ma'am."

"I jus' tryin to tell you how it is."

"You'll get your chance."

Opal stopped talking; she'd evidently decided that civilized behavior might further her case.

The ranger nodded to his partner. "Get his shotgun, Bill. And cuff him. Then untie the woman and cuff her, too."

"Look, the bodies were on Lard Can," McCleary said. "I've been in the Glades since Wednesday. This woman's friends took my wife and the other couple we were camping with. They—"

The ranger frowned. "Took them? Took them where?"

"I don't know. I got away. I was stuck on an island back there and then she and her buddy came along and—"

"He's lyin!" she screamed again. "He killed my son!"

The two rangers exchanged a look that didn't bode well for expediting things, McCleary thought.

"We'll sort this out back in Flamingo," the man with the rifle said.

"I ain't goin to no Flamingo," Opal spat.

"Ma'am, I'm afraid you don't have a choice."

2.

By the time they neared Lard Can campsite, Benson was ready to call it quits.

He was wet and tired, he'd been bitten by countless mosquitoes, he'd seen two alligators, and now he was knee deep in muck the color of shit because George couldn't get the airboat past the tangle of branches in the channel. If he never *saw* the Glades again, much less set foot in it, it was just fine with him.

"Should've brought a canoe," George muttered, trudging along at the head of the line and swinging his machete at the overhead branches.

Nice time to think of it.

"Should've gotten on the radio before we came in here and given Joe our position," George went on.

Good planning.

"Should've come straight here and then worked our way north."

For this I'm paying you twenty-five bucks an hour?

"Should've—"

"Christ, George, just shut up, will you?" Benson snapped.

He did.

They had checked the Wedge Point Chickee and the one on Hell's Bay, but both were as empty as the chickee on North River had been. He didn't doubt that Lard Can was going to turn out to be a zero as well, and he didn't intend to search any further.

When they reached land, it was hardly any drier than the muck they'd been treading through. The campsite was a river of mud and looked barely hospitable enough for animals, much less human beings. The light was gloomy, the air smelled faintly of urine, and why anyone would *choose* to spend a night here was beyond him.

"Hey, take a look at this," George called.

Benson walked across the clearing and into the trees on the far side, where George had cut an arrow out of one of the trunks. An arrow, for Christ's sakes. It was ordinary enough, but it had a steel arrowhead that was ridged, rather nasty-looking. "Kind of a weird thing to find," he said.

George nodded and flicked the colorful feathers with his thumb. "Weird, yeah. It's definitely weird." His gaze wandered toward the trees on the far side of the campsite. "Let's check in there. If the Crawfords were here, they probably took shelter in the trees, and maybe they left something behind."

"Even if they did, I wouldn't know if it belonged to them."

"It won't take long."

He took off. Benson stood there with mud in his shoes, mud caked to his jeans, his arms itching from bites, mosquitoes whining around his head. All he wanted to do was get in his car and drive home. But home evidently wasn't in the cards just yet. He swore to himself and hurried after George.

Into the woods. Into cabbage palms and buttonwoods, mangroves and pines. The light dimmed. The air changed, thickening, tightening, rippling with the strange, elusive undercurrents of invisible wildlife. The ground was mush. Rich, dense scents assaulted him: water, soil, moss, and something else—something that never left you once you'd smelled it. The odor of decaying flesh.

The bodies had been buried in a makeshift grave of leaves and mud, which the rain had partially washed away. Judging from the decomposition, they'd been here a while, a couple of days at least. The woman had been shot; most of her shoulder was gone. Benson wasn't sure what had killed the man. Whatever it was, it looked like he'd taken it through the back.

"An arrow," George said.

Who would know better than an Indian? Benson wondered as George pointed to the flesh that had been torn when the arrow was jerked out.

"These the people you looking for, Captain?"

"I don't know."

"I'd better go radio Ranger Joe."

179

As he walked off, Benson wondered if the Seminoles had ever used bows and arrows.

3.

The old man was busy in the kitchen.

Quin watched him through a square in the hammock's netting, her neck twisted back at an uncomfortable angle. He was stirring something that was boiling in a pot on the two-burner wood stove. Now and then he turned away from it, chopping up things on the counter, pulling other things from jars, dropping items into the pot. Steam rose up around him; the wind from the open window dispersed it and carried a peculiar aroma toward her. An unpleasant aroma. Indescribable. It wasn't food.

She relaxed her neck and kept working her hands up and down, again and again, over and over. He'd tied her wrists so that her hands faced each other, and every time she moved them, shoots of pain radiated up the insides of her arms.

Quin rested to the count of ten, then started moving her ankles. They seemed looser, but so what? Just where the hell did she think she was going if she freed herself? Out the front door where Ticker stood guard? Ticker with the shiner and the lump on his head the size of a walnut that McCleary had bestowed? Even if she got past Ticker, the only place to go was down into the water. Without a canoe. The old man, after all, had made a point of leaving the front door open whenever he left enabling her to see what lay beyond it. And he'd left and returned numerous times, and each time she'd seen the neighboring chickees, the water, the mangroves. Miami Tommy was crazy, yes, but he wasn't stupid.

He knew she was lying here thinking of escape. He knew that her stomach was shrieking for food, that her bladder was filled to bursting, that she hurt, that her fear had eaten up whatever energy the drug Josie had given her hadn't sapped. He knew it, and he used it against her. He made her wait in the silence, with only the noise of the rain and the wind and the echo of his voice to keep her company.

It isn't time yet.

Time for what?

For the rules to be explained.

But what he really meant was that it wasn't time yet for the retribution.

Now he shuffled into the room, brushing past her, carrying something in a straw basket, his bare feet whispering against the rough pine floors. He opened the front door. Rain streamed off the roof, creating a curtain of water between him and the two men outside. Ticker and Weston the Ugly.

"Call the children. I am ready."

Ticker walked to the edge of the chickee and hollered. Weston the Ugly stepped through the curtain of water behind the old man. "She's first." He spoke to the old man, but his eyes were on her. "It's only fair."

Miami Tommy smiled. "Nothing is ever fair. But I agree, she should be first. The others should watch, though. I'll open the door."

As he moved toward the door that had been closed since she'd awakened, the door to the room where the Nicholses were, Weston went into the kitchen. He returned with a collapsible canvas chair, a stool, and two strips of colorful fabric that looked like they were cut from the same bolt as the blouses Josie and the other women wore.

He stopped in front of the hammock, grabbed her by the chin, and snapped her head toward him. She jerked it free and he grabbed it again, his fingers digging into the skin at her jaw, forcing her lips to pucker. He leaned so close to her, she inhaled his sour breath and swam in the deadness of his eyes.

"Listen good, lady. He took my boots, my belt, my airboat, my wife, and I almost didn't get back here because my canoe was way the fuck out in the canal. My son's dead, my wife's gone. And all of you are goin to pay. Got it?"

McCleary. He's talking about McCleary. McCleary got away. "Yes." It came out as "Ye," because he was still squashing her lips with his hand.

"Good." He pulled her into a sitting position, then tossed her over his shoulder and carried her to the canvas chair. He dropped her into it, shoved her forward, cut her hands free. He took hold of either wrist and fastened

181

each one against an armrest with the strips of cloth. Then he moved the stool in front of her, sat down, hooked his ankles behind the footrest at the bottom.

He stared at her.

Quin stared back, her heart racing, skipping beats, leaping again. She heard the door open but didn't look in that direction. Didn't dare.

"I seen women like you when I was in the world," he said. "I seen them in them fancy cars. I seen them in them fancy clothes, them fancy houses. I seen them prancin through the malls and I says to myself. 'Wes, someday you can have yourself a woman like that.' And for a long time, I thought about that. How soft her skin was gonna be." He touched a fingertip to her cheek; the blood drained from Quin's face. "How her mouth was gonna taste." His finger slid along her lower lip. "How her throat was gonna be smooth and white." His finger glided over her chin to her throat, lingered at the soiled collar of her shirt, circled the first button. "How her tits was gonna look. . . ."

Please don't let this happen. Aw, Christ, please.

He undid the button. Her skin crawled. She swallowed and knew he heard it, blinked and knew he expected tears, rolled her lips together and knew he waited to hear a plea.

He unfastened the next button. He was smiling now.

The door opened again; she saw it peripherally. A warm, muggy wind rushed into the room. It stank of swamp and mud and the sweat of her own skin. Then the door slammed and Weston's hand froze. His eyes held hers for a moment longer, then flickered away toward the old man, who was standing in front of the other door, holding it partially closed; she couldn't see inside. Something happened between the two men, something silent, a brief struggle of wills, a struggle for power in which she'd become the pawn. She held her breath, waiting.

When Weston's arm dropped to his side, she realized he'd lost. She let her breath out slowly, knowing that he heard the soft exhalation of air and now clearly understood the depth of her fear. His smile touched only his eyes, then he turned and looked at the five small children who'd crowded silently around him.

Two girls, three boys, none older than eleven or twelve. Each had some small deformity—a lazy eye that rolled as loose as a marble in a cheek, a lopsided mouth, a leg that was shorter than its twin, fingers without nails, a missing toe. Their faces were uniformly odd in the same way Judd's had been.

"The children." Weston said it as though they were royalty, exalted beings worthy of worship. "They got to start learning about the old ways. They need to know. Right, Ticker?"

Ticker, standing behind them like a proud father, grinned. "Yeah. But why we startin with her?" He pointed at Quin. "Other one's prettier."

"That's got nothin to do with it."

"Pa ain't here. He oughta be."

"For what?"

" 'Cause the pretty one's his."

"We let the children decide who should go first," said Miami Tommy, allowing the door to the other room to swing open as he moved away from it.

The only things in it were twin mats woven of palm leaves, where Lydia and Nichols were bound and gagged. He was lying on his side, blankets and tarps bunched up behind him preventing him from rolling onto his back. He wore only a shirt and shorts and was groaning into his gag. Quin realized she'd been hearing the sound for some time, but it hadn't registered.

Lydia was also on her side, facing Nichols. She was dressed in a brightly colored caftan made of the same material as the strips of fabric that bound Quin's wrists. When she lifted her head, her eyes slid through the room, seeing none of them. Her face was utterly vacant.

"She don't look so pretty now," Weston said.

Ticker wiped the back of his hand across his mouth and looked at Tommy. "You done something to her. Pa's gonna be pissed."

The old man held out his hands, palms up. "I have done nothing except give her clean clothes."

"What's ailin him?" Ticker gestured toward Nichols.

"He does not like the treatment I have prescribed for his leg."

183

"Yeah?" Again Ticker's lips drew back over his teeth in a grin. "What don't he like 'bout it?"

"The leeches," the old man said, and smiled.

Sweet Christ.

"Leeches, huh," said Ticker, and walked over to Nichols. He pressed the sole of his shoe down against Nichols's leg, so the thigh was clearly visible; Nichols screamed into his gag. Quin glimpsed a squirming gray mass on his thigh before she jerked her head in the other direction, her stomach promising to heave if she looked again.

A couple of the children giggled and looked at each other. Then, as though something had been decided, the little girl with the lazy eye approached Quin. She was picking her nose and continued to pick it as she stood there, the lazy eye lolling in her cheek while the other one regarded Quin with vague interest. The old man addressed her in a language that sounded like a mixture of Spanish and something else, perhaps an Indian dialect. The girl looked at him, glanced toward the room where Lydia and Nichols were, then focused on Quin again.

"Her," she said in English, in a tiny voice thick with congestion. She pulled her finger out of her nose and stuck it in her mouth.

Weston ruffled her stringy hair and smiled at Ticker. "There, see? The kid's no dumbass."

"Other four gotta vote." Ticker leaned forward, his hands against his thighs as he spoke to the other four children. "Who's gonna be first? Who's gonna be purged first, huh?"

Four pairs of eyes fixed on Quin.

4.

The ranger at the Flamingo station who questioned McCleary was named Jim Bogie—as in "Humphrey's nickname," he explained in his good-ol'-boy voice, "Or as in Hoagie," like the sandwich. He had a lot to do with the erosion of McCleary's relief at having been found by the good guys.

He was young and ebullient, and this was obviously the most exciting thing that had happened to him since he'd started working as a ranger. He kept interrupting

McCleary's story, asking him to clarify details, and frequently repeated things he'd said.

"So this boy Judd carried a bow and arrow? Is that what you said?"

"He wasn't a boy, and no, he didn't carry a bow. The woman did. Judd had a spear."

It was a ploy to trip him up, something he'd probably learned in ranger school that worked well on TV but not in real life. When McCleary called him on it, Bogie combed his fingers through his crew cut and acted like he didn't know what McCleary was talking about.

"Look, I've told you what happened, okay? And the longer we sit here playing games, the harder it's going to be to find my wife. So how about trying Metro-Dade again? The sooner Benson verifies who I am, the sooner I can go look for my wife."

Bogie shook his head. "Oh, I'm afraid it's not that simple, Mr. McCleary. The woman's telling us one thing and you're telling us another. It's my job to find out what really happened. We've got two men on their way up to Lard Can now and one of my men is in talking with the lady. She's sticking to her story, that you killed her son."

"No one killed her son. He tripped on his own goddamn spear."

Bogie flashed a Pepsodent smile of capped teeth. "It's still your word against hers, Mr. McCleary, and I—"

A knock cut him short. The door opened and a ranger poked his head into the room. "Uh, Jim, can you step out here a second?"

"Sure. Be right back, Mr. McCleary."

One more delay.

He got up and walked over to the map of the Glades on the wall. Whitewater Bay bordered Cape Sable, which occupied most of the bottom southwest curve of Florida. It was ten miles long as the crow flew and perhaps seven miles across at its widest point. Besides the numerous rivers that fed into it, the area around the bay was intersected by literally hundreds of inlets, creeks, and channels. Even if he knew for sure that the crazies lived somewhere near the bay, it would take him months to explore it. By air he might have a slightly better chance of sighting a village, if one existed, but only if it were built in the open, which he doubted.

He located Midway Pass, the only passage that ran between two islands. It was smack in the heart of the bay. Although he couldn't be sure, he guessed they'd been headed west through the pass last night when he'd escaped because vast areas on the western side of the bay were unmarked. There was only one chickee, on the Joe River, and no official canoe trails. So if he confined his search to the west side . . . Hell, it would still take him months to search it.

No matter how he looked at it, Opal was his best bet, and he had about as much chance of getting an answer from her as he did of winning the Florida lottery. The odds for the lottery, in fact, were probably better.

He stared at the map again, hoping for the burn of a hunch that would at least send him in the right direction. But the longer he stared, the less certain he felt about everything.

Behind him, the door opened. *Go away, Bogie.*

"Mac?"

McCleary spun around. Standing in front of him was Benson.

II

I WAS MAD, *you got to understand that. My boy was dead, my wife was gone, and the outsiders had caused it. I figured if Lee-dee-uh and Big Man seen what was going to happen to the skinny woman, they would fear like I feared, hurt like I hurt. It was only right. So I pulled their mats into the front room.*

Pretty Lee-dee-uh screamed into her gag, tried to roll off the mat, and I busted her one in the side to make her shut up. I woulda hit her in the face, but it was such a pretty face and I didn't want to spoil it for later. For tonight. For the ceremony of the gold box.

The big man wasn't much better. His eyes was rolling back in his head, his cheeks was bright red, he was still making noises. I hate big guys who're wimps and told him he had about ten seconds to shut the fuck up or I was gonna give him something he could really moan about. I started counting and the children joined in, giggling and laughing, making a game of it. Tommy clapped his hands to every count—

. . . four, five, six . . .

and Ticker stood there with that stupid grin on his face and the skinny lady watched with them wide, terrified eyes—

. . . eight, nine . . .

and Lee-de-uh squeezed her eyes shut and curled up like a baby, and the big man didn't shut his mouth—

. . . ten . . .

so I did what I promised. I reached inside Tommy's straw basket and I pulled out the jar that had the leeches. They slithered over and around each other, a rippling gray mass. I spun the cap. The children giggled and clapped and chanted, "Yes, yes," as I stripped off Big

Man's shorts, peeling them down over the wound where leeches was already feasting.

"Oh, God," whispered the skinny broad; she looked like she was going to puke.

"God's got nothin to do with any of it," I told her, and reached into the jar.

I didn't much like the feel of them leeches. All slippery and cold, like a dead man's skin, and I didn't much like the soft sucking sound they made; they was always hungry for blood. But I didn't much like them outsiders, neither. I picked out two of the biggest leeches and kicked away the blankets and tarps that kept Big Man on his side. He rolled onto his back, silent now, his eyes huge and fixed on my hand.

"Now you're gonna have somethin to groan about, Big Man," and I dropped the leeches into his groin.

They found where they needed to go, all right, and Big Man went nuts. He rolled off the mat, shrieking into his gag, rolled over on his wounded thigh, and went right on rolling across the room. I loved it. I thought of my Opal and I loved it, and the children loved it, whooping and scampering around him, laughing and pointing and pushing at him with their hands.

Lee-dee-uh freaked. She somehow managed to lift up onto her knees, fell forward, lifted again, and writhed like a snake toward the big man. I snapped my fingers at Ticker. "Take care of her."

Ticker was moving forward, but the old man stepped between him and the woman and barked, "Enough," and Ticker stopped dead.

The children went still and quiet.

Lee-dee-uh toppled forward again, her body thumping loudly against the floor. She lay there sobbing into the gag. The big man kept rolling and shrieking, and in the sudden quiet, it clawed at my nerves.

I turned on the old man. "What'd you do that for?"

"This is not why the children were brought here."

"They gotta learn the old ways."

"This is not the old way."

"Who cares," muttered Ticker. "It's fun."

"You put leeches on him." I heard my voice rising, but I didn't care none. I was sick of him. Sick of his demands, his tests, his silent accusings that I was a bad seed like my brother; sick of his magic that'd done nothing for Opal. "But when I do it you say it ain't the old way."

"You do it for sport." His terrible eyes pinned me. "I do it for the purging."

"Bullshit. You ain't foolin me. You do it 'cause you like seein people in pain."

"Wes," Ticker said softly, shrinking back. "You better not—"

"Mind your own business, Ticker. You just like all the rest of 'em. You scared shitless of him. But what's he gone and done for us, huh? Jus' tell me that. His magic ain't done a blue crap in hell for Judd or Opal. It ain't done nothin for the band, neither. You see children bein born that don't got somethin wrong with 'em? You see new places for us to go? You see tons of food on your table? You see our little farm out there producin anythin worth a shit? Huh, Ticker? You see any of them things?"

Before Ticker could reply, the skinny woman, the one whose name I can't never remember, except that it rhymes with sin, suddenly shouted, "Do something! He's dying, for God's sakes, he's dying!"

Everyone's attention went to the big man. His face was red and bright with sweat, his mouth was open, and he was sucking hard at the air, trying to pull it in around the edges of the gag. Tommy rushed over to him, pushing the children out of the way. He fell to his knees, tore off big Man's gag, and pulled hard at his shirt. The top buttons popped off.

He barked at Ticker to untie his arms and legs—Fast, do it fast—and then he leaped up and hurried into the kitchen. He came back with a wet cloth and wiped Big Man's face. He lifted his head so he could breathe easier. But it was too late.

Big Man was as dead as Judd.

III

1.

THIS ISN'T HAPPENING.

But it *was* happening. Those *were* leeches, Nichols *was* dead, her arms *were* strapped down to a canvas chair, her legs *were* tied, she *was* surrounded by crazies. And now the room had gone dead silent. A silence that deafened. A silence that made her long for noise. Anything would do. Nichols's dreadful shrieks; the weird, cruel laughter of the children; Weston's angry voice; the thump and scratch of Lydia's body as she languished against the hard pine floors, trying to reach her husband.

But no one moved, no one spoke; she wasn't even sure that anyone was breathing. They were figures in some bizarre photograph, frozen in time, in this one small instant of time, while beyond them the Everglades flowed and moved around them, just as it had done for millennia.

Then one of the children coughed and everything spun forward again. The old man stood and threw the washcloth down; it slapped Nichols's face. Ticker muttered, "Shit, aw shit, man," and raked his hands through his hair as he looked about frantically for someone to tell him what to do. Weston jammed his fingers into the pockets of his jeans, shook his head, muttered, "Ain't my fault his heart stopped. I didn't even touch the fucker. Ain't my fault, no siree, no one's pinnin this shit on me." Lydia looked like a political dissident in a third-world country: body hunched over, hands bound behind her, forehead touching the floor as she awaited execution. Her shoulders shook with muffled sobs.

The children seemed confused and then afraid, and then one of them started to cry, which set off the bunch of them. Weston yelled at Ticker to get them out of the chickee. The old man shouted at Weston to remove the body now, immediately; he didn't want this tortured spirit in his house. The children's cries, the shouting, the pandemonium, brought more crazies to the door.

Quin recognized Pa, Rusty with the squashed nose, Josie, and others from the hammock where they'd camped last night. There was a lot of shouting. Accusations were hurled. She was in the middle of a verbal brawl that was rapidly approaching a knock-down-drag-out punching match. The only thing Quin gleaned from any of it was that Nichols's death had broken some delicate balance, a necessary balance for something the old man had in mind.

The children were herded out, Nichols was hauled away, and Weston, Pa, and the old man remained. They argued in the pidgin Spanish or whatever it was that she'd heard earlier, the three of them rooted in the middle of the room, locked in what she knew was a struggle for power of the band. She didn't think it would affect her situation one way or the other who won. They were all certifiable. The end result to her—and to Lydia—would be the same.

Torture, mutilation, death, or all three.

Not that Lydia would know it, Quin thought, glancing over at her. Her mind had snapped like a toothpick. She was slumped on her side, rubbing her cheek hard against the floor, saliva drooling from a corner of her mouth, stuff oozing from her nose. *So if you're planning on busting out of here, don't count on help from Lydia.*

Or from McCleary. Or from anyone else, for that matter. No one would find them in three million acres of swamp. Three *million*, not three, not thirty-three, not even three hundred. Or was it four million? Did it matter?

She looked at the three men. She looked down at the strips of fabric that held her arms to the chair. She looked at the rope that bound her ankles. Then she looked slowly around the room, memorizing where the windows were, what was on the walls, what she might use as a weapon, how the light and shadows had changed since she'd awakened in the hammock, and she thought hard, her gaze fixed on the skull.

*I had to get it after he'd been buried. . . . A rather
unpleasant job. But necessary. One does what one must.*

Yes, one does, she thought, and felt the skin at the
corners of her mouth cracking as she smiled.

2.

McCleary was seated outside the room where Opal had
been taken. The door was closed. Benson, Bogie, and
another ranger were inside with her.

Every so often he heard her witch voice shouting an
obscenity, but compared to earlier it was tame stuff. He'd
expected more. He'd expected an endless stream of ob-
scenities, threats, promises that the crazies would cut
them all into pieces and feed them to the 'gators. And
yet she hadn't even mentioned the crazies, an omission
that seemed significant, although he was damned if he
knew why. He felt he should pursue the thought, catch
up to it, let it lead him. But he was too tired. The circuits
in his brain weren't working right.

One of the rangers—not Bogie—had given him a towel
and a bar of soap and shown him where the showers and
the staff kitchen were and told him to make himself at
home. Another ranger—not Bogie, whom McCleary suspected had a germ phobia of some kind—had lent him a
pair of jeans and a cotton shirt and offered the couch in
his office. McCleary declined the couch; he was too wired
to sleep. But the hot shower and clean clothes and the
leftover stew he'd found in the kitchen had gone a long
way toward restoring his equilibrium. Now all he wanted
to do was get the hell out of here and start searching.

But there were steps to follow, Benson the cop had
reminded him. There were procedures that might lead to
information that might provide shortcuts. Yeah, yeah,
McCleary had replied. He'd been a cop, too, remember?

Just an hour, Benson had replied. Two hours max. He
had given McCleary the kind of look that crossed a man's
face when he realized the person he was talking to might
not have things together. That he might, in fact, be rapidly approaching the point where he would do something
irrational. Like steal an airboat and a gun and the most
complete map of the Glades he could lay his hands on.
That kind of look. And since it was precisely what

McCleary had been thinking at the time, he'd shut up and sat down and watched the hands of the big clock on the wall in front of him quivering from one moment to the next.

Sixteen minutes now since that door had shut. But who was counting?

"Mr. McCleary?"

His gaze dropped to the ranger seated across from him. The one who'd lent him the clothes. Frank Someone. Young, bored by desk duty out front. "Yeah?"

"Did you see that woman kill Crawford?"

"No."

"Then how do you know she did it?"

McCleary explained briefly what had happened that first night at Lard Can. Frank rubbed his jaw. "They *admitted* killing them?"

He nodded. "They apparently came back to get rid of the bodies."

"I got a glimpse of her before. She's wearing some rings my wife would kill for. And when they brought in the Crawfords, I noticed that some of the lady's fingers have white bands on them, where she once wore rings. I mentioned it to Bogie, but he didn't seem to think it proved anything."

Buffalo George glanced up from the magazine he'd been paging through. "Bogie's an asshole. He doesn't have any idea what he's dealing with."

McCleary caught the unstated postscript to the declaration: *But I know. Just ask me.* So he asked. "Do you know?"

"I think so. She's one of the clan."

"The who?" McCleary asked.

"The clan of white Indians." George explained what he knew, which wasn't much, and what he suspected, which was a great deal more. "Your descriptions of their appearance, their dugouts, the way they speak . . . it all fits. Also, according to people who've traded with them and their medicine man, they favor bows and arrows, especially the kind you described, with ridged arrowheads. It's high on their list of trade items."

"Don't bother telling Bogie," said Frank. "He thinks the clan is a figment of the tourist imagination."

"Like I said, he's an asshole," George replied.

"These sites you've come across," McCleary said. "Where the chickees are. Could you find them again?"

"Probably. But they were abandoned when I saw them. They're also inaccessible by airboat, and by canoe it'd take days to get to them. They're spread out all over the Glades. And there're no guarantees that your wife and friends were taken to any of them. There're thousands of places to hide here."

"Do you think these sites would be visible from the air?"

"No."

"The woman could probably tell you where to look," said Frank.

"She probably could, but she won't. Kin don't snitch on each other."

He said it as though it were fact, not speculation, McCleary thought. As though he *knew*. Or maybe that was just the way he hoped it sounded.

McCleary got up, drank from the water fountain, went into the men's room. He wet a handful of paper towels and held them against his face.

Inside his head, he saw the gun in the top drawer of Bogie's drawer, the map on Bogie's wall, the keys to an airboat on Bogie's desk. He knew about the keys because Bogie, in his good-ol'-boy voice, had told McCleary *all* about the three new airboats the state of Florida had just bought for the Flamingo ranger's station and, Christ, were they fast and efficient. Sometimes, Bogie had said, when he felt real uptight, all he had to do was take that airboat out for a spin to clear his head and then he could put in a *real* day's work, the kind of work the state was paying him for. Did Mr. McCleary ever have days like that?

Yeah, since he'd gotten here his days had been like that.

He knew how this one was going to play if he hung around, waiting for Benson and the rangers to pump Opal dry: the delays that would result as the wheels of the bureaucratic machine began to grind forward; the paperwork Bogie would insist upon; the fine-tuning of a million irrelevant details. Afternoon would roll inexorably toward evening before anyone started talking about a search, and then it would be delayed again because Bogie wasn't the type who would want to do it in the dark.

But it wasn't Bogie's wife out there.

He wadded up the paper towels and stared at his reflection. The man in the waist-high mirror looked like he'd crawled out from under a tree somewhere. Stubbled jaw, circles that ringed his eyes. He lifted his shirt and looked at the nasty bruise across his stomach and part of his right side where Rusty had punched him. "You got anything to say?"

"Nope," replied his reflection. "Go for it."

George strolled into the restroom just then, parked himself at the sink next to McCleary, and spoke to his reflection. "I think I can help you find your wife."

McCleary just stared at him in the mirror, waiting for him to continue.

"There's only one place she'll end up, if she's not already there, and I think I can find it."

"Maybe you'd better explain."

George unbuttoned his shirt, pulled it off.

"Jesus," McCleary whispered.

Dozens of raised, x-shaped scars covered the insides of his arms. Scars crisscrossed his chest and back, scars that were thick and old and made him look as though he'd been mauled by an animal. But an animal wouldn't have left such neat injuries, such precise and deliberate injuries.

"Rather grotesque, isn't it," George said. "The scars on my back and chest were inflicted with snake's fangs. The ones on my arms were caused by a knife." He put the shirt back on quickly, as though the sight of his own body shamed him. "I was eight when it happened. It's what they do to people who choose to leave."

"They? The clan?"

"That's their folklore name. They refer to themselves as the band. Or the family." He buttoned his shirt. "This way, you're marked for life. You're the outcast, the sinner, just like in biblical times. Other Indians you meet know what it means. You don't fit anywhere." A bitter smile creased his mouth.

"You don't look like these people," McCleary said, remembering the eerie sameness in their features.

"Only because I wasn't the product of years of inbreeding. My mother was a full-blooded Seminole who they captured specifically to introduce new blood into the clan. They were very careful about who mated with her. She eventually fell in love with my father, and when he died, she wanted out. In those days, the price was what I've just shown you. It happened in a place called Snake Mound. You won't find it on any map. It's considered a sacred place and their darkest ceremonies are held there. I think it's where they've taken your wife."

"I don't suppose you told Benson or the rangers this."

"No."

"Why not?"

"Look, I suspected from the beginning that the band was behind the Crawfords' disappearance. I told Benson stories about them. He was polite, maybe even mildly interested, but basically he figures I'm just a superstitious Indian. With an attitude like that, why the hell should I tell him anything?"

There was more to it than that, McCleary thought. "Why should you help me? You don't know me. You don't know my wife."

"I have a score to settle, and I don't want to go in there alone."

"So you waited thirty years?"

"Twenty-five."

"And what am I supposed to do in return?"

"Just go with me and be there when I'm ready to leave."

It sounded too simple. But McCleary didn't want to know the rest just now. If this man could take him to Quin, that was enough for him. He'd worry about the rest of it later.

3.

The men had left five or ten minutes ago and had neglected to put her back into the hammock. Into her little net prison. But Quin hadn't moved. It might be a trap. Someone was probably outside the door listening, waiting for her to attempt an escape, to speak to Lydia. Then the person would report to Tommy, who would breeze in to punish her.

With the leeches. Or worse. A POW trick. Of course.

But as the minutes wore on and the door didn't open, she wondered whether, in the chaos following Nichols's death, they'd simply gotten careless. It was possible, wasn't it? They weren't infallible.

"Lydia?" she whispered. "Hey, Lydia."

No response. No movement. *No one's home.*

"Lydia, c'mon, snap out of it."

Nothing.

Quin worked her ankles until the rope around them loosened enough to allow her to press one heel and then the other against the floor. By using them as leverage and manipulating her hips and buttocks, she slowly—very slowly—began to move the chair around. Right heel, left, wiggle, shift, over and over again, the legs scraping against the pine floor until she'd turned the chair forty-five degrees and stopped.

She was now facing Lydia.

Who was still out to lunch.

Quin rested a few moments, straining to hear voices outside. Surely if someone was at the door, the person would have looked in on them by now.

Don't just sit here.

Right heel, left, wiggle, shift. Once she got the chair turned so it faced the kitchen, she discovered it was more difficult to go forward than it was to shift directions. Sometimes the legs caught in the cracks between the boards or the legs wouldn't move at all and she had to push herself back or sideways and try again. Once, she heard voices outside, voices that skipped across the water like stones, and she stopped dead, blood chilling in her veins, head in an uproar with visions of leeches.

Her eyes fixed on the knife in the kitchen, sitting on the tiny counter, the knife she would somehow use even without her hands, and she struggled forward once more, blocking out everything but the knife, the knife, the knife.

Two feet short of the kitchen doorway, when she could almost feel the spray of rain from the open window and see it glistening against the blade, one of the chair's legs snagged on a board. In a fit of fury, she jerked the right side of her body to free it and suddenly toppled backward. Her head smacked the floor, the air rushed from

197

her lungs, her ears rang. She lay there on her back, gasping for breath, legs jackknifed above her, the ceiling blurring as tears sprang into her eyes.

Laughter, fear, frustration—all of it welled inside her and lurched into the air as a dirty, little sob, a stupid sob, a ludicrous sob. Christ, if she was going to cry, the least she could do was to let out a whopping shriek of a sob, a long, mindless wail. Instead, all she could muster was this tiny squeak, this pathetic whimper. It disgusted her.

She tensed her muscles and rolled right. Her cheek was now squashed against the floor, and the vision in her right eye shot straight out across the pine, zeroing in on a bug that had frozen three feet from the end of her nose. A very big bug.

A roach, she thought. Let it be something harmless like a roach.

Sweat tracked down her temples and along the edge of her nose. She blinked. The bug moved and it wasn't a roach but a spider. And it was scampering toward her with the speed of light, its legs carrying it so high off the floor, she could see bits of dust beneath it, motes swept along in the breeze of its movements. It was headed right for her, closing the gap between them with astonishing speed. It was almost as if it sensed that this tremendous shape on the floor was not capable of smothering it in Raid, stepping on it, squashing it, and hey, it might even make a fairly tasty supper. And my, wouldn't it last a mighty long time? Things were sure looking up for the spider, Quin thought, and frantically whipped her body along the floor, trying to get out of its way.

Two feet, shit, it was only two feet away.

The chair was an impossible weight, an albatross, and her right arm, the arm she was lying on, had gone dead and numb beneath her, and sweat kept rolling into her eyes and dust swirled up her nose, making her sneeze, and oh, God, here it was, eighteen inches from her. Those hideous legs seemed to rise up and down, painted ponies on a merry-go-round, carrying it closer, closer. Her breath erupted from her chest. Her cheek scraped against the floor. Something got caught in her eye and it started to water, stealing half her vision. She lost sight of the spider and for long, black seconds she thought she felt something scrambling across the back of her neck, into her hair, along the ridge of her ear. She jerked her legs out again and jerked the upper part of her body toward them, moving like a giant clam would move, and then something slammed down against the wood inches from her ear.

Quin craned her neck back. The spider's legs stuck out from under the heel of a mud-caked shoe. Hairy legs that quivered. A shoelace swam into focus. Then part of another shoe.

She tilted her head back farther. Lydia stared at her with vacant blue eyes. She was sitting with her legs bent, chin resting on her knees, hands still tied behind her. But her ankles were free. *Free.* "Lydia, Jesus . . ."

"Bad spider," she said. "Lydia not like spider. Lydia mush spider." She giggled, kicked the spider away, then stretched out on her side, dirty face even with Quin's. "Game? We play game, Quin?"

A kid. She was nothing but a kid, talking like a three-year-old. "That's right, we're going to play a game. But Lydia has to help Quin first, okay?"

Another giggle, then: "Okay."

"I want you to go into the kitchen, Lydia. There's a knife on the counter. If you turn around, you can pick it up with your hands. Then bring it in here to me. Okay? Can you do that?"

Her mouth was twitching. She looked like she was going to cry.

"Lydia? Can you do what Quin asked?"

"Lydia wants to go home." Her face squashed up and she started to whimper.

"If you get the knife, we'll go home. I promise." They would go home and never come back. "Okay? You understand, Lydia?"

She sniffled, rubbed her nose against her shoulder, glanced toward the kitchen and back at Quin. "Lydia can do."

"Good. Now hurry."

Please hurry please.

4.

"There were twelve of them, Tim. Backwoods weirdos in dugouts who were equipped with bows and shotguns. They were taking us somewhere . . ."

Benson's conversation with McCleary before he'd come in here ran through his head like a broken record as he listened to Bogie question Opal. "Ma'am, it's going to be easier for you if you cooperate," Bogie said for the umpteenth time. "Now what's your full name?"

"I jus' finished tellin you, sonny. Name's Opal. That's it."

"What's your address?"

She puffed on the butt one of the rangers had given her, blew smoke at Bogie, and smiled. "Got no 'dress."

Benson watched the snake tattoo on her cheek quiver as she spoke. "Where do you live?"

Her dark eyes darted to his face. "None of your business." *Yo bizness.*

"Do you understand what you've been accused of, ma'am?" asked Bogie.

The paragon of goddamn politeness, Benson thought, and felt like taping his mouth shut.

"You got it all mixed up, sonny, I ain't killed no one. That man out there . . ." Blood rushed into her face as she wagged a finger at the closed door. ". . . done killed my boy."

"Then where's his body?" Benson snapped.

"What difference do that make?" *Wha' difference d'dat make?* "I done told you what happened." *Done tole . . .*

"We need proof," Benson replied. "You know what proof is?"

Silence.

"Who's Weston?"

"Man I married."

"Where the hell is he?"

Silence.

"What were you doing at Lard Can campsite?"

Silence.

"Look, lady, you're going to be booked for murder one unless you start talking."

"Don't need no book."

Wiseass. "Then you're going to need a lawyer."

"A what?"

There was something about the way she said this, about the expression on her face, that made Benson think she really didn't know what a lawyer was. But even hillbillies knew what a lawyer was, didn't they? "Who's Pa?"

She laughed. "Pa's Pa." Paw-paw. "Everyone knows Pa."

"Where'd you get the airboat?"

"In a trade." In a tray.

"A trade? With whom? For what?"

"None of your business." Yo bizness.

"Where do you live?"

"Lots of places." Lotto plazes.

"Do you understand what you're being accused of?"

Silence.

"Do you?"

"Captain," said Bogie.

"Shut up!" Benson barked. "Let's go through it once more, Opal."

"Fuck yourself." Fu' yoself. The snake on her cheek did the jitterbug.

"Captain, I don't need to remind you that this isn't your jurisdiction. In the absence of the state police, *I'm* head of law enforcement here and I—"

"And I don't need to remind *you* that we've got two bodies out there, a witness who's told us what happened, and three missing people. That's more than enough evidence to arrest her for suspicion of murder. Now either *you* call the state police or I will, Mr. Bogie. I don't have any more time to waste. I want to start searching for these people before it gets dark."

"Four of my men are already out there."

"Out where?"

"All around Whitewater Bay, where Mr. McCleary was picked up."

"That's admirable and real efficient of you, Mr. Bogie. But I want *her* taken care of." Benson stabbed a finger toward Opal. "And if you can't do it, I will. Do I make myself clear?"

Bogie drew back like he'd been struck. A muscle twitched fast and furiously under his right eye. "I got news for you, Captain. Just because you've vouched for who Mr. McCleary is, doesn't mean he's above suspicion. And quite frankly, Captain, I find *his* version of what happened pretty incredible. I mean, c'mon, a dozen men and women in dugout canoes who abducted him, his wife, and the couple they were camping with? Bows and arrows?'' He gave a nasty little snicker, an almost feminine snicker.

"An arrow didn't kill the woman. A shotgun blast did.''

"Exactly. And when my boys pulled in that airboat McCleary and this woman were on, *he* had a shotgun, Captain.'' Bogie's small, self-satisfied smile said I rest my case.

A TV sleuth, Benson thought. *Spare me.* He glanced at Opal. It was obvious she'd been paying close attention to their conversation. Even if the finer points eluded her, she most certainly understood the broad strokes and was having a mighty fine time watching the cop and the ranger act like assholes. "Where's a phone I can use?''

"In my office.'' Bogie hurried after him with short, urgent footsteps. "Just who're you calling?''

"The state police.''

"Look, Captain, before you call them, there're a few things Mr. McCleary needs to clarify. I'm sure you'll agree that—''

"Fine, fine. You can talk to him while I'm making my call.''

"But—''

Benson slammed the door behind him.

5.

"This knife?'' Lydia asked in her little-girl voice, tilting her head toward the counter. "Is this the knife Quin wants?''

She lifted her head from the floor but could only see Lydia's feet. "Yes, that knife's fine. Just bring the knife over here, Lydia.''

A few moments passed.

"Lydia? Is something wrong?''

"Mommy says Lydia can't play with knives.''

Fuck Mommy. "You're not going to play with the knife.

You're helping me. Remember? You're going to help Quin get loose so we can play our game. Your mommy would want you to help Quin.''

"She would?"

Quin pressed her lips closed against the scream that was rising in her throat. "Of course she would. It's like helping an old lady across the street." *Don't I look old, Lydia? Don't you see this street we've got to cross? Huh? Don't you?* "It's a good thing to do. A nice thing."

"Well, if you're sure it's okay . . ."

We're dead otherwise. We may be dead, anyway. "I'm sure it's fine. I'm positive it is."

Something clattered to the floor. "It fell."

So pick it the hell up. "That's all right, Lydia. Just pick it up. Just crouch down and pick it up. Can you do that?"

"Uh-huh. I think so." A pause. "There."

"Good girl. Now bring it over to Quin."

6.

"Where're Mac and George?" Benson asked the ranger at the front desk.

"I don't know," Frank replied. He was watching something on a small portable TV. "Last I saw them, McCleary was headed for the men's room and the Indian went to get a soda out of the machines. How's it going in there, Captain?"

"It's not."

"Troopers are going to have their hands full with the likes of her."

"If your boss doesn't release her."

Frank made a face. "Yeah. Well. He's not that stupid."

Benson had his doubts. He started toward Bogie's office to use the phone, but Frank called him back.

"Did you ask her about the white Indians?"

"No."

"Maybe you ought to. George thinks she's one of them. He was telling Mr. McCleary and me that the bow is the weapon they favor. Maybe if you confronted her with that . . ."

Maybe the clan got them. . . .

"What makes him think *she's* one of them?"

Frank related their conversation, and yes, it all made a weird kind of sense. Maybe Opal wouldn't give her last name because she didn't have one (or didn't know it) and maybe the same was true for her address. It would explain the way she talked, why she didn't seem to know what *booked* or *lawyer* meant. It would explain a lot of things.

But it would also raise a number of questions.

"You think George is right?" Frank asked.

"I don't know."

No, absolutely not, he thought as he stepped into Bogie's office. Someone would have seen these people. Anthropologists or sociologists or whoever would have been looking for them, studying them, something. The Everglades was a wilderness, yes, but it wasn't the Amazon. Or Africa. Or Timbukfuckingtu. It was too accessible. Opal and the group McCleary had described were probably just a bunch of rednecks from someplace like Frostproof or Yeehaw Junction who were down here.

For a little target practice with their bows and shotguns.

He stopped midway across the room. *"George said he knew where those abandoned chickee sites are. I think Mr. McCleary believes his wife is being held at one of them."* Wasn't that what Frank had just said?

Benson doubled back toward the door and made a bee-line for the men's room. It was empty. And no one was at the soda machine.

"Shit, man. It wouldn't have taken *that* much longer," Benson mumbled, and hastened outside, already knowing what he would find.

And he did. The airboat was gone.

7.

Even the sound of Lydia's footsteps seemed small, like a child's. When she reached Quin, she turned, showing her the knife clutched in her bound hands. "See?"

"Great. Perfect." The blade was facing up. "Now sit down here by me . . . uh-huh, just like that. Turn around and hold the knife real steady, okay? I'm going to try to slip the blade under the piece of material."

Quin shifted her shoulder, maneuvering her right arm, the arm that was against the floor, until the tip of the blade touched the fabric. Then she moved it another fraction of an inch and held her breath as the blade slid sideways under the fabric.

"You finished yet?" Lydia asked.

"Stay real still. Don't move the knife or your hands, Lydia."

"But my hands are tired," she whined.

And mine aren't? "I know. Just stay steady for a little bit."

Quin pulled her arms back, then pushed them forward, back, forward again. The blade was sharp and the fabric frayed quickly and then popped and her arm was suddenly free. It just lay there for a beat, white, motionless, dead. Then blood rushed into it, spreading through her wrist and each of her fingers as they curled and uncurled and reached for the knife.

She sliced through the ropes around Lydia's wrists, freed her left arm, her feet, kicked the chair away from her. She was so weak that when she sat up, her head spun. *Water, food, sleep, please, and in exactly that order.* Quin pressed the heels of her hands against her eyes, sucked air deeply into her lungs, rolled back onto her heels.

"Quin? Can we play the game now? Can we, Quin?"

She looked at Lydia, veteran of acid, mescaline, speed, twenty-plus years of pot, and Christ knew what else. But decades of substance abuse had not done what three days in the Everglades had: turned her inside out like a dirty sock.

"Sure. Sure, we can play the game now." She looked around; her eyes settled on the skull. She unhooked it from the wall, placed it carefully in Lydia's hands.

"Gross." She wrinkled her nose. "It's so *ugly*."

"What I want you to do, Lydia, is go over to the door and listen. If you hear any sounds—anything at all—whistle very softly. Like this."

Lydia watched Quin's mouth as she whistled, then imitated her.

"Good. That's real good. If anyone comes through the door, you press back against the wall and raise the skull over your head, and as soon as the person steps inside, you smash the skull over his head. Okay? You think you can do that?''

She lifted her gaze from the skull and something changed in her eyes. A spark, brief and bright, blazed with full awareness of their situation, of everything that had happened, of everything that might happen from here on in. Until this moment, Quin hadn't realized just how badly she had wanted to see that understanding, even from Lydia, or how desperately she needed it to bolster her own faltering courage. She felt like throwing her arms around Lydia and apologizing for every shitty thing she'd said to her and thought about her. She wanted to tell her she was just fine in her book, wanted to weep with her over Beau, eulogize him, pray for him, whatever, it wouldn't matter as long as she had the support of another aware, functioning adult.

But the light went out as suddenly as it had appeared and the aloneness that swept through Quin nearly overpowered her. A hot, acidic taste filled her mouth. A fever burned at the backs of her eyes. Her skin felt as if it were loosening from her bones again. Her knees went soft and spongy, and, Jesus God, she was suddenly so afraid, so consumed with terror at what lay beyond the door, the chickee, that her mind turned as white and blank as a hot summer sky.

She didn't know how long she stood like that, paralyzed, lost in a fugue as deep and ubiquitous as Mc-Cleary's amnesia last summer. But when Lydia giggled, it broke. ''Smash the skull on a head, uh-huh, I understand. I like this game, Quin.''

She patted Lydia on the shoulder, then moved quickly across the room, the knife clutched in her hand, the spark of light she thought she'd seen now forgotten.

IV

1.
THE RAIN HAD stopped.

The afternoon sun was struggling to show itself through mountains of clouds the color of blueberries. Everything McCleary looked at possessed an eerie, almost preternatural luster—the saw grass, the mangroves, even the water. Especially the water.

It eddied around clusters of hyacinth, shimmered against moss and leaves, rushed from pockets of shadows. The rains had replenished it, renewed it, and it was everywhere and nowhere, this water, an entity unto itself, a kind of god.

As the airboat sped across it, through it, sometimes barely touching it, McCleary understood something that had eluded him before. If you expected to survive in here, you had to do more than acknowledge the *fact* of the water; you had to become part of it. You had to move as it moved, reflect what it reflected. You had to be grateful for what it gave and not demand that it give more.

That had been their mistake.

They had not been grateful. They had fought the water from the moment they'd set their canoes adrift. They had tried to protect themselves and their gear from it, had cursed it when it didn't behave the way they expected it to, had tried to hide from it. But Weston and his band understood the secret of the water—and thus of the Glades—and that made them formidable. It endowed them with a power that others simply didn't have. It was something he intended to remember.

George steered the airboat into a cove where three other airboats bobbed in the water like wingless silver insects. He pulled up to one of the three docks that jutted out from shore; a pair of rusting gas pumps bore the faded words PROPERTY OF PAUL ABBOT. MESS WITH THESE AND YOU'LL HAVE MORE THAN THE LAW TO WORRY ABOUT. Beyond them was a bait and tackle shop, a storage shack, and a parking lot with more puddles than cars.

As they hopped down from the airboat, an elderly man limped out of the shop. Bounding alongside him was a black lab that shot forward as soon as it saw George. It galloped down the dock and leaped up, nearly knocking George back, and covered the Indian's face with wet, sloppy kisses. "Meet Diogenes," George said with a laugh. "Di for short. She's been living out here with Paul since I moved into town so I'd be closer to the campus."

"She's a beauty," McCleary said.

"Say hi to Mike, Di."

The lab sat back on her haunches, tail thumping the dock, tongue lolling from her mouth, and lifted her paw. McCleary laughed and took it.

"Nice to meet you, Di."

She barked and rolled onto her back, offering her belly for a scratch. "No, girl," George said softly, as if answering a question the dog had asked that McCleary hadn't heard. "Not this time."

"Hey, Buffalo," called the old man as he limped toward them. "What brings you this way?"

"Some gas, a canoe, and a few other things."

The man jerked a thumb over his shoulder. "It's all in the shack." He stopped, looked down at the dog, and shook his head. "Fickle, Di. That's what you are."

Di whimpered and slapped his shoe with her paw; the old man laughed. "Shee-it, dog, you think you can fool an old man? I know who your first love is. But I'm willing to share you."

George chuckled and made the introductions. Paul Abbot probably wasn't as old as he appeared to be. But a lifetime of Florida sun had weathered his face, and his body looked as tough as a strip of beef jerky. "You got yourself the best guide in the Glades, Mr. McCleary."

"He hasn't hired me as a guide, Paul. The band's got his wife," George said. "We're going after her."

Abbot's expression was that of a man who believed in

the bogeyman and had just heard it was coming for him. "That's crazy, Buffalo."

"Maybe."

"What's the point?"

"It's time, that's the point."

Abbot stared at George a moment longer, as if debating whether an argument would change his mind. He evidently decided it wouldn't, because he turned his attention to McCleary. "How'd it happen, son?"

He briefly explained as the three of them walked to the shop, Di prancing beside George. Abbot didn't say anything until they were inside and George had gone on to the shack to get supplies. "He tell you about his connection to them? To the clan?"

"Yes."

"I figured he must have. All these years, it's eaten away at him, festered inside him." He walked over to a rusting fridge. "How about a cold root beer?"

"Great, thanks."

He pulled two from the fridge, opened them, gestured toward the line of stools in front of the lunch counter. "You hungry? Can I get you something to eat?"

McCleary started to say no but realized he was famished. Other than the stew he'd had at the ranger's station, he hadn't eaten anything since . . . Well, he couldn't remember. "If it's not too much trouble."

"No trouble at all." Abbot scooted behind the counter and went to work. "Talking about the clan always makes me want to do something ordinary, you know? It's like the American who goes overseas for the first time and everything's so strange and all that he hits a McDonald's the first chance he gets because it's familiar. That's how the clan makes me feel. And I've known about them for a good while."

When Buffalo George and his mother first got away, he said, he was running a bait and tackle place out near the Seminole reservation. "His ma came in one day and asked if I needed any help around the shop. She said she'd do anything—clean, wait on customers, it didn't matter. I didn't need any help, but I felt right sorry for her. She was a pretty little thing with the widest, saddest eyes you've ever seen. And I knew that if she was looking for work, chances were good that she was widowed.

"Turned out she wasn't even living on the reservation. She didn't feel like she belonged. She and the boy were working on a farm for room and board. I moved them off the farm and into the garage apartment next to the shop." He paused, flipped the eggs sizzling in the frying pan, popped bread into the toaster. "I reckon I probably loved her from the first time I saw her. The boy, too. But it was a long time before either of them told me about the clan. About what had happened. And even longer before she consented to marry me. She was afraid the clan would somehow find out about it and come looking for me."

"Did they?"

"Naw."

"Is she marked the same way George is?"

"Was." His voice softened. "She died two years ago."

"I'm sorry."

His smile was thin and sad. "Not half as sorry as I am. And yeah, she was marked." He worked silently for a few minutes and McCleary sipped his root beer. Cold and sweet. He couldn't remember the last time he'd had one of these.

When Abbot set the plate in front of him, he said he'd made the biscuits just that morning. Besides the biscuits, he'd fixed two eggs over easy, bacon, grits, and had squeezed a glass of fresh OJ. The sight of so much food made McCleary think of Quin, who could have eaten twice this and then some. He wolfed the meal down as Abbot poured two mugs of coffee and claimed the stool next to him.

"These clan people have lived in the Glades for nearly ninety years, Mr. McCleary. They don't just *know* the area. It's almost like they *are* the Glades. I mean, if the Glades was going to be human, it would be the clan, if you get what I mean. The place is in their genes. And maybe because of that and because of all their inbreeding, they've got certain advantages the rest of us don't have."

"Yeah, you might say that."

"I mean advantages that aren't obvious." He rubbed a

210

hand over his jaw, stirred more cream into his coffee. "I guess what I'm trying to say is that they *sense* things, like an animal does, and what one of them senses, the rest of them can sense. Not always, but sometimes." It was similar to what happened in a hive of bees when the queen was threatened. Or in a colony of ants. That was how George's mother had explained it to him.

"Also, they seem to have a pool of knowledge about the Glades—its wildlife and plants, its history, its people—that they tap into when they need to. I imagine men in the Stone Age had something like it. A survival mechanism. And some of that's in George. It's part of what makes him such an excellent guide. He couldn't get lost out there even if he wanted to. His sense of direction's too good."

When George was small, Abbot said, he'd sometimes come on the boy outside, sitting real still, like he was listening to something. "I'd ask him what was going on and he'd say, 'We got to find a new place to hunt.' Or 'So and so's got rat fever.' Or 'This drought's like the one that happened back in '28. . . . ' Then he'd look at me with those big, frightened eyes and want to know how come they wouldn't leave him alone."

It sounded like a kind of racial memory, McCleary thought. But in this case it was highly specific.

"His mother and I tried to explain that the band wasn't *doing* it to him, just that a part of him was still connected to them. He used to call it Kin Dread."

"Is he still like that?"

"Naw. By the time he was twelve, thirteen years old, he grew out of it. But there're things about the band, about what powers it, that he's never told anyone. He's afraid if he does, they'll know and they'll come looking for him. He says it's the only time they'd look for an exile. That's how deeply ingrained the superstition is. Anyway, just keep all this in mind when you're in their territory."

Uttered like a warning.

When he and George left a while later, a dugout was strapped to the floor of the airboat. Under it were sandwiches and water Abbot had given them, camping gear, gasoline, and a pair of Ruger Super Redhawk .44 Magnums with Bausch & Lomb night scopes. Not exactly your run-of-the-mill weapon: George wasn't taking chances.

2.

From what Quin could tell, the chickee stood alone and in front of a line of chickees that were clustered in pairs of threes, creating a small village on stilts. It appeared to be in a lagoon or an inlet bordered to the back by a hammock and was well hidden by branches, saw grass, and the crescent shape of the cove. But even if it weren't, she sensed it was so deep in the Glades, it was unlikely that weekend canoeists would stumble upon it. She also doubted that it was visible from the air; the tin roofs were covered with thatch that blended with the awning of branches.

But a hammock meant dry land. If they could somehow get to the hammock . . . *And then what?* It would only lead to more water. It probably wasn't very big. They would find her. And this time they'd kill her for sure.

But they'd be killed if the old man found them like this, so what was the difference?

Quin peered out the kitchen window again and wished it were still raining. Rain would have camouflaged them. But it would be getting dark soon, which would shield them even better.

Shield us while we're swimming through the muck, the swamp. In the dark.

Her gaze dropped the five or six feet to the water, then darted the two or three hundred yards to the hammock. She swam six times that distance a couple of times a week, but in a pool, not in waters like these, not in water that was . . . *I can't do it.*

They'd find another way out, she thought, and turned away from the window. She saw Lydia at the chickee's front door, waiting, the skull in her hands. She had found her dirty shorts and shirt and put them on again. Quin saw the canvas chair. The strips of fabric. Ropes. The hammock. The mats where Lydia and Nichols had lain. She saw the straw basket that held the bottle filled with leeches. Everything was utterly clear and still, as if preserved under glass. Or like a police photo of a crime scene.

The victims were Quin St. James of . . . and Lydia Nichols of . . . who were . . .

Here or there. Some choice.

She looked around for anything besides the knife she clutched that might prove useful. But the kitchen wasn't a kitchen in the ordinary sense of the word. Not surprising, since nothing here was even remotely ordinary.

The little two-burner woodstove was the only luxury in the room. No faucet, no fridge, no drawers, no cabinets, no shelves. The counter was just a row of wooden boxes turned upside down that were covered with old mason jars. Some of the jars were stuffed with herbs and cash. Others had knives of various lengths sticking out of them and utensils that had no doubt come from an unsuspecting camper's backpack. But when she upended one of the boxes, she discovered a cornucopia of small treasures. Coconuts, mangoes, bananas, tomatoes, onions, even some papayas.

"You see our little farm out there producin anythin worth a shit? Huh, Ticker?"

That *little* farm, as Weston had called it, was apparently producing enough to feed the old man. She peeled one of the bananas, wolfed it down. Her stomach woke up, rolled over, and shrieked for more. She stabbed the knife into a ripe papaya, sliced herself a generous piece, and devoured everything but the peeling. The agonizingly sweet juice dribbled down her chin. She wiped it away with the back of her hand and cut herself another slice and ate it as she went through the other boxes.

She found slices of dried fish (very salty, but who cared) and stuffed some in her pockets. She uncovered a bag of trail mix, a jar of honey dry-roasted peanuts, a bottle of Evian water, which she gulped at, then set aside with the other items, and numerous canned goods. Some were home jobs, packed tightly in mason jars. But most were from those oh-so-familiar spots like Winn Dixie, Publix, even a 7-Eleven.

She hurried to the doorway and called softly to Lydia. "You hungry? Thirsty?"

Lydia's childlike eyes lit up. "Quin has food?"

She laughed. "Quin's got a ton of food. C'mon, Help me eat some of this stuff."

She came running, the skull tucked under one arm like a stuffed animal, her footsteps as quick and eager as a second-grader's. But Lydia the child wasn't interested in dry fish or fruit or honey-roasted peanuts. She wanted chocolate. She wanted ice cream. She wanted strawberry shortcake. And water? No way. Where were the Cokes? The Pepsis? The Kool-Aid? Where was the finger-lickin'-good Kentucky fried chicken? Where was the fat, dripping McDonald's burger?

Oh, she sampled and picked all right—the adult Lydia lost inside her was too hungry not to—but she also made faces and disgusted noises and then she got fed up and started to cry. Long, deep sobs, like a kid with a broken heart. Quin just stood there, watching her knuckle her eyes, watching urine drip down the insides of her legs as she sobbed, "Lydia has to pee, Lydia can't hold it no more," watching and wondering how the hell she was ever going to convince this child in a woman's body that their salvation lay outside these walls.

3.

While Bogie was on the phone alerting his fellow rangers to be on the lookout for George and McCleary, Benson went in to talk to Opal. She was still sitting at the table, calm as you please, looking through the magazines stacked on a bookcase under the window. A handful of magazines were already scattered across the table in front of her. A butt from the pack of unfiltered Camels one of the rangers had left burned in the ashtray.

She glanced at him as he sat down, sipped noisily from her can of Coke. Benson couldn't take his eyes off the weird tattoo on her cheek. She said, "Got nothin to say to you."

"You want something to eat? There's a machine out in the hall with sandwiches in it."

She was instantly suspicious of the offer. "You ain't foolin me none, boy."

"Hey, no tricks. I just figured you might be hungry."

"Nope."

She paged through an issue of *Redbook*, skipping over

the printed matter in favor of the ads. Her fingers slipped over the glossy pages, lingering on the depicted objects with a kind of longing. It was like watching a kid in a toy store, Benson thought.

"You know what that is?" He pointed at the neat, square container of eye shadow in a Revlon ad.

Silence.

"You don't, do you. You can't read what it says."

A corner of her mouth plunged as she gave him a look that could have fried the balls off a bull. "It's color, boy. Pretty colors."

"It's called eye shadow. Color for the eyes." He tapped another object in the ad. "And that's mascara. For your lashes, to make them darker and longer. That's lipstick. To paint your lips. And that—"

She shoved his hand away. "Stop botherin me, boy."

She flipped through more pages, stopped at an advertisement for color TV.

"You know what that is?" he asked.

That look again. "I ain't stupid, boy. It's a gawddamn sin box."

Benson picked up an issue of *People*, where the ads were longer and more interesting than the articles. He pointed at a refrigerator. "What's that?"

"A big box."

He pointed at a typewriter. "And this?"

Silence.

Benson went through a slew of ads and, before long, had a fairly accurate picture of the depth of Opal's ignorance. A hair dryer was a gun; a floor lamp was a hat with a stick on the end; a phone was sorcery that spoke to you; eyeliner was a pencil; a microwave was a box; a clock was something that told you what part of the morning, afternoon, or night it was; a VCR was a long box.

Some ordinary things had obviously been explained to her. Others—like guns, knives, boats, rifles—she had no problem with at all, and still others were totally beyond her comprehension. With certain things, she seemed to grasp the concept but not the reality. An airplane, for instance, was a "gawddamned noisy machine that done took you places by flyin through the air." A car was "a dugout you rode on land."

"I'm a policeman. Do you know what that is?"

"Yeah, an asshole," she cackled. "Just like them rangers."

"You know what we assholes do?"

She leaned forward, her tiny eyes now spitting fire. "You go where you don't belong, mister, 'cause you ain't got a lick of sense, and since you don't know what you're messin with, you're goin to git yourself killed." She started to page through the magazine again, but Benson slapped it shut and kept his arm over it. She glared at him, reached for another magazine, and he swept the bunch of them to the floor.

"Listen real good to me, Opal. My friend left here a while ago with an Indian who knows where your people live. He knows about the different places in the Glades that you travel to. And he knows where your people are holding my friend's wife. I don't want to think about what's going to happen to your people when the Indian and my friend find your village. But I can tell you this. My friend's not going to give a damn about who he has to kill to get his wife, Opal. So while you're sitting here sipping Coke and looking at the pretty things in magazines, your people are going to get slaughtered. So you think about that for a while."

He pushed away from the table, flung open the door, and stepped into the hallway before she said, "Hey, boy."

He turned. "Yeah?"

She grabbed the ashtray and hurled it at him. Her aim was lousy. It struck the wall behind him and shattered against the hallway floor, littering it with glass and butts. "Fuck you."

Benson smiled at the lack of conviction in her words. "Right," he said, and shut the door, locking it behind him.

V

No one liked to be around Pa when he was mad, least of all me.

And he was mad, all right. Mad at me, at Grandpa, at Ticker, mad at how things got so fucked up that we lost one of them outsiders and Opal too. But most of all I think he was mad because of Lee-dee-uh. With Big Man dead, he figured he didn't have no hold on her, that he couldn't make her do things by threatening to hurt her mate.

I never followed his thinking when it done come to women. Any man, with the exception of Ticker, maybe, could make a woman do what he wanted. That wasn't how we treated our women, but Lee-dee-uh was an outsider and we captured her fair and square, and outsider women was easy to scare. I just didn't see that Pa needed Big Man to get what he wanted from her. Looking back, I think he was using Big Man's death for an excuse to rally the band against Tommy—maybe even to exile him—so he could head the band.

But when it come to Tommy, most of the band was like me. They was scared of him, scared he would turn his sorcery on them, even if they didn't admit it. He'd headed the band since before I was born, and that's a lot of history to fight.

He joined at a time when the fever sickness was raging and the drought was baking the Glades and sucking up so much water that the fish was dying. The sickness had killed so many, the band was smaller than now. Them that was left was looking for a miracle and I guess Tommy was it. He brought his magic, his medicine, his power, and for a long time the band did real well.

But for the last ten, eleven years, nothing'd gone good

217

for us. Fifteen pregnancies, and of them only five children born and we had to drown all but two of them. We'd lost adults, crops, two settlements that wasn't hid deep enough, and there wasn't nothing Tommy's magic could do to keep the world from coming closer every year or to keep the fires controlled when they started. I heard a lot of talk about how Tommy was too old, too weak, that we oughta get him to step down for someone younger. But no one dared say it to his face.

Now it was about to be said. I could feel it building here inside Pa's chickee the way you can sometimes feel a storm stirring out over the Atlantic. I could see it in Pa's face, in the thin line of Josie's mouth, in the way Rusty was looking at Tommy, like he wanted to bust his bones, in the wild tic under Ticker's eyes.

We was six in that front room, where we'd been ever since we tied rocks to the big man's body and dumped it in the swamp. Pa's whiskey—real whiskey from Christ knowed where—was getting passed around while we talked about what to do with the outsider women.

"We also got some other bizness to chew," Pa said, and the air went dead still. "I reckon we all know what it is."

"Reckon we do," echoed Josie, nodding.

Eyes turned to Tommy. He sat back on his hands, legs crossed, white hair flowing down his back, and smiled—smiled—like it was some kind of joke. "This business you speak of should be handled by majority vote. That is the way."

"Fuck the way," Rusty said, clenching his fists against his thighs.

Pa held up his hand for silence. "We ain't got time for a vote tonight, old man. Some of the women say that rangers got Opal and that the things of the world could tempt her to direct them here, to the outsiders."

I knowed that was wrong. Had to be. And I said so. "Opal ain't never been into the world. She don't care about the world. Never has. And she wouldn't break the pledge and tell outsiders how to find us."

"I'm just tellin what the women tole me, Wes," said Pa. "But I've a mind to agree with you. Opal ain't tole nothin. But Josie and some of the others feel outsiders

218

might be comin. Now maybe they found someone who knows the way or maybe they just thinks they knows the way. In either case, we need to be thinkin about that, because if outsiders are comin, it's the women they want."

"Yeah," said Josie. "They's doin what we oughta be doin. Comin for their own."

Pa shook his head. "You know the rules. Anyone in the band who gets took is on his own. That's the way it's gotta be."

"Let them come," the old man said. "We are well hidden."

"We was talking about somethin else," I reminded them. "About how we got no time for a vote."

The old man turned them terrible eyes on me, and for a second, I forgot what I was going to say. I forgot everything except them eyes digging down inside me, looking for my fear, my weakness, that bad seed.

"And what's that mean, Wes?" He sounded like he was going to laugh. "Why don't you tell all of us here"—he held out his arms—"what you mean and why you used the leeches and why you wanted to kill the big man. Why don't you just tell us, Wes?"

"I didn't want to kill him." I could hardly spit the words out. "I was teachin him a lesson and showin the children the old ways. I didn't know his heart was no good."

"No. No, of course you didn't." The old man's voice was softer now, and I knew it was a trick, but some part of me, the boy in me, needed to hear that softness. "You had no way of knowing. But the fact is, the big man's dead because you literally scared him to death, Wes. And he died in my house. That will bring bad luck down upon the band unless I prepare a magic to fight it."

I suddenly understood the trick, but I didn't have the right words to describe it. Tommy talked better than me. Better than all of us. It was part of his power. But even if I'd had the words, I wasn't fast enough. Tommy's eyes was on Pa, whispering, You got the power for such a magic, Pa? You want to risk bringing bad luck down on the band? Now Tommy's mouth was opening and his

219

words was coming out, but they wasn't the same words his eyes spoke.

"One of the things we need to discuss, Pa, is a defense. Just in case the outsiders find us." His smile now was just as soft as his voice. "With our luck turning sour, we can't be too careful." He paused, letting them words sink into us all, letting us think about what would happen to us without his magic. "I think there's something else we need to consider," he went on, and now his eyes darted around the circle, finally resting on me. "We wouldn't be in this situation if Wes and Opal hadn't killed the man and woman on Lard Can."

"Accident," Pa said. But his voice was weak and scared.

"Maybe so. But it doesn't change what's happened since then, does it?"

Tommy's eyes was moving again, skipping around the circle, challenging us. You got something to say? them eyes whispered. How about you? And you? Anyone ready to cast a vote?

Rusty looked at Pa. Pa looked at Tommy. Tommy looked at Josie, who looked at me, and on like that around the circle, all of us yellow-bellied cowards again.

"That man and woman on Lard Can didn't do what me and Opal told them," I said.

No one spoke. I looked at Josie. Like Opal, she'd always supported me, and me, her. But now she just looked down at her hands.

"And we brought supplies from Lard Can," I rushed on. "Supplies the band needed."

The hiss of a lantern answered me.

"And the only reason Opal, Judd, and me went back there was because Tommy told us to. He said we should get rid of them bodies in the saw grass. That's what we was going to do, but them other outsiders came and . . . then Judd got himself killed and everythin went bad from there. Wasn't my fault. Wasn't Opal's fault."

"No one's blaming you, Wes." That soft voice again. "We're just stating the facts. You and Opal started this and now we've got to finish it."

He kept saying we, like it was him and the band against me, and sure enough, when I looked around, that's exactly how it was. I could see it in their faces. "It was Tommy's magic that failed." My voice was high and strange and sounded scared. But I didn't care. "He ain't got magic. All of you know it same as me. His only power is words. Words and us being too scared to say what we think. Well, I'm saying what I think. He ain't got it no more."

"Calm your voice, boy," snapped Pa.

Pa sounded like the wind in the saw grass; he always did when he was mad. And it shut me up real fast. "Tommy's right. We need to be ready in case they come." We need his magic, his eyes screamed. "What do you think we oughta do, Tommy?"

The old man's scarce white brows fanned together. He seemed to be thinking, but I knew it was just pretend, that he'd already thought everything out. Fact is, I think he knowed what he was going to do with the outsiders from the time they was brought here. Maybe he didn't know the details—like about the big man's heart giving out, no way he coulda knowed that—but he had a general idea how he could use them to make himself look good. And that meant Snake Mound. Hell, even I could figure that out.

"We should take them to Snake Mound," he said, and oh, yes siree, everyone nodded what a good idea that was, like they wasn't thinking the same thing themselves. "At true dark, we leave."

"At true dark," Pa agreed.

"The entire band should go. For the ceremony."

"I ain't likin the idea," Josie said, glancing over at me to show me she was on my side, even though she was still scared of the old man. "We don't need to do nothin to the women. I think if the outsiders find the way here, then we oughta make a trade. Their women for Opal."

"She's right," I said.

I could tell Pa liked the idea and maybe he woulda said so if Tommy hadn't shaked his head just then. "A trade's a fine idea, but it won't work. We've never allowed a true outsider to find his way here and then leave. We—"

"Poachers come here," I said. "Traders."

"They're different. We have business with them.

They're not true outsiders. But these people are. They'll tell other outsiders about us, and pretty soon the rangers would come and that would be the end of the band.'' Them words, end of the band, hung in the room as his cold dark eyes touched each of us.

"But what about the exiles?'' Josie argued. "They know about us and we let them leave.''

Tommy sighed; it was as good as saying Josie was stupid. "It's not the same. An exile would never dare speak of the ceremony or bring outsiders here.''

"He's right,'' Pa said. "Exiles 're as good as dead when they leave.'' Pa's mouth curled around exile and spat it out like bad food. "They don't count.''

Ticker touched his swollen eye, his cut cheek. "True outsiders and exiles ain't like us. No reason we should go bein nice to them. It'll just bring us trouble.''

Tommy smiled at him like he was the new favorite grandson, then looked at me to make sure I'd noticed. In the long moments after that, when silence quivered against the bruised light that filled the open windows, I felt the band's death in the air.

Night

I

1.

THE AIRBOAT SPED into the dusk, skimming saw grass
and sloughs, crossing several bays and wide rivers. The
lush, rich odor of the Glades permeated the air. Even
though it was drizzling, patches of soft purple sky
streaked the treetops in the distance—the first McCleary
had seen in three days.

But by the time they approached the mangroves on
Broad River where George wanted to stash the airboat,
dusk had bled into a rapidly vanishing twilight. A lone
star glimmered against the skin of the sky, a jewel bright
enough to varnish the dark waters in pale light.

They tied the airboat to some trees about a quarter into
a channel, then put the canoe into the water and trans-
ferred their gear. McCleary settled in the bow and George
took the stern, with the gear in between. Once they were
out of the tunnel of mangroves, a healthy breeze kicked
up behind them and they moved along at a swift clip. It
stopped drizzling. Stars popped out everywhere, and for
a long time their light was all the illumination needed.

As the river widened, loud splashes off to their left
made George turn on his flashlight. "Dolphins. There.
At eleven o'clock. Two of them."

McCleary saw them, a pair swimming side by side,
surfacing, diving, surfacing again, water spewing from
their blowholes. For a few minutes, they slowed down
and made wide, graceful circles around the canoe. Then
they shot off through the channel.

"I didn't realize they came into the Glades," Mc-
Cleary said.

"Sure. All these rivers feed into the gulf. But you don't see many dolphins in here this late in the spring. They're more common during the winter, when they're seeking warmer waters. It's a good sign, Mike."

As though he were fully inside his Indian skin now, reading portents in the wind, the waters. McCleary supposed it was similar to what happened to him sometimes during an investigation. There was a point he reached where things suddenly started clicking together, where everything he did and saw and heard somehow related to the case.

"You ever thought about investigative work?" McCleary asked.

"You mean like private-eye kind of investigating?"

"Right."

George chuckled. "Nope."

"I think you'd be good at it."

"Yeah? Why?"

"Because it's not all that different from what we're doing now."

"I'm good at this because it's important to me personally. And I know the Glades. I don't have much use for cities, to be quite honest with you. That the line of work you're in?"

"Yes."

"You don't seem the type."

"Is there a type?"

"Sure. And you're not it. I had you pegged for some sort of businessman, like an IBM dude who wears three-piece suits during the week and roughs it on weekends."

McCleary laughed. "IBM. Jesus."

"What's your wife do?"

"The same. We have an agency." *Sort of.*

"What about your two camping buddies?"

"They own a sporting-goods shop in Atlanta."

"Are they outdoors people?"

"Not really." He told him briefly what had happened before they were captured by the group of crazies.

"Shit," George muttered. "What about your wife? How'd she hold up?"

"Good." He had the impression the questions weren't idle, that George, in fact, was not the kind of man who ever asked idle questions. "Why? What is it you really want to know?"

"I'm just trying to get a feel for what kind of people they are. The band doesn't fuck around, Mike. If they think you all killed one of their own—and from what you told me, that's what it sounds like they believe—then they're going to get their pound of flesh. They've had your wife and friends for nearly a day now and they may already be dead. You'd better be prepared for that eventuality."

He said it simply, matter-of-factly. The possibility, of course, had prowled through the back of McCleary's thoughts ever since he'd escaped. But when he dwelled on it, tried to think it through, it filled him with such despair he backed off. He was *not* prepared for that reality, would *never* be prepared for it, and refused to consider it now.

"But on the other hand," George went on, "if they sense that outsiders are coming to *them*, they may not be in such a big hurry to kill your wife and friends."

"They must know by now that I got Opal. Won't they try to find her?"

"No, not if band rules are the same as they used to be. And they probably are. Everything's slow to change with them. They're a superstitious lot and rarely act quickly. That's in our favor. And if your wife's clever enough and fit enough and doesn't scare easily, she may have a chance."

He noticed that George didn't mention the Nicholses this time. "What powers the band, George?" he asked, remembering what Abbot had said.

"You don't want to know. There're things I can't tell you, McCleary. They'd know. You have to see for yourself."

Can't tell you. As if he'd taken an oath he was powerless to break. "Who heads the band?"

"Unofficially, a renegade medicine man. He intermarried with the band and has called most of the shots for years." In the same soft, factual voice, he recounted the complex and often lurid history of Miami Tommy.

"How do you know he's still alive?"

'Stories I've heard from people who've traded with him.''

''He'd be ancient.''

''In his late eighties. He's been making band decisions for about sixty years now.''

''And you're sure it's him?''

''Yes.''

''Why?''

''I *feel* it.''

''Hunches have been wrong.''

''This one isn't.'' He paused. When he spoke again, bitterness riddled his voice. ''That fuck inflicted the punishment of exile on my mother and me.''

So they were coming full circle, McCleary thought. The band's vengeance for Judd's death had gotten them into this, and now Buffalo George's vengeance for something that had happened to him nearly thirty years ago was, he hoped, going to get them out. ''So he's the reason you're doing this.''

''Yes.''

''But why did you wait all these years?''

His answer to that was simple. ''Fear.''

''Of the medicine man or the band?''

''Both.''

''And now you're not afraid?''

His laughter was a swift, beautiful sound. ''Of course I am. And in some ways, the fear is even deeper now than it was when I was a kid. But it had gotten to the point where it was starting to become a handicap. I found that every time I was out in the Glades I was uneasy, always looking over my shoulder and expecting to see someone from the band. I knew I was going to have to confront the fear, but I wasn't sure how.''

The day Benson had shown up at the ranger's station, he explained, he was supposed to be in class. But all that day he'd been feeling that he should be somewhere else, so he'd cut his evening class. That in itself was strange, he said, because in two years of college it was the first class he'd ever cut. He drove over to the park, where he hired out as a guide, to see if Ranger Joe had any trips for him.

He and another Seminole were sitting on the porch of

226

the ranger's station when Benson arrived. The second George saw him, he knew Benson was the reason he'd cut the class. "It didn't make any sense. I didn't know who he was, I'd never seen him before, and I didn't have any idea why he wanted to see Ranger Joe. Then later, when we were driving over to the entrance to Hell's Bay Trail and he told us about the Crawfords, I had the strongest feeling that the band was behind their disappearance. I realized that Benson was somehow going to be the vehicle for my confronting my fear." He lifted his paddle from the water and pointed off to the right. "Just ahead is the cutoff for the Wilderness Waterway. We follow it for a while."

McCleary nodded, and for a few minutes, neither of them spoke. The water lapped at the sides of the canoe. A bank of clouds climbed the sky, blocking the stars. Heat lightning flashed in the distance.

"Abbot told me about this, uh, psychic connection that exists among members of the band."

A note of circumspection crept into George's voice. "It seems to be strongest among the women. Or at least it used to be. And it isn't psychic so much as instinctive. It's something that's developed over the generations."

"So you think they've sensed, through Opal, that someone's coming?"

"It's possible."

"And what about you, George?"

"What about me?" His caution had turned to downright caginess.

"Can you sense them?"

"I've been out of the band for a long time."

"That doesn't really answer my question." He waited for George to reply. When he didn't, McCleary added, "I know about Kin Dread, George."

The incessant chirring of insects along the shore poured into the brittle silence. "That was a long time ago."

There was something about the way he said it that indicated the passage of time had only dimmed the connection between himself and the clan, not killed it, as Abbot believed. But McCleary let it pass.

2.

Throughout the settlement lanterns, flickered like fire-flies in the light, steady rain. Quin could see figures moving around on porches, standing in doorways, getting into canoes. It was as if the darkness had brought all of the crazies out of the woodwork, and now, like vampires or werewolves, they were preparing themselves for a night of hunting.

Or a night of something else.

She stepped back from the window and zipped up the windbreaker she'd found in one of the rooms. It was too big for her, but it provided ample space for everything she'd stuffed in the zippered pockets. The navy-blue color would also camouflage her.

"Quin?"

Lydia's small, frightened voice drew her away from the window. It was too dark to see her and Quin didn't want to risk turning on the flashlight she'd found in the kitchen. "I'm right here. Did you get those shoelaces tied?"

"Uh-huh. Lydia ready. But it's so *dark*."

Quin followed the sound of her voice and knelt beside her. "You want to get out of here, right?"

"Bad place. Lydia want to leave."

"Then you have to do what I tell you."

"Lydia be good."

"Promise me, Lydia."

"Cross my heart."

Cross my heart and hope to die: Yeah, count on it if we don't get out. "Okay, give me your hand."

Quin helped her up, then held tightly to her hand as they made their way into the kitchen. "Quin, door is back there."

"We can't use that door. Someone might see us." They stopped in front of the window. "So we're going to climb out here and—"

"Skull is too heavy for Lydia. Quin want to carry it?"

She hadn't realized Lydia was still holding the horrid skull. "Here, let me have it," she said crossly, and set it on top of a box. "Now listen to me. We're going to climb out the window, drop into the water, and swim very quietly toward the trees. You can do that, can't you, Lydia?"

"Water? The *yucky* water? No. Lydia not go." She wrenched her hand free of Quin's and stepped back. "Lydia not like yucky water."

"You either go out *this* way or you stay here alone. Those are the choices."

"Lydia not want to stay alone," she whined.

"Then you'll have to come with me, because I'm not sticking around."

She picked up the kitchen knife and started to climb onto the sill. Lydia began to cry. The cries quickly turned into loud, noisy sobs, then wails. "No, don't leave Lydia, don't leave Lydia alone."

Quin dropped the knife, spun, and grabbed Lydia by the arms. She jerked her forward, around, and slapped a hand over her mouth, locking her arms behind her. Lydia grunted, squirmed, struggled, but not very hard. It was like trying to hold on to a hyperactive five-year-old, and after a moment or two she slumped against Quin, her breathing noisy and labored, as if she'd been running.

"You want to end up like Beau?" she hissed. "You want leeches sucking at you, Lydia? Because that's what they're going to do to us before they kill us. You remember the leeches? You remember what happened to Beau? Huh? Do you?"

Quin heard voices outside the chickee. She couldn't tell exactly where they were coming from—the porch, the water just below, maybe even another chickee. But they were close. "It's them," she whispered. "If you make a sound, we're dead. You understand?"

Lydia's head bobbed once.

Quin let go of her, patted around for the knife, found it. She moved to the side of the window, heart beating wildly in her chest, and peered out. Flickers of light glided through the blackness, but none of them was close. *Out, quick.*

But as she was about to tell Lydia to move, she heard the voices again, louder this time, and knew they were coming from the front of the chickee. The medicine man was home, and he had company.

A cold, white fear slammed into her. Her heart shot for her throat. Sweat sprang across her skin in waves. The knife she held suddenly weighed a ton and slipped out of her hand, clattering against the floor. Her fear screamed through her, and for a beat, she didn't move, didn't breathe, didn't blink, didn't swallow, didn't twitch a muscle. Her body had shut down, and any second now she would just fold up like a marionette whose strings had been severed.

If they jumped now, they'd be dead.

If they didn't jump, they'd be dead.

A wild laugh gurgled in her throat. She swallowed it back, scooped up the knife, hissed, "Out the window, fast!"

Lydia lurched forward, scrambled onto the boxes, and onto the sill, where her body filled the window. She hesitated only an instant, but it was an instant too long.

The door to the chickee swung open. Light from a couple of lanterns washed through the front room. Someone—*Ticker, it's Ticker*—said, "Hey, what's happened here?" His voice was slow and stupid with disbelief, as if it were inconceivable to him that Quin and Lydia had gotten free, therefore what he was seeing was wrong.

The medicine man, old but not stupid, shouted, "The kitchen!"

Lydia jumped from the window. Before she'd even struck the water, Quin had clambered onto the boxes, but she wasn't fast enough. Ticker was suddenly right there, behind her, his hands a vise around her ankle. She kicked, but he held on, clinging to her like one of the old man's leeches. She twisted around, stabbed blindly with the knife, felt herself slipping, and stabbed again. This time the blade struck home, sinking, and Ticker fell away from her shrieking, "My arm, you bitch, my arm!"

Quin hurled herself out into the night. The darkness rushed around her, through her, into her, an eternity of darkness steaming with the smell of mud and saw grass, mangroves and silt and water, the primordial odors of the Glades. The she hit the water and it closed over her head.

Bubbles fizzed and popped around her. Her shoes sank into the muck on the bottom. Weeds and grass tangled, serpentine, around her shoes, her ankles, and when she tried to swim for the surface, they held her there, laughing. She could hear them, Jesus, she could, a soft, throaty laughter, the sound of wind through the saw grass, the voice of the Glades.

Too bad, Quin, it laughed. *You weren't quick enough, Quin. You weren't smart enough. Bye-bye, Quin.*

She clawed at her legs, trying to tear the weeds loose with her hands. But it was too slippery, too strong, and now strands of it were wrapping around her shins and calves. Her lungs were about to burst, dots swirled in front of her eyes, she was starting to panic. She tore off her shoes, jerked her legs again, jerked hard, and suddenly slipped free.

She didn't swim toward the surface; she lunged, panic propelling her. As her head broke through, she gasped, sucking at the air, pulling it into her lungs. Those smells, now so familiar, flooded through her. Shouts rang out. Paddles slapped the water. Her head snapped right, left. She didn't see Lydia. She didn't see anything but the blurred, ghostly glow from what seemed like hundreds of lanterns bleeding across the water, through the lagoon, illuminating the dark shapes of chickees, canoes, and land, oh, Christ, land.

She dived.

3.

Benson watched as Ranger Bogie bit into an American cheese sandwich on white bread. It was stuck together with gobs of mayo that oozed out the sides like pus; a fleck had settled on Bogie's square chin.

Benson looked away, his stomach queasy, his patience worn so thin that he knew it was going to take maybe another fifteen seconds for it to snap completely. Then he was going to tell Bogie to shove his American-cheese-and-Wonder-Bread sandwich and inform the boys from the state police that he would be out in the Glades doing what should have been done hours ago.

The four state troopers who'd arrived nearly an hour ago had questioned Benson and Opal, said they wanted to talk to McCleary and the Indian when they were found, then booked Opal on suspicion of murder. She was now under guard in the next room, awaiting transport to the Dade County jail. It was, of course, under Benson's jurisdiction and where he'd wanted to send her in the first

place. But thanks to the carefully defined parameters between county and state, which put the state police in
charge of the park, approximately three hours had been
wasted just to get Opal to where she would have ended
up if shit-for-brains Bogie had cooperated to begin with.

The troopers, however, weren't any more enthusiastic
to get involved in a search in the Glades at night, in bad
weather, than Bogie was. Their arguments were reason-
able enough—the area was too vast for a night search,
even with choppers, and more thunderstorms were supposed to move into the Glades within the next two hours.

But the bottom line, Benson thought, was that they
were content to let a handful of Bogie's minions do the
dirty work. Never mind that these foot soldiers didn't
have the slightest idea where to look. Yes, they'd found
the Crawfords easily enough and brought the bodies back
here. But Lard Can was on a marked channel; the place
where McCleary and the Indian had gone, the place
where Opal's people had taken Quin and the Nicholses,
was not. But in all fairness to everyone—even shit-for-
brains—was *he* ready to head off into a world as foreign
to him as the surface of the moon? Hell, the moon would
be easier than the Glades at night even if Opal drew him
a goddamn map.

So here they were, a bunch of bureaucrats with their
thumbs up their collective ass, pretending they were trying to figure out their next move. With the exception of
the youngest trooper, who'd been tapped to transport
Opal, and the trooper who'd already left with the Crawfords' bodies, the rest of them were probably going to
sit around drinking coffee until first light.

Benson looked around the table. Bogie was leaning
back in his chair, feet propped at the edge of the table,
as he told a condom joke. It was the fourth one Benson
had heard in the last hour and all of them were along the
same lines as the old Polack jokes. One of the troopers
was listening with what seemed to be inordinate interest
while the other was cleaning his nails. One of Bogie's
boys—Benson couldn't remember his name, they all
looked alike to him—was making another pot of coffee.
A real lively group.

As he pushed away from the table, Bogie fell silent. "My jokes boring you, Captain?"

"Yeah."

The two troopers chuckled. "His jokes'll do that, all right," said one.

"Sure will," agreed the other.

Bogie looked offended. "*Reader's Digest* published one of my jokes and paid me five hundred bucks."

"*Reader's Digest* buys jokes?" asked the first trooper.

"Not jokes exactly, but funny things that happen. You know, in that section about life in America."

Like this turkey knew about life in America. "That's nice, Bogie. Where's the radio? I want to check in with your guys on the airboat," Benson said.

"Down the hall, take a left, first room on the right."

Benson nodded. As he left, Bogie was telling his audience of two the tale that *Reader's Digest* had published.

The station was oppressively quiet. Benson's footsteps echoed as he walked out to the front desk to get change from Frank for the sandwich machine. He didn't know that he could stomach another one, but, Christ, he was hungry.

Lightning flashed in the long window in front of him. It froze the reflection of the ranger behind the desk who was watching TV, caught his own shadow self moving forward, and illuminated the shapes of two men outside who were headed for the front door.

Ranger Joe and Billy Tiger darted inside, rain glistening against their slickers. "Hey Sergeant," said Farrel, smiling. "George around?"

"Nope." Benson didn't feel like explaining, and besides, he still hadn't quite forgiven Farrel for setting him up for that twenty-five an hour he'd paid Buffalo George. He dropped a buck on the counter and asked for change. "He left a while ago. Why?"

"A mile ago?" Farrel said, frowning. "What do you mean?"

Billy Tiger shook his head. "A *while* ago, Joe. He left a while ago."

"Oh." He grinned at his mistake. "Did he say where he was off to?"

"Why?"

Farrel and Billy Tiger looked at each other. Billy shrugged as if to say it was Farrel's ball game; he'd go along with whatever the ranger decided. "Well, uh, his last contact with me was this afternoon, after you found those bodies on Lard Can. I was kind of wondering why I hadn't heard from him since—he usually lets me know when he's finished with a job. Then I was listening to the radio a while ago and heard Bogie's APB bulletin about George and someone named McCleary and reckoned I'd better get down here and see what's what."

Took him long enough, Benson thought. Bogie's last contact with the airboats had been an hour and a half ago. "So you knew he wasn't here. Why ask?"

"He wants to know what's going on." Billy Tiger looked embarrassed about the old man's concern. "That's all."

Benson picked up his change and glanced at Billy Tiger. "What I've been wondering is why you never bothered mentioning that you'd given the Crawfords a ride to the Hell's Bay Trail from the canoe shop."

Billy's hard face went even harder. "Because I knew what you'd think."

"Yeah? And what's that, Billy? What am I thinking?"

"That I had something to do with them disappearing."

"That night, we didn't even know for sure that they'd disappeared."

Billy was starting to look real uncomfortable. He shifted his weight from one foot to the other, jammed his hands in the pockets of his slicker, and glanced at Farrel as if for support. But the ranger was staring at him with something close to contempt in his eyes and said, "If you've got something to say, boy, then say it now."

"I haven't broken any laws."

"No one's saying you have," Benson replied. "I'm just asking a simple question."

The Indian's expression was that of a man who was weighing his options and finding that none of them was particularly good. He glanced at Farrel. "You know that airboat that exploded?"

Impatience deepened the creases in the ranger's face. "What about it?"

"I was, uh, near there fishing when it happened. I went out to see what had happened and picked up these two guys."

"Two guys," Farrel repeated. "Uh-huh. And who the hell were these two guys, Billy?"

"I only know one of them."

"And what's his line of business, boy?" Farrel's voice was sharp. Benson noticed he didn't seem to be having any trouble hearing things now. "Poaching? Moonshine? What?"

"A little of both."

"And did he happen to enlighten you about why the airboat had exploded?"

Billy's hands sank deeper into the pockets of his rain slicker. Frank had switched off the TV and was sitting forward, listening with rapt attention. A crack of thunder and the patter of rain against the front windows filled the silence.

"Did he?" Farrel snapped.

Quietly: "Yeah. It was an accident. They were, uh, supposed to be keeping an eye out for these people in canoes and—"

"What people?" Benson demanded.

"Two couples."

Aw, Christ. "And who were they supposed to be doing this for, Billy?"

"For this guy they trade with."

"What guy?"

"He's, uh, a medicine man who lives out in the Glades. Or at least he used to be a medicine man. Now he's just a crazy old man. I mean, I've never met him, but that's what these guys tell me. That he's crazy. That—"

"Stop beating around the bush, boy," Farrel barked. Identical bright pink patches of agitation bloomed in his cheeks. "What medicine man and where does he live and what do these acquaintances of yours trade with him? C'mon, let's have it. Let's have all of it."

Billy looked scared now. "He's supposedly Miami Tommy, but that's gotta be bullshit. It couldn't be him. . . ."

"I'm not interested in why you think it's bullshit. Where's he live?"

"I don't know exactly. But these poachers said it's somewhere north, off the waterway. They trade kerosene and jeans and shit for 'gator skins, deer hides, like that."

"All that from one old medicine man?"

"I guess so."

"You *guess* so?" Farrel laughed. "C'mon, boy. If this medicine man is Miami Tommy, he'd be nearly as old as the Glades. How's a man that old catching 'gators and hunting down deer? You got any ideas about that?"

Billy looked as if he were hoping the floor would open up and swallow him. "I don't know."

"You don't know or you aren't saying?" Benson asked.

"Hey, man, I'm just relating some conversations, okay?" The Indian's eyes blazed. "According to these dudes, the old Indian lives in a settlement of chickees on a lagoon somewhere off the waterway. They say he lives there with some white people."

"With the clan?" Farrel prodded. "Is that what they're saying?"

Billy shifted his weight from one foot to the other and looked down at the floor. "Yeah. And I know that's gotta be bullshit, Joe, because the clan doesn't exist, except in tales and in George's head."

Benson grinned. "C'mon. You're going to meet someone, Billy. And I'm going to tell you exactly what to say to her."

II

1.

QUIN CRAWLED INTO a barrier of tall weeds that lined the shore and collapsed, her breath erupting from her chest in short, hot bursts that she tried to stifle.

Some of the crazies were nearby, trampling through the drizzle and the brush. The light from their lanterns swept across the tips of the weeds and bled down between the blades. It seemed she could feel the heat of that light against the backs of her legs and the soles of her bare feet. It cradled the base of her skull like hands.

Ha-ha, Quin, whispered the wind. *They're gonna get-cha*.

A couple of them passed within a foot of where she lay, so close she heard them breathing. One of them said: "This happens when you bring outsiders. Pa shoulda killed 'em."

"They's Wes's. He couldn't."

"I woulda killed them."

The other man laughed. "That's why you ain't in line to head the band."

"Wes ain't in line, even if he thinks he is. Pa'll head it when Tommy's gone."

"Tommy ain't goin nowhere."

And neither was she.

They moved on past her but were still too close for her to get up, to move. Quin squeezed her eyes shut and started bargaining with whomever might be listening— God, saints, dead Mormons with clout, it didn't matter. If she survived this, she would—what? Just what would she do? Sell the agency and give all the money to charity? Join the Moonies? Go to church? Move to India to work with Mother Teresa?

She would try to be a better person.

It wasn't much, but it was the best she could do.

And just what do you mean by better, Quin? asked the voice of the Glades.

Better meant no lies, not even white ones, to clients she didn't like. It meant more tolerance toward people. It meant forgiving.

Forgiving who?

Lydia. If she was still alive.

And? whispered the voice.

She went through a mental list of people against whom she'd held grudges, sometimes for years, and forgave them all. Forgave them again and again. But the voice was persistent. It kept saying, *Who else? Who else?*

McCleary. Okay, she would forgive McCleary for sleeping with Callahan. For forgetting her. For moving out of the house. She would forgive him for every bloody thing he'd ever done to her, both real and imagined. But not right now.

To forgive him now, before she knew whether she was going to survive, to get out of here, would be to surrender just as she had in the past.

They're gonna getcha, the wind cackled again.

"Let's check them weeds," called one of the two voices she'd heard minutes ago.

Quin dug her toes into the wet soil, pressed the heels of her hands down, and inched backward, toward the water. She didn't know what the hell she was going to do when she got there; the lagoon was thick with canoes. But she couldn't stay where she was, either.

I woulda killed them.

The two men bulldozed into the weeds. She could see the glow of their lanterns. It sounded like one of them had a machete and was hacking off the tops of the weeds as he moved. She crawled back faster, as fast as she dared.

Her blouse hiked up, bunching beneath her, and her bare belly scraped through weeds, across twigs and pebbles. Mud pushed up under her fingernails. Something wet and slippery slithered across the bottom of her foot, something living, a slug, a worm, a reptile. She kicked it away with her other foot, twisting her body right, and kept sliding down, down toward the water. The men's voices, drawing steadily closer, were punctuated by the *whack, whack* of the machete.

Water rose up around her ankles. Her calves. Her knees. *Whack*, sang the machete. *Whack, whack*. Thunder exploded across the lagoon and lightning blazed blue through the trees. There, three feet from her, was one of the men, frozen like a deer, his dark figure looming above the tall weeds.

He sees me.

"I seen something!" he shouted.

A floodgate opened inside her, pouring adrenaline through her muscles, her blood, her very bones. She shot to her feet, stumbled through the last strip of weeds, and hit the water. She swam a frantic, uneven breaststroke just beneath the surface and knew that, from shore, she was probably a cinch to track. But when she tried to go deeper, weeds stroked her cheeks and curled insidiously around her hands, arms, and feet.

Too shallow. Too close to shore. She could see the luster from the lanterns riding the surface of the water, a glowing oil slick, and heard splashes around her. She came up for air, rain pelting her face, took a quick look around, and wished she hadn't.

Dugouts were closing in on her—two at the front, one from the right side, another behind her. To her left, where the shore was, a man swam toward her, arm over arm, his feet kicking up a storm. Lights struck her in the face and she dived again, shooting down into the weeds, and swam toward what she hoped was the space between two of the canoes.

But her fatigue, the things in the pockets of her windbreaker, her wet clothes, slowed her down, and when she came up for air again, she realized she'd miscalculated how far she'd gone. She was dead center in a tight circle of dugouts. A bright, white light impaled her like a fish, something whizzed past her head—*An arrow? A spear?*—someone shouted, and she ducked under again and headed for the bottom of the lagoon, the light pursuing her.

The muscles in her arms shrieked for a respite, her legs had turned to wood, her eyes burned from the salt in the water, her lungs clamored for oxygen. She knew she wasn't going to make it—*Make it where, Quin?* laughed the voice of the Glades—and a heartbeat later someone grabbed her ankles. She kicked, she twisted, she flung herself around and clawed at the man's face. But he locked his arms at her waist, trapping her own arms under them, paralyzing her as he swam toward the surface, straight into the light.

2.

Opal was stretched out on her back on the couch, snoring. One arm was flung behind her head, the other was against her waist, the hand curled into a tight fist. Her mouth was slightly open. She was uglier asleep, Benson thought, than when she was awake, and the snake tattoo on her cheek seemed even more bizarre.

"Time for the lady to split?" asked the ranger who'd been guarding her.

"Not just yet," Benson replied. "Wake her up."

The man made a face. "Shit, so much for the peace and quiet." He leaned over Opal and shook her. "Hey, you got visitors."

She muttered something that sounded like "Mofo."

"Nice mouth," Benson said. "Throw that pitcher of water on her. The one with the ice cubes in it."

There was no pitcher of water in the room, but Opal didn't know that. Her eyes snapped open, tiny and black. "You ain't tossin shit on me, copper boy." She sat up, smoothing her hands over her wrinkled shirt, her jeans. Her gaze flickered from Benson to Farrel to Billy and back to Benson again. "We leavin?"

"It's her," said Billy.

"You're sure?" Benson asked.

"Yeah. I'd know her anywhere," Billy replied, following the script Benson had given him. "Last time I traded with Tommy, I saw her around."

Opal's wrinkled forehead wrinkled even more. "That's shit you's sayin. Ain't never seen you before."

"What'd you trade with him?" Farrel asked.

"A couple of bows, some kerosene, some canned food."

Farrel: "And where'd this trade take place?"

240

Billy: "Up north along the waterway and then east a ways."

Benson: "Could you find the place again?"

Billy: "Sure thing. There're some chickees in a lagoon. Real well hidden, but yeah, I could find it again."

Opal: "You's lyin, boy."

Benson: "And you're sure you saw this woman when you were trading with the old man?"

Billy: "Absolutely. She carried a bow. She was with a tall, skinny dude."

Opal: "You ain't gonna find shit, boy, 'cause there ain't nothin to find."

Benson, feeling good for the first time since Stevie Ibson had walked into his office, smiled at Opal. "I think your people are about to join the world, Opal."

Her knuckles were white from gripping the armrest so hard, her face was bright pink, her eyes had shrunk to black dots in her cheeks. "He's lyin!" she shrieked, and flew off the couch toward him, fingers hooked into claws and aimed at Billy's face. The ranger caught her, restrained her, but it didn't shut her up. "It's west not east, and it's off Lostmans Five Bay, not—"

Her mouth clamped shut, her head snapped toward Benson, her eyes bulged until he thought they were going to pop out from their sockets. "You tricked me." The words were a deadly hiss.

"You got it, lady."

Her face squashed up as she struggled to free herself from the ranger. She grunted, swore, tried to bite him. But he squeezed hard at her waist and lifted her. Her feet were still kicking impotently at the air as they rose from the floor. He tossed her onto the couch, grabbed her wrist, and cuffed it to the armrest in seconds flat.

"Good thing she didn't bite you. No telling what kind of diseases she carries," Farrel remarked drolly.

"Rabies, for one." Billy grinned at her, then glanced at Benson. "You ready to roll?"

Opal's animal sounds pursued them into the hall.

3.

The canoe twisted through a maze of islands, mangroves, and fields of saw grass, moving sometimes west,

241

sometimes east, then north again along the Wilderness Waterway. The rain wasn't a deluge yet, but McCleary guessed it wouldn't be long, if the lightning ahead was any indication.

It crackled through the thunderheads in a dazzling display of energy and raw power, filling the clouds with blue and silver neon. Occasionally, a bolt shot out and cut a jagged, horizontal path across the treetops, making the sky look as if a chunk had been bitten out of it by a pack of wild dogs.

When there was no lightning to watch, when they were sealed up inside the darkness and the rain, McCleary's anxiety had a field day. It churned through the tight, crowded space inside him, knocking loose old memories of marital transgressions: small betrayals that burned with the brightness of white lies, things said that could not be taken back, events that should never have happened. The man that he had been was holding up a mirror to the man he had become, and within these juxtaposed reflections, he glimpsed the various men he might become *if* . . .

If Quin were dead.

If Quin were alive.

If they reconciled.

If they didn't reconcile.

If they didn't find Snake Mound.

If he got through this endless night.

If he didn't get through it.

With each possibility, there was a different future version of himself. It was as if his chromosomes were doing what his memories had done—shifting around, changing shape, rearranging themselves. Before the end of the night, he would dissolve as surely as aspirin in water or he would solidify again.

"McCleary?"

"Yeah?"

"Have you slept in the last three days?"

"Some."

"How much?"

He thought about it. "A few hours a night, I guess. Why?"

"If you're tired, catch some sleep now."

In the canoe. In the rain. Again. No thanks, he thought. "We'll make better time if I'm paddling, too."

"In that case, I think we should first check out the village closest to the Mound. It'll give us some idea about what's going on. If I'm right—and if your wife is still alive—nothing will be happening at the Mound before midnight. That's when their ceremonies always started."

"Twenty-five years ago, you mean."

"Like I said, McCleary, they're slow to change. And their ceremonies will be the last thing to change."

"How far is this place from the Mound?"

"Depends on the route you take."

McCleary asked how many people were in the band; George didn't know. He'd only seen two settlements and that was about six years ago. Both had far fewer chickees than the place where he'd lived as a boy, but that could mean that families were doubling up until more chickees could be built.

"Before my mother and I were exiled, there were forty-six adults and ten children under twelve. In the band, you go through a series of initiation tests when you're twelve and if you pass them, you're then considered an adult. But you don't have a vote in band affairs until you've passed a final test at seventeen, where you track down and kill the creature of your choice." He paused. "That 'creature' is often human."

"Human?"

"Sometimes it's a member of the band who's done something unforgivable, like take another man's woman. Sometimes it's an outsider. Twice that I know of, it was a band woman who'd given birth to too many deformed children. It's the way."

"Is their punishment for someone who's killed a member of the band always death?"

"Ultimately, yes."

McCleary heard the *but* in his voice. "What kind of death?"

That secretive, evasive tone crept into his voice again. "It depends. There're different punishments for men and women."

"Such as?"

"You don't want to know, McCleary."

He realized it was true.

4.

Chickee, water, canoe, chickee: she'd come full circle, for what it was worth.

Quin stood in the middle of a room in another chickee, water puddled at her feet, arms hugged against her. They'd taken the windbreaker but left her in her wet clothes, and now she was drenched and cold and weary beyond belief. She wanted nothing more than to sit down and close her eyes and wait for whatever was going to happen next. But she was afraid any movement at all would spook Ticker, who was already jumpy, and he'd let loose the arrow he'd had trained on her for the last ten minutes. Neither he nor Josie would tell her whether they'd caught Lydia or what they'd done with her if they had.

"C'mon, woman," he said to Josie. "Hurry up."

"Yeah, yeah." She was jerking articles of clothing from a Styrofoam cooler as though they were tricks in a magician's hat. Her shotgun was on the floor near her feet. "Okay, I got somethin." She turned, a bundle of clothes in her arms, and tossed them at Quin. "Strip them wet things off and put on that stuff there."

Quin glanced at the clothes at her feet, then looked up. Ticker smirked. The lambent light painted one side of his face a pale gold, illuminating the rapid tic at the corner of his mouth and the bandage around his arm, where her knife had pierced it. Shadows claimed the other side and made black hollows of his eyes. "You not hearin so well? She told you to strip."

Josie laughed; the space of her missing tooth gaped in her mouth. "You know how them outsider women are, Ticker. Modest and all. She don't want you watchin. Go on outside."

"Tommy said to stay. He said you and me was s'posed to guard her."

"I can do it. You go on now."

Ticker planted his feet firmly against the wooden floor, the bow slack now as he and Josie glared at each other. Quin sensed something going on here besides sibling

244

competition for the upper hand, something that involved the old man. But her situation was already so bad, she didn't think this little spat was going to change anything. She waited, the cold, sharp blade of fear twisting in her gut.

"I'm s'posed to stay," Ticker said again.

Josie exploded with laughter. "You thinkin you can git it up if you sees her naked, Ticker?"

His face turned to stone; the blade in Quin's gut slipped in a little deeper. "Stop sayin shit like that."

"It's true, ain't it." She snickered and shook her head. "And if you git it up, what then, Tick? You ain't allowed to touch her. Only Wes can say who touches her."

"And no one's listenin to him." Ticker smirked again. "The rules say—"

"You goin against Tommy?"

Something changed in Josie's face; shadows snaked through her strange, luminous eyes. When she spoke, her tone was sharp, deliberate. "Put on them clothes."

Ticker's smile was slow, triumphant, and Josie saw it. "And don't worry none about him," she added, jerking a thumb toward Ticker. "He don't know tit from twat."

"I'm gonna tell Pa what you said."

"Good. Tell Pa. And he'll laugh. C'mon, Miss Bones, hurry up." She stepped in front of Quin, her back to Ticker, blocking his view. Her eyes telegraphed messages Quin couldn't decipher. "Here, I'll help you. Them fingers are kinda stiff, huh."

"Get outta the way, Josie."

"I'm helpin her."

Over Josie's shoulder, Quin saw Ticker move to the left. Josie also moved left. Quin quickly peeled off her blouse, grabbed the cotton one off the floor, pulled it on. She sensed a change in the dynamics among the three of them, but didn't allow herself to define it, to qualify it.

"I'm gonna tell Tommy what you done."

"I ain't done nothin. We gotta leave soon. I'm just hurryin things along, Tick, just hurrying things along."

As Quin was zipping up the jeans, the door opened and the old man shuffled in with the rain and the wind. Josie turned quickly, like a child who knew she'd done something wrong and realized she probably wasn't going to get away with it. Tommy—old but not stupid, Quin reminded herself—looked at each of them, looked slowly and carefully. He stepped into the light and Quin saw the straw basket on his arm. Leeches. The blade in her gut turned hot.

"Is she ready?" the old man asked.

"Yeah," Josie replied.

"Josie said things 'bout me," Ticker whined.

"Josie's always saying things about you." Tommy shook the rain from his white hair. "Bring her into the front room."

He's going to put leeches on me.

"She ain't just Wes's, right, Tommy?"

"What do you mean, boy?"

"Wes ain't got the only say 'bout who touches her, right?"

"You want to touch her, son? Even though she's all bones?"

Ticker rubbed his jaw, considering this, then wrinkled his nose as though he'd smelled something malodorous and shrugged. "I guess not."

"Bring her into the next room."

Josie picked up her shotgun; her hand closed around Quin's arm. "You heard the man. Move."

"Why? What're we going in there for?" She looked at Josie as she said it, hoping to see sympathy, something that would indicate she was on Quin's side. But her face was hard and flat, and it was Ticker, not Josie, who answered her.

"For the purge. It don't hurt." Then he laughed. "Not much."

Josie gave him a dirty look and Ticker laughed again. He poked the arrow at the air in front of Quin's face; she rocked back away from him. "It only hurt so much you wish you was dead," he said softly, and grabbed her other arm, jerking her forward. "Git goin."

5.

As they approached Third Bay, the thunderheads seemed to be almost directly overhead and the rain was uneven. Sometimes it was barely more than a soft weeping, a residue, as though the clouds were practically dried

246

up. But other times it fell in quick, violent bursts that made the canoe pitch and roll and sent McCleary or George or both of them scrambling to keep the supplies covered.

The bursts never lasted for more than fifteen or twenty minutes, but it was impossible to make much headway through them and it slowed them down considerably. During one lull, George explained that from here the waterway wandered west through the bay, then drifted lazily north. "There's a shortcut we could take. We won't be able to use the outboard, but we'd still save some time. It veers off the waterway and through an area where there're a lot of 'gators. But I'm willing to risk it if you are."

"What do you mean by a *lot* of 'gators?"

"It's a breeding ground."

Great. "How much time are we talking about saving?"

"At the rate we've been moving, at least an hour. The village is probably another hour beyond it. It's ten now."

In other words, McCleary thought, if they didn't take the shortcut, they'd be cutting the midnight deadline for Snake Mound a little too close. "Okay, let's do it."

6.

Her purge apparently had nothing to do with leeches.

But from the look of things, it involved a variety of rather ordinary objects, which, in the wrong hands—and these were definitely the wrong hands—could be lethal. A straight-edged razor, a hammer, a pair of scissors, a wrench, a pliers, a couple of heavy-duty sewing needles, a dozen or more long, thin wooden splinters, a Bic lighter, a container of lighter fluid, a hunting knife. At the end of the line was another box, face up. And because she couldn't see what, if anything, it contained, it frightened her more than all of the other items combined.

"Tie her arms to the chair," the old man said.

Ticker grinned. "Yessuh." He picked up two lengths of rope from the far side of the basket.

"Wes oughta be here," Josie said, biting at her lower lip as she watched. Her expression told Quin more about what was going to happen than she cared to know. "She's Wes's, Tommy. The rules say—"

"I make the rules," Tommy snapped, and picked up one of the splinters.

"You didn't make the first rules. They existed before you joined the band. No one can change 'em."

"Shut up," Ticker told her, squashing Quin's arm against the armrest as he lashed rope around it.

"Josie, Josie, Josie." The old man's voice was as smooth and slippery as butter; he touched the edge of his thumb to the tip of the splinter and drew a drop of blood. "I *am* the rules, don't you know that by now?" He smiled at Quin, a warm, perfectly crazy smile that seemed to cut the lower half of his face away from the rest of it. "Miss Bones knows it, don't you, dear?"

His voice seemed to speak to some unreachable place inside her. She pressed back into the chair as the old man held the splinter up close to her face. He allowed her time, too much time, to see how sharp the ends were, to contemplate the various ways this simple object could inflict pain.

A bead of sweat rolled down the side of her face.

"The purging devices are numerous, and all have a rather singular beauty, don't you think?" He set the splinter down and picked up the hammer. Quin stared at it as he tapped the heavy end against his palm. "One blow from this against the end of the nose and the cartilage is driven up into the brain. Very effective. But also usually lethal." He set the hammer down, studied his neat row of objects, and reached for the straight-edged razor.

"This has long been one of my favorites." He swished the razor through the air; it whispered past the tip of her nose, light glinting against the shiny metal. "I used this on one of our adulterous women." He looked over at Josie, who was standing very still, watching. "That was long before you were born. The woman's no longer with us. She and her young son chose to be exiled." Now his gaze shifted back to Quin. "In those days, exile had a price. Now people just leave when they feel like it. It's much too easy. I think people should pay for what they want, don't you, my dear?"

He touched the razor to her throat but exerted no pressure. It just rested there, cold and sharp, and he smiled—that slow, seething, crazy smile.

The light licked at the sides of his face and coiled inside his dark eyes. "In those days, the punishment for adultery was quite specific."

He dug his fingers into her wet hair and jerked her head back. Her awareness shrank to the size of a pea; the only things that existed were his eyes and her heart falling through her chest. She expected last-minute flashes of her life, a rush of memories, faces, things that would never be. She waited for the hot lick of pain across her throat. Instead, he pulled on the clump of hair he clutched, pulled so hard it felt as if he were yanking it out by the roots, then sliced the razor through it.

Hair fell into her lap. A flurry of hair.

He grabbed another bunch, chopped it off, and pretty soon her wet umber hair was everywhere. It stuck to her jeans and her arms and the front of her shirt. It littered the floor. It curled against the surface of the wooden boxes like commas, like question marks. It slipped down the back of her shirt and made her neck itch. It caught on her lips, her cheeks, her lashes. Tears marched down her face, but she didn't know if she was crying from relief or rage or something else.

Ticker was laughing, Josie just stood there with her hands over her mouth, and the old man was talking in that same steady voice, telling her about the adulteress. ". . . since a woman's hair is one of her greatest vanities, this is the perfect punishment for an adulteress, don't you think? And, of course, if you have someone's hair, it can be used to create a very powerful magic against them. Helen of Troy knew it when she cut off Samson's hair. Voodoo shamans know it. Santeros know it. Does it surprise you that a simple ex–Seminole medicine man should know about such things?" He laughed, and the razor went *whack, whack,* sounding very much as the machete had earlier.

"Ticker, get me her wet clothes." The old man set the razor aside and brushed some of the hair into a neat little pile on the surface of the box. When Ticker had brought over her clothes, he picked up the blouse and, with the razor, sliced off a patch of fabric in the front. "Now we add this . . ." He dropped the square of fabric on top of the hair and told them all how privileged they were to witness the making of magic.

Wind gasped through the open windows. It caused the lanterns to hiss and spit, blew loose hair across the boxes and the floor, lifted the swatch of fabric. The old man slapped his hand down over it, smoothed it out with his thin, nimble fingers so it covered the pile of hair, then weighted it with the wrench.

Now he turned back to his tools, hemmed and hawed, then picked up one of the needles. Before Quin had time to think about what ingenious way he might inflict pain with it, he pricked her index finger and squeezed several drops of blood onto the pile. "The best magic always demands a little blood." He smiled. "And a little pain," he added, and picked up the pliers. He snapped them open and shut quickly, like castanets, then moved toward her again.

Some part of her knew what he had in mind but didn't quite believe it. There were, after all, levels of belief to all acts of horror. The Jew who denied that the shower would expel gas instead of water, the death-row inmate who believed his eleventh-hour appeal would come through before the switch was pulled, the lone jogger who thought the gang of thugs ahead wouldn't harm her.

Not until he took her hand and trapped her thumb between his own thumb and index finger did she begin to believe it. She tried to pull her hand away, but between the ropes and his grip on her hand she didn't have a prayer. "Please," she rasped as he opened the pliers. "Jesus, please don't. I didn't kill Judd. I didn't do anything."

"But Judd is dead, isn't he." The old man touched the pliers to the tip of her thumbnail.

She heard herself explaining, tripping over her own words as her eyes flew to Josie, who'd turned absolutely white, and then to the old man, who was smiling, and then to Ticker, whose smirk whispered, *Do it, do it.*

Then the pliers closed over her thumbnail and the old man jerked his hand to the right, tearing the nail off to the quick.

III

I HEARD HER *scream. Only a deaf man coulda missed it.*

I was over near Pa's chickee, loading up a canoe, and that scream raced out through the dark, over the water, through the rain, and yeah, I knowed what that old fucker had gone and done. Hell, I could feel *it, almost like she was one of our own.*

I threw down the rest of the shit I was holding and started to climb down the ladder to the dugout when Pa's head poked over the side.

"Don't," he said.

"She's mine."

"No, she ain't. For tonight, she's his." He crouched down, the rain slapping his head and streaming down his face. He looked old right then, near as old as Tommy, and I could see what the last years had done to him. Pa was the one the band went to when things wasn't going the way they should. He was the one who tried to set things right. He was the one who decided which newborns was going to live or die. Pa. Not Tommy. The old man supposedly had magic, but Pa had brains. Pa also had fear and love for the old man and that made him weak.

"We need what he can do, Wes," he said. "And he'll do right by us. He's got to and he knows it. And after tonight it'll be different. You'll see. We'll be havin more food, more tradin, more children, more. Believe me, boy. Let it be. And after tonight, if Opal ain't come back, we'll go lookin for her. We'll forget the rules and go look for her. You got my word on that, Wes."

It was lies, but I didn't know that then. And because he was Pa, I listened and I believed and I climbed back up onto the porch, that scream still living in my head.

IV

1.

THE SHORTCUT WAS a channel a mile and a half long and about five feet wide, with a ceiling of branches maybe eight inches above their heads. It cut between two mangroves that had probably been joined at one time, and much of it was thick with weeds and hyacinth.

George turned off the motor and tipped it back out of the water as they entered the passage. Branches swung into their faces like rambunctious chimpanzees. The air exploded with the deafening chir of insects, hundreds of insects, perhaps thousands. George sprayed repellent into the air and it helped, but only until they'd paddled beyond it. Then the insects dived in again, ravenous, relentless.

They were like armed sentries at the entrance to some mythical, forbidden place, the first line of defense in a boobytrap of more defenses. Even the texture of the air here seemed different. It was slick, thick, almost greasy with the extreme humidity, and suddenly, all McCleary wanted was to get through here as quickly as possible. He paddled harder, faster. Weeds and grass clawed at the sides of the canoe and whipped around the end of his paddle.

"Check the width of the channel ahead, Mike."

He turned on his flashlight. Burning from the mangroves to his left were a pair of 'gator eyes, luminous red gems fixed in all that blackness as though marking its very center. When the beam skimmed past them, he thought he could still detect an afterimage of those eyes, a ghost light, motionless, watching. Four feet later, he saw another pair of eyes. And then another and another and another, dozens upon dozens of the soft, lustrous orbs.

His fear turned to a hard, pulsing lump just under his jawbone. "Shit, this place is *infested*," McCleary whispered, switching off the light.

"There're more on the other side."

He flashed the beam on the mangroves to his right. The little globes were everywhere, bright as Christmas lights, multiplying like bacteria. McCleary realized that the only thing he knew about alligators came from the press: the 'gator in a Fort Lauderdale lake that snapped an arm off a five-year-old child; the eighteen-footer in a Davie canal that turned a cocker spaniel into chopped liver; the hungry 'gator that came ashore at a lake in Stuart, just up the coast, and chased a sunbather who escaped only because she hung a sharp left and 'gators had trouble negotiating turns on land.

Fact number one: 'gators moved faster in a straight line when on land.

Amazing what trivia the mind tossed up when faced with the unimaginable.

And this particular fact wasn't going to do him much good, since he wasn't on land. "What're we going to do if they all decide to take a swim at the same time, George?"

"We'll be fine as long as we don't make any sudden moves."

As long as. If. But. Unless. So many qualifiers and conditions. "But just suppose . . ."

"They'll only attack if they're hungry or provoked or if people have been feeding them. With all the rain, there've been plenty of fish, so they're not going to be hungry, and no serious canoeist would feed a 'gator."

But what about the unserious canoeists?

"Turn off the light."

He did. The darkness swam around them again.

They paddled slowly, evenly. The sounds they made were surely too benign to offend, weren't they? And the 'gators weren't hungry, right? And no *serious* canoeist would feed a 'gator, so what could there possibly be to worry about?

Nothing. Nothing except that splash off to his left and

that second splash to his right and a third splash around eleven o'clock. The 'gators were swimming. Yes siree, the unthinkable was about to happen. Now what, George?

"Fuck," George whispered.

"Pass me a gun."

"No. You'd never get them in the dark and gunshots might just throw them into a frenzy. Take this." George thrust one of the cans of gasoline into his hands as McCleary turned. "Splatter it around the front and sides. They won't swim through it."

More splashes.

McCleary spun the cap on the can and fumes poured out of it, fumes so thick that if he even *thought* fire this shit would go up in his face. He splashed it around the front of the canoe, heard a 'gator uncomfortably close on his left, and splashed gas in that direction, too. The reptile swept away, its powerful tail kicking up a current strong enough to rock the canoe.

And then suddenly it doubled back. McCleary heard its tail slapping the water as it turned, heard water parting as it swam furiously toward the canoe—and rammed it.

The canoe pitched savagely to the right, throwing McCleary off balance and nearly hurling him and their supplies into the water. George shouted, "Light a match to it!" The echo of his voice bounced like a jai alai ball against the mangroves.

Before McCleary could steady the can of gas between his feet so he could look for the matches, a second 'gator struck them from the right, dived, and tried to come up beneath them. It lifted the bow high enough to catapult McCleary's stomach into his throat, then slammed its tail against the aluminum side. The vibration seared through the soles of his shoes like an electrical shock and sped up his spine, a chill of death.

"*Hurry!*" George yelled.

He jerked on the outboard's cord again and again, but the engine didn't catch. Another 'gator slammed into the side of the canoe. McCleary twisted the cap on the can, jammed it between his feet, dug desperately in his poncho for matches. A white desert filled McCleary's head and Death galloped across it on a black horse, whipping

254

the reins from one side of the horse's neck to the other. McCleary found the matchbook and tore off two matches. They were damp and disintegrated in his hands. Death roared with laughter and his horse galloped faster, faster, its hooves kicking up clouds of dust. McCleary fumbled for more matches, struck them, and felt a rush of triumph when they flared. He tossed them overboard, but they went out before they hit the water. Death was now nearly hysterical with glee, the rictus of his grotesque smile filling McCleary's inner vision like a black moon, a decaying moon, the last moon.

McCleary lit the whole matchbook and dropped it over the side. The gasoline caught with a loud *swoosh!* Fire raced across the surface of the water, a deadly missile seeking targets that lay beyond its center. It leaped spots where the gas hadn't reached and turned the inside of this tunnel of leaves and branches a bright Halloween orange. McCleary grabbed the paddle, thrust it into the water.

There were 'gators everywhere, the ridges of their primeval snouts burning with light, their eyes reflecting the flames like tiny mirrors. And all of them seemed to take flight at once, their mighty tails shooting them through the blazing water like torpedoes. They headed for the mangroves. They dived. They churned wakes around the canoe that nearly tipped it.

"Get that engine cranked up!" McCleary shouted, paddling furiously. But it wasn't fast enough. The fire had found pockets of leaves and branches that weren't damp enough to make them impervious to the heat, and pretty soon flames hissed and crackled overhead. Embers rained down on them.

A flaming branch fell into the canoe. He thought of the gas he might have spilled, imagined the can igniting, saw himself flailing in the burning strait. He flung himself forward, hurled the branch over the side, and stomped out the sparks on the floor of the canoe. Only later would he discover the burns on his palms.

The engine suddenly caught and the canoe lurched forward. Moments later, it burst free of the tunnel, the flames, and raced out into the blessed rain, into air that smelled clean and rich again, into a darkness that seemed to welcome them. Death's crackle echoed in his head, then died to a whisper, a faint memory of desert and dust.

2.

Quin knew where she was. She knew what had happened. She knew she would now be taken someplace else. But she didn't know what would happen then, in this other place. And no one was telling.

She stood behind a curtain of rain, under the awning of the chickee's porch, wondering where Lydia was, fighting the effects of whatever the old man had forced her to drink. A downer of some kind. It hadn't made her drowsy but had turned her limbs to rubber and her brain to mush. She had trouble following a thought to completion, couldn't quite connect people's words when they spoke, but at least the drug had reduced the pain in her thumbs to a dull throb.

Josie's hand was on her arm, gripping it. Ticker had just climbed down the ladder and was doing something in the canoe bobbing in the water below. She didn't know where the old man had gone. It was enough that he was no longer near her, doing things to her, speaking to her in that soft, crazy voice.

Around her, dozens of lanterns winked in the rain, telegraphing messages she wouldn't have been able to decipher even if she were straight. She could detect dark shapes moving about on other porches, moving past chickee windows, climbing down ladders to waiting canoes. An exodus was in progress. But why people were leaving or to where remained as inscrutable to her as the complexities of the old man's madness.

"Them thumbs still bleedin?" Josie asked.

"No." She didn't know for sure because she couldn't see her thumbs; Josie had wrapped them in strips of cloth. But she didn't feel like talking.

"Still hurtin?"

Quin looked at her, wondering if she was really as stupid ass he seemed to be. "Tear off your own goddamn thumbnails and then ask me that, Josie."

It was not the way you spoke to someone here—she'd learned that much—but she was beyond caring. She expected a blow to her face, her head, but it didn't come. Instead, Josie touched the side pocket of Quin's jeans and whispered something. It sounded garbled to Quin and she said, "What?" then watched Josie's lips as she spoke, trying to read them.

"You're goin to be needin that."

"Needing what?"

"What I put in your pocket."

Quin's hand moved toward her pocket, but Josie stopped her. She spoke softly, without looking at her. "Don't go touchin it. It's a key chain. It's got one of them fancy knives with lots of blades, includin one that'll fold out to 'bout six inches. There's a bitty light that looks like a ceegar, and one of them compasses.

"Ticker's goin to tie your hands once you're in the canoe, but I'll try to loosen 'em when he's not lookin. When you can git free, do it, and use the knife on whoever you have to. Then run like hell to the east, always east, for 'bout two miles. It's easy runnin, through trees. You'll git to this live oak with tons of moss hangin down from it. It's near a river and a dugout's hid there. Use it and go straight east"

Quin just stared at her.

"You understand everythin I jus' said, Bones?"

It was difficult to form words and Quin stuttered a couple of times, then said: "How do I know it isn't a trick?"

"You think I'd go and give you a knife if I was tryin to trick you?"

"You might."

"Well, it ain't no trick."

"Then why're you doing this?"

" 'Cause you and your friends was a mistake."

She'd been called a lot of things in her life, but never a mistake. "Wes's mistake, you mean."

"His and Opal's, yeah. But I ain't blamin them 'cause it was Tommy who told 'em to go back to that campsite. So it's *his* mistake, see. And he's made too many mistakes. There ain't goin to be nothin left of the band if he keeps makin mistakes."

Power, this was about power, Quin thought. "He's just one man. Get rid of him."

"Ain't that easy. Too many got the heebies 'bout him.

They's scared of his magic. But I don't think he's got no magic now. I think his magic's dried up. Thing is, the others got to see it that way, too.''

"Git 'er down here, Josie," shouted Ticker.

"Yeah, we're comin." More softly, she added: "Can you remember everything I jus' said, Bones?"

"Yes."

"You're sure? That stuff Tommy gave you really got a kick."

"I'm sure."

"This place is goin to be weird. You got to understand that."

It couldn't be any weirder than what had already happened. "Right."

"And you got to understand that if you don't use that knife, if you don't git out, they goin to kill you."

It didn't surprise her, but it wasn't a particularly encouraging thing to hear.

"And when we're gone from here, I ain't goin to be able to help you."

"Where's my friend?"

"Pa's got 'er. He used her the way Ticker wants to use you."

A shiver crawled through her.

"And there ain't nothin you can do for her, so don't even think 'bout it."

"Where're you taking me?"

"Snake Mound."

"Is Lydia going to be there?"

"Reckon so. That's the final place."

"What's going to happen there?"

"Lots of things. Whole band's goin, even the children. That's why I can't help you when we leave here."

"Hey, Josie," Ticker shouted again.

"Yeah, we're comin, jus' hold on." More softly, she added: "Ticker's the one you gotta watch out for. Now git goin, Bones. And remember. Do what you gotta do with that knife."

The final place, Quin thought as she started down the ladder. *Final*, as in *the final act* or *the final resting place*. F-i-n-a-l: end of the line. It couldn't get any clearer than that.

3.

It was a little over an hour shy of midnight when George announced that they were nearing the village and switched off the motor. From here on in, he said, it would be best to use only the penlights.

McCleary didn't sense anything different about this particular spot. The mangroves looked the same. The field of saw grass to their left was just as tall and eerie as any other field they'd passed. The rain here fell just as hard, the air was the same implacable black. But what had he expected? Markers? Neon signs? BAND HOTEL: CHEAP ROOMS, BREAKFAST INCLUDED, FIRST LEFT OFF LOSTMANS FIVE BAY.

They paddled a long time with saw grass on their left, the wind plucking those long, nasty leaves as though they were musical instruments. A harp, a guitar, a piano, a sitar, notes that sometimes created a voice that was hauntingly human, the sound of someone in pain. Other times, the voice of the wind wasn't human at all, but something animalistic and menacing, perhaps a warning.

The grass ended as suddenly as it had begun. They turned right and followed its edge across the width of Lostmans Five Bay. Now its voice was a sibilant whisper, sometimes gravelly, sometimes shrill, always eerie. McCleary wondered what stories the grass could tell if he understood the language. Would it tell him of the distant past, of the millennia before man? Would it spill tales of the Calusa Indians? The Spanish conquistadors? The Seminoles and the Miccosukees? Would it reveal the band's secrets? Their dark rituals? Would it tell him if Quin was still alive? And if the voice, like the grass, was timeless, could it tell him the future?

Was this going to end? How would it end? Tell me that.
But the voice fell silent and they paddled on.

4.

They entered a pass in the trees that was cloned from the dozens of other channels McCleary had traveled in the last three days. Mangroves on both sides, hyacinth floating on the dark waters, drooping overhangs as flabby as bellies. He didn't know how George could find his way here in daylight, much less at night in the rain, and realized he had not faltered even once since they'd left Abbot's. Maybe the Indian, in fact, had lied. Maybe, in fact, he'd been here a lot more recently than six years ago. Like maybe as recently as last week.

"Where's this lead?" McCleary asked.

"To the lagoon."

"You're sure?"

"Yes."

"I guess the Glades haven't changed much in six years."

Silence.

"Hey, George."

"I heard you the first time."

"So?"

He hesitated, then: "I *feel* them, dammit. I've been feeling them since we left Abbot's. At first it was just a little tickle. But it's gotten stronger. The closer we get, the stronger it is. It's like I can't shake them, okay? If I think left, then I get this tickle that says no, we should go right. It seems like once I made up my mind to try to find this place, the last thirty years never happened. Like I'm a kid again, hooked into them. Or them into me." He let out a soft, bitter laugh. "It's that feeling, Kin Dread, all over again, McCleary."

A chill burrowed through him. He knew what it was like to be connected like that, to feel as if you were inside another man's skin, buttoned up in his bones, seeing what he saw as though he were your dark brother, an evil twin. It had happened to him during the case that had brought Callahan back into his life, with a man who had killed for sport. He knew, and he didn't have the foggiest notion what to say to George, so he said nothing at all.

A few minutes later, the canoe bumped up against the shore and they scrambled out. They removed what they needed of their supplies and put everything in a large backpack that George shrugged on. As McCleary pulled the canoe into the trees, he thought he saw George put something else in the pack. Extra ammo, probably. Or maybe another canteen of water.

They stashed the rest of the gear under the canoe. "Which way?" McCleary asked.

George stood absolutely still. His penlight was aimed at the ground and its meager beam cast a circle of light barely larger than a quarter. But it was enough for McCleary to see the blankness in his face, in his eyes. *He's checked out.*

Then George started to turn, a radar dish seeking a signal. "This way." He moved ahead, his gait jerky, uneven, almost as if he were being yanked along on a leash.

"Like I'm a kid again, hooked into them. Or them into me."

The obvious question, the one McCleary didn't ask, the one he couldn't bring himself to ask, was whether he could tell if the clan was hooked into *him*.

5.

At first, the darkness was so black and so wet, McCleary saw nothing at all, not even the veil of rain that moved across the lagoon. Hell, he couldn't even see the lagoon. But gradually, as his eyes became accustomed to this greater darkness, he identified shapes. Inside the shapes were flickering lights. Lanterns, he guessed. They helped define the shapes, broadening their parameters until they turned into chickees.

There were a baker's dozen of them, clustered like flowers along the border of the lagoon. Chickees with walls, roofs, windows, the works. That sense of unreality swept through him again. "They *are* the Glades," Abbot had said of the band. And this was where they lived. Here. In the heart of a landscape so forbidding, so foreign, an ordinary man would need magic to get him through a single night.

None of it vanished when he blinked. None of it dissolved. None of it melted together like objects in a Dali painting and became something else, something he understood, something that was within his grasp to understand. Of course not. The chickees remained after he'd blinked a dozen times, after he'd crawled closer to the water on his belly, even after he'd muttered something unintelligible, to which George replied, "Yeah, that's how it is, all right. And no one's home."

"How do you know?"

"The lanterns. They're in every third window. In their absence, the lanterns are supposedly the magical eyes that guard the place. It means they're at Snake Mound. It's the only time the entire village leaves at once. More than thirty people, I figure."

Short of massacre, McCleary thought, they didn't stand a ghost chance in hell against that many. "How're we supposed to thwart thirty people?"

"I don't know yet. Let's go take a look."

"Why?"

"Because I want to be sure I'm right about the Mound. If that's where they've gone, there'll be some sign in Tommy's chickee that your wife and friends have been there."

McCleary didn't like the idea of getting any closer to the village, much less stepping foot inside one of the chickees. But neither did he want to waste time getting to the Mound if the band and Quin weren't there.

"I'm right behind you," he said.

6.

The settlement was built in a half moon, with the pair of chickees in the middle of it closest to shore. That was where they would enter the village.

As McCleary followed George into the water, he felt vulnerable and exposed, and kept the Magnum tight in his hand and well above water. His eyes darted about. His senses had sharpened, shifted into a higher gear, a kind of hyperalertness. But he neither heard nor saw anyone.

They waded out to the chickees—a distance of no more than ten yards—through water that was rarely more than a foot deep. George was first up the ladder, scaling it with a simian deftness and speed, while McCleary remained at the foot, covering him. Just in case. When he vanished over the top, he whispered, "C'mon, it's empty up here," and McCleary climbed up after him.

Water dripped from the lower part of his jeans. Rain drummed soft and steady against the hood of his poncho; the wind blew rain into his face. But he was so accustomed to the rain, the wetness, he scarcely noticed it. These things were simply a fact of his existence now, like sore muscles, like wet feet, like the submerged rumble of anxiety that never entirely went away.

When he reached the top of the ladder, George wasn't waiting for him. He was scurrying along the wooden walkway that connected the chickees, crouched over like a soldier in the field who was expecting an assault of gunfire at any second. He looked like a man who had a definite destination in mind, who knew exactly where he was going and couldn't get there fast enough.

McCleary sprinted after him, his nerves strung like thin wires, the soles of his soggy running shoes slapping against the wet wood. He didn't like the feel of this place, didn't like being here, wanted nothing more than to get in and out as fast as possible. Suppose there was no evidence in the old man's chickee that Quin had been there? What then? And just what sort of evidence were they looking for?

Bodies.

Yes, of course.

He wouldn't think about that one.

He stepped into the last chickee. A lantern hissed and winked in an open window and George stood in a pool of its light, looking around slowly, very slowly, as if comparing the reality to whatever image existed in his mind.

"It's almost exactly like I remember it," he whispered. His left arm swung up; a finger pointed. "That's a *human* skull. It belongs to his wife's first husband." Now the arm swung down; the same finger pointed at a straw basket on the floor. "And if my memory's right, that basket has a jar in it that's filled with leeches." The arm flew left again. "That's the hammock of punishment. My mother spent three days there, McCleary. Three fucking days. She was never untied, never fed anything but water, and she was tortured—with leeches, snakes' fangs, burning splinters—each torture worse than the one before it. And the children were brought in to see it. To teach them the way, the goddamn *way*." He let out a harsh, terrible laugh. "Welcome to the inside of the crazy fucker's head, McCleary."

McCleary barely heard him. He was moving toward the makeshift kitchen, where the floor was blanketed in hair and clothes were puddled under the window. His throat closed as he scooped up a shirt from the floor. Blood pounded in his ears as he pressed his thumb over the monogrammed *Q* on the pocket. Even without the monogram he would have recognized this blue-and-white-checkered shirt anywhere. A swatch had been cut from the front.

He crouched and ran his fingers through the hair on the floor. Bits of it stuck to his fingertips. "Christ," he whispered.

"One of his favorite punishments for women is cutting off their hair," George said, coming up behind him. "He probably did this with a razor. It always happens when the woman is alive."

"And this?" McCleary held up the blouse, indicating the square of fabric that had been cut out. "What's this mean?"

"Something personal. For the magic."

McCleary dropped the blouse and knuckled his eyes, pressing hard on the lids, trying to blot out the insidious pictures that swam across the dark screen in his head in three-dimensional Technicolor. But his imagination had gone haywire and spared him nothing.

He didn't know how long he remained like that, crouched under the window, watching and listening to the movie in his skull. But suddenly he smelled gasoline and he glanced back. George was moving quickly, splashing gas from a coffee tin around the front room. He splattered it everywhere: the floor, the hammock, the straw basket, the walls. His long black hair stirred in the wind as he passed by a window. In the flickering light, he no longer seemed Westernized at all; he looked every inch the Indian he was.

"What the hell are you doing?" McCleary hissed, hurrying over and grabbing his arm.

George wrenched it back. Gas splashed over the side of the coffee tin. His black eyes pinned McCleary like a moth under glass. "What I should've done a long time ago."

"We didn't come here to burn the village."

"This isn't your battle, McCleary. Get out of here."

264

"They'll smell the fucking smoke, George. They'll know someone's here."

"I don't give a shit what they smell." George brushed past him on his singular mission, tossing gas here, there.

"Then tell me where the Mound is, George. I'll go alone." He spoke to the Indian's back.

"Just a few more minutes, that's all I need. I want to make sure this place is soaked in gas. Because of the rain. And then I'm going to soak the . . ."

"No."

". . . walkway outside and the . . ."

"No."

". . . chickee on the other side . . ."

McCleary grabbed him by the shoulder and George nearly lost his balance. The coffee tin slipped out of his hand and rolled across the gas-drenched floor. He went for his gun, but it was too late. McCleary's Magnum was up against his throat and now his hand tore George's weapon from the waistband of his jeans. When McCleary spoke, his voice was quiet. He did not need to raise it. "The. Mound. Tell. Me. How. To. Get. There."

"You can't find it without me. Don't be crazy, man. You won't be able to find it."

"You got to the count of five."

George told him.

McCleary removed the ammo from George's weapon and set it and the gun on the windowsill. Then he backed slowly away from him.

He was out the door before the Indian had moved, for all the difference it was going to make. The way to Snake Mound sounded like the directions to Never-Never Land.

PART FOUR

Never-Never Land

May 12

"There's something damn strange about it. Something you can never find out. It's something that's been here since the beginning. . . ."

—H. M. TOMLINSON

Snake Mound

EVER SINCE I was a boy, when my ma and others would tell us children that they was going to take us to the Mound if we wasn't good, the place spooked me.

At Snake Mound, nothing felt right—not the air you breathed, not the ground you walked on, not the trees that hid you. And it didn't make no difference whether the sun was shining or the moon was bright and ripe because light couldn't touch the badness there.

The Mound done existed long before the band. It went way back to the first Indians, who buried their dead here, buried them straight up like they was standing and still living. They covered the bodies with shells and vines and sand. Then later, other Indians found the Mound, almost like the voice of the dead called to them, leading them here. Them Indians boiled the flesh from their dead, tied the bones together, and buried them over the bones of their mothers and fathers and grandparents. If you dug deep enough here, dug way down under the centuries of mud and silt and decay, I reckon you'd find a village of bones. Maybe a whole city of bones. More bones than you'd ever want to see.

No one knows for sure when the real bad things started happening here. Some say they was going on right from the beginning, when the first Indians carried out punishments. Others say it started with the Spaniards, when they supposedly ambushed a bunch of Indians here during one of their burial ceremonies and killed every last one of them, killed them in bad, painful ways. They say the badness you felt was the spirits of them Indians. I didn't much care about why it felt bad. All I knew was that Snake Mound spooked me, plain and simple.

I was sitting with Pa and Lee-dee-uh in the circle. Lee-dee-uh had her legs pulled up against her real tight, her arms wrapped around her knees, her face buried in her arms. She was rocking back and forth and making funny sounds. She wasn't tied up; Pa didn't think she had sense enough to try to get away. But it didn't have nothing to do with sense; I could see that the one time she looked at me. She just wasn't there. It was like whoever Lee-dee-uh was had stepped out, leaving nothing but bones and hair and skin behind.

The rain was coming down real light through the trees, a rain that woulda been friendly anywhere else. But here it seemed cold and ugly, rain that was just teasing us, promising something worse. Much worse.

We was waiting for the drink to be passed around. The special lanterns was lit, the ones with the blue glass, and they throwed off that weird light that made me feel like I was underwater. It turned Tommy's white hair that same shade of blue them old ladies on Miami Beach dye their hair. But he didn't look old no more. He never did at the Mound. Josie once told me she believed Tommy got power from the Mound the way other people got it from food, and that was why he'd lived so long. Whatever was true, I believed what I seen with my own eyes: Tommy wasn't the same man when he was here.

He was moving around the circle with the bottle that held the drink, moving like a man twenty years younger, his blue hair blowing out behind him, sparkling with raindrops. Now and then he looked my way and them eyes seemed to be laughing at me and saying, Too bad, Wes. You lost.

It was true enough. As long as the others believed in his magic, he would lead the band. The thing to do was to show them he didn't have no more magic than me or anyone else. But not tonight. The timing had to be perfect, otherwise the band would turn on us. On Josie and me. And, deep inside, we wasn't ready for that yet. Maybe we never would be.

While I waited for the old man to get around to us with the drink, I watched Rusty and another one of Pa's boys getting the pit ready. When we wasn't using the pit, we put a huge sheet of plastic inside it, weighting it down *with rocks and logs so the dirt would stay packed. Then it was covered with another sheet of plastic that kept off the rain. But even so, there was always some digging that needed to be done, and since Rusty was so strong, he usually did it.*

Now Gimp, the oldest of the children, the boy with the limp, and his ma came up to the outside edge of the circle and stopped. They was carrying the gold box that had tiny holes punched in the top. Gimp said something to Tommy in the old tongue, stumbling a little with the words. It was only the second time he done this. Tommy answered, and a gap appeared in the circle as people moved aside. Gimp and his ma came through and set the box on the ground near the pit, then he went and stood by one side and his ma at the other.

This was the way Tommy had taught them. Tommy's way. Not the *way. There's a difference. Everyone except me and Josie seemed to have forgotten that, but I was going to make them remember. Somehow.*

The old man was in front of Pa now, holding out the bottle, murmuring words in the old tongue. Pa grasped the bottle with both hands and tipped it back to his mouth and drank deep. It was supposed to be a form of respect, a way of showing the old man that you believed. But, hell, Pa always drank deep and it didn't make no difference whether it was magic or firewater.

"Pull the woman's head back," Tommy said.

But Pa looked up at Tommy, Tommy with his wild blue hair blowing in the wind, and was brave enough to shake his head. "No. We let her be."

"You know the rules. Everyone in the circle has to drink."

"Not this time. She ain't all here."

In the blue light, the old man's grin was the badness of the Mound. "That's even better. Pull back her head, Pa."

Pa didn't look so sure of himself now. If Josie hadn't said her mind just then, he probably woulda jerked on Lee-dee-uh's hair, yanking her head back so Tommy could pour the drink down her throat.

"Outsiders never take the drink," Josie said. "That's a rule, too. Your rule, Tommy."

271

He turned his dark, terrible eyes on her. I could see her shrinking back, pulling in her shoulders, her spine curving in on itself like she was just going to fold up and let the wind carry her off. She was terrified of him. But Josie's got guts. "Your rule," she said again.

I could feel people go tight and hard inside themselves, waiting to see what he would do. I heard murmurs. If the old man backed down, the others would see it as weakness. But if he broke a rule he had made, then the others would think they could break rules, too, and that was worse. I felt these things going through Tommy's head, that he was thinking about what had happened earlier in Pa's chickee and trying to figure how things would be if he went one way or the other.

"Don't forget we got two outsiders," said Ticker, his eyes going to Miss Bones. She didn't look none too good, neither, her hair all short and weird. But at least she was all there. "And it's not like they's going to be leaving here once they drink, right?" he finished.

A few people nodded and I suddenly wanted to slam my fist in Ticker's stupid mouth.

"We'll vote on it," Tommy said.

"Good idea," someone agreed.

"Takes too long," said another voice.

"Makes no difference one way or the other if they's not leaving nohow," someone else said.

"Bet your ass it makes a difference," I said. "We're talkin 'bout rules."

Tommy hit me with one of those looks like Opal sometimes gave me. "A vote. Who among you thinks the outsider women should partake of the drink?"

His fancy words made me want to puke. Among you . . . partake.

A few hands went up. In the blue light, people's faces seemed thin and hungry, the kind of faces hoping for a magic powerful enough to put food on their tables.

"Who among you thinks the rule on outsiders and the drink should be followed?"

A lot of hands went up.

"Guess that's it," Pa said, smiling.

Tommy didn't look none too happy about it, but if he went against the majority vote, it wouldn't matter how much magic he had: No one would believe in him then. So he didn't say nothing more to Pa. He just stepped up to me and held out the bottle.

In his horrible eyes, I saw the blue light dancing hot and strong, a light that had once leaped from his eyes and into me like a knife. But no more. I wasn't no boy now. And I wasn't the same man who'd sat in his kitchen two mornings ago and let him drive splinters through my wrists.

"Your drink, Weston." His voice was soft and real formal, like you hear on them TV shows in the world where some guy in a suit says, "Pass the wine, please."

I took the bottle, but I sure as hell wasn't going to drink none of the stuff. I knew Josie wasn't neither. Once you drunk it, there was no going back because they was all inside your head then, all of them back to the beginning, nearly ninety years of the band. And somehow, Tommy or one of his people, even someone as stupid as Ticker, would see that Josie and me wasn't with them.

So I raised the bottle and opened my mouth to it. It was too dark for Tommy to see that I didn't swallow. But some of the liquid pooled under my tongue and stayed there until Tommy had moved on. Then I rubbed my jaw against my shoulder and let the gawddamned shit dribble out the side of my mouth and run down my raincoat. The taste was still there, of blood and spices and herbs, but not enough of it had gone down my throat to matter.

When I looked up again, Josie caught my eye.

She was smiling.

Final Paces

1.

THE AIRBOAT HAD gotten them farther than Benson had thought it would. And compared to the canoe they were in now, it had done it at the speed of light. But they were at least another hour from Lostmans Five Bay, Farrel said, and that was if the weather didn't get worse. If they didn't get lost. If there were no surprises.

In other words, if Murphy's Law didn't rear up and kick them in the ass.

"There's one other alternative," Billy Tiger said. They were at the edge of a mangrove, where Farrel had steered the canoe when the engine started to sputter. Now he held the flashlight as Billy cut through the weeds that had tangled around the outboard. "It's a small chance—real small—but maybe we ought to check it out. There're some dudes not too far from here who've got a seaplane."

"What dudes?" asked Farrel, ever suspicious.

"Dudes, okay, Joe? Just dudes. You go pulling ranger shit on them and they aren't even going to talk to us."

Poachers, Benson thought. But what the hell. "Would they fly in weather like this?"

"I figure they've flown in worse."

"These the same *dudes* you helped out when the airboat went sky-high, Billy?" Farrel again.

"What difference does it make, Joe?"

He swung the beam into Bill's face. "Just answer my goddamn question."

Billy winced and pushed the flashlight away. "Jesus, you don't need to blind me, man. Yeah, they're the same dudes, okay? They owe me. Not only that, they know exactly where these people live. They got a place not too far from here.''

A place. He made it sound like a cottage on the beach, Benson thought. ''Let's try it.''

''You aren't a cop then, Captain.''

''Fine. I sell socks. Insurance. Whatever.''

''Joe?'' Billy looked at Farrel, who rubbed his hands over his jeans.

''I hear you, boy.''

Billy dropped the engine back into the water. ''Give me your word.''

''Shit,'' he muttered.

''That's not your word.''

''Okay, okay, you got my word. Now move aside so I can get us out of here, boy.''

2.

When McCleary reached the shore, he glanced back toward the village. No sign of fire yet. George was probably dousing the walkway or the neighboring chickee right now. McCleary didn't doubt that the chickees were going to go up like so much tinder when George lit the gas. And once the rain hit the flames, the smoke would probably be visible in downtown Miami. But the wind was blowing away from him, and with any luck, it would hold at least until he reached the Mound.

He took off through the trees, his penlight penetrating the dark just enough so that he didn't stumble over his own feet. It didn't take him long to reach the canoe. He stopped to get a few things from the gear they'd stashed that might come in handy, including a pair of heavy-duty rubber boots George had packed.

He pulled them on over his running shoes and tucked his jeans inside them. They reached to his knees and felt as awkward as the old galoshes he'd worn as a kid during the rainy springs in Syracuse. But George had placed the boots up there with water and rifles in terms of important supplies, so McCleary kept them on.

He headed right, parallel to the channel, just as George had instructed. Compared to some of the places he'd trudged through in the last three days, the terrain here was as easy to negotiate as a shopping mall. But a quarter of a mile in, when he reached the fork in the channel, all of that changed.

Palmetto scrub brush and tremendous ferns burst from he ripe soil, their leaves hiding other smaller plants— cactuses, spider lilies, ferns. The ground was mushy and swarmed with insects that scurried over the tops of his boots on urgent business of their own.

His light seemed brighter here, but it was probably because the darkness seemed darker, bleeding from trees like new limbs, seeping upward from the ground with the slow movement of fog. Despite the warmth of the night, the place chilled him. It felt like Miami's Overtown had a decade ago, right before the race riots had broken out, when he was working the streets in a cruiser. There was a certain crackling tension in the air, as though it were infused with electrical static from an impending storm. It felt . . . well, bad, that was all. Just bad.

And it got worse as he stepped into the channel and waded the twenty yards across it, the muck on the bottom sucking at his boots like a vacuum cleaner. But the water level never rose above the tops of the boots, which was no small thing to count among blessings.

Once he was on the other side, he followed the channel for five or six minutes, until it started twisting left. Then he turned in place, a turn of ninety degrees, and shone the penlight around, hoping to spot a pair of buttonwood trees. *Bloody doubtful.* It was like trying to pick out a Toyota in a parking lot filled with Japanese cars. Everything looked the same.

"If you can't see the buttonwoods, go about fifteen paces straight forward from the water and look to your right," George had said.

Fine. Fifteen paces. Easy enough. He glanced right. No goddamn buttonwood trees.

McCleary retraced his steps and tried again, taking smaller strides this time. When he still didn't spot the buttonwoods, it crossed his mind that George might have lied just to get even. But the more he thought about this, the less probable it seemed. The Indian might be a flake when it came to the clan, but he wasn't a malicious liar.

He veered right and moved slowly, examining every tree. Fat trees and thin, tall trees and short, trees with

276

orchids sprouting from the branches, trees with flowers, trees blanketed in snails.

"The trunks of the buttonwoods are covered with snails."

McCleary let out a soft, triumphant laugh, stepped between the pair of trees, and pushed through the tangle of growth on the other side. For a few minutes, the brush was waist high and thick. Insects and frogs filled the wet, breezy darkness with incessant noises. Mosquitoes dive-bombed him. That feeling of *badness* persisted and changed, becoming something else, a sense of imbalance, a malaise of the spirit, a psychic dizziness.

It was as if he'd suddenly walked into another dimension or had slid sideways in time. Any minute now, a saber-toothed tiger would shriek from one of the trees, a man from nine hundred years before Christ would stumble into his path, wild and nearly naked. He would suddenly realize that time and space had somehow shifted, that neither he nor Quin had yet been born, that they didn't even exist as an idea in anyone's mind. He would realize that his world would not come into being for another three thousand years.

That kind of imbalance.

He moved faster, faster, stumbling, swearing, sweating, keeping one step ahead of panic. Then the brush ended, the terrible tightness in his chest popped like a boil, his inner world tottered back into balance.

He was in what looked like a grove and realized this was the place George had referred to as "the band's garden," as though it were a two-by-four patch surrounded by a white picket fence at the back of someone's house. Trees and bushes grew in neat, precise rows on ground that was slightly elevated. He identified coconut palms, papaya, mango, and coco-plum trees, wild potato bushes, pond apple and wild tamarind trees. Although there was an astonishing variety of plants, few of them were thriving.

Hard times for the clan, he thought. So they pillaged campsites and hoped the magic of a crazy old man would reverse the trend. Understandable. But not forgivable.

When the grove ended, the ground sloped into a deep depression stuffed like a cooked turkey with all sorts of surprises. There were balloon vines exploding with swollen seed capsules, wild poinsettia, orchids—and a pair of Key deer drinking from a puddle of rainwater. They were no larger than children and fleet as the wind, shooting off into the trees when they heard him. He wondered if George would consider the deer a good or a bad omen or if deer were simply too benign to be considered as either.

Whatever. He was going to need all the help he could get. The deer, he decided, were a good sign.

But as he moved through the depression, the trench, whatever it was, the reality of his situation reduced portents to an embarrassing absurdity. He needed a miracle, and the more biblical it was, the better: a flaming chariot appearing above the treetops, the voice of God speaking to him from a blazing bush, the Magnum multiplied like loaves and fishes into an arsenal. And if he couldn't have any of those things, then a plan would be acceptable. Any plan. It didn't matter how outrageous it was as long as it had a chance of working.

But nothing took shape in his head. There was no urgent burning between his eyes that signaled the birth of a hunch. There were only the walls of dirt and brush on either side of him, blocking out the noise of the breeze, the drizzle, the night.

And the feeling of badness had thickened in the air.

3.

Quin hoped something familiar would insinuate itself into her vision. It didn't have to be anything startling; the more mundane, the better. The tiled roof of a house, the white dividing line on a highway, a cat. Dear God, yes, a cat. And she wouldn't even care if it wasn't one of *her* cats; any cat would do. An unneutered tom that marked his territory every few feet, an alley cat that left gifts of dead mice on the doorstep, a stray whose ribs you could count.

But there were no cats here.

And regardless of how much she wished for something else, the scene in front of her didn't change, didn't become familiar, didn't become anything other than what it was. Trees: tight and close, washed in blue light, their upper branches bending inward under the weight of the

278

wind as if to hear something below. Ground: cold and damp and hard beneath her, turning her legs to stone. Her thumbs: no pain at all. The drug had killed it. Her hands: the left wrist was now tied to Ticker's right, thanks to Pa, and there was no way she could get to the knife in her left pocket that Josie had given her without his knowing about it. The silence: thick and oppressive, the result of whatever the band had drunk.

And then there was the circle: twenty-nine band members, four children, Lydia, and herself. She'd counted four times to make sure. Inside the circle were a woman, a boy with a limp, the old man. One of the adult members of the band was missing; that bothered her. But what bothered her even more was the gold-painted wooden box in the circle.

A rather ordinary box, really, except for the color. And for whatever it contained.

For some time now, she'd been hearing a noise that she knew came from inside the box, but which she couldn't identify because it wasn't consistent. Sometimes it was a rustling, like leaves. Other times it was a wet, sloppy sound. And now, as the boy and the woman pushed the box across the ground, closer to the pit, the noise seemed dry, harsh, like sandpaper rubbed hard and fast against hot concrete, and she suddenly knew what it was.

The woman and the boy in the circle crouched next to the box. The woman lifted one side of the lid and the boy the other. They moved in complete syncopation with each other, as though the drink had welded their nervous systems together, their muscles. They slid the top to the left and it struck the ground. The boy glanced at Tommy, who nodded, then looked back at the box. His tongue slipped slowly across his lower lip, wetting it. He rubbed his palm against his thigh, then raised his arm toward the mouth of the box.

As his hand vanished inside, excitement rippled around the circle. It was a soundless, living thing as real as the hardness of the ground, like an electrical current that raced from one person to the next and the next until the circuit was complete.

Then the boy slowly pulled his hand out and held up

a snake that was perhaps three feet long, thick-bodied, and dark. He gripped it behind the head, its fangs clearly visible. Quin didn't know what kind it was, but the species hardly mattered. That it was a snake was bad enough. That it was probably poisonous was even worse.

That it was going to involve her was unthinkable.

4.

It was not a house. It was not a chickee. Benson wasn't even sure that the place belonged in the Western world.

The poachers' shack looked like it had been slapped together from saw grass, thatch, mud, and pine. It was shaped like a mushroom and rose on stilts from the edge of a field of saw grass. A dock jutted out from the front, into the bay, and the seaplane was tied at the end of it.

The single-engine plane, Benson noted with a sinking feeling in his stomach, didn't look any sturdier than the shack. The windshield was smeared with squashed bugs that even the rain hadn't washed away, and the wings seemed to sag beneath the weight of the tip tanks at the ends. As they climbed out of the canoe and onto the dock, Benson smelled gasoline.

"You sure that thing flies, boy?" Farrel asked as they hurried down the dock through the rain.

"Yeah, it flies," Billy replied. "Just keep your opinions to yourself, okay, Joe?"

"You know I'm not much good at that."

"Just do it."

The door to the shack was opened before they reached it. A man the size of a small horse stood there with a lantern in one hand and a rifle in the other. "That's far enough," he said.

They all stopped. "Hey, Nick, it's me. Tiger."

"Yeah. Who's with you?"

"Couple of friends."

"Kind of late for a visit, Tiger."

"Got a job for you and Rick, if you're interested."

Nick and Rick: It sounded like a bad vaudeville act, Benson thought.

"What kind of job?"

"The seaplane."

"Only crazy men fly in shit like this."

"How much they paying?" called a voice inside. "Ask him that."

"How much you paying?" Billy looked at Benson.

"I thought this was a favor," he said softly.

"Offer them a hundred," Billy whispered.

"I don't *have* a hundred. My wallet's in the trunk of my car."

"I got about sixty," the ranger said. "If you can come up with the rest . . ."

Benson patted his pockets, where he often stashed a twenty or two, and dug out the forty.

"Yeah, okay, fine."

"They're paying a hundred," Billy said.

"How's a hundred sound, Rick?" called Nick.

The man inside the shack replied: "For what?"

"Could we come inside and discuss this?" Farrel asked. "It's wet out here."

"I guess that'd be okay." Nick stepped aside and motioned them into the shack with the rifle.

5.

Quin watched the boy as he moved slowly around the pit, his back to it, the snake high enough for everyone to see it. The old man stood nearby, smiling, pleased with how things were proceeding. When the boy glanced his way again, Miami Tommy nodded once more and the boy stepped away from the pit and walked up to Pa.

Lydia raised her head, but the boy's body then blocked her from Quin's view.

Pa reached out and touched the snake's tail. No, he didn't touch it, Quin thought, he *stroked* it, *caressed* it, a strange, almost intimate gesture. In the light, his hand looked dry and scaly, just like the reptile's skin.

When he stopped stroking the creature, Pa held the back of his hand still against its skin for a moment, the underside of his wrist exposed. The air tightened with expectation. Ticker sat forward, his eyes riveted on Pa and the snake. And since their wrists were tied together, Quin had to sit forward, too.

The boy moved to the next person; Pa looked disappointed.

What the hell's going on here?

The knife in her pocket seemed suddenly heavy, weighted, warm. *Use me*, it whispered. *Do it and live.* But the knife was wedged at the bottom of her left pocket, and to get her fingers down that far inside, she would have to stretch out her left leg. With Ticker sitting as close to her as he was, she wouldn't be able to do it without him noticing.

"The snake didn't want him." Ticker's voice was soft, almost dreamy, like his eyes.

"What?"

"The snake didn't want Pa."

Lucky Pa, she thought, swallowing back the slippery bubble of hysteria rising up in her throat.

"It's a sign."

You bet it is.

"Of what?"

"That Pa's growed weak."

Pump him. Keep him talking. The more you know, the better off you'll be. She wasn't so sure that was true, that knowledge in this situation would lead to salvation, but she said, "I don't understand."

He looked at her with those dreamy eyes, eyes so loose and liquid, they threatened to slip out of the sockets and slide down his cheeks. "The snake picks who's gonna speak for the band. Sometimes it's one person, sometimes more." He smiled then, his lips an ice-blue as they pulled away from his stained teeth. "Them people then pick who's gonna dance with the outsiders."

Dance: she was missing something here, definitely missing something.

"Dance? Dance where?"

"In the pit."

In the pit, with the snakes: got that, Quin?

"Suppose the snake doesn't choose anyone?" The words felt cold and awkward on her tongue. Like stones. Like marbles. Like chunks of ice that refused to melt. "What happens then?"

"That ain't never happened. The snakes always choose."

"But suppose it doesn't?"

He frowned; apparently he couldn't understand why

she kept asking the same question. "This is the way. The snakes got to pick someone."

"His eyes were nearly all pupil. Whatever was in the drink, she thought, was potent. Maybe potent enough to slow down Ticker's reflexes and to turn the rest of the band into whipped cream when they were on their feet.

"Does it ever pick Tommy?"

He laughed; it was the same dreamy sound as his voice. "Tommy ain't gonna be picked. He can't be. He's a medicine man."

"What kind of snake is that?"

"Water moccasin," he said, and turned his attention back to the circle.

Her mouth moved soundlessly around the word and she spelled it out in her mind, as though breaking it down into letters would somehow mitigate its venom and her terror. But it didn't. *M-o-c-c-a-s-i-n.* As in, a rattler without a rattle. Otherwise known as a cottonmouth.

As the boy moved around the circle, the woman reached into the box with the same care the boy had. But there was polish to the way she did it, a certain flair for the dramatic that suggested she'd done this before. This was her act and she was good at it.

When her hand reappeared, it was holding a small snake with yellow, black, and red rings, a snake every schoolkid in Florida could identify by the time he or she could talk. A coral snake.

Now she started around the circle as Tommy stepped up to the box. He didn't hesitate and didn't bother with dramatic posturing. He simply reached into the box as though it contained candy and brought out the largest snake yet, five feet or more. Even if Quin hadn't heard the rattle, the distinctive diamond pattern on the creature's back was a dead giveaway. This was an eastern diamondback.

And Tommy was bringing it toward her.

Bright, cold blades of fear poked at her spine. She was suddenly giddy with fear, drunk with it.

"Do you like her?" The old man stopped in front of her and held the snake close enough to her face for her to see its triangular head and those eyes, oh,

Christ, those eyes. "I named her Mariella, after my wife."

"Nice." Fear dug between her vertebrae, triggering a sequence of involuntary twitches throughout her body. She didn't want to jerk back, didn't want to show just how afraid she was, but she couldn't help it when he brought the snake to within a foot of her face.

"Do you like Miss Bones, Mariella?"

The rattle shook furiously; the snake's tongue hissed from its mouth. Blood drained from Quin's face.

"I believe that means no. Too bad." He laughed.

Beside Quin, Ticker snickered. "Mariella knows she's an outsider."

"That must be it. But she loves her Tommy, don't you, sweet thing," he cooed.

Then he brought his left hand, his free hand, up in front of the snake's snout. It struck fast and savagely at the heel, those fangs sinking in and holding on. The old man didn't wince, didn't show any sign of pain at all. He simply tightened his grip around the back of the snake's head again and pulled his hand away.

For a beat, maybe two, his gaze held Quin's and his eyes were laughing at her. *Got it figured yet, outsider?* they seemed to say. *Is there venom in those fangs? Have I been bitten many times before? Or is it really magic you're seeing here?*

Then he laughed out loud and spun around, his long white hair shot through with blue, his arms rising above his head in that familiar, almost prototypical stance of all dictators, all conquerors. The snake dangled parallel to his left arm, its rattle shaking, its tail wrapping around his elbow.

"Let it begin!" he shouted. "Let the snakes choose!"

Ticker and the other men started drumming their palms against their thighs as they chanted, "Now, do it now; now, do it now," over and over. Her own hand, the one tied to Ticker's, flopped around spastic, uncontrolled.

Her right hand inched toward her left pocket.

Toward the knife.

6.

The chanting had fluttered up through the trees, filling the Glades like water, like air, and McCleary had followed it. Now he was flattened out on his stomach on the edge of a mound peering down into the source of it. Into an eerie blue light and a scene so bizarre, it took him a few moments to assimilate what he was seeing.

When he understood, when he had somehow managed to shuffle the pieces around in his mind like pawns in a mental game of chess, Death cackled in his ear. Death laughed at him. Death galloped on his great black horse across that blazing white desert, his laughter rising and falling inside McCleary's head.

We may not get out of this one, Quin. But we're going to give it a bloody good fight.

He slid down the bank of the trench, rolled onto his back, checked the ammo in the Magnum. He mounted the night scope, sighted through it, adjusted it. *You're going to need more than bullets for this one.*

He looked down into the clearing again, sighting through the scope until he found Quin. Her face swam into focus, and a lump the size of a grapefruit lodged in his throat. Her hair had been chopped off practically to the roots, so her head was covered by little more than fluff, like an infant's. Her features seemed diminished by fear, damaged by it, changed by it.

He moved the scope to the man next to her. Ticker. A bow and a quiver of arrows lay on the ground beside him. His wrist was tied to Quin's.

McCleary sighted on Lydia and recognized the vacancy in her face. She'd looked the same way on that acid trip twenty years ago, when she'd lost it bad.

There was no sign of Beau Nichols. He set the gun on the ground and rubbed the heels of his hands against his burning eyes. He couldn't bring down so many people, not alone, not with the ammo he had.

McCleary glanced over the edge of the mound again. The chant had hit a momentary lull, and now he could hear the snakes, hissing like a hundred teapots on a hundred stoves in a hundred empty, silent houses. He knew it couldn't all be coming from the three snakes in the circle, which meant the box was teeming with them.

He sighted on the box but couldn't see inside it.

He sighted on the pit; it was empty.

But it wouldn't be for long.

The chanting rose again in pitch, in volume, and the woman and the boy moved more quickly around the circle, borne along by the fever. When the snake the woman held suddenly struck at one of the men, a cheer went up.

"It picked. It picked," they chanted. *"One more, pick one more."*

The man, clutching his arm where he'd been bitten—by a coral snake, McCleary thought—flopped forward at the waist. Two men moved quickly toward him as he jerked back, and pulled his arms out to his sides, trying to restrain him as he thrashed on the ground.

A moment later, the boy's snake struck at one of the women. She reacted just as the man had and was handled just as he was. The old man with the white hair—*It's him, Miami Tommy*—was the only person left in the circle. McCleary sighted through the scope and focused in on the snake Tommy held.

It stood out perfectly.

A diamondback.

"The scars on my back and chest were inflicted with snake's fangs": George's voice.

"Is their punishment for someone who's killed a member of the band always death?"

"Ultimately, yes."

"What kind of death?"

"It depends. There're different punishments for men and women."

"Such as?"

"You don't want to know, McCleary."

Snake's fangs.

Snake tattoos.

Snake Mound.

Snakes.

The band was a snake cult.

Reckoning

1.

BENSON COUNTED BILLS into Rick's outstretched hand. He was as big as his brother, but in both men the bulk was mostly fat. Their bellies attested to a love of beer; their double chins and wattles hinted at diets of fast foods as greasy as the kitchen counter Rick was leaning against.

He wondered what conditions their hearts were in. After all, he was going to get into a plane with these bozos and suppose one or both of them had a coronary while they were in the air? What then? Benson didn't know the first thing about flying a plane and he suspected that Farrel and Billy didn't either. Hell, he didn't know if these guys even had their licenses.

"Eight-five, ninety, a hundred." Benson dropped the last bill into Rick's hand. "You both pilots?"

"Nope. Just Nick." Rick folded the bills, stuffed them in an inside pocket of his raincoat, and whipped a baseball cap off the counter. He slapped it at a long trail of marching ants that were carting bits of food back home, and the insects broke formation and scurried everywhere. "Goddamn fuckers," he muttered. "You live out here and there's no way in hell your life is ever bug free." He plopped the cap on his head, picked up a flashlight, then they went outside, where the others were.

"How long does it take to get there?" Benson asked, hunching his shoulders against the rain.

"Depends on the winds." Rick tugged the cap down low over his eyes. "I guess you know those clan people are about as inbred as rabbits."

"So I've heard."

"True enough. And that Indian medicine man is a crazy fucker. Smart, but crazy."

"You know him?"

"Done business with him. Sometimes he does favors for us, so we do favors for him." He glanced up and grinned. "Good public relations, you know? But I don't think Nick and me are going to be having much to do with him after this. There's some sort of power thing going on in the clan, and I figure the old man is so ancient, he's going to lose. And the rest of those people are too creepy for me. I got no interest in dealing with them. They'd just as soon stick you in the back as look at you."

"I thought the clan was just one of the local myths."

Rick laughed. "Yeah, that's what they want people to think. But every year they need more and more from the outside world, so it's just a matter of time before people realize the clan is real."

They'd reached the end of the dock. Nick was scrubbing bugs from the windshield with a brush as he jabbered to Billy, who was holding up a lantern. Both men seemed oblivious to the rain. But Farrel looked as if he was rapidly approaching his limit.

"Safe to fly in weather like this?" he asked Rick.

"I'm not the pilot, man, ask Nick."

Farrel repeated his question to Nick, who glanced at him as if he'd lost his mind. "You kidding? The Glades aren't a picnic even in daylight with a visibility of twenty miles and no winds. You always got to be thinking about what you're going to do if the engine fails and you're not high enough to get to one of the open bays. And at night, with zip visibility and tricky winds . . . Shit, no telling."

"Then why're you willing to fly in this?"

Nick tossed the brush onto the dock and rubbed his hands over his jeans. The lantern's light glistened against his damp, plump face. "You might say we're evening up a score. Right, Rick?"

The brothers laughed, then Nick patted Farrel on the shoulder. "Don't you worry none, Mr. Farrel. Blaze will get you there in one piece." He slapped the wing with his open palm. "She don't look like much, but once she's in the air, there's no other plane quite like her."

Benson found no comfort in that thought.

2.

The chanting had stopped.

It was so quiet, McCleary could hear the wind moaning across the clearing and the soft tap of the rain against the leaves. Gooseflesh crawled up his arms; the hairs at the back of his neck literally stood on end. Everyone's attention was centered on the man who'd been bitten.

Through the scope, McCleary watched the man rock back and forth, arms clasped around his knees, head lolling on his neck. The sounds he made seemed to mimic the wind. Suddenly, his head snapped back, his eyes rolled until only the whites showed, his mouth literally fell open, and he started to babble. His voice rose and fell with the wind, and although McCleary didn't understand a word of what he said, the clan apparently did.

A feverish chanting erupted from the circle. It rolled through the air like the hard, hypnotic beats of a drum, touching off a frenzy below. People in the circle were now thrashing about just as the bitten man had moments ago. This primal pulse, this vestige of ancient worlds, pounded against some deeply buried center of nerves inside him, making them twitch and tighten until they threatened to burst. The urge to surrender to this sound, to let himself go wherever it took him, swept through him—powerful, visceral, unrelenting.

McCleary pressed his face against the wet ground, into leaves, into weeds, into the suffocating odor of the Glades. He pulled the scent into his lungs, deeper and deeper until it coated the bundle of quivering nerves, immunizing them against the seductive sound.

As he raised his head, something cold and hard pressed against the back of his neck and a voice said, "You ain't goin to live long, Lover Boy, 'less you set that gun nice and easy to your right and roll to your left."

McCleary froze.

The end of the rifle dug into his neck. *"Move."*

He pushed the gun to his right; a hand scooped it up.

"Roll over. Arms straight out from your sides."

He rolled left onto his back. The rifle was jammed against his throat. The dark shape of a head loomed over him. There wasn't enough light to see the man's face, but when he spoke again, McCleary recognized his voice from last night. One of Pa's boys.

"Outsiders ain't allowed to see the ceremony. The ones who do don't live long enough to tell about it."

"I'm not interested in your ceremony. My wife's down there."

"You got that right. And I reckon I'm goin to take you down there to join her."

The chanting went on, but it seemed distant now, not connected to him, to this. "Don't you think that's right nice of me, Lover Boy?" He placed a foot on either side of McCleary's body, straddling him. "You and the little lady together?" He dug the end of the rifle harder against McCleary's throat. It put pressure against his Adam's apple and cut off his air. "Huh? ain't that a nice thing for me to do?"

He couldn't breathe, and the bastard was pushing the rifle down harder, harder, as he repeated, "Huh? Ain't that nice?" McCleary heard Death's soft, mocking cackle to his left, his right, and suddenly jerked his knees toward his chest and slammed his feet, encased in the heavy boots, into the man's groin.

The rifle snapped up, scraping a path from McCleary's chin to his forehead as the man fell back, his shrieks swallowed by the noises in the clearing. McCleary scrambled forward, sucking at the air, coughing, rubbing at his throat, then rocked onto his knees and stumbled to his feet. He grabbed the man by the front of his raincoat, jerking the upper part of his back off the ground, and sank his fist into the guy's mouth, silencing him. He slumped to the ground when McCleary let go of him.

Magnum: He pulled it out of the man's belt and dropped to his knees, his breathing sharp, ragged, blood oozing from the scrapes on his chin and mouth. He rose to a crouch and for long seconds afterward, he pivoted slowly in place, his eyes sliding here and there through the surrounding darkness.

But he didn't see or sense anyone else nearby. McCleary quickly gagged the man on the ground, rolled him onto his stomach, pulled one of his arms back and one of his legs up, and tied them together. He did the same with the other arm and leg. Even Houdini would have trouble getting out of that, he thought.

Then he flattened himself against the ground again and peered into the clearing. The chants had gotten more frenzied. The old man was lifting the diamondback above his head, where its skin glistened in the ghastly light, then he dropped the snake on the ground.

It whipped through the dirt toward the edge of the circle, toward the people who were still seated there, chanting, and none of them moved. None of them even attempted to get out of its way. It struck at a man seated about four feet from Quin, then hesitated, as though considering its next victim, and darted toward a woman another few feet to the left.

"Blessed, blessed," they chanted.

Tommy scooped up the snake with the impunity of someone wearing iron gloves and hurled it into the pit. Now the man who'd been bitten by the coral snake earlier lurched to his feet and stumbled around the circle, pulling people into the center with him.

He should be dead. He's got to be dead if that was a coral snake.

Unless it was a look-alike species. Or maybe its venom sacs had been removed. But if not, that meant he was looking at a race of people who were apparently immune to the most deadly bites. Perhaps the immunity had been built up through decades of inbreeding or, in an even more bizarre fashion, by introducing small doses of venom from birth, for instance, the way children were vaccinated against tetanus and measles and polio.

The chant abruptly changed to "Out-siders, out-siders," and someone, a man, jerked Lydia to her feet and pulled her into the circle. She didn't fight, didn't try to wrench free, didn't even scream. McCleary realized she'd been drugged. She didn't seem to have any idea what was happening to her until another man—Pa, he thought, sighting him through the scope—started tearing off her clothes. Then she shrieked and kicked and struck him with her fists until two other men restrained her and pushed her toward the pit.

"Out-siders, out-siders," they chanted.

"Sweet Christ." He sighted on the man to Lydia's right and squeezed the trigger.

3.

The explosion rocked through the clearing and Quin saw the man on Lydia's right clutch his shoulder and fall back. The chanting stopped instantly and there was a moment of utter silence. It was as if the clan, collectively, couldn't believe what it had heard.

Quin smelled smoke. She didn't know where it was coming from and had no time to think about it because a second shot—from a different direction, there were two people out there—brought down the man to Lydia's left. Chaos broke loose. Everyone in the circle—including the people who'd been writhing on the ground—seemed to move at once, a battalion of insects scurrying for cover. But apparently no one had any idea where to go. They were like a swarm of bees awaiting orders from the queen, who was silent.

Even Ticker, who'd leaped up, jerking Quin with him, now paused and looked wildly around to see what everyone else was doing. He was muttering, "Aw, shit, aw, fuck, man," and raking his fingers through his hair, a violent, desperate gesture.

Quin seized the opportunity to do what she hadn't been able to do before: She jammed her fingers in her left jeans pocket and dug down deep and pulled out the Swiss Army knife.

A third shot rang out and Ticker hit the ground. Quin landed hard beside him, and at first she thought he'd been hit, that he was dead. But then he started to crawl toward the pit, snapping, "C'mon, c'mon, hurry up," and yanked her by the wrist.

As she crawled, her fingers worked frantically to pull the knife's blade from its casing. But the drug had stolen most of the sensation from her hands; her fingers belonged to someone else. Her mind wasn't much better. It moved with the lethargy of a snail and seemed to be independent of her thoughts, which fluttered lazily through the air like pigeons seeking someplace safe to roost. At some point, her mind and her thoughts merged again and attempted to find McCleary, but couldn't. She tried to reason out what had happened, but couldn't get beyond the gunshots. Who had fired them?

Not McCleary. He'd never find this place.

And where is Ticker crawling to?
And where's Lydia? And the old man?
He's the key. The old man is the key.

The blade suddenly came free in her hand. The metal was cool and hard against her palm. She yanked her hand back, the hand connected to Ticker, her albatross, her nemesis, her goddamn jailer. "What the hell you doin, woman," he hissed. "Don't give me no hard time now. . . ."

The blade tore up through the rope, cutting her free, and then kept on going.

Unfortunately for Ticker, his chin was in the blade's way. It sliced a nasty path to the corner of his mouth, and in a second or two of absolute clarity, Quin saw blood pouring out of the gash, saw the astonished look on his face, saw his hand fly to his jaw and come away covered with blood. Then the pain hit him.

He bellowed, he howled, he slapped at the gash with one hand to stem the flow of blood and lunged at Quin with the other. But she was already out of reach, scooting back on her buttocks. She was dizzy from the drug, blind with panic, and her legs wouldn't listen to her. They refused to push her up. They were fake legs, hollow legs, bad legs. She grabbed her right leg under the knee and pushed the lower half out. It swung like a broken thing, and she sobbed, "C'mon, please, please work," and suddenly it did.

She was up. She spun. She saw Lydia less than a yard away, cast in blue stone at the lip of the pit, her thumb stuck in her mouth. *Aphrodite on a bad acid trip.* She wanted to laugh at the thought but couldn't. She wanted to erase the thought, it was unkind, it was mean, but it wouldn't go away.

Quin grabbed her arm, pulled her away from the pit, and stopped dead.

They were surrounded by snakes.

Someone had tipped the gold box.

Someone had let the snakes loose.

Someone.

She heard Ticker laughing.

Brothers

WHEN I HEARD *gunshots and smelled smoke and every-*
one started running around so crazy, I didn't wait to see
what was happening. I took off for the village.

But there was nothing I could do back there. There
was nothing no one could do. Four of the ten chickees
was burning bright and hot like we'd never had rain.
Tommy's chickee was nearly gone. Pa's porch had crum-
bled. The roof on the chickee where Rusty and Josie lived
had caved in. My place was smoking bad, with fire leap-
ing out the windows.

But that wasn't the worst.

The worst was the seaplane bobbing out there on the
waters of the lagoon. I didn't know where it'd come from,
who it belonged to, or what it was doing here, but it
meant outsiders and that was all that mattered. Its land-
ing lights was brighter than the fire and them lights
showed everything: the burning chickees, people throw-
ing their things in dugouts, the band scattering fast. I
seen men getting out of the plane, into rafts, and I knowed
then, right then, that the band was dying.

I seen Josie running along the shore and shouted at
her to wait. When I reached her, she grabbed my hand
and pulled me along beside her. She looked half wild,
firelight dancing in her eyes, dirt streaked on her cheeks
and forehead, her snake tattoo quivering like it was alive.

"I got us a dugout stashed at the live oak, Wes. Hurry.
There's some crazy people in them trees, shootin, and
more outsiders are here."

"I'm goin back for the old man."

"Fuck the old man. His magic's dead. The band's
dead. You and me can git someplace safe." Another shot
rang out and she jumped. "C'mon."

"Give me your bow and quiver, Josie."

"Forget *Tommy*."

"Please. You've still got a shotgun."

She looked at me like I was as crazy as the old man, then shrugged the bow off her shoulder and unstrapped the quiver. "I'll wait for you at the live oak."

I said yeah, okay, but I knowed I was never going to make the live oak.

I strapped the quiver on my back, slung the bow over my shoulder, and took off into the trees, away from them lights, them outsiders, back to the Mound. Where the old man was. He was mine.

Long as I recall, a gun's been my weapon. It's clean and fast, and if your aim is good, it's deadly. Course, the same thing could be said for a bow, but not in my hands. I was never much good with a bow, maybe because I knowed that no matter how much I practiced, I wouldn't be as good as Opal. But the bow was perfect for this. For the old man.

I charged through the trees, the devil on my ass, and stopped just short of the clearing to fix an arrow in the bow. Some of the blue light from the Mound oozed over the branches and leaves and spilled onto some guy I never seen before. He was just ahead of me and to my right. He had a bow over his shoulder and was doing an old band trick—wrapping cloth just behind the arrowhead on an arrow. Once it was lighted and flying, that burning arrow would arch through the dark, bright as a falling star. Before it reached its mark, the arrow would be burning and whatever it hit would catch fire.

I sneaked up behind him and hissed, "Hold it right there, man, or this here arrow's goin through your back."

He stopped cold. He held up the arrow and turned, real slow-like. When I seen his face, something cut through me and I knowed he felt it, too. It was in his eyes.

"You," he whispered.

"I know you?"

Very slowly, his fingers went to his poncho, opening it, then to his shirt, undoing the buttons, laying it open so I could see his chest. I stared at those marks, all those

295

marks, remembering that night here at the Mound like it was yesterday.

This man was my brother and he looked more like our ma than I ever did. I could see her in his eyes, his mouth, his Indian face.

Tears burned hot at the backs of my eyes. "Buffalo," I whispered. "But how . . ."

"Doesn't matter," he said, and closed me up in his arms just like he done when I was a boy.

I went all weak inside. I didn't want to move. I just wanted to stand there with Buffalo's arms around me, protecting me from the stink of the smoke, from the old man's madness. The place where Tommy's splinter'd gone started aching real bad, like it was reminding me that he had taken everything from me, even my brother.

"I came for the old man," Buffalo said finally. "To settle the score. Will you help me?"

I pulled back, looking at him, at the arrow with the cloth wrapped around it, then at him again. So many years had passed, years where his life went one way and mine went another, but here we was, at the same place. Aiming to do the same thing.

"Yeah," I told him. "I'll help you."

But I ain't never telling which of us fired that flaming arrow.

Pyre

1.

McCleary didn't know who had fired the second shot. Maybe George. Maybe someone else. But he wasn't about to charge into the clearing and risk getting killed. Dead, he was no use to Quin.

When she'd broken free of Ticker, he'd lost sight of her for several seconds as the members of the band scattered like startled gulls, all of them squawking at once. Some were headed toward the clearing. Others didn't even seem to know where they were and stumbled about like drunks.

He scanned the clearing, picked out Ticker and the old man. Then he saw Quin and Lydia and the snakes—dozens of them, perhaps as many as fifty, maybe more.

His blood turned thick and cold in his veins.

2.

"Snakes, Quin," murmured Lydia, saliva drooling from her mouth. "Bad snakes. Lydia should mash snakes, but Lydia afraid."

Oh Christ oh God get me out of this.

She looked up and saw Ticker and the old man on the other side of the pit, staring at her. At them. At her and Lydia. The only thing she noticed about Ticker was the blood streaming over his jaw. It was the old man who captivated her, held her. Wind played with his blue hair. His blue face was hideous and old. His blue lips were smiling. He looked like a mad guru in the midst of a gathering of followers who'd just realized the world was ending and they better take cover. Even Ticker was tugging on his arm, saying, "C'mon, Tommy, we need to get back. C'mon."

But the old man didn't move and Ticker took off without him. Now there was only a handful of people left in the clearing, and they weren't paying any attention to the old man. They were running. Panicking. Shouting.

In his arms was one of the children, the little girl with the runny nose. The noise around Quin seemed to recede and she heard him clearly, heard him as though he were standing right next to her, whispering in her ear. "Do you like my friends, dear?"

She smelled smoke again and, for a wild moment, thought it was the short-circuiting of her own nerves and synapses that she smelled. The old man sniffed at the air as though it was just another day at the beach, another day of perfect weather, clear skies, friendly surf.

"The wind changed and I think one of your friends found the village." He nodded to himself. "It was predicted, you know. That the clan would end in fire and smoke. But I didn't think it would be this soon."

The snakes around her and Lydia hissed and twisted through the mud, drawing closer. Lydia kept murmuring, the unintelligible words tumbling out around her thumb. She held tightly to Quin's hand, trusting.

"I don't understand," Quin managed to say, her eyes on the ground, watching the snakes, then sliding toward the pit, where there were more snakes.

"Of course you don't." He spoke in that soft, soothing voice, the voice that addressed the drug in her. "You aren't expected to understand. Some things aren't meant to be understood." He crouched and picked up a snake. It was not the diamondback and it wasn't large, under two feet. But its tail rattled.

Pygmy rattler.

"My battle with your world has been going on longer than I care to remember." He rubbed his old face against the snake's back. It hissed. It writhed in his hands. The little girl giggled with delight. "Aren't they lovely creatures? So maligned, really. Unjustly so. Do you realize that the only man in the world who's been bitten by more snakes than I have is that fellow who used to own the Miami Serpentarium?"

The Miami Serpentarium. We're standing here about to die and he's talking about the Miami Serpentarium.

Giddiness welled in her throat; she couldn't speak. "And I've seen to it that my people are well protected. We start the children quite young, when they're about two months old." He stroked the snake like it was a small dog with incredibly soft fur. "They don't appreciate it. Not really. And most of them don't even like me very much these days. But that doesn't matter. I can handle them. And next week this will all be just another bad dream for them. But only if you and your friends aren't around. You should have let well enough alone, my dear. You would have lived longer."

Then he shouted, "You with the gun! They're all yours. If you can get to them." He laughed and tossed the snake across the pit. It struck the ground within a foot of where Quin and Lydia stood and lay there, perhaps wounded, thrashing, hissing.

Lydia started to cry and huddled next to Quin, who couldn't take her eyes from the snake. A part of her believed that as long as she watched it, the snake wouldn't move closer, wouldn't strike. But if she watched it too long, maybe the other snakes would know it and strike en masse. It was possible, of course it was. Anything was possible here. Anything at all. And yes, sure enough, when she looked around, it seemed that the rest of the snakes were a little closer, edging in toward them, toward the pit.

"It's my duty to wait," Tommy said. He sat down close to the lip of the pit with the girl. "Until it's over."

"You're afraid one of them will shoot you."

"They wouldn't dare. Not with the child right here." And he smiled again.

3.

It's a trap. It's got to be a trap. McCleary thought.

He was flat on his stomach at the edge of the trees behind Quin, no farther than a hundred yards from where the ring of snakes began. But it might as well have been a hundred miles.

Would the old man just sit there while his village is burning? Yes, if this was a trap. Yes, if Quin and Lydia were the bait and members of the band were hidden in the trees, in the pockets of shadows the blue light didn't reach, waiting to ambush him when he stepped out.

But he didn't know-for sure. He couldn't second-guess these lunatics.

And he couldn't just do nothing.

McCleary pushed up from the ground. The boots seemed to weight the lower half of his legs and were going to slow him down if he needed to run. He started to kick them off, then looked down at them. He pinched the upper rim, testing the rubber's thickness, and smiled.

You knew, didn't you, George. Of course you knew.

McCleary stepped out of the trees.

4.

"Well, well, what have we here," the old man said.

Quin's head snapped around. She saw McCleary coming toward them, a McCleary who looked like he'd been to hell and back.

"Mac."

"Just stay real still." He stopped on the outer fringe of the snakes and reached down to one of his boots. "There're too many to shoot without startling the bunch of them, so I'm going to toss you these boots, Quin. Put them on. They're thick. They'll protect you. Then when you're out, we'll throw them to Lydia."

"She won't understand. She's gone."

"Oh, I'm afraid we can't have this," said the old man, shifting the little girl in his lap.

"Don't move," McCleary barked, swinging the Magnum up, his boots temporarily forgotten.

"I don't think you're the sort of man who would shoot a child, now, are you." The light painted the old man's skin in shades of blue as he held the child directly in front of him. An offering. A threat that said she was expendable. "I must insist that you not interfere. If you don't put the gun down, I'll have to drop the child into the pit, which will enrage the snakes. As I was telling your lady friend here, the snakes are drawn to the pit. They'll converge on these two very lovely ladies. Do I make myself clear?"

A pulse beat at his temple. "You're bluffing."

"I assure you I never bluff. Ask your friend."

McCleary looked at Quin. *He means it,* said her eyes. *He's capable of worse.*

The old man was close enough to the pit so that even if McCleary shot him in the head, the child might tumble into the pit. He couldn't chance it and he sure as hell wasn't going to kill a kid. And Tommy knew it. He looked as comfortable as an old man with his grand-daughter at a baseball game and smiled when McCleary said, "Okay," and set the Magnum on the ground.

5.

Just as he set the Magnum on the ground, a flaming arrow shot out of nowhere and slammed into the old man's back. His head jerked up. His eyes widened with surprise. As his hair caught fire, he made a noise that was only remotely human and shoved the little girl off his lap as he tried to stand. He lacked the strength to get her as far as the pit and she tumbled to the ground, crying and sniffling and looking around for someone to help her. The old man's hands flailed behind him, trying to reach the arrow, but now flames were consuming his shirt, zipping over the top of his head. The air filled with the stench of burning fabric, hair, and skin.

He shrieked as he twirled through the flickering blue light, a human torch. His back was on fire. His arms. His legs. The flesh melted off his face, exposing tissue, muscles, then finally bone. The sockets of his eyes turned black. Fire leaped into his mouth, silencing him, but he was still alive, still spinning, when he toppled into the pit.

It hadn't taken long, maybe two minutes, but it was the longest two minutes of McCleary's life. And now, as he scooped up the Magnum and moved toward Quin and Lydia, he could hear the snakes in the pit. He heard them burning, hissing, rattling, slithering over each other as they attempted to escape. The snakes around Quin and Lydia, excited by the fire, smoke, and noise, were now a quivering dark swell, five and six deep. They didn't seem to know whether to move toward the pit or away from it, and he wasn't about to wait around for them to make up their minds.

He stepped into their midst, praying the boots were

thick enough, and winced as the first snake struck. Then another. Another. Lydia started to scream and jump around. McCleary shouted at her, Quin tried to restrain her, but she was so consumed with terror that she broke free and lurched forward, kicking aside a few snakes before she was struck in the ankle. She screamed. The snake held on and she tried to knock it off with her hand and another one bit her in the arm. Then a third. A fourth. They quickly brought her to her knees, snakes striking her every few seconds now until she was supine in the dirt. Then the shuddering mass simply covered her.

Dear God.

He tore his eyes away from the place where Lydia lay, and saw that Quin was backed up to the pit. She was holding her arms tightly against her chest, her face was ashen, her attention was fixed on a pair of rattlers coiled inches from her feet. McCleary shot the closest one, crushed the head of the other with the heel of a boot, then grabbed her hand, jerked her against him, and flung her over his shoulder.

He flew away from the pit, Quin bouncing on his shoulder like a bag of food, and didn't stop until he was in the trees. He dropped the gun and set Quin on the ground. She was shuddering and crying, her hands moving mindlessly over her arms, up and down, up and down, again and again.

McCleary tore off his poncho, wrapped it around her, and held her against him, warming her. She smelled of dirt and smoke and unspeakable things. Her skin felt gritty. He looked at her hands and saw the dirty bandages on her thumbs. He couldn't bring himself to ask her about Nichols, about what had driven Lydia over the edge, about what had happened in the chickee where he and George had found her clothes.

Someday he might ask, but not now. Right now, it was enough that she let him hold her, that she kept saying, "Let's go home."

Epilogue
July 3

I

IT'S ALMOST FUNNY.

If George hadn't been in the trees that night, if I hadn't seen him, if we hadn't talked, and, even further back, if Opal and me had just kept going instead of stopping at Lard Can, then I wouldn't be sitting in jail.

Opal ain't sitting in jail.

She escaped from the trooper who was supposed to transfer her to Miami. Into the world. She did what I shoulda done that night, woulda done, if it hadn't been for George. He kept me around long enough for them men from the seaplane to get to us and then he said, "This is Weston," and just walked away. I think he cared that we was blood, I really do, I can still see that look in his face. But what Tommy done to him and Ma all them years ago was too bright and fresh in his mind for him to separate me from the rest of the band. I want to blame him, but I can't.

Sometimes that copper, Benson, comes in and asks me about the band. Do I got any ideas about what happened to them? About where they are now? I don't think he expects me to tell him. I reckon he's just curious about where all them people disappeared to. And yeah, I can figure easy enough where they are. And I know that Pa heads the band now and that things are going to get worse as the Glades shrinks smaller and smaller. I know because I feel them at night, when it's still and quiet here in the jail. I can hear Opal whispering to me. I can hear the voice of the saw grass. I know.

But it's my secret.

II

RIGHT ON TIME, McCleary thought, watching the Toyota squeeze into a space at the curb that didn't look large enough to accommodate a motorcycle. The rise and fall of civilizations could be timed by Quin's promptness. It was noon on the nose.

She hopped out of the car and hurried through the heat in a sleeveless sundress. She'd regained the ten pounds she'd lost during those days in the Glades, and although her hair was still very short, it was slowly growing back. She looked almost normal again; the scars were in places that didn't show.

Quin tipped her sunglasses back into her hair as she stepped inside the café. She spotted him and strolled over. This was the third time McCleary had seen her this week, more than any other week since they'd separated. Progress. They were even talking about his moving back into the house.

"Neat place," she remarked as she sat down. "This another one of your Cuban haunts?"

As though his life in Little Havana were a map with Xs marking buried treasures. "There aren't that many. You had lunch?"

"Before I left the office. But I'd love whatever the house specialty is."

He laughed and signaled the waitress, who came over to take their order. "You want an espresso, too? The coffee here is great."

"Just tea."

Tea? The only time Quin took tea over coffee was at night or if she was ill. "You sick or something?" he asked after the waitress had left.

"I just feel like having tea. Why? Do I look sick?"

"You look terrific."

She combed her fingers self-consciously through her hair. "I still can't get used to not feeling hair on my neck."

"I like it short."

The compliment seemed to embarrass her and she looked relieved when he changed the subject. "Benson said Weston's trial is set for November."

"Good."

"The prosecutor wants you and me to testify."

She nodded. "I expected that. He wouldn't have much of a case without us."

"You'll also have to testify about what happened to Beau."

She nodded and patted at the back of her neck, seeking hair that wasn't there. "I expected that."

"You going to feel up to testifying?"

"Sure. Why wouldn't I be?"

"I just thought . . ."

She smiled. "Don't worry about it, Mac. I'll be fine. Really. I won't freak out on the stand and blow the case."

The waitress brought over a plate of *arepas* and a bowl of chilled gazpacho soup. Quin ate like someone who hadn't had a meal in weeks. "What kind of case does the defense have?"

"Not much, as far as I can tell. George's testimony on the band should help the defense considerably."

She buttered an *arepa* with what seemed to be an extraordinary amount of interest. "You free for dinner in the Grove on Friday night?" he asked.

"Hmm. I think so."

"You okay?"

"Why do you keep asking me that?"

"You seem distracted."

"Do I?" She shrugged. "I was just, uh, thinking about how big I'm going to be in November if I keep eating like this."

"C'mon, you haven't gained a pound in twenty-five years."

"I've never been pregnant before, either."

He nearly choked on a mouthful of soup. "Pregnant?"

307

His mouth curled around the word as though it were unfamiliar, a word he'd never heard before.

"I got the results of the blood test about half an hour ago."

"Blood test?"

"You don't have to repeat everything I say, Mac." She leaned forward. "Look, I'm not telling you this so you'll feel pressured about moving back in, okay? I just want you to know, that's all. I mean, I'm perfectly capable of doing this by myself. Lots of women do it by themselves, and they do it with more than one child, so don't feel obligated or anything about—"

He started to laugh.

"What's so funny?"

"I think it's great."

"You do?"

"Of course I do."

"I'm forty years old, Mac."

"So?"

"I'll be nearly sixty when she's going to college."

"She?"

"She, he, whatever. Did you hear what I said?"

"And we'll both be in our eighties when he's our age now. So what?"

"She'll be an only child."

"Is that bad?"

"I don't know." Another *arepa* vanished into her mouth. "Maybe she'll grow up spoiled because of it."

"Maybe he'll be a prodigy because of it."

She laughed. "Maybe both."

Their meals arrived and they fell silent. McCleary pushed his food around on his plate, waiting for her to mention the obvious. When she didn't, he said, "I was wondering about something."

She raised her eyes. "What?"

As though it hadn't crossed her mind. As though it was the farthest thing from her mind and she really hadn't given it much thought at all because she wanted things to remain as they were. "What do you want to do about us?"

"What do *you* want to do?"

"You know what I want."

308

"What's that?"

She wants me to say it. To ask. "I'd like to move home."

Her gaze held his for a moment. She was going to say no, to shake her head. And if she did, he couldn't blame her.

"But only if that's what you want," he added quickly.

"It is," she said, and smiled.

About the Author

T.J. MacGregor lives in South Florida. She is the author of four other books in the Quin St. James/Mike McCleary series: KILL FLASH, DEATH SWEET, DARK FIELDS, and ON ICE.

The T.J MacGregor series continues as St.James and McCleary join forces again.